Praise for D.B. Reynolds's Vampires in America . . .

"D. B. Reynolds always tells a fantastic story with all sorts of twists and turns in her complicated worlds that you can't help but love! I can't wait to see what her genius-self cooks up next!"

—Cassandra Lost in Books on QUINN

". . . another can't-put-down book, so clear your schedule and hunker down for a terrific read."

—La Deetda Reads on RELENTLESS

"This is a power read, and fans will not be disappointed in the latest installment of Reynolds's tantalizing series. Top Pic! 4 1/2 Stars

-RT Book Reviews of LUCIFER

"Captivating and brimming with brilliance, CHRISTIAN is yet another defining addition to the ever-evolving world of Vampires in America created by D.B. Reynolds."

—KT Book Reviews

"Did I mention that the sizzling sex factor in this book is reaching the combustible stage? It is a wonder my Kindle didn't burn up."

—La Deetda Reads on DECEPTION

"D.B. Reynolds has outdone herself with this exhilarating story; and VINCENT is a worthy addition to Reynolds's always excellent Vampires in America series."

—Fresh Fiction

"Terrific writing, strong characters and world building, excellent storylines all help make Vampires in America a must read. Aden is one of the best so far." A TOP BOOK OF THE YEAR!

—On Top Down Under Book Reviews

Other Titles by D. B. Reynolds

D.B. Reynolds VAMPIRES IN AMERICA

Raphael * Jabril * Rajmund

Sophia * Duncan * Lucas

Aden *Vincent

Vampires in America: The Vampire Wars

Deception * Christian * Lucifer

The Cyn and Raphael Novellas

Betrayed * Hunted * Unforgiven

Compelled * Relentless

Vampires in Europe

Quinn * Lachlan

The Stone Warriors

The Stone Warriors: Damian

The Stone Warriors: Kato

The Stone Warriors: Gabriel

Lachlan

by

D. B. Reynolds

ImaJinn Books

This is a work of fiction. Names, characters, places and incidents are either the products of the author's imagination or are used fictitiously. Any resemblance to actual persons (living or dead), events or locations is entirely coincidental.

ImaJinn Books
PO BOX 300921
Memphis, TN 38130
Print ISBN: 978-1-61194-947-6

ImaJinn Books is an Imprint of BelleBooks, Inc.

Published in the United States of America.

ImaJinn Books was founded by Linda Kichline.

We at ImaJinn Books enjoy hearing from readers. Visit our websites
ImaJinnBooks.com
BelleBooks.com
BellBridgeBooks.com

10 9 8 7 6 5 4 3 2 1

Cover design: Debra Dixon
Interior design: Hank Smith
Photo/Art credits:
Man (manipulated) © Fotorince | Dreamstime.com

:Llok:01:

Dedication

To Jane Sanderson and Jean Blair, two fascinating women who made my first visit to beautiful Scotland a trip I'll never forget.

Look for me, because I'm definitely coming back.

Prologue

The Highlands of Scotland, 1846

LACHLAN MCRAE woke on his first night to bloodshed and death. He lay on a rough bed in the deep, dark basement where all McRae vampires were left to rest after being turned. It was a clan tradition to turn the strongest of their warriors, a tradition so old that no one could say when it began. Lachlan was proud to have been chosen, but by all the saints, he ached in body and bone, the pain made worse by the small bed being such a poor fit for his long frame. But none of that mattered now. It was the sound of screams, the clash of blades, that drew his gaze to the stone ceiling overhead.

Minutes dragged by before he could force his reluctant body to move, as if his head didn't know how to control his legs and arms anymore.

"What's happening, Lachlan?"

He turned slowly at the sound of his cousin's groggy voice. "Don't know, Fergus," he managed, his mouth drier than bracken in winter. "But I'll be finding out. Is Munro stirring yet?

"Aye," a scratchy voice responded. "I'm with ye."

Lachlan raised his head when everything went nearly silent up above. He'd have rather the sounds of battle than this ominous quiet. "Grab blades soon as ye can, lads," he murmured. "But stealth is th' watchword. Follow my lead."

His cousins didn't say a word. They didn't have to. They'd been following Lachlan's lead since the three of them had been babes barely able to crawl.

Lachlan climbed the twisting stairs, footsteps silent despite his stature. He was a big man, even by McRae standards. Tall and broad, both. But he'd always moved like a ghost through the heather, his uncle's favored scout for all that you wouldn't know it to look at him. And now, with the newly born vampire gift coursing through his blood, he was quieter even than a ghost, and one hell of a lot faster.

He paused at the basement door and glanced back. His cousins were right behind him, their eyes glowing red in the dim torchlight. He blinked at the unfamiliar sight and wondered if his own eyes were as bloody. The thought didn't last as a furious roar rose over fresh screams from above. He pushed the round, wooden door upward. Hinges squealed, but the sound went unheard in the empty kitchen. Where was everybody? He could hear the renewed clash of blades from the courtyard, but the women and children should have been taking shelter here, deep within the fortress. It had been years since they'd endured any serious assault, but memories were long. The clans weren't a peaceful brotherhood. Friends could become enemies in a fortnight. All it took was a single setback, and they'd start looking beyond their borders for something better. And so the women and children, who were the future of the clan, drilled as hard as the warriors. But their duty was to survive, not to fight.

He shoved the overhead door all the way open, catching it just before it would have crashed to the floor. Most likely there was no one to hear it, but his body acted without thought, aiming for stealth, just as he, too, had been taught since childhood.

The three of them climbed into the kitchen, not yet as graceful as they were accustomed, but warming with every step. Following the growing sounds of battle, they made for the main passage, heading for the courtyard. They'd no sooner taken the first twisting turn than Lachlan froze, his gaze swinging to stare in disbelief at the heavy door that hung open on the resting place of the elder vampires of the clan, including their Chief. But it wasn't the open door that made his breath catch in his lungs. His nostrils flared at the dusty scent. He didn't need his newly born vampire senses for this. It smelled like death. Vampire death.

"Lachlan?" Fergus whispered, his gaze following Lachlan's. "Is that . . . ?"

"Aye. But we don't know who yet, so . . ." He paused. "Let's go."

They found the first bodies next. Two McRae warriors, human not vampire, the smell of their blood so strong that Lachlan could hardly think. He was a day-old vampire. He'd woken starving, and blood was blood. But he would not lick the death's blood of his own kin. He might be vampire now, but he was still a McRae.

The next body was a woman, small, with long dark hair covering her bloody face, arms clasped around a wee child who lay perfectly still. He went to one knee, heart in his throat as he brushed the woman's hair aside. Fergus bit back a choked cry and pushed forward to kneel next to her, anguish creasing his face at the sight of his sister and her child. "Sara." It was an agonized whisper, barely heard against the battle still raging outside.

Lachlan forced himself to be practical, to shove down his own grief. His lovely, laughing cousin was dead, her barely-born son along with her. But her spirit was screaming for revenge, not tears. He stood and offered Fergus his hand. "Come, laddie. We'll mourn her properly, after we kill th' bastards that did this. Their dead souls will pave her way inta that paradise th' priests prattle on about."

Fergus's jaw clenched as he covered his sister's face with her shawl, then gripped Lachlan's hand with a grim nod, and stood.

Discarding stealth, they raced for the courtyard. A quick glance showed an uneven battle as their remaining human cousins faced off against a band of vampires wearing the Ross tartan. Lachlan roared as he waded into the battle. That the enemy was Clan Ross didn't surprise him. They'd been enemies of the McRae a hundred years over, for all that they'd both kept the truce of their last bloody battle. What surprised him was that the Ross vampires had made it to the fortress this soon after sunset. Granted, he and his cousins were so newly made that the sun had set some hours past, but even so, the Ross vampires must have slept nearby to attack so quickly. It spoke to considerable planning, but it wasn't the secrecy that bothered Lachlan. It was the troublesome fact that the McRae guards set about during the day must have been killed before the fighting even started. For there was no way they could have missed this many fighters on their doorstep.

But the dead could be tallied later. It was time to save those he could from an enemy so craven that he countenanced the killing of women and children, not to mention the slaughter of vampires in their daytime beds. Such acts could only be avenged with death.

Lachlan rushed into the courtyard, breaking through to the front of the line with ease, stout McRae warriors moving aside without being asked, like water parting before him. It was an odd thing, but Lachlan didn't squander thought on it, as he hefted his broadsword and blocked a blade that would have beheaded a clansman. In the next moment, he dropped his metal shield and instead drew on his newfound vampire strength to wield a second blade in a deadly dance that laid waste to his enemies. Blood flew as the screams of Ross warriors joined the cacophony of battle, as vampire and human warriors alike fell to his blades. But these weren't the deaths he hungered for. His two swords rose and fell in a whirl of steel, but even as he fought, he scanned the ranks of his enemy, seeking the ones who were behind this cowardly attack. The ones who had to be there.

His dark gaze locked on the man—the vampire—he sought. Erskine Ross, who styled himself a vampire *lord* and thought he could rule all the Highlands. McRae had no interest in that kind of an alliance, one that would set Ross above all others. Highlanders had long memories, and the Ross clan had a habit of turning on their friends as readily as their enemies. But their tendency toward perfidy had nothing to do with their strength. Erskine Ross, in particular, was a powerful vampire. He was also dishonorable enough to have devised this dastardly attack on sleeping vampires, and on women and children.

Blades whipping around him, Lachlan shoved his way through the crowd, careless of his own safety, determined to confront the black-hearted Erskine. The powerful vampire stood his ground, grinning as his gaze locked with Lachlan's, while around them, the retreat sounded and the Ross fighters fled.

Lachlan finally came within shouting distance of Erskine, the battle dying between them, blades dripping as they stared at each other. Erskine wasn't as big as Lachlan, but his tremendous vampire power made up for it, making him seem twice his size. Lachlan had power, too, but he had barely begun to unleash it. He wasn't as weak as some he'd observed in the past, vampires who had to learn to walk again, much less to wield a blade. At some future date, he might even fight Erskine and win, but not this night. That didn't mean he'd bend his neck and surrender, however.

"This will not stand, Erskine," he called as the field cleared. "McRae will have our revenge."

The vampires to either side of the powerful Erskine snickered. "End him now, my lord," one of them drawled. "We killed the elders, why leave this babe at our backs?"

Erskine's grin became a laugh. "For my amusement," he said finally, his accent pure lordly English, as if he considered himself too high and mighty to speak his born tongue. "Look at him. He's so fresh, he still stinks of humanity. It will be entertaining to watch the great Clan McRae stumble and fall under his leadership. Assuming he survives his first blood." He scoffed and started to turn his back on Lachlan.

"You're right," Lachlan said. "McRae's revenge will not be soon, but it will come. And when it does, it will be my hand that ends you."

Erskine shrugged. "Be a good lad, or we'll kill the others."

Lachlan stiffened. "What others?"

The self-styled vampire lord jerked his head at the lackey standing next to him. The man gave a loud whistle and suddenly, there was a shuffle of feet near the ruined front gate. He heard a chorus of soft cries, and then a dozen McRae females were shoved into the shattered opening, none of them older than sixteen, while the youngest was barely ten, clinging to her sister's waist. Lachlan had no siblings, but he had cousins aplenty and he recognized every fierce scowl and tear-stained face.

"You would do this cowardly thing? Take women and children prisoner?"

Erskine Ross shrugged. "Hostages are common enough in war, as are slaves. But these will be treated well and released at edge of McRae lands, as long as you mind your place." He smirked, then glanced at the sky. "Dark's a wasting and we've a fair ways to go," he said to his fighters, then paused to toss a warning over his shoulder. "Mind what I said, Lachlan McRae. Before the next new moon, I *will be* Scotland's first vampire lord. Your clan chief and his council refused to see it, so they had to die. But it will take every sword we can muster to defend our lands. Be smarter than they were. I would welcome your strength in the coming battle. But know this . . . I would just as easily wipe you from the earth if you continue to oppose me."

Erskine gave him his back then, as if Lachlan was nothing. No threat, no warrior. Nothing but a baby vampire with no power.

He growled, muscles tensed, but Fergus stopped him with a hand on his arm. "It grinds my heart too, cousin. But you'll only get yerself killed, and we need ye."

Lachlan swung his head to stare at his cousin. "Ye think so little of my skills?"

"Uh course not," Fergus snapped. "But th' facts remain. Let th' arse think ye weak. It will only help us when we finally kill him."

Lachlan stared after the departing enemy, torn to the roots of his soul.

"There's dead here what deserve a proper send-off, 'n' someone has to organize a defense of th' living," Munro said somberly, walking up to join them.

"Surely, Taskill—"

"Dead," he said flatly. "And the others with him. The faithless bastards began their attack in daylight. They arrived as human traders, two of them. One made his way into the elders' resting place 'n' murdered . . . everyone. We're all that's left, cousin. Th' three of us are th' only McRae vampires still livin'."

Lachlan stared. Granted, he'd known some vampires had died. But all of them? Taskill had been nearly 400 years old, and he'd led Clan McRae from the shadows for most of that time. If Lachlan and his two cousins were truly all that were left . . . . "Why did Erskine Ross let us live?" Grief made the words little more than a rasp of noise. "Why didn't he kill me?"

"He said it himself," Fergus said grimly. "For one, he needs pure tough warriors t' keep th' Highlands in Scottish hands. But beyond that, he doesn't know ye, cousin. He doesn't see yer strength, not only t' wield a blade, but t' lead. He believes this is th' end of Clan McRae as anythin' but a memory. But he's wrong. If it takes two years or two centuries, ye will rebuild Clan McRae, 'n' when that happens, revenge will be ours."

Chapter One

Washington, DC, present day

JULIA HARPER shoved her water bottle into the curve of her elbow, holding it above her purse as she dug in a pocket for her key . . . and didn't find it. "Shit," she cursed softly and switched everything to her other arm to dig into the opposite pocket. She kept telling herself she was going to put the damn key on her key ring, but she hadn't yet. She'd only moved in last week and there was a mountain of higher priority tasks demanding her attention. Finally finding the elusive little sucker, she shoved it into the lock and pushed into her townhouse, letting the door slam behind her.

The four-bedroom townhouse was too big for her, but her dad, and his accountant, had insisted she needed a bigger tax write-off, whether she needed the extra bedrooms or not. It was either that or pay more taxes, her dad had explained. And because she trusted him, especially when it came to the substantial family trust that he managed, she'd bought a townhouse she never could have afforded on her salary as a cubicle dweller for the CIA. Some of her colleagues, knowing she came from old money, had asked why she was working for the CIA at all. She usually brushed it off with some comment about needing something to do, but the truth was that she'd joined the CIA for the challenge of working as a field agent. She'd almost gotten there, too, but that was a story for another time. A time when she wasn't wearing workout clothes that were still damp with the sweat she'd earned in the dojo that night, trying to keep up the fighting skills she'd learned before her dream died.

Shivering, she hurried to her upstairs bedroom, stripping off damp clothes as she went. When she hit her bedroom, she tugged off her pants and socks, and dumped the entire, disorderly bundle of clothes into the hamper. But with her mother's gentle voice still clear in her head, one of the few distinct memories she had to cling to, she dutifully slid her shoes neatly onto the closet shelf designated for athletic shoes, and headed for the bathroom.

She turned on the hot water first, letting it fill the room with warm, wet heat. She could feel her pores drinking in the moisture, like a dried mushroom soaking in wine. Stepping under the spray, she simply stood for a while, loving the heat, the pounding of water on tired muscles. When she found herself nearly nodding off, she washed her pale blond hair, slathered on some body wash, then did a quick rinse and turned off the water.

By the time she left the bathroom for her bedroom, she had a towel on her head and was wrapped in an oversize terry bathrobe. She was just considering whether to skip dinner and go straight to bed, when her cell gave a distinctive ring.

Surprised, she crossed to the side table where she'd left her phone. There'd been a time when she'd heard that ring several times a day, but she and Masoud had had a falling out a couple months ago. She hadn't heard from him since, and she'd missed him. He was her oldest friend in the world. They'd always been close, but after her mother and brother had been killed in a car accident when she was a child, she and Masoud had become even closer. They'd grown up together, even when their parents' jobs had taken them far apart. He'd been her best friend, the one person she could always talk to.

Until she'd discovered that he thought what they had was much more.

"Hey," she said, answering. "Did you finally get tired of refusing my calls?"

"Julia." His voice was hushed and tight with some emotion she'd never heard from him before.

"Masoud? What's happening?" The emotion was fear. And not simple fear, but something much more.

"I don't have time—" he said, but not impatiently. More like he really meant it. "I need you to do something for me."

"Anything. But tell me what's going on. Where are you?" Dread crept up her spine. She'd known Masoud bin Abu almost her entire life, and she'd *never* heard him like this.

"London," he said shortly, giving her the first real piece of information since she'd answered the phone. "Meeting a client. But it went bad, Jules. Very bad." He practically whispered the last two words.

Julia's chest squeezed, her heart in her throat as she asked, "Where in London? Do you need the embassy?"

"I'm trying to get there," he confirmed, and for the first time she paid attention to the sounds of traffic behind his voice.

"Damn it, Masoud, don't be walking in the open. Get a fucking cab."

"Don't swear," he said absently, as if he'd told her the same thing a million times. Which he had. "I'm only a block away."

That told her two things. First, he was aiming for the Saudi embassy, which was in an expensive neighborhood of London not far from the palace and lots of other embassies. Masoud had dual citizenship, but the US embassy was some distance, on the other side of the river. He wouldn't be going there if he was in a hurry. But she also knew he was lying. She could hear it in his voice. He had more than a single block to go.

"Masoud, grab a cab. They're everywhere in that—"

"Listen," he said urgently. "I need to tell you this. Go to my house—you have a key. In my office, you know the safe."

"Of course, but—"

"The combination is our numbers, you remember?"

"Yes, but—"

"There's a blue expandable file in there. Erskine Ross. That's the name. The folder has a few written notes, but also two flash drives. Make sure you get those. They have all the docs, all my notes on the data trail."

"Data trail. What are you talking about?"

"Money laundering, I think. I should have turned it over to enforcement, but I wanted to be sure. He's a big client, very high profile, been with the firm for years. I wanted to be wrong." The words were tumbling out, and he was breathing heavily now, as if he was running. "Put that file somewhere safe. You understand?"

She understood, all right. Masoud wasn't supposed to know she worked for the CIA, but he did. He was too smart to fool for long, and besides, she'd trusted him. He wanted her to take this blue file to her office in Langley and lock it up.

"Masoud, please. Are you safe?"

"Don't know. Don't think so. Not yet." The words were distracted, forced out on heavy breaths. "Be careful. Don't let anyone know. He's a vampire."

"What? Who?"

"Erskine Ross. He's a vampire."

"What the hell? Masoud, you're scaring me. I don't want—"

"Julia," he said, his voice suddenly unnaturally calm and even, as if he'd stopped running. "I love you, *habibi*. Don't ever forget that."

The squeal of tires and gunshots. Later, she'd remember there were three shots. But in that moment, all she could hear was the sound of Masoud's pain as he grunted into the phone, the dull thud of his body hitting the ground, the crack of his cell phone falling to the sidewalk.

"Masoud!" She screamed his name over and over, until finally the phone cut off with the crunch of a heavy boot.

Chapter Two

London, England, six months later

JULIA SIPPED HER whisky, eyes raised over the rim of her glass to watch the young woman sitting across the table.

"I couldn't believe it when Fergus called," Catriona McRae nattered cheerfully. "I mean, what are the chances that all these years later, someone would be asking me about Cyn?"

Pretty slim, Julia thought, worried about the coincidence that some vampire in Scotland would be nosing around about her friend Cynthia Leighton just as she arrived in London to investigate Masoud's death. She stifled the shock of pain that still touched her heart every time she thought about him. She couldn't believe he was dead. That she'd never have a chance to hug him again, to smooth over the pain they'd caused each other before he died. She knew coming to London was a longshot. She was no hotshot investigator. She couldn't even count on the cooperation of local authorities, since she had no official standing. In fact, if anyone bothered to dig out the fact that she worked for the CIA, they'd be investigating *her* instead of Masoud's death.

She took another sip of whisky. She was the one who'd agreed to this meeting, but that didn't ease the combination of suspicion and curiosity at a call from someone she hadn't seen in ages. Someone who'd been a little *too* interested in Cynthia Leighton. She herself had been speaking to Cyn almost daily since Masoud's death. She'd needed to learn about vampires and how to find one *particular* vampire in a country she barely knew, and Cyn happened to be mated to the most powerful vampire in North America. Which brought up one more chance connection . . . that Cyn had suggested *Julia* reach out to Cat. And that was simply too many coincidences. So she'd agreed to Cat's out-of-the-blue invitation, though she'd insisted on a public location in a hotel that was very protective of its guests.

Catriona (pronounced *Katrina*, though everyone at school had simply called her "Cat") had been a year behind Julia and Cyn at the

French prep school they'd all attended. Students there had hailed from all over the world, but with one thing in common—their families had enough money to afford the privacy and security the school offered, while also delivering a first-rate education and an international cultural experience. But Cat had stood out, even in a school population that included its share of royal offspring—both European and Hollywood. Mostly because she'd made no secret of the *vampires* in her family tree. At the time, Julia had figured at least half of Cat's stories were fictional, but it was the other half that had made her consider Cyn's suggestion seriously.

So there Julia had been, looking for a rich and powerful vampire, wondering how she could possibly find him, thinking about calling Cat. When suddenly Cat reached out first, saying her vampire cousin wanted to talk to her. Supposedly because *he* needed an inside line to *Raphael.*

Julia didn't know much about vampires, other than what she'd learned from Cyn and her own research over the past six months. She'd discovered Erskine Ross was reported to be the big boss of all Scotland's vampires. The so-called Scottish Vampire Lord, though she hadn't managed to find a single picture of him, other than a distant profile that was so blurry she wouldn't have recognized him on the street. But the fact that he *was* the ruling vampire begged the question of why another wealthy vampire—which she assumed Cat's cousin to be, given the family money which had qualified her for the French prep school—would need *anyone* to serve as a go-between if he wanted to talk to Raphael. The timing and facts just didn't ring true.

But she couldn't pass up the chance. *If* Cat's cousin was on the up-and-up, he might be very useful to her own investigation. And if all it took to secure his help was a phone call to Cyn . . . well, hell, she could do that. Although she'd want to know *why* first. After all, Cyn was a good friend, while Cat's cousin was not only a stranger, but a vampire. And it was vampires who'd killed Masoud. She knew it, even if no one else believed her. Of course, that might be because she hadn't shared Masoud's files with anyone, not even his father. Hell, *especially* not his father. There was too much money involved. Masoud had gone against his father's dictates most of his life. The two had never been close, a situation which had only worsened as Masoud got older. He'd never trusted his father enough to make him a part of his life, and there was no way in hell she was going to trust him with his death. She knew without asking that his father would never pursue Masoud's killer if it meant losing a lot of money.

"Of course, I've kept up with Cyn from afar," Cat was chattering on. "Can you imagine Madame Martel's reaction when she heard that Cynthia Leighton had hooked up with"—she lowered her voice to a whisper,— "a vampire?" She laughed. "And not just any vampire, but the big honcho himself—Raphael."

Julia nodded agreeably. "Old pinchface probably had a severe case of the vapors." She smiled, despite herself, at the not-so-secret nickname that her fellow students had all used for the headmistress at their very elite prep school. At the same time, she gave her phone a casual scan to check the time, wondering when Cat's curious cousin was going to show. He was already overdue, which made her nervous. She'd been very careful in her investigations, but if someone wanted to shut her down, she'd be an easy target.

Glancing up when there was a stir around the entrance to the tony bar, her gaze sharpened, every bit of her training and instinct telling her this could be very, very bad. A man stood just inside the wide doorway, a slight bulge under his leather jacket betraying the weapon concealed there. Tall and broad, with long, black hair and eyes that scanned the crowd with careful precision, his gaze lingered on the most crowded tables, as if assessing the risk. Or calculating the death toll.

"Cat," she said in a quiet voice. "When I give the word, I want you to hit the floor. Don't ask questions, don't panic. Just duck under the table."

Catriona gave her a puzzled look. "Why would I—?"

"Just do it," Julia hissed, seeing the man begin to make his way between the tables.

Cat, of course, ignored her warning, standing instead, her gaze lifted over the heads of their fellow drinkers as if searching for whatever had set Julia off.

Julia cursed silently. This was no time for gawking. Damn Cat was going to get them both killed.

"Over here!" Catriona called suddenly, laughing as she lifted both arms and hugged . . . .

Well, fuck. Julia closed her eyes briefly, feeling stupid. The leather-clad gunman was Cat's vampire cousin? He sure as hell didn't look like the rich Scottish lord of anything. What he looked was fucking deadly, rather like her personal vision of a vampire.

"Here goes," she whispered to herself, then raised her eyes to meet a piercingly intelligent stare.

LACHLAN MCRAE spotted Catriona before he'd taken two steps into the bar. She was hard to miss with that shock of red hair down her back, but even without it, his wee cousin drew a man's attention. Especially when she stood up and yelled at him, as if he hadn't the wits to find her himself. He started toward her, then stopped, scowling when the crowd parted and he saw the cool blond sitting at the table. This was a surprise. He'd been expecting to meet his cousin to discuss using her contacts to get hold of Cynthia Leighton. The get-together wasn't even his idea, though he'd agreed to it. What he really wanted was to meet with Raphael, the vampire lord of North America's Western territory. He didn't give a fuck about North America, but Raphael was the most powerful vampire alive right now, one who'd taken a personal interest in Europe. Not that Lachlan could blame him. Not after several European vampire lords had done their best to kill him and take over North America. Idiot arseholes were all dead now, of course. But their stupidity had led Raphael to undertake some vampire king-making in Europe to ensure it didn't happen again. He'd begun by wiping out almost every powerful vampire in France, and then taken it a step further by installing his own candidate as Ireland's new vampire lord.

To be sure, the American, Quinn Kavanaugh, had overthrown and killed Ireland's longtime vampire lord on the strength of his *own* power and abilities. By all accounts, he was one cold and scary motherfucker. But it had been Raphael who'd handpicked him for the job.

Lachlan, seeing long-overdue change taking root in Europe, had decided it was finally the right time for him to get some revenge of his own, by killing Scotland's vampire lord—one Erskine Ross—and seizing the country for himself. He didn't *need* Raphael's approval, but he and his cousins had decided it would be smart to pay the powerful vampire lord a courtesy visit, just to be certain that Raphael wouldn't clog up the works with a candidate of his own.

Hence this meeting with Catriona, who'd somehow ended up at the same fancy French boarding school as Cynthia Leighton, who happened to be Raphael's mate. He'd assumed Catriona would reach out to Leighton on her own and provide an introduction for him to make his call. All he'd wanted was a good phone number and an intro. It hadn't seemed like a monumental task, so when Catriona had suggested meeting for drinks, he'd expected nothing but a slip of paper with the necessary information.

What he *hadn't* expected was a surprise guest, and he was not a man who liked surprises. Even when they came in attractive packages. He scowled down at his wee cousin, for all the good it did.

"Lachlan," she said cheerfully, her tone saying she'd sprung one on him.

"Catriona," he growled, half greeting and half warning, even as he reached down to hug her much smaller frame. Lifting her off the ground, he bent his head to her ear and said, "Who the fuck is this?"

She tugged at his hair. "Fergus said you wanted to meet Cynthia Leighton. This is Julia, and she knows Cyn way better than I do. Now behave, you heathen."

He set her back on her feet with a smacking kiss to her cheek, then turned to the unknown blond as his cousin made introductions.

"Julia, this is my cousin Lachlan McRae. Lachlan, Julia Harper. We went to school together," she repeated. "Julia, me, and Cynthia."

Lachlan leaned across the table to shake, careful of the woman's slender hand as he wrapped his thick fingers around hers. A tingling heat warmed his palm when their hands touched, and his eyes shot up to meet hers, seeing her pupils widen in surprise as if she'd felt the same heat. She managed to confine her reaction to her eyes, keeping the rest of her face coolly polite, which was fine with him. Keeping his tone the same, he said, "Ms. Harper."

"Julia," she supplied, as she slid her fingers out of his grasp.

Lachlan's own distrustful nature had him following her hand, and so he noted the quick glance she gave her palm, as if seeking a logical reason for that moment of sizzling heat. When she caught him watching, she brushed invisible crumbs from her skirt instead. He bared his teeth and met her gaze. *Nice legs beneath that skirt,* he thought intentionally, letting the appreciation show in his eyes.

Catriona slapped his arm. "Be nice," she hissed under her breath, then smiled for the blond's sake and indicated a chair between them. "Have a seat, cuz."

He gave her a look that said she'd pay for this, but pulled out the chair and sat, grateful that at least she'd chosen a meeting place with real chairs, so he didn't have to squat on some fancy frippery of a thing.

"So what's this about?" he asked bluntly. He didn't have time for any of Catriona's games, cousin or not.

She pretended to be puzzled. "Fergus said you wanted to meet Cynthia Leighton. Julia here—"

"I don't need to meet her," he interrupted. "I just want to get hold of her."

The blond leaned closer, suddenly interested. "What do you want with Cyn?"

He shifted his attention, drawn by her scent, even as he said, "It's business."

"What kind of business?" she responded.

"The private kind."

Her eyes narrowed as she gave Catriona a look heavy with meaning he didn't understand.

"Lachlan," his cousin said impatiently. "Julia here was the same year in school as Cyn. I was a year younger, and when you're a teenager, that year matters."

"What's your point?" he growled.

She made a frustrated noise. "Julia and Cyn were best friends."

"That's an exaggeration," Julia corrected. "We're close but—"

"Closer than I ever was, anyway," Catriona interrupted. "I haven't talked to her in years, and even then, you guys were upper-classmen. You had—"

"Class ladies," Julia corrected primly, then she and his cousin both laughed at some inside joke. Great. Just what he needed.

"Catriona." One word, but it said everything that needed saying.

She made a face. "Fine, Mr. Grumpy. Julia can do what you want."

Lachlan let a smile play around his lips as he caught the delicate blond's gaze. Her cool façade was firmly in place, but a pink flush on her fair skin gave her away. She'd caught the unintentional double meaning behind Cat's announcement, same as he had. He blinked lazily, and she looked away, her blush spreading to the glimpse of delicate skin visible in the open vee of her black silk blouse. He'd bet the tops of her breasts were flushed, too. He lifted his eyes and gave her a knowing look.

Catriona squeezed his forearm, having been around her male cousins enough to figure out what he was thinking. "Julia thought you were a terrorist," she confided, shifting his attention.

But only for a moment. He swung his gaze back to Julia, one eyebrow raised in question.

"You have to admit, you do make an entrance," Julia accused.

"So does fucking Prince Charlie, but you wouldn't call him a terrorist."

"You're not exactly a prince," she said, fighting a smile.

"You don't think so?" he argued, finding himself intrigued. She gave off an ice princess vibe, but there was a real person beneath those sophisticated, blond looks.

"Prince of what?" She gave him a speculative look.

He laughed, then turned to Catriona. "Does she know?"

"Uh, well. I was just getting to that when you walked in."

"Know what?" Julia persisted.

Lachlan gave his cousin a pointed look. She cleared her throat and said, "You know how I was talking about Cyn having a big vampire for a lover—"

"Mate," he corrected.

Catriona stopped and stared at him. "What?"

"She's Raphael's mate, not just his lover."

His attention swung back to find Julia studying him intently, those blue eyes more intrigued than anything else. "And *you're* the vampire cousin," she deduced.

"One of many, but yes." He said it matter-of-factly, but was still surprised by her reaction. Or lack of one.

"Yes," she repeated. Her voice matched his tone, but she couldn't conceal the sharpening of her gaze or the slight increase in her heartbeat that indicated more than a casual interest.

"Definitely not a terrorist," he added, not quite knowing what drove him to push her.

She sat forward. "You think vampires are immune to that sort of thing?"

He could have told her that vampires didn't need to terrorize humans, that they could *persuade* humans to do whatever they wanted, to *give* them whatever they needed. But that wouldn't have been the whole truth. Because a lot of vampires engaged in violence, simply because they could.

She continued before he could say anything. "I can name a very powerful vampire who's the worse kind of criminal, stealing whatever he wants and killing anyone who gets in his way." There was real pain in her voice this time. They'd finally struck at the heart of the matter. At least, for her.

Catriona stood abruptly, her chair tipping slightly in her hurry to leave. "Okaaay," she said with false cheer. "I've made the intros, so my job is done. You kids try to avoid bloodshed now, all right?" She leaned over and kissed Lachlan's cheek, then waved her fingers at Julia. "Cheers for now. Maybe we'll catch up later."

Lachlan and Julia both watched Catriona leave, almost as if they wanted to avoid dealing with each other. Which certainly wasn't true on his part—he was more than intrigued by this Julia Harper, with her delicate blond looks and steely will. He wanted to know why she was here, and why the hell she thought he could help her. Because it was obvious to him that she hadn't agreed to this meet out of the goodness of her heart. He turned around, hitching his chair closer to her side of the table. "What did she mean by that?" he asked.

"She said many things," his cool blond answered breezily, clearly avoiding the question. "To which are you referring?"

Lachlan gave her a speculative look. If this was all part of some game on Catriona's part, he was going to lock her in the dungeon for a year. He smiled. "What *exactly* can you do for me, Julia?" he drawled lazily.

"In your dreams," she drawled right back at him.

He was amused by the attitude, and frankly, liked the fact that she didn't wilt in his presence the way most women did. There was iron inside that slender frame. But he was beginning to doubt she knew anything that could help him, and he didn't have the luxury of time. He went to push his chair back, but her next words stopped him.

"If you want to meet Cynthia Leigh—" She held up a hand when he opened his mouth to correct her. "Fine, fine . . . you don't need a meet, you just want her phone number. But I assume you'd also like her to answer when you call," she added with smug sweetness.

He stared at her. "And you can make that happen, because you're her best friend."

She shrugged. "Not her *best* friend, but one she'll pick up the phone for."

Lachlan studied her. She could probably deliver on her promise. She didn't strike him as a woman who played games, something else he appreciated. And then there was his attraction to her. Not only physical, although God knew his body wanted her. But it was more than that. She was smart and confident and wasn't intimidated by what he admitted was his less than charming personality, at least when he met new people. But he didn't have the luxury of courting a woman right now, no matter how much he wanted her. Too many vampires had put their faith in him, taken serious risks to support him.

She tilted her head and gave him a tiny smile, as if waiting for an agreement she already knew was coming. Fuck it, he thought. She could provide the inside track to Raphael that he needed, and if it brought them closer together? Well, hell, he wasn't a damn monk. Catriona had delivered the access he needed. And if it came in a tidy package of long legs and flushed breasts, not to mention a pair of plump lips that just begged to be bitten, then he'd just have to take one for the team, he thought, with a very private laugh.

"And what price would you ask for a simple phone call?" he asked calmly.

She gave him a teasingly prim glance. "By price, I assume you don't mean anything so crude as currency."

"Oh, aye, mustn't be crude," he agreed. "But you're right. I'm thinking your price will be something other."

She nodded in agreement, suddenly all business. "We shouldn't discuss it here. You never know who's listening."

"Maybe *you* don't," he muttered, but continued before she could react. "I have a room."

"I'd rather *my* place." The way she said it, the look she gave him, told him she thought he had some dank flat off a dark alley. The idea amused him.

"I'm sure you would," he replied. "And I'm guessing you have a plush office somewhere nearby, but I don't like office buildings. Too much security these days, eyes and ears everywhere."

"I meant my apartment. I don't have an office in London." Her gaze sharpened. "Why would you think I do?"

"Instinct. I figure you for some embassy type, possibly a lawyer, but definitely on the bureaucratic side. I can't see you with a 9mm on your hip."

She gave him a curious look. "Why not?"

"No gun with you."

"How do you know I didn't leave it at my supposed office? Or maybe it's in my purse."

He leaned in. "First," he said quietly, "you Americans love your guns far too much to leave them in the office. And second, I'm a vampire. If you had a gun on you, I'd smell it."

She blinked, showing genuine surprise. "Even in a crowded place like this?"

"Even so, especially when you're sitting right next to me."

She breathed a soundless, "Oh," then asked, "Okay. How far is your room? And how do I know I can trust you?"

"Not far, but we won't be walking. I have a car waiting. As for trusting . . ." He stood and held out a hand. "You've no way of knowing, but life's more exciting that way."

She stared up at him, their eyes locked in a silent test of wills. Lachlan didn't so much as blink. He was a vampire, over 170 years old. A few minutes meant nothing in the scope of his lifetime.

Finally, she drew a long breath and stood, ignoring his hand. The small rebellion made him want to smile, but he kept his face blank and gestured with one arm toward the door. "Lead on, princess."

"My name is Julia," she corrected firmly as she passed him.

He smiled at the rise he'd gotten out of her. She was far too controlled for his taste, but he was beginning to suspect that was only the surface. How much heat was hidden behind that cool façade? And what would it be like if he stoked that fire?

JULIA WALKED AHEAD of Lachlan, out of the bar and through the small lobby of the Goring hotel. She was exquisitely aware of the big vampire behind her, could feel his eyes on her back . . . and lower. If it had been any other man, she'd have turned and given him a look guaranteed to freeze his balls. But for some reason, Lachlan McRae made her want to add an extra swivel to her hips. What the hell was happening to her? Sure, there'd been that odd sizzle of heat when their hands first touched, but that was just static electricity or something. Wasn't it? He *was* a beautiful male specimen . . . *Good God, Julia, listen to yourself!* Beautiful male specimen? Who talked like that? He was a gorgeous hunk of sexy man, that's what he was. And once he'd gotten over the whole terrorist misunderstanding, he'd been charming in a dark, broody way. A way she found entirely too attractive. Especially given the spark of intellect in eyes that were strikingly pretty in such a masculine face—hazel, but the kind that would change color with the light. She reminded herself that intellect was way more important to her than looks, but put it all together, and . . . well, hell.

Of course, he *was* a vampire. She couldn't be attracted to a *vampire,* could she? Sure, she'd heard plenty from Cyn about how close she and Raphael were, how violently protective he was. Then there were the fan magazine reports she'd read as part of her research for this trip. Reports of vampires' charisma and spectacular sexual prowess. She'd hadn't believed any of those, figured they were exaggerations by people who'd never met a vampire in their lives, other than the ones they read about.

But having met Lachlan. . . . Given her family's wealth and the resulting business and political connections, she'd met a lot of powerful men in her life, and not only the rich ones. Money brought influence, but power was something else. It came from inside a person. And Lachlan McRae had it. His power slid over her like that first, unexpected, pulse of electricity, a subtle pull that made her want to find out more about him, to get close enough to wrap herself in the sheer heat of him. She didn't know any other way to describe it. It wasn't sex. Okay, maybe some of it was sex, but it was also . . . safety. She'd seen the way he'd held Catriona, surrounding her in his arms, letting her know that she was loved, despite his gruff teasing, and without squeezing the air out of her, despite his overwhelming physical strength. How would it be to have a lover like Lachlan? A big, dangerous vampire watching over her, making her safe, making *himself* safe *for* her. The seductiveness of it nearly took her breath away, because Julia knew too well how cruel the world could be. How the people you loved could be there one day and gone the next. No warning, no good-byes. Just gone forever, the way her mom and brother had been. A careless driver had wiped away their lives in an instant, then ended up burned to death in his own car, which had crashed into a ditch a couple of towns farther along the same road.

She shoved those thoughts away, forcing herself to remember who she was—the woman life had taught her to become, the woman she'd made of herself.

No man could protect her. They couldn't even protect themselves. People died. Even rich and powerful people—like her own family, or like Masoud—people who thought their money or position bought them security. She didn't want or need someone else to worry about her, someone for *her* to worry about. She had to protect herself. And she would. She might look like a good wind would blow her away, but the truth was far different. Lachlan had been right about her job, even though he didn't see, couldn't *know*, the truth of it.

Sure, she was nothing but an analyst now. A data troll for the CIA, who spent her work hours in a cubicle reading intelligence reports and looking at grainy photos until her eyes watered. But when she'd first been recruited, they'd wanted her for more. Her intellect and adaptability, her language skills, which included Arabic, had all made her a candidate for field work. She'd even trained on the CIA's infamous "farm." Few people meeting her for the first time ever guessed at the strength hiding inside her slight frame.

And no one had been more surprised than *she'd* been when they'd abruptly pulled her out of field training and stuck her in a cubicle. Their reasons had all been terribly logical, but she'd known the truth. Her father had paid off the right politician to make sure his baby girl remained safe. She couldn't even blame him for doing it. Half their small family had been killed on that highway in Florida. Julia and her dad had both lost too much to risk losing each other.

So she'd accepted the transfer and spent her days safely ensconced in an office. But she'd never stopped training, never stopped keeping herself strong and capable. And now, it had paid off. Because she had a purpose. It was vengeance for Masoud that got her out of bed in the morning these days, vengeance that kept her awake late into the night searching for his killer.

So yeah. She'd get Cyn on the phone for Cat's vampire cousin. And then she'd extract her price. Lachlan McRae didn't know it yet, but he was her ticket to a very dead Erskine Ross.

She was still contemplating that, telling herself it was far too early to feel even the first, tiny twinge of the satisfaction she'd know when Erskine was dead, when a big, black Range Rover slid up to the curb, surprising her into taking a step back, right into Lachlan. Damn, but his body was big. And she did love big men. As a tall woman—she was a hair under five feet ten inches—it was difficult to find men who made her feel feminine and delicate, despite her very slender build. She'd spent most of her prep school years mourning the absence of boys tall enough to date. Of course, the school she'd attended with Cyn and Cat had been all girls, so there hadn't been too many boys to worry over. Just the occasional French lad they'd come across after sneaking out of the dorm, looking for evidence that the real world still existed outside the ivy-covered walls of their prep school prison.

"That's our ride," a deep voice murmured in her ear.

She stifled her jerk of surprise, but couldn't do anything about the shiver that slid over her skin in response to his voice. He might use it mostly to grumble and growl, but it was a wonderful voice. Deep and masculine, with a velvet undertone that was like a sensuous caress. Lachlan McRae was probably the kind of man who could make a woman feel all sorts of things.

In front of her, someone opened the back door of the SUV. Wondering if she was being reckless in going alone to Lachlan's place tonight, but committed to her pursuit of Erskine, she climbed into the vehicle and settled herself into the backseat with prep school grace. At least until Lachlan shoved in behind her, his broad shoulders taking up far more than his share of space. She gave him a scowling glance and scooted all the way to the far door, but he wasn't paying attention to her, occupied instead with something his driver was saying. They were speaking English, but with such a heavy Scottish accent that she could only catch the occasional word. Odd, because that accent had been completely missing when Lachlan had spoken with her and Cat earlier. If anything, he'd sounded American, with just a touch of England. She made a mental note to do a deep dive on Lachlan McRae when she got back to her apartment. There was obviously more to him than he wanted the world to know.

His hotel wasn't far, but traffic was so congested that they probably could have walked faster. She didn't have to wonder why he'd insisted on driving, though. The Range Rover might appear to be a normal vehicle, but to someone who knew what to look for, it was obvious that it had been enhanced for security. She'd have bet money that the body was armored and the windows bulletproof. And *that* made her wonder about his enemies. What was there about Lachlan McRae that had people trying to kill him? There were the usual suspects of money and power. Those always drew enemies. Or maybe it was just a general vampire thing. Not all humans were happy to welcome vampires into their midst.

She was startled when the Rover finally stopped at Claridge's. He was a vampire, for fuck's sake. Shouldn't he be staying at some small boutique hotel with dark lights and velvet walls? She did a mental eye roll. She knew better than that, but Claridge's still seemed awfully busy for a guy who wanted to keep a low profile.

Lachlan stepped out when the valet pulled open the door, then waited, holding out a hand to help her. It might have seemed polite, gentlemanly even, if not for the knowing smirk flirting around his lips. He somehow knew she'd been surprised by the hotel. She frowned slightly, thinking about vampire telepathy. Cyn had warned her that some vamps had remarkably strong telepathic abilities. Was Lachlan one of those? She made a mental note to research techniques for keeping her thoughts private. There might not be much in mainstream journals, but she'd bet the government had invested in more than a few studies. It was all a matter of knowing where to look.

Lachlan continued his courtly ways, letting her precede him into the hotel to a chorus of various staff offering respectful greetings of "my lord" this and "my lord" that. It was everything she could do not to stop and stare. What the hell? Were they all vampires here? Or could he have some ancient landed title that she didn't know about?

One of the staff held an empty elevator for them, reaching in to insert the key card for a penthouse floor with yet another murmured, "My lord." Julia studied the porter as she walked past him and into the waiting car, but couldn't find anything to distinguish him as a vampire. Lachlan certainly didn't offer any clues. He simply nodded at the man, then did what seemingly every person on earth did in an elevator. He went to the back wall, then turned and watched the numbers as the door closed and the car started upward. And if she detected a touch of humor on those sensuous lips, it was probably just her imagination. But there *had* been that casual implication earlier that he might be a prince or something.

She decided to go for a direct approach. "I didn't know Cat's family was noble."

He smiled, but didn't look away from the numbers. "We're not."

She studied his profile, trying to figure out if he was playing with her. "But then why . . . ?"

"You mean the lads downstairs."

"Well, yes," she said in frustration. She was no protocol specialist, but she wasn't ignorant either, especially when it came to simple matters of titles.

"A couple of the lads here are vampires who're loyal to me, rather than the current Scottish lord. I'm not currently a vampire lord, but they believe I will be, and so they grant me their respect. The rest of the staff here are sensitive to titles and such, and they follow suit, rather than risk offending me."

"Do they know you're a vampire? The others, I mean."

He grinned, still without looking at her. "No."

Julia couldn't help smiling, but managed to swallow it before the elevator opened onto the lush silence of an expensive penthouse lobby. A door opened down the hall as they exited the elevator, and a man stepped out, his eyes skimming over her, before lifting to Lachlan behind her. "My lord."

Another one, she thought. But this guy didn't work for the hotel. Instead of a natty uniform suit, he was dressed much like Lachlan, in jeans and a long-sleeved T-shirt. Except that *unlike* Lachlan, his weapon was carried openly, and he eyed her with suspicious care as they approached.

"It's all right, Fergus, Lachlan said. "This is wee Catriona's friend, Julia."

Fergus didn't look convinced, but he moved back and let her enter the room, waiting until Lachlan followed, before stepping in and closing the door. "Where's Catriona?" he asked.

"Off on her own, as always," Lachlan replied casually. "She stayed only long enough to introduce Julia here, who's good friends with Cynthia Leighton."

Fergus's glance shifted her way briefly, then back to Lachlan. "And?"

Lachlan chuckled. "And we're negotiating. Julia's American."

Julia frowned. What the hell did that mean? "Look, if this is all too much—"

"Patience. Julia Harper meet Fergus McRae. And don't take his doubt personally. It's his job to be suspicious. Julia and I are going to chat, cousin. You can join us—"

"I'd rather he not."

Both vampires turned to stare at her. Lachlan raised his brows in question.

"Some of the details are . . . personal," she told him.

He shrugged. "We can speak in private if you'd like, but I'll tell Fergus everything anyway."

She wasn't thrilled with that response, but years of experience with bureaucratic bullshit kept both her expression and her words mild. "Then you're welcome to join the party, Fergus."

The cousin gave Lachlan an amused glance and walked to the door, saying, "I'll be just across the hall."

Julia watched him go.

"You can't lie to a vampire, you know."

She spun at Lachlan's words. "Who says I was lying?" He scoffed noisily, and she shrugged. "All right, I'll bite. Why can't I lie to you? Where I work, lying's considered normal conversation."

"Because vampires have greatly enhanced senses. Hearing, sight, smell. And as normal as you might think you're acting when you lie, your body knows better. It reacts, and I can detect those reactions no matter how hard you try to conceal them. Unless you're a sociopath, or a pathological liar."

She tilted her head curiously. "I didn't know that about you. About vampires, I mean."

"We don't publicize our talents."

She snorted. "That's putting it mildly. Your friend Fergus—"

"Cousin."

"Your cousin," she corrected. "He can still stay if you want, though I'd rather you decide what to share *after* we talk. Even if you tell him everything, it might be better if he didn't know where it came from."

Lachlan eyed her carefully. "Which agency?" he asked casually.

Julia didn't so much as twitch in surprise that he'd narrowed in on her profession correctly. "I work for the State Department, same as your Foreign Ministry, not—"

"CIA then. You're not the only ones who play coy, but you all like to pretend you're foreign trade ministers or some shit."

She just looked at him. There were other agencies who did the same, and he probably knew it, too. But she wasn't going to play that game with him. "My job doesn't matter. This is personal, and all you need to know is that I want Erskine Ross dead. And since he's the current Scottish vampire lord, and your people plan on *you* taking that title, I'm guessing *you'd* like him dead, too. Which is why you're telling Cat that you want to talk to Cyn. You don't want her at all, you want Raphael."

He studied her a moment then said, "Have a seat, princess. Let's be civilized, even if we aren't."

Julia chose to ignore the "princess" comment, for now, and sat on one of two elegant sofas, skirt tucked beneath her thighs, legs together, ankles crossed. She assumed the position without thinking, then immediately wished she hadn't when she caught him watching. He sat on the sofa across from her, taking up as much room as he could, an arm stretched along the back, and one ankle propped on the opposing knee. She wondered if he'd done it on purpose, to contrast her own tidy posture. Damn it.

"What do you know about Erskine?" he asked.

"I know he rules every vampire in Scotland, and—"

"Not every vampire."

She gave him a questioning look. "No? Vampires don't exactly share, so my information is imperfect, but I thought he was your vampire lord."

"Nominally, yes. But not everyone accepts his authority."

"You mean you and your McRae cousins?"

He nodded. "And others. Close allies of McRae who hate Erskine Ross and his lackeys as much as we do."

"I know vampires are secretive, but can you tell me how long he's been in charge?"

"A hundred and fifty years, give or take."

"A hundred and fifty years," she breathed. "How *old* is he?"

"Older than that. Two hundred? Two-fifty? Before my time, anyway."

Two hundred and fifty years. She couldn't imagine what it would be like to measure a life in centuries, much less to actually *live* that long. And not to age. That was the key. She studied Lachlan abruptly. He looked about the same as her own twenty-nine years. Did she dare ask his true age? Maybe she should call Cat instead.

"Can I assume, then, that you have no objection to me going after Erskine?" she asked.

He regarded her from beneath half-closed lids. "That might not be good for your health. The vamp's an asshole, but he's not without power. Or supporters."

"Which is where you come in."

His brows shot up. "Do I? And why would I do that?"

"Because I can get you to Cyn and Raphael."

He made a dismissive noise. "It might be *easier* for you to call Leighton for me. But if push comes to shove, I can simply call Raphael's estate myself."

"And get the digital equivalent of a switchboard. I can do better."

"Maybe. You could also get me dead. What's your plan?"

"I'll tell you that once we agree to work together."

"Look, princess—"

"Julia," she interrupted to say.

He smiled. He'd been baiting her again. "Julia. I'm not some sheep herder fresh off the mountain. You want me to help you out, I need to know what I'm signing up for."

She considered his response and sighed, knowing she'd have to come clean. "I don't know exactly. That's what I need you for. I have a general plan to lure Erskine into what he'll think is a lucrative financial deal along the lines of what he's gone after in the past. But as yet, I don't know enough about how he works to be more specific than that."

His eyes crinkled slightly in what might have been amusement. "And once I've helped you, and Erskine is dust . . . what then?"

She blinked, confused for a moment. What then? She hadn't really thought beyond getting her revenge on Erskine. Not just killing the bastard, but destroying everything he'd built.

"Someone has to rule Scotland's vampires when he dies," Lachlan said quietly. "It's necessary."

"Necessary for whom?" she asked suspiciously.

"For every vampire in Scotland. It's not only necessary, it's vital. You'll have to trust me on this."

"Trust? I don't—"

"Look, if you want me to trust *you*, you'll have to return the favor. It's a two-way street."

Julia didn't like it. Didn't like having no options. Didn't like her plan being completely dependent on a vampire she'd barely met. But if she was honest with herself—and she liked to think she was—it was more than she'd expected. She'd had a vague plan to engage a disgruntled vampire or two in her scheme, but she hadn't known when she'd met Catriona this evening that the sexy answer to her prayers was going to walk through the door.

Wait. Who said anything about sexy? Well, fuck. No, no fuck. Okay, so he *was* sexy. But that was irrelevant. What mattered was that she needed him more than he needed her, and he knew it.

"All right. Two-way street. Where do we start?"

"You tell me everything you know about Erskine Ross. And I want details, including what you said earlier about people he's killed. Which I take to mean humans," he added pointedly.

She bit her lower lip, hating the idea of laying her broken heart on the table for his perusal. Not to mention his cousin's. But what choice did she have? "I'll need my research materials," she said quietly, buying herself another day of privacy. "Can we meet again tomorrow night?"

"Sure. But we call Leighton tonight."

Julia started to protest, then sighed. "Fine."

He grinned. "See how easy that was?"

It didn't seem easy to her. In fact, it went down like a rock in her throat, but she swallowed it anyway and pulled out her cell. "My phone or yours?" she asked, feeling her chest tighten with stress, even though this was what she'd wanted. She'd plotted and planned for this since she'd been forced to listen while Masoud died thousands of miles away, unable to do anything to stop it. But now that it was really happening . . . . It was as terrifying as it was exciting.

"Yours," Lachlan said. "We want Leighton to recognize the caller."

She nodded wordlessly, then asked, "Are you going to talk to her?"

He seemed to think about it. "Depends. Tell her why you're calling, that I'd like a meeting with Raphael. If she asks to talk to me, I'll take over."

Julia's spine stiffened at the "take over," but she didn't say anything. It wasn't as if Cyn needed her protection. She did a quick time zone calculation. "It's afternoon in California. I'm guessing Cyn will need to check with Raphael, so you won't get your answer tonight."

"I'm familiar with the concept of time zones," he said dryly.

"All right. You ready?"

He winked. "I'm always ready," he deadpanned.

She feigned a gagging noise and picked up her phone.

LACHLAN STOOD behind the sofa where Julia sat, listening as she exchanged pleasantries with Cynthia Leighton. She'd put the phone on speaker without being asked, which he'd appreciated. He didn't want to seem like a paranoid fuck, but his life had taught him to trust very few people. And those few all shared blood or clan, or both.

Julia had been right about Leighton's response to her call. Raphael's mate had answered on the second ring and had seemed very happy to catch up with how things were going in London. So happy that Lachlan was going to lose a few teeth if he didn't stop clenching his jaw at the unnecessary delay. He was about to grab the phone when she finally got to the point of the call.

"Listen, Cyn. I met up with Cat tonight, and she brought her cousin with—"

"Oh, my God, is he as gorgeous as she always said?"

"Cyn! He's—"

She cut herself off at the sound of his choked laughter, which was more about Julia's response than Leighton's question. He was fairly certain she'd even paled a few shades. Good thing she was sitting down. She twisted around with a threatening glare, and he wondered how she expected to follow through on that threat . . . and if it involved getting naked. He blinked in surprise at his own thought. Did he really want her naked? Sure, he was attracted, and she was a beautiful woman. But she was also the perfect product of a rich girls' prep school, with her cool looks and tidy skirts. Did she even know how to get sweaty in bed? He tried to picture her losing control, her clothes hanging half-off, blond strands of tangled hair falling over her shoulders, cheeks pink and glistening with effort while he pounded between her firm thighs to the music of her screaming his name. He smiled at the image, and some of what he was feeling must have shown in his eyes, because her gaze went wide, and she lost track of what she was saying to Leighton.

"Sorry, Cyn, I almost dropped the phone." She turned her back to him with a forced laugh, then covered her mouth with her hand and spoke in a hushed voice, clearly not remembering what he'd told her about a vampire's enhanced hearing, much less that she was still on speaker. "He's standing right here, so maybe we can discuss that later."

"Oh, shit! I didn't know." Leighton laughed. "You know he can probably hear every word you're whispering. I've given up trying to keep secrets from my darling vampire. He's so nosey."

"Are you happy?" Julia asked abruptly, and Lachlan's attention sharpened at the note of . . . was it longing that he heard in her voice? Wistfulness?"

"Delirious."

"I'm glad," she said, sounding completely sincere. "Anyway, like I said, he's here with me, and that's why I'm calling." She shook her head, as if to clear her thoughts. "He'd like to meet with Raphael to discuss . . . well, I'm not sure what he wants to discuss. He hasn't shared that part with me. Vampire business, I guess."

"So Cat really does have vampire cousins. Huh. I only half-believed her back then."

"I think we all did. Shows what we knew." Julia gave a little laugh. "Anyway, the cousin's name is Lachlan McRae."

"Obviously from Scotland," Leighton said dryly.

"More than you know. Anyway, he's here if you want to talk to him."

"No. I'll check with Raphael first, see what he says. But I've got to tell you, Jules, it's an odd request."

"Preaching to the choir. I'm just doing a favor for a friend."

"A friend, huh?"

"I was talking about Cat."

"Sure you were," she snickered. "Okay. Sun's in the sky, so it'll have to be later, but one more thing, Jules. If Raphael agrees to meet, it'll have to be here."

Julia glanced up at Lachlan to get his response. He nodded agreement. What choice did he have? If he'd had the power to force Raphael's hand, he wouldn't have been going through her in the first place.

"That would be great, Cyn. Thanks for doing this."

"Oh, it's my pleasure. You know me. I love stirring things up." She laughed. "Talk to you soon, Jules."

Julia disconnected the call, then stared down at her phone for a moment before turning to him. "Was that what you expected?"

"Pretty much," he agreed, walking around to sit next to her. "If I got a call like that, I'd be wary, too."

"What do you think will happen?"

"Depends on how much Raphael knows about me, or how much he can find out. He won't waste time if he doesn't think I'm worth it."

"And are you? Worth it?"

He eyed her for a long moment, then said with perfect seriousness, "Oh, yeah. Worth every minute."

She looked away quickly, but not before he caught the confused expression on her face—a combination of irritation and pleasure. She *liked* that he was intrigued enough to tease her with sexual innuendos. Well, well.

She stood abruptly. "It's late," she said, then made a hapless gesture with one hand. "Well, not for you, maybe, but I was up for hours last night, dealing with DC. Give me your cell number and I'll contact you as soon as I hear from Cyn. And then maybe we can get started on your half of the deal."

He rose next to her, intentionally standing close. If she breathed too deeply, their bodies would touch. Predictably, she took a half-step back, putting enough space between them to eliminate that possibility, but without looking as if she was retreating. She clearly understood body language and how to use it.

"Let's see what Raphael says first. If he agrees to a meeting, it'll take a few days for me to travel to Malibu and back."

"Shit," she cursed. "Can't you just—?"

"What? You think I'd give you Erskine's address and send you off on your own to get killed, or worse?"

"No, no, I just forgot you'd have to go to California."

"I don't think Raphael would settle for Skype. It's a vampire thing."

"I know. You're right. It's just . . ." Julia looked down, shaking her head in disgust. "I've been planning this for . . . ." She sighed. "But that's all right. It's not as if you're never coming back." She raised her head to give him a close look. "Don't forget, vampire. I did my part, and I'll know when you get back."

"You think you can track me?" he asked, amused at her arrogance.

"You better believe it."

"Might be fun to watch you try. But don't worry," he added, his voice going hard, "we made a bargain, and I keep my word."

"I wasn't questioning—"

"Yes, you were. But you'll learn better. Come on, Fergus will walk you out."

"That's not necessary."

"It is in my world."

JULIA FOLLOWED Fergus into the elevator, wondering why she felt . . . ashamed. As if she'd done something wrong, something she wasn't proud of. So she'd reminded Lachlan of his promise. So what? She barely knew him. Why should she automatically trust that he'd keep his word? Especially once he had what he needed from Raphael. He wanted to overthrow Erskine Ross and assume leadership of Scotland's vampires. That happened to dovetail nicely with her own plans, but she somehow doubted Lachlan would be willing to take her along when he went after Erskine. She snorted softly, drawing a glance from the otherwise silent Fergus. These McRae vampires apparently had a lot to learn about women. Or maybe they were accustomed to dealing with curvy village maidens who blushed at every kind word and appreciative glance from the big, bad vampires.

Whatever they were used to, she wasn't it. But they had to understand her need for vengeance. They were Highlanders, for God's sake. Anyone who'd read Scottish history knew that Highlanders had perfected revenge to a self-destructive art. As old as Lachlan, and probably his cousins, were, they'd have lived it several times over. But if they thought she was going to sit back and watch while they took care of Erskine Ross on their own, they were sadly mistaken. Lachlan seemed willing to do more than give her Erskine's address and walk away, as he'd said. But she *needed* this. Needed to be the one who shot that evil bastard in the heart, so that Masoud's life wouldn't end on a tragic footnote. Maybe she was selfish. Maybe this was for herself as much as Masoud, a balm to the guilt that haunted her. But whatever it was, she *would* have her vengeance. And not even big, bad Lachlan McRae was going to stop her.

She gave Fergus a polite smile as the elevator moved downward. He was a good-looking guy, too, of course. What was it Cyn had called them? *Sexy fuckers.* She grinned privately. That was Cyn for you. Her habitual cursing had been the absolute bane of Madame Martel's existence. She had a point about vampires, though. Lachlan's image filled her mind. Not just his face, though he was brutally handsome, but that body . . . and what he could probably do with it. She'd bet he'd insist on taking charge in bed. Not like the ambitious and social-climbing guys she usually dated. Guys who were more concerned with pleasing her than dominating her. She was never sure if they were after her or her father's money and connections. She sometimes thought they should just give her dad a blow job and skip her altogether.

She sighed. Yeah, Lachlan was a fine piece of manhood, but it would be messy. Not in the body fluid way—although she was sure that would certainly be true—but in terms of messing up her plan to get Erskine. She'd dreamed and schemed about killing that bastard, and she wasn't going to let even the sexiest vampire on earth get in the way of that.

The elevator door opened, and Fergus stepped out, his gaze sweeping the lobby quickly before he reached back to hold the door open for her. The vampire bellman, or whatever he really was, took over then, giving a nod as Fergus faded back into the elevator and the door closed.

"I'm Lennon, my lady," the vampire said easily.

"And I'm Julia Harper, no title necessary. So 'Lennon,' was your mum a Beatles fan?"

He gave her an amused look. "Lennon McRae, Ms. Harper. Born long before the Beatle version."

Julia's face heated with embarrassment. "That was stupid of me. I apologize."

"No need. I get it more than you might think. Here we go." He opened the front exit door to a wash of cold, wet London air, just as a dark sedan pulled up to the curb.

LACHLAN STEPPED out onto the balcony to watch Julia leave. He'd called Lennon, wanting him to be ready for her. The vamp was another McRae cousin, albeit a generation or two removed. He was perfect for bellman duties whenever Lachlan came to London, because he looked to be no more than in his early twenties, and with a face that screamed his innocence. All of it was a lie, of course.

He heard Lennon's voice as the door opened, and a black sedan pulled to the curb. Julia must have ordered a private car service. She appeared a moment later, but hesitated on the sidewalk in front of the hotel, her head turned to say something to Lennon.

Everything happened at light speed after that. Front and back doors on the sedan opened and two men jumped out, both reaching for Julia at the same time, one on each arm. Lennon gripped one of the men by his hair and yanked him away, as Lachlan leapt from his balcony. He was forced to drop the distance in two stages, too high up to be certain of a safe landing. But he moved so fast that it hardly mattered. He hit the ground just as Julia produced a short baton from somewhere, gave a sharp jerk to snap it open, and began beating her second attacker with it. Lachlan grabbed the guy she was beating and threw him against the building. Bones crunched and the guy's head cracked against the wall loud enough to be heard over the first assailant's yells, as Julia and Lennon both laid into him. Lennon, aware of Lachlan's arrival, was taking his time and giving his fists a workout, while Julia joined in with her baton.

Lachlan had thought to grab the driver, but the man had gunned away from the curb when he saw Lachlan land, and was already well down the block, with no thought for his comrades. Lachlan could have caught him anyway, but it was a busy street with too many witnesses, and there was no need. The attacker he'd thrown into the building was dead, gray brain matter already leaking to the sidewalk, but the other was still alive, and one was all he needed . . . assuming he could stop Julia and Lennon from beating the man to death, that is.

"Enough!" Lachlan ordered, putting a punch of power behind it to be sure both Lennon and Julia obeyed. They turned as one to stare at him, breathing hard and looking more than a little pissed that he'd stopped them. "We need answers," he explained. "And the other is dead." He spoke with no inflection at all, as if a man's death meant nothing. Which it didn't, in this case. Whatever his reasons for trying to kidnap Julia, they hadn't been altruistic. He'd made his play and lost. "Lennon, you know what to do. Fergus is on his way down. He'll deal with the police. Julia, let's go."

"Go where?" she demanded. "I have to wait for the police." One hand was still fisted around the baton, her eyes bright and her chest heaving with effort. She was both gorgeous and incredibly fuckable at that moment. Lachlan's cock twitched, but this wasn't the time or place.

"You're not waiting for anyone." He slid his hand over her arm. "I don't want you involved in this."

"But I *am* involved," she protested, but she didn't fight his hold. It would have been pointless, and she was smart enough to realize it. "What if they were kidnappers? My father needs to be warned."

"And what if you're wrong? What if Erskine knows what you're up to and decided to stop you before you started? That's something we should know, don't you think?"

He turned her down the next street, where the Range Rover was waiting for him. He and his cousins never used garages if they could help it. He dug the key fob out of his pocket and unlocked the doors. "Get in." When it looked as if she was going to argue with him, he opened the passenger door and said, "Don't fight me on this, Julia. You won't win. Now get in the fucking car. Please."

Lachlan thought it was probably the "please" that did it. She had no trouble bashing a guy on the head with that vicious baton of hers, but one must observe the courtesies. Women were such a strange and wonderful mystery.

"Where are we going?" she asked tightly, as he pulled into traffic. A lot had happened since the sun went down, but it wasn't all that late.

There were still plenty of cars on the road, which now served his purposes just fine.

He didn't answer her question directly. "Where are you staying?"

"You're taking me home?" She seemed surprised.

"Depends on where you live. Is it secure?"

"Yes. It's my father's place in Kensington. It's a newer building, with a 24-hour concierge and the latest security tech. And there's a company I can call if I need more."

"Why would you need more than that?"

"I don't. It's my dad's idea. It's just the two of us, and he worries about me."

"Hmm."

"What does that mean?" she groused.

He glanced at her sideways, then back to the road. "It means 'hmm,'" he replied mildly. "What's the address? I'll take you there."

"Tell me where *you're* going instead. Where'd Lennon take that other man? The one you didn't kill, that is."

"You have a problem with killing men who try to kidnap you?"

"Not at all. I'm just not accustomed to handling the dead bodies myself."

"Good thing you didn't have to, then."

"What about the one who survived? Where's Lennon taking him?"

"To someplace it's better you don't know about."

She didn't settle for that. He hadn't thought she would. "Does that mean you're going to interrogate him?" she asked, pushing.

"Something like that."

"Something like that," she said mimicking his much deeper voice. "Look, *I'm* the one they wanted. I should be there. I *want* to be there."

"No, you don't. What I'm planning isn't entirely legal." Lachlan could feel her staring at him.

"You think I can't handle it." It was a statement, not a question, but he answered anyway.

"I don't know what you can or can't handle. But in this case, there's no reason you need to do either. I'll give you whatever I get from him, but I need to know if it's connected in any way to Erskine. And the human police won't get that out of him, because they won't know to ask." Privately, he thought it unlikely, since the kidnappers had been human, but Erskine had used humans in the past when it suited his purposes.

She exhaled deeply. "All right. Will I see you tomorrow?"

"Depends on your friend Leighton. If it's daylight when you hear from her, leave a message, and I'll call back after dark."

"Okay."

She sounded resigned, maybe even a little sad. He glanced over. "You okay?"

"Sure. I'm always okay."

Lachlan scowled. In his experience, people who said they were okay were usually far from it. But he didn't have the luxury of psychoanalyzing Julia Harper right now. The night only lasted so long, and he still had to question the damn kidnapper and dispose of the two bodies. Because there *would* be a second body. Lachlan wouldn't let the man live, no matter how willingly he gave up everything he knew. One might think a big city like London would offer lots of places to dump a dead thug, but it wasn't that easy. These days, London's city police were much more tuned in than they used to be when it came to vampire activities. It was always better to go farther afield, out into greater London or one of the suburbs where personal crime was so prevalent that the authorities didn't even try to keep up.

But first, he had to make sure Julia was home and safe. Making a final turn, he pulled up in front of a tall, modern building in Kensington. Both the concierge and security guard in the lobby took note of his arrival, and at least two cameras were recording the glass-fronted entrance. He'd have to remember those cameras for future visits. Vampires had come a long way from the days of skulking through alleys for victims, but that didn't mean they wanted their every step to be noted. Like most of his brethren, he preferred to stick to the shadows.

He became aware that Julia was staring at him. "How'd you know my address?" she asked.

It took Lachlan a second or two to figure out what the problem was, but then he cursed his own lack of attention. He'd taken the location from her thoughts when she'd been answering his questions about where she lived. Shit. He hadn't meant to do that. Or at least he hadn't meant to let her *know* he'd done it. His telepathic ability was strong, but he usually controlled it better than that. Obviously, he'd been more distracted than he realized.

"I recognized the building from your description," he lied. "There aren't that many newer tower developments in Kensington."

She gave him a look he couldn't read. Well, he could have, but he wasn't going to eavesdrop on her thoughts again.

"I guess." She sounded both tired and resigned. "I'll call you—"

He was already out of the vehicle and moving around to open her door. After all his talk about her safety, did she really think he was going to drop her at the curb like a bad date?

She gave him a surprised look. "The guard—"

"I'm sure he's a great guy and very diligent," he interrupted.

She sighed impatiently and muttered, "You're worse than my father." But she didn't say anything more until the security guard had the door open for them. "Thank you, Gerald."

"Everything okay, Ms. Harper?" the guard asked, not even trying to conceal his scrutiny of Lachlan.

"Just fine," she said quietly, then gestured. "This is Lachlan McRae. He's a friend." She gave a little wave to the concierge who'd remained behind his desk. "Welcome back, Mickey," she called. "It's good to see you again. Mr. McRae will be in town for a bit, so you should put him on my approved visitors' list."

"Will do, Ms. Harper."

Lachlan was taking in several things at once. First, Julia was clearly accustomed to dealing with a serious level of security at her residence. Or at least, her father's residence. The fact that she'd gone to that fancy French school with Catriona told him her family had money, and she'd also hinted at living in more than one country growing up.

But while she seemed to know both the guard and concierge well, they were strangers to *him*—strangers whose loyalty, as far as he knew, could be bought. Then there was the lobby itself. He noted the number and placement of doors and windows, and the bank of two elevators, neither of which required a key to enter. But none of that kept him from taking note of Julia's comment to the concierge, putting him on her visitors' list. He *hmm'd* silently, not wanting another interrogation as to the meaning of his non-verbal observations.

The elevator doors opened as soon as the guard pressed the call button. He would have joined them inside, but Lachlan lifted a hand to stop him. "I've got this," he said, touching the words with just enough power that the man gave him a respectful nod and stepped back.

"What'd you do to Gerald?" Julia asked quietly, as the elevator started upward.

"Just assured him you were safe with me."

"And am I?"

He gave her a sideways glance, but she wasn't looking at him. "Depends on your definition of safe."

Her breath came out in a soft rush, and her heart kicked a beat, which she probably didn't remember he could hear. But she didn't say anything. Not until the doors opened to a wide, marbled hallway on the penthouse floor. Directly opposite the elevator was a mahogany wood table that looked expensive, topped by an arrangement of fresh white flowers with just enough scent to be elegant, but not overwhelming. Roughly twelve yards to either side of the table were matching sets of heavy, double doors in an identical dark wood.

"This way," Julia breathed, then walked over to the leftward doors and slipped her hand into a niche containing a very sophisticated, full palm, biometric lock.

Lachlan glanced at the set of doors at the opposite end of the corridor, and found a more typical keyed deadbolt.

Julia noticed his glance and said, "I told you. My father worries."

He tipped his head toward the neighboring unit. "Who lives over there?"

"Some Russian oligarch or other. He's rarely in London. At least I haven't seen him, but I'm not here that often, either." She pulled out her hand and tapped in a code. The lock made a discreet burr of sound, but the door remained shut until she gripped the handle and pressed the old-fashioned thumb latch. "Come on in," she said, as she pushed the door wider and walked inside.

"You didn't mention tonight's attack to Gerald or Mickey downstairs," he said, "even though you seem friendly with both. Why not? Don't you think it's something they should know?" He strolled into the penthouse behind her, noting the immediate drop in air temperature. The place had an empty feel to it, as if no one was living there.

"They'd only tell my father." She raised a hand to forestall any comment. "Even if I asked them not to." She gestured at the spacious rooms. "This is all Dad's, not mine. And they take their cues from him. They're very protective."

"Maybe your father *should* know," Lachlan said, watching for her reaction.

Her mouth tightened just slightly before she spoke. "That's a very paternalistic thing for you to say, only I don't need any more fathers. The guys downstairs are bad enough."

He fought back a grin, glad to see she still had some spirit left. She'd seemed far too disheartened on the way over, as if all the air had drained out of her. Maybe she was just tired, as she'd said earlier.

Julia walked over and pressed a rocker switch, turning on a bank of very bright LED lights overhead. She immediately touched the dimmer, but before she did, he got a good look at her face and noticed something he hadn't caught earlier.

He strode over as she turned, her eyes going wide when he reached out and brushed away a thick lock of blond hair which had escaped the tidy chignon she'd worn all evening. He'd noticed the loose strands earlier and had assumed they was nothing more than that, a chunk of hair that had been tugged out of place during the attack. But the bright light had revealed something else.

"You're injured," he said quietly, holding the hair back from her face, resisting the urge to rub the silky strands between his fingers. "You're going to have a black eye." He gently touched the swollen ridge of her brow, already inflamed a bright red, but rapidly turning blue. "You should ice this."

She reached up, as if to grab his hand, but placed her own hand against his chest instead. "It's fine," she murmured, her eyes meeting his as she gave a rueful smile. "It's not my first black eye."

His lips crooked in a half grin. "Are you a hooligan, Ms. Harper?" He was still touching her face, his thumb brushing gently on the growing bruise beneath her eye. It would only get worse as the congested blood drained downward.

Her smile grew. "It's not my first black eye, but it *is* the first one I got in a real fight. The others were all from working out."

"You bash each other with the dumbbells at your gym?"

She rolled her eyes, then winced. "Shit, that hurts. And, no. I take kickboxing, which is a greatly exaggerated term for what I do."

His fingers slid down to cup her cheek, and he was abruptly aware of how close they were standing, the velvet softness of her skin, the warm brush of her breath over his hand . . . the clenching need in his gut, and growing heaviness in his groin.

Shit.

He took a deliberate step back, trailing his hand down her arm to ease the separation. "You'll be okay here?" he asked, glancing around. "You should turn on some heat."

"It's not worth heating the whole apartment," she said, resuming her cool façade, taking her cue from him, damn it. "There's a fireplace in the bedroom," she added. "That's enough for me."

Lachlan had a sudden picture of Julia naked in the firelight, pale blond hair tangled over her shoulders, fair skin painted gold by the flames. He shook his head against the raw appeal of the image. What the hell was wrong with him tonight?

"All right. Good," he said, to convince himself as much as Julia. "I'll check in with you tomorrow night."

"I don't know if I'll hear from Cyn that quickly. She might—"

"I'll check in anyway," he said, walking back to the door. "Lock this behind me."

"Yes, Dad."

"Very funny. Lock the fucking door."

Her soft chuckle drifted over him as the door closed, but he didn't call the elevator until he heard the electronic lock snick shut.

JULIA WATCHED THE video monitor as Lachlan strolled down the hall and waited for the elevator. He was beautifully put together, his body turning that simple walk into an anatomy lesson of how a man's muscles were supposed to move. He seemed relaxed enough, and yet there was a coiled readiness that said this man, this *vampire*, could shift gears at the drop of a hat, going from relaxed to deadly in an instant.

She sighed as he disappeared into the elevator. They'd had a moment there, when he'd noticed her bruised eye. His hand was so big. He could have crushed her head like an egg. And yet, his touch had been careful, so very tender against her sore face. She sighed again and turned away, passing quickly through the echoing emptiness of her father's ultra-contemporary entertaining space, and into the other half of the penthouse which was private and designed for people to *live* in. Not that she or her father did so in any meaningful way. At opposite ends of the long hallway were two master suites, one for each of them, separated by two nice, but much smaller, guest bedrooms. The masters each had a fireplace and a ridiculously big bathroom, which made the suites more like apartments than bedrooms. Neither she nor her father lived here permanently, though he was here on business far more often than she was. What she hadn't told Lachlan was that her father didn't approve of the two-month leave she'd taken from the CIA, supposedly to put Masoud's affairs in order. He couldn't deny that she was executor of Masoud's estate, nor that Masoud had assets around the world, including London. But he didn't see why she couldn't handle it just as well from the relative safety of Washington, DC. Nobody denied Masoud's murder, but London authorities had concluded he'd been the victim of a random crime. Julia knew better, but hadn't told anyone of her suspicions, because she'd known they'd immediately seize everything she'd found in Masoud's safe and warn her away from it.

Her father, with his connections around the world, accepted the official finding, but she could tell he had his doubts. If he found out about that evening's attack against *her*, he'd be in London tomorrow, packing her up and carrying her right back to the States, believing the only way to keep her safe was to keep her close. It was a little claustrophobia-inducing sometimes, but it wasn't his fault. Julia had only been eleven when her mother and brother had been killed by that hit and run driver. Her family had money—*old* money, as they said—and her father would have spared no expense in searching for the man. But the police found him first, dead in a ditch and burned beyond recognition, the victim of his own reckless driving.

After that, her dad had become paranoid about the safety of his only remaining child, and in turn, Julia had done her best not to cause trouble, because she had her own fears. Her father was all she had left. And if her mother and brother's deaths had taught her anything, it was that nothing could keep you completely safe. Not even all the money in the world.

She turned off the lights as she passed into the hallway, leaving the big, dark room behind. Maybe she'd take a bath to soothe muscles gone stiff from the unaccustomed fight. Or maybe she'd take a handful of ibuprofen and a hot shower, then crawl into bed and dream of a hot vampire who stalked down the hallway like a beast in the jungle.

LACHLAN NODDED pleasantly to the two men stationed in the lobby of Julia's building. The concierge, Mickey, stuck to a professional nod, while Gerald, the security guard gave him a far more cautious scan.

"Gentlemen," Lachlan said. He was tempted to advise them to keep an eye out for strangers lurking about, but mindful of Julia's comment about her father's likely reaction, he held his tongue. He had reasons of his own for wanting her to remain in London. He told himself it was simply business, that he needed her to smooth the way with Raphael, but he wasn't that blind. He was attracted to her on a whole different front, which surprised the hell out of him. If someone had told him when he'd walked into that bar and seen the cool, controlled blond sitting with his cousin, that he'd want her before the night was over, he'd have laughed in their face. But there was more to Julia Harper than icy discipline. He didn't know what in her life had convinced her that a frosty façade was the way to go, but he knew that's all it was. She was no colder than he was, although it was possible he concealed his emotions just as effectively as she did. What a pair they made, he thought. Probably a good thing they weren't a pair at all, then.

He did a careful scan as he approached the Range Rover, using every sense he had, including his telepathy, to detect anyone lingering where they shouldn't be. He also used the remote to unlock the doors and start the engine, while standing in the small space between two buildings. He hadn't lived this long by letting bravado rule over reason. Erskine Ross had wanted him dead for a very long time. He'd tried and failed more than once since the Ross attack on Castle McRae, ever since he'd realized that Lachlan wasn't the weakling vampire he'd thought he was leaving behind to twist in the wind while the clan withered around him. Maybe Erskine hadn't understood that the battle had taken place on Lachlan's first night as a vampire, or maybe he'd let his overweening ego and cruelty get the better of him. But as Lachlan had matured into his power, the vampire lord had understood his mistake . . . far too late. Lachlan was too cautious and too powerful not to detect Erskine's various schemes. It was impossible to get an assassin close enough to do damage, and the one time he'd managed to slip a bomb into a small pub where the McRae cousins had liked to meet, Lachlan and every one of his cousins had emerged from the rubble unscathed. He was convinced it had been that display of power that had finally made Erskine back off his assassination attempts and pretend friendship instead, thinking Lachlan would live out his life in the obscurity of the far northern highlands, if simply left alone. Lachlan snorted at the thought as he slid into the driver's seat. Neither he, nor any living McRae, would ever forget the craven murder of their clan. Vengeance might come slowly, but he was a vampire. He could wait centuries to destroy his enemy.

He punched up his cousin on his cell as he pulled away from the curb.

"Yeah," Fergus answered. No names. It made Lachlan smile. His cousin made paranoid people seem careless.

"You've secured the prisoner?"

"Yes. You on your way?"

"Twenty minutes out, less if the streets stay quiet."

"Good. He's already terrified. Show him some fang, and he'll probably wet himself."

"Great. Why don't you do the honors, then hose him off before I get there?"

Fergus laughed. "Sorry, but duty comes with power."

"Who the fuck said that?"

"Me. See you soon, cuz."

Lachlan growled half-heartedly as he disconnected. Fergus and

Munro were both utterly loyal to him. The three of them had been the only McRae vampires who'd survived the attack all those years ago. It had taken decades to re-build the clan, not only the vampires, but the humans. Other clans had married in, and weaker clans had joined with them against the common enemy that was Erskine Ross. With the exception of his two cousins who, like Lachlan, had been reborn the night before Erskine's attack, every McRae vampire now living was Lachlan's child. More than one of them had proved to be a strong master vampire, and he'd brought in a few very strong vampires from other countries, or parts of Scotland, who'd sworn loyalty to him long ago. He wasn't a coward like Erskine, who liked toadies and vampires too weak to pose a threat. Lachlan wanted strong men and women by his side. Vampires who could help him hold the territory once he disposed of the cowardly Erskine.

He made the drive to the safe house in half the time he'd told Fergus. The streets had been empty, and the one police vehicle he'd seen had been going the other direction on a side street. If they'd wanted to stop him, he'd have been gone by the time they'd have turned around. He didn't even know if they'd tried. Didn't care, either. If they *had* managed to stop him, he'd have fuzzed their minds until they forgot all about him. He didn't feel guilty about that. There were better uses for public tax money than chasing down a single driver for speeding on empty streets.

It was Munro who buzzed him into the safe house. Although "safe" was a relative term. The house was furnished to look quite ordinary, if a bit more comfortable than most, but if one knew where to look, the enhancements were obvious. The house was *safe* for him and his cousins, because they'd installed a high-tech security system and a basement vault that was triple secured against intrusion. It was not so safe for the human kidnapper wanna-be who waited in the next room. That room wasn't so nicely furnished, but it *was* specially insulated. Unfortunately for their prisoner, that insulation was designed to keep something *in,* rather than out. Like the screams of people Lachlan interrogated there. Although admittedly, the screamers were usually vampires. In fact, he couldn't remember the last human they'd brought here. He was about to ask Munro about it, when Fergus opened the door to the next room.

"I thought I heard your voice," he said, then called over his shoulder, "Hey, Dave, look who's here. It's the guy who's going to scrub your brain until he gets what he wants."

A whimpering sound slid through the open door, and Lachlan

shook his head, a slight smile on his face at Fergus's sense of humor.

"Let's get this over with," he said. "Did *Dave* tell you anything at all?"

"Just that he was paid to grab her. He insists that's all it was. An ordinary ransom kidnapping. There's something more, but I'm not sure he knows what it is."

Lachlan gave his cousin a sharp look. "He was programmed?"

"Something like that, but subtle. Whoever did it knew what he was doing. I can't get it out of him."

"I will." He shrugged off his jacket and tossed it on a nearby chair. "What's his full name?"

"Dave Hill. We ran him. He's got a record, but it's small time stuff. Burglaries, some minor racketeering."

Lachlan took that in then said, "All right. Let's go."

Fergus accompanied him into the next room, but remained back by the door where the prisoner couldn't see him, since the chair he'd been tied to faced outward toward a large window. That window had a view of a church across the street, as if to taunt the prisoner with his salvation. The view was fake, just like the window, but it was a very good imitation.

Lachlan walked slowly around the prisoner and leaned against the wall next to the supposed window. The man looked up at him with wild eyes above the gag tied over his mouth.

"What's with the gag?" Lachlan asked Fergus.

"I got tired of his begging."

The prisoner shook his head almost angrily, as if he objected to Fergus's statement.

"Untie it," Lachlan said.

The man sucked in a gasping breath. "Thank you," he whispered. "I couldn't breathe."

"Your continued breathing isn't exactly high on my list, Dave. Tell me about tonight."

"I told the other guy—"

"So tell me."

Dave licked dry lips, his hungry gaze going to the bottle of water Fergus had placed in plain sight.

"Here," Lachlan said, handing him the bottle. "Wet your throat. This will go a lot faster."

Dave gave Lachlan a desperate look.

"Oh, right. Your hands are tied. Okay. One sip. I'm not going to stand here all night holding a fucking bottle, like feeding a baby." He put the bottle to Dave's mouth, and the man drank greedily, sucking in as much as he could before Lachlan pulled the bottle away and placed it back on the table.

"All right. Now talk."

"Like I said, I told the other guy. I was paid—we all were, the three of us—to grab the lady and hold her. That's it. We were given an address—"

Lachlan glanced at Fergus, who shook his head.

"—where we were supposed to take her."

"What's the address?"

Dave rattled it off and Fergus left the room. One of their vampires would check the place before dawn, but Lachlan didn't expect to find anything. Whoever had set Dave and his pals on Julia would know by now that their plan had failed. If the hideout had contained anything incriminating, it would have been sanitized already. But they had to check, anyway.

"How long did they want you to wait to be contacted?"

"He said no more than three days. We weren't going to hurt her, I swear. Her rich daddy was supposed to pay the ransom, and we'd set her free."

Lachlan straightened from his slouch against the wall and gave the prisoner a piercing look. "Who's 'he,' Dave? Who's the guy who hired you?"

Dave's face scrunched down with effort, and he shook his head. "I've tried, I swear. But I can't remember. It's like . . . it's right there, or it used to be, but now . . . ." He stared up at Lachlan. "I don't know anymore."

"We'll see about that." Lachlan didn't move, but power suddenly filled the room, like a charge of electricity abruptly sparking on every molecule of air. The walls groaned as if it was too much—too much pressure, too much weight—to bear. A thread of Lachlan's power stretched out and touched the prisoner's mind. Dave groaned and his head fell forward as Lachlan slipped into his thoughts. A quick surface scan showed nothing more than what the man had told him, but Lachlan had no interest in that. He probed deeper and found a memory of sitting in a dark pub earlier that night. He and his friends were having a pint, waiting. Waiting for what?

Dave glanced up as someone entered the pub. The room was dark and crowded, and the new arrival had something obscuring his face. A hat, maybe. Or one of those hoodie things the local thugs all wore. The man, if it was a man, walked by and tossed a piece of paper on the table. Dave's friends grabbed for it, but Dave turned in time to see the man disappear into the shadows of the pub. He blinked and stared harder—the guy hadn't just gotten lost in the crowd, he'd honest to Christ disappeared. But that was impossible. Maybe he'd had a pint too many. His friends were standing. They had their assignment. It was time to go.

Lachlan skipped over the next several memories, tedious in their detail. Either Dave was obsessive, or he was stupid and had to think about even the tiniest act before he moved. Whichever it was, Lachlan wasn't interested. He scrubbed Dave's brain as he went, careless of the damage he was doing. Poor Dave wasn't going to survive the night, so it didn't matter. He shouldn't have gone after someone in Lachlan's circle, even if he'd only met Julia tonight. She'd been with *him* before Dave and his buddies had attacked her, and that made it personal.

Dave moaned as Lachlan dug deeper, his moans turning to a keening noise when Lachlan detected a familiar scent. Not an *actual* scent, more of a mental signature. But in his own mind, he was a predator who'd caught the scent of his prey. And it was one he knew. Erskine Ross. Now why the fuck would Erskine be sending a trio of incompetent humans to grab Julia Harper? Of course, if she'd been alone, without Lachlan's vampire guard detail, the kidnapping scheme might have worked. Julia was deadly with that little baton of hers, but it wouldn't have worked against the two big men who'd tried to grab her. Dave might be whimpering now, but he was a big man, just like his dead buddy. But the real question was, did Erskine ultimately want Julia dead or alive? And why did he want her at all? Did he know Julia was after him? How? Lachlan himself only knew because Julia had told him, and they'd only met because of the coincidence of their individual goals. But even if Erskine had somehow found out, what threat could one human woman pose to such a powerful vampire? And why go to such lengths to take her alive? Was there something else he wanted from her?

But those were questions for Lachlan's cool blond, because he didn't give a damn whether Cynthia Leighton trusted Julia or not. Lachlan intended to get answers before *he* trusted her with anything to do with Raphael. There was too much riding on his plans for Scotland, and he wasn't the only one who would suffer if he didn't succeed. Erskine would wipe out the McRae clan for good if Lachlan failed this time. Not just the vampires, but every human clan member as well. Including lively wee Catriona and many others just like her. He couldn't let that happen. If he took on Erskine, he had to know he would win.

And he had to know if there was a snake in the grass who might cock it all up for him.

Lachlan's mind was racing, his planning already ten steps ahead when he felt Dave's brain rupture in a massive, fatal hemorrhage. He pulled his own awareness out of Dave's head, just before death claimed him. He'd slipped up when he'd been younger and still experimenting with his powers. He'd been curious enough that he'd remained in a prisoner's thoughts while the nothingness that was death stole everything that made him human. It had been both terrifying and depressing. Terrifying, because for a moment he'd confused his own thoughts with those of the dying man, and depressing because he'd realized that death was literally nothingness.

He'd never done it again, and he didn't do it tonight either.

He looked up as Fergus reentered the room. "Put the body on ice. It's too late to dispose of it safely tonight."

Dave wouldn't truly go on ice, but they had a cold room that would keep his body from beginning to decompose before they could get rid of it. It wasn't pleasant, but it was a fact of life they had to deal with in a big city like London.

"I could hit the hospital incinerator before dawn. It's a good time for it. All those tired workers ready to go home," Fergus said.

But Lachlan shook his head. "No need to chance it. You can do it tomorrow."

"What'd he tell you?"

"Pretty much what we suspected. Erskine was involved in this, and I need to have a chat with Julia Harper. The sooner the better."

"Let's hope she's a late sleeper, then."

"I don't give a damn what time she opens her eyes. I'll find her, and she'll damn well answer my questions, one way or the other."

Chapter Three

Malibu, CA USA

"I GOT A WEIRD call from my friend Julia, today."

Raphael glanced up at Cyn's reflection in the mirror, where he was tying his tie. "Weird how?"

She stepped in front of him and took over the task with a quiet smile. He was perfectly capable of knotting his own tie, but his Cyn seemed to enjoy it, and he loved having her take care of him. He rested his hands on her slender hips.

"Weird how, *lubimaya*?" he repeated.

"She and I went to prep school together in France." She lifted her gaze to his. "I told you about that school."

He nodded.

"We were close back then. Her father was some diplomat or other. One of those mega-rich guys who becomes an ambassador mostly for the prestige and because they meet people they can later negotiate business deals with over cocktails. Anyway, he lived in Paris at the time, so she went home more than I did—which was never—and I'd go with her. We've stayed in touch over the years. Birthday calls or, more often now, emails, and the occasional meal together when we're in the same city, which hasn't been for a while. She pretends she followed her dad into the diplomatic corps, although, to be honest, I think she's CIA and the State Department thing is a cover."

Raphael made a wordless sound of agreement, not sure where all of this was going.

"Anyway, Jules lost someone important to her a few months back. She was on the phone with him when he was shot on a street in London, and she heard the whole thing." She shuddered, and he dipped his head to kiss her upturned face. She gave him a soft smile before continuing, her gaze once more on his tie. "It gets worse. Just before he died, he warned her about some client he was investigating. A *vampire* client. Jules is convinced this vampire's the one who killed him, and she's out for blood."

"That's a dangerous route to take."

"Exactly. That's what I told her when she first called me. But she was determined to do it, even though she knew next to nothing about vampires. So what else could I do? I answered her questions, told her what to look out for, that sort of thing." She glanced up. "Don't give me that look. I warned her every single time we spoke that this was too dangerous, that she should let the police handle it. But you don't know Julia. She looks like some rare and precious orchid, all fragile and lovely, but there's a spine of steel hiding underneath. Once she's decided on something, she will *not* be dissuaded."

He tugged on her hips, bringing her against his body as she smoothed the length of perfectly knotted silk tie. "And you're telling me this because . . . ?"

"Because when she called *today*, she asked about *you*. She was calling on behalf of some Scottish vampire named Lachlan McRae, and he wants a meeting with you."

Raphael blinked in surprise as he ran the vampire's name through the database in his head. There were a lot of vampires in the world, but only a very few with the power to seriously propose a meeting with him. Especially one from that part of the world, with the currently hostile climate between the ruling vampires of Europe and North America. Lachlan. The name clicked into place with a mental snap.

"Where does he propose to meet?" he asked mildly.

Cyn studied him a moment. "I told her that if this guy was worth your time, and *if* you agreed to meet with him, it would have to be here." Her expression was set into stubborn lines, as if expecting an argument from him.

He smiled. "I assume you want the meeting to be here for my safety?"

"Damn right."

"So you think this Lachlan can best me?"

"No." She gave him a withering look. "But I don't trust anyone these days, so why take chances? Besides, he's the petitioner; let him come to you."

"I'll take the meeting. No one except Lachlan, no other vampires, not even to North America. Your friend can come, if you'd like, though. In fact, I insist on it. If she's CIA, then I want to make sure this isn't all a cover for the American government snooping into vampire affairs."

Cyn shook her head. "It's not. But I'll pass your requirements along. Can't be too careful."

Raphael's smile broadened into a grin. "I'm glad you approve. By the way, I have a business meeting tonight, right here on the estate. Would you like to sit in on it? To ensure my safety, of course."

Her eyes rolled. "Very funny." She rose onto her tiptoes and gave him a lingering kiss. "I'll pass on the meeting, but I'll see *you* later."

"Yes, you will."

She laughed, while he crossed to the elevator and stepped inside. As the doors closed behind him, he considered Lachlan's request. There was only one reason for the Scottish vampire to want a meeting—he was planning to take out Erskine Ross, who was the current Lord of Scotland. Before he'd left Europe for North America, Raphael had met the Scottish lord, but only once, a very long time ago. He'd thought Erskine vulnerable enough at the time that he'd briefly entertained the possibility of taking over Scotland for himself. Fortunately, he'd recognized the extent of his own ambitions and left for America instead.

As for Lachlan, Raphael knew of his existence and that he was strong, but nothing else. It would be interesting to see if his ambitions matched his abilities. Or if he'd die before he left Malibu.

Chapter Four

London, England

JULIA WOKE ABRUPTLY, her heart pounding, her body drenched in sweat. Damn it. She'd thought the nightmares would ease up once she set her plan in motion, but if anything, they'd gotten worse. Tears filled her eyes and spilled over. She hated this. Hated the fear, the aching loss . . . the guilt. Sometimes she wondered if it would ever go away. If even Erskine's death would be enough to ease the pain.

She rubbed at her eyes impatiently, ignoring the mental voice that told her she shouldn't. Fuck "shouldn't." She was exhausted, her nerves stretched so taut that she was surprised she managed to function at all. She shot a blurry glance at the clock and saw it was just past noon. She'd slept later than usual—even if she hadn't slept soundly. She'd probably have to get used to even later hours if she was going to be hanging around with vampires. Which it seemed she was, if she was determined to pursue her revenge against Erskine. She possibly could have hunted him on her own, maybe even killed him without getting herself killed in the process. She wasn't above using so-called feminine wiles to work her way into his good graces, and then blasting his heart to smithereens while he slept. But since she preferred to survive this venture, working with Lachlan was probably—no, *definitely*—the better route.

Besides, now that she'd met him, she was intrigued. He hadn't been at all what she'd expected in a vampire. Especially now that she knew he had significant power of his own. Somehow, she'd thought every powerful vampire would be more like Erskine. Rich, slick, and unbearably superior. The thought of cozying up to an asshole like that had made her want to vomit, but she would have done it, if it had been the only way to get to him.

But now that she'd met Lachlan, she wouldn't have to, although she was more than a little conflicted about that. She was attracted to him in a very fundamental way, and he seemed to like her, too. She paused. Jesus, she sounded like a twelve-year-old with her first crush. Maybe she should complete the ridiculous scenario—call Cat and ask *her* to ask her *cousin* if he liked Julia. Right, like *that* was going to happen.

The reality was, however, that she had an agenda that Lachlan didn't know about. Oh, he clearly suspected there was more to her story, but he didn't know the details. Didn't know how personal this was for her, how she'd lain awake every night, plotting her revenge, figuring out a way to get to Erskine. She'd have to tell him. Not the sweaty night details, but the rest of it. And sooner rather than later, because despite her reluctance, she knew the longer she waited, the less likely he'd be to trust her enough to include her in his plans. And she *had* to be there, had to be the one to fire the fatal shot that took that evil fucker out of the world. It was the only thing that would alleviate the guilt she felt.

Her cell rang at that moment, and her first thought was that it was Lachlan, that he somehow knew she was thinking about him. But that was impossible. It was barely past noon. Checking the caller ID, she blinked in surprise when Cyn's name popped up. She hadn't expected a call-back so soon, much less at this hour.

"Hey, Cyn," she said, putting the phone on speaker. "It's not even the crack of dawn there, yet."

"Life among vampires. You should probably get used to it."

"Why?" Julia asked, willfully ignoring the fact that she'd just been thinking the same thing herself.

"Because you're coming to California. Raphael's willing to meet your friend Lachlan—"

"He's not really my—"

"Hey, you made the call. Raphael says he'll meet Lachlan, but he wants you come along, and no one else. None of his vampire buds."

Julia stared at the phone. "Why me? I don't have anything to do with—"

"I repeat," Cyn said cheerfully. "You made the call. And don't give me that innocent crap, Jules. I know where you work. If your bosses are involved in this, we need to know. Raphael's not crazy about governments in general, but especially not when they poke into his business."

"There's been no poking," she insisted immediately. "The State Department has no interest—"

Cyn made a loud scoffing noise. "Puh-leeze. You forget who you're talking to. Besides, you're kidding yourself if you don't think Lachlan knows everything about you, too. Vampires have connections everywhere. Believe it."

"I don't *want* to go to fucking California. I just got used to *this* time zone."

"There's my Jules. For a while there, I thought you'd forgotten how to swear."

"Come on, Cyn, can't you—?"

"Nope. Think of it as a visit with a dear old friend who's not that old. Me. And it's not as if Malibu is hard to take this time of year. Much better than rainy old London."

Julia sighed. "I don't even know if he'll do it without his cousins. They seem tight."

"He will if he wants the meeting. Raphael won't do it any other way."

"But why does he want *me* there? Hell, why would *Lachlan* want me there?"

"What's not to want? You're a beautiful woman. Persuade him."

"I can't believe you, of all people, just said that to me."

"Oh, right, because you've never used your looks to get what you want. Remember Monsieur Leveque? You had him so worked up—"

"He used to look up our skirts in class! The man was a pig."

"And yet, you sweet-talked him into an A."

"Fine. I'm a slut. Is that what you want—"

Cyn's laugh cut her off. "Not a slut, Jules. Just a woman who knows what she wants. Nothing wrong with using the pig's perversions against him."

"Yeah, well, I'm not sure that'll work with Lachlan," Julia grumbled.

"Use your dad's jet as a bribe, then. Vamps hate flying across time zones."

She thought about that a moment. "I can try. When is this big meeting supposed to happen?"

"Whenever you get here, I guess. You're the ones who wanted to meet."

"Okay. I'll talk to Mr. Gloomy and see what he says."

"Gloomy?" Cyn laughed as she continued, "Oh, God, this ought to be a great meeting. Broody meets Gloomy."

"I'll call you back. And stop laughing, you bitch. It's not funny."

Cyn was still laughing when Julia disconnected and tossed the phone aside. "Damn it," she muttered, dropping onto her bed. She was going to have to tell Lachlan the full truth a lot sooner than she'd planned. She knew Cyn, and there was no way she wouldn't dig out the truth, even if Raphael's people didn't do it for him. Plus, Cyn had a head start. She knew some of Julia's past, enough to know where to start looking anyway. Forget what the vampires might know, Cyn's *personal* connections were as good as Julia's. She'd know the whole tragic tale by the time Julia arrived in California. With Lachlan.

Fuck.

LACHLAN'S EYES opened, and it took him a moment to remember where the hell he was. He'd slept in no fewer than five different places in the last few weeks, as he'd traveled to London from his clan fortress in the mountains of Kintail. Even in London, he'd moved between two different safe houses, and this one wasn't his favorite. For that matter, the Claridge Hotel was far grander and more comfortable by far.

He might be a bit spoiled, he admitted privately. But he was old enough to deserve a little comfort. That thought made him laugh. The day he felt so old that he needed a soft bed was the day he'd lie down in a nice sunny spot with the dawn.

He threw off the comforter, which he probably didn't need. It wasn't as if vampires ever got cold. When he was out, he was *out*. No sensations at all. But he still had enough humanity to crave the warmth of a good comforter on a cold, wet day. Which pretty much defined London this time of year. Scotland, too, so he couldn't complain much. He padded naked to his private bathroom and turned on the shower as hot as it would go. He had a list of things he wanted to accomplish tonight, and first on that list was a reckoning with Julia Harper.

In fact . . . . He picked up his cell. No messages. That might mean she hadn't heard from Leighton, or she might be waiting until well after sunset to call him. She struck him as an efficient person, so maybe the latter, but he didn't feel like waiting. He hit her number.

"Lachlan." Her greeting was cool and businesslike, and it made him want to do something to rattle her. Maybe when they got together later, he'd fist his hand in her long blond hair and kiss her breathless. Just to fuck with her.

"Princess," he replied smoothly. She sucked in an irritated breath, which amused the hell out of him. "Any news for me?" he asked blandly.

"As a matter of fact, yes. We should meet."

"I agree. But tell me what the news is first."

"Raphael has invited you to Malibu. Which I'm sure you expected," she added tartly.

That made his grin widen. He did love getting on her nerves, though he didn't stop to wonder why.

"There are conditions," she said.

His grin faded. "What are they?"

"You have to come alone, without your cousins or other vampires. And . . ." She paused. "He insists that I come with you."

Lachlan digested that last bit of news, trying to decide if he trusted her enough to accept her word on this. The demand for her presence seemed random. Why would Raphael want her there? Hell, maybe the two women had conjured up this supposed requirement so they could visit. He dismissed that thought almost as soon as he had it. Both women were wealthy enough that they could travel anywhere they pleased. Julia hardly needed to hitch a ride with him to visit California. Besides, she didn't sound any happier about it than he was.

"Why do you think that is?" he asked, truly curious about her response. It might tell him more than she knew.

She sighed. "I suspect it has to do with my job. Which is why we need to meet. There are things you need to know."

Now, *that* surprised Lachlan. He'd been all ready to turn the screws and demand she tell him the truth, but now it seemed she'd beat him to it. He was almost disappointed.

"All right. Let's meet. Your place or mine?"

"I was thinking someplace else, like a restaurant or a bar."

"Don't trust me, princess?"

"Stop—" She exhaled a sharp breath, before continuing in her usual cool voice. "You're right. It's probably better if we keep this private. Let's make it my place, if you don't mind."

"Not at all. See you in an hour." He disconnected before she could respond, figuring she'd try to change the time to regain control. But he wasn't a man who let others control him. Not when it came to meetings, and sure as hell not in bed.

He frowned. He was having an awful lot of sex-themed thoughts about Julia Harper this evening. He considered the possibility. She'd be a challenge, but he was always up for one of those. Ha ha. He was still smiling as he stepped under the shower's pounding spray.

JULIA STARED AT her cell phone, wishing she could slam it down properly. Older phones were far more satisfying when it came to hanging up on people. But the bastard hadn't even given her that much. He'd hung up on her. And that after announcing he'd arrive in an hour. This was *her* apartment. Shouldn't she be the one to set the time? What if she'd had another engagement? What if she wasn't ready to entertain *anyone* in an hour, much less a fucking vampire?

"And if he calls me 'princess' one more time, I'm going to stake him," she muttered, then cocked her head, thinking she should check with Cyn about that. She'd done some research about what it took to kill a vampire, because she fully intended to see Erskine Ross brought to dust by her own hand. What she'd found indicated the idea of a stake was pure myth, that a gun would do the job just as well, though it might be a tad less satisfying. Still, Cyn would have insider knowledge, so maybe it was good luck that Raphael had insisted on her presence. It would give her a chance to pick Cyn's brain before she undertook the dangerous hunt for Erskine Ross.

She crossed to the wall of floor-to-ceiling windows and reached for the pull to shut out the night. She studied the street far below, her gaze traveling over the surrounding buildings, and the river in the distance. Her eyes caught for a moment, not by the London skyline, but at a reflection of the rumpled bed behind her. Her first thought was that she needed to make it before Lachlan arrived, but she shook her head defiantly. No way he was going to see her bedroom. She might need him to fulfill the promise she'd made to herself over Masoud's grave, but she didn't *need* him. The memory of Lachlan landing a four-story leap to fight off the kidnappers played in her brain, but she forced it away. Who cared if he was strong and brave and . . . whatever the fuck else he was. He *still* wasn't going to see her bedroom. Not tonight.

She sighed as she headed for the bathroom and a hot shower. Hell, maybe she should make it a cold shower instead. But no, he'd made a point of telling her about vampires' enhanced senses when they'd first met in the bar. She wouldn't want to offend his highness with the scent of her nightmares.

LACHLAN STRODE through the lobby of Julia's building, not pausing on his way to the elevators. "Evening, Mick, Gerald," he said with just the right note of friendliness. Pleasant, but not too familiar. He was good at judging social niceties among humans—another benefit of his telepathic abilities. It didn't hurt that he'd dressed for the evening, looking every bit the professional gentleman in a dark gray suit and white shirt, his deep red tie bearing the faintest trace of the McRae tartan.

The two men acknowledged him with similar greetings, calling him by name. A second guard, just entering through a door behind the front desk, gave him a careful scan. Lachlan could have greeted him by name, too—having read it in Mick's mental response to the guard's entrance—

but that would have freaked out the three men, and he didn't want to take the time to smooth over their thoughts. So he settled for a friendly nod, figuring since the other two obviously knew him, the new guy wouldn't question it.

He was right, of course. He cruised over to the elevator, which Gerald already had keyed in and opened for him.

"Thank you."

"Should I let Ms. Harper know you're on your way up?" Mickey called.

Lachlan paused in the open elevator door. "No need. I called her from the car. She's expecting me." Figuring that might be against the building's rules, he added a small push of power to make sure the man didn't make the call. He wasn't sure why he bothered, except that it would probably throw Julia off her stride when he showed up at her door unannounced. And he'd decided she needed more spontaneity in her life, whether she wanted it or not.

The elevator didn't stop on its way to the penthouse floor, and the silence that greeted him on arrival was just as hushed as it had been the night before. The neighboring apartment was still empty of life, and Julia's wasn't much better. A human observer would probably judge both residences to be empty. There was a coldness to the entire level, as if no one had lived there for a very long time.

But then, he wasn't human. To his senses, Julia's presence was a warm spark in the otherwise elegant austerity of the penthouse atmosphere. He walked to her door with vampire stealth and knocked. He still had the life spark that was Julia in his mental sights, and so saw the slight flare of her reaction when he knocked without warning. The click of high heels sounded on the marble floor a moment later, and the door opened.

She gave him a narrow look. "How'd you get up here?"

"The elevator," he said, doing his best innocent impression.

"Did you jinx Mickey?"

"Jinx?" he repeated in amusement. "I don't *jinx* people, princess." He pushed forward into the apartment, forcing her to either move back or bodily stop him from entering. He put a steadying hand on her hip when she teetered slightly on her skinny heels. She didn't brush his hand off, but he could tell she wanted to, as she took a step away instead.

"I thought you needed an invitation to enter a home?"

He shrugged. "You invited me in last night. I'm afraid you're stuck with me now."

"Can I rescind it? Make it a one-time deal?"

He laughed. "I'm wounded. I thought we were friends." When she just stared at him, he said, "The answer is 'no.' That only happens on TV."

"Well, that sucks," she muttered and turned away, heading for a small sitting area where there was a fire burning. She was wearing another one of those tight skirts, and he admired the round swell of her ass, the sway of her hips, and the elegant curve of her calves above those sky-high heels.

She turned when she reached the sitting area, giving him a withering glance when she caught him watching. Lachlan hadn't even bothered to conceal his appreciation. He simply raised his gaze slowly to her face and smiled. "The fire's nice," he murmured, walking right up to her again, forcing her to tip her head back to meet his eyes.

She stared at him for a moment, then drew a quiet breath and said, "Thank you. This room's too cold without it."

He trailed two fingers carefully over the soft skin under her bruised eye, the discoloration barely noticeable beneath expertly applied makeup. "Does it hurt?"

She slanted her gaze to the side, as if embarrassed. "A little, but I heal quickly." With that, she turned away, walking past a small sofa to sit on one of the chairs, gesturing for him to sit wherever he wanted. Lachlan took the sofa, sitting on the end closest to her, while draping his arm over the back, claiming the entire space for himself.

"Would you like wine?" she asked, indicating the bottle and two glasses on the small table between them. One glass was already half-full, with a slight lipstick smudge on the rim.

"No, thank you," he said politely. His gaze drifted to the pulse of her blood visible beneath the open neckline of the cashmere cardigan she was wearing instead of a blouse. She must have caught the shift in his attention, because she twitched the opening of the sweater, as if trying to cover her neck. It didn't matter. She could have been wearing a turtleneck up to her chin, and he'd still have known exactly where the plump vein was located.

He looked up and caught her staring at him. Their gazes met and held, and in that moment, Lachlan knew he wanted this woman. And he was a man accustomed to getting what, and whom, he wanted.

JULIA'S BREATH caught when her eyes met Lachlan's. A heavy fringe of black eyelashes made his pretty hazel eyes seem darker than they were.

There was none of the otherworldly glow she'd read about in descriptions of powerful vampires. But there was a power that defied common perception. She couldn't have said how, but somehow, she knew that if she touched his skin, she'd feel it simmering just beneath the surface. Just as she had earlier, when he'd been walking behind her and she'd sensed his perusal like a wave of heat traveling over her body. He'd done that from the very beginning, studying her, not saying a word, just waiting. But waiting for what?

She lifted her glass and took a sip of wine, breaking the eye-fucking going on between them and wetting her dry throat enough that she could speak. "We should finalize the details for California first, so I can make arrangements. I've already made inquiries about the jet's availability and I think it will work for us. But I'm not sure—"

"What jet?"

"Oh, right. Sorry. I discussed this with Cyn earlier. She said vampires don't like crossing time zones, given all the problems with daylight arrivals and such, which rules out commercial flights. My dad has a jet, which he lets me use whenever he doesn't need it, and depending where it's based at the time. So I thought we could fly that way."

His mouth curved the tiniest bit into a crooked smile. "Aye. And will you be the sexy flight attendant, then?"

Julia was tempted to toss the wine in his face, but she'd only have to clean up the mess. And besides, she didn't believe for one minute he was really that uncultured. Oh, sure, one could argue he'd been born in a time when women were little more than property to be traded between clans and families like cows. But Lachlan didn't fool her. He was educated and very in tune with the modern world. He had to be if he was seriously considering the takeover of all Scotland's vampires. So she only smiled back at him. "The plane comes with a professional attendant. Usually a man," she added, though it wasn't true.

His expression shifted, going from teasing to serious in an instant. "Not on this flight. There'll be no one in the cabin but you and me."

She frowned, genuinely confused. "Why?"

"You said it yourself. We'll be flying through daylight at some point, which means I'll be out of it. I can't have strangers poking around."

"But the pilots—"

"Will be busy flying the plane, one hopes."

Julia sucked her lips into a flat line as she studied him, and saw him smile.

"Don't do that," he said quietly.

"Do what?"

"Your mouth's too pretty to suck your lips like that."

Her breath caught again. He liked her mouth? She barely stopped herself from immediately pushing her lips back out. "We were talking about the plane," she said sternly.

Lachlan's smile grew. "Aye. And we'll need no flight attendant. I'll get my own drinks. When do we leave?"

Julia's heart was racing. She hated this part of meeting a new guy. The uncertainty, the 'does he/doesn't he' stupidity. And Lachlan wasn't even a new guy, not in that sense. Yes, he was male and new. But he was a business associate, not a *guy*. He was also a vampire who could hear her heart racing. She tried to slow her body's response. The last thing he needed was any ego stroking on her part.

"We're in luck, actually," she said lightly. "I got an email from my dad overnight. He always lets me know when he's traveling. He left DC for Paris a few hours ago. Once he arrives, the jet will be sitting idle in France for a week or two, waiting for him. But I thought I should wait to call him until I spoke with you. Just in case." She sipped her wine. "When would you want to leave?"

"The sooner the better. Did Raphael specify a date?"

"No. I'll check with Cyn to be sure, but I got the impression he'd make time whenever we could get there."

"Okay, then. Tomorrow night."

Julia winced. "Tomorrow?"

"Problem?"

"No, no. I just hate jet lag."

Lachlan snorted. "Don't we all? Unfortunately, delaying won't make it any better."

"I know," she said with a resigned sigh. "Okay. I'll talk to my dad, get the jet over here for tomorrow night. The pilots probably won't mind. They get bored sometimes, just hanging around."

"They get bored in *Paris*?"

"Yeah, well. It's not the first time they've been there, and they have families back home."

"Let me know when it's confirmed, then." He shifted to scoot forward, elbows on his knees, his big body suddenly much closer as he met her gaze. "Now, what else do you need to tell me, Julia Harper?"

FOR THE FIRST time since he'd arrived that night, Julia avoided looking at him. She took a long drink of wine, as if she needed the liquid courage, then leaned back in her chair before glancing up, and away again.

"Okay," she said. "Hear me out, all right? Don't jump to conclusions and don't interrupt."

Lachlan's eyebrows lifted. "That's a lot of assumptions on your part, princess."

Her head shot up, her expression narrowed in irritation. "Maybe I'm getting to know you better."

He sat back and assumed a deliberately relaxed posture, ankle crossed over the opposite knee. "No promises, but I'll try to be good."

She shook her head with an exasperated noise, then took another sip of wine and began her story. "I told you I want Erskine dead, but I didn't tell you why. Honestly, I wasn't planning to tell you at all. When I asked Cat about meeting you, I only thought to get information, nothing else." She started to say more, but then turned to stare out the apartment's wall of glass, as if thinking of what to say next.

"And I didn't expect to find anyone but my wee cousin," he said, encouraging her to continue. "She forgot to mention you'd be there."

Julia seemed surprised at that. "Oh." She scowled, though whether it was meant for Cat's machinations, or because it changed whatever she'd planned to tell him, he didn't know. Finally, after what seemed like an internal debate on her part, she shrugged and said, "I guess . . . . Well, I'm not sure how much you know about my dad, so I'll start at the beginning. Forgive me if I'm telling you things you're already aware of."

Lachlan waved a dismissive hand. He'd listen to just about anything if it would get her started.

"Dad sticks closer to home these days, which means the States generally. Mostly the house in New York, but he also . . . Never mind, that's not important." She blew out a breath and started over. "When I was younger, he worked for the US State Department . . . . That's our foreign affairs people, ambassadors and stuff. You know that, right?"

Lachlan nodded his head and tried not to be insulted. The truth was that a lot of people didn't understand the various cabinet ministers and departments from country to country.

Encouraged, she continued. "Well, back then, he was kind of an ambassador at large, going wherever they needed him. He wasn't a career diplomat or anything, but his family was wealthy, with a wide range of investments, and so," she shrugged, "he knew people. Depending on which administration was in office, they'd give him a title and he'd go swing some trade deals with his friends. Good for both sides, and yeah, he made money, too. He wasn't in it for charity. Anyway, that meant my family lived overseas a lot—which is how Cyn and I ended up at that French school together, but that's not part of this story.

"Over the years, my dad met up with a lot of friends who had kids my age. One of those was Masoud." Her lips curved in a private smile. "Later on, he told his friends to call him Max, especially in the US. But he was Masoud when I met him, and that never changed. He was two years older, same as my brother, and just about the handsomest boy I'd ever met."

Lachlan's jaw tightened in inexplicable irritation, as she continued.

"Of course, I was only six at the time, so I hadn't met that many boys, at all."

He grunted something close to a chuckle, because it seemed appropriate, though he wasn't all that amused.

"Our families kept in touch through the years." A shadow crossed her face. "Especially after my mom and my brother were killed."

"I'm sorry. How—?"

"A car accident, when I was eleven." Her gaze turned bleak for a moment, before she continued. "Anyway, Masoud had never known his mom—she'd been a much younger mistress of his dad's—and while he had a bunch of half-siblings, they were all much older. So we stayed close. We saw each other on and off through prep school—"

"By 'saw,' you mean dated?" Lachlan didn't know why he asked the question. Wished he could take it back.

She blinked at the interruption, then nodded. "I guess you could call it that. We weren't always in the same country, much less the same city, but we were close enough that when it came to choosing a university, we both knew we wanted to go to the same place. Cambridge first, of course, since he was in London at the time, and two years older. And then, eventually, Harvard. Law for me, because I figured I'd do something in government, although I had no idea what. But Masoud, he was brilliant, and far more dedicated than I was. He'd always had to be, because his dad had expectations. The family was in private banking and investments, and it was assumed that Masoud would join them. He ended up with two master's degrees—in finance and economics—though the second one was mostly so he could stay in Boston until I completed law school. When I moved to DC—"

"Wait up, lass. You're a barrister?"

She shrugged. "I have a law degree, and I passed the bar. But I've never tried a case in court and probably never will. I'm an analyst."

"What do you analyze?"

She met his eyes. "That's classified."

He snorted. "Right. Because you're with the American State Department."

"About that . . . I shouldn't tell you this, but I think it's why Raphael wants me there, and I don't want you going in there blind." She winced, seeming reluctant to continue, then spoke quickly, as if to get it out before she changed her mind. "I'm not State, I'm CIA. But I'm just an analyst," she added insistently.

Lachlan studied her for a long moment, trying to decide if it was good or bad that she worked for America's spook factory. And then, he tried to decide if he cared either way. Finally, he asked, "And where's Masoud in all this?"

She stared at him for a long time, then said, "Masoud is dead."

Lachlan went perfectly still. Talk about burying the lead. He had a feeling Masoud's death was central to Julia's hatred of Erskine Ross. "How did he die?"

"Erskine Ross killed him."

JULIA'S INITIAL reaction to Lachlan's casual inquiry regarding Masoud's whereabouts had been a burst of red hot rage. How dare he trivialize Masoud's death, his *courage*? But in the next moment, she was glad the big vampire had interrupted her story. She'd gotten so caught up in the telling that she'd have bared her soul to him in a way she never had with anyone else. Sure, she'd shared her grief with others, shared even the terrible loneliness she'd felt after Masoud was gone. But she'd never told anyone about the horrible, gut-wrenching guilt. It was the same guilt that drove her now, that would guide her hand when she stabbed Erskine Ross in his black heart.

"Like I said," she continued quietly. "Masoud was brilliant. He'd always wanted to be a physicist, and he had the brains for it. But that wasn't acceptable to his father, so he went the finance route. At least he got to work with numbers, which he loved. He was head of risk management for a very exclusive, very private investment firm. That sounds ordinary, but at that level, risk management is—"

"I know what it is. He analyzed hundreds of daily transactions, maybe thousands depending on the size of the firm, looking for irregular patterns, missing pieces. Money that disappeared without a paper trail, market responses that didn't add up, that sort of thing."

"In a nutshell," she agreed. "I would have gone crazy, but he loved it. And it killed him. Your friend Erskine—"

"*Not* my fucking friend," he snarled.

"Right, sorry. Masoud was convinced that Erskine was laundering money through the firm—presumably ill-gotten, although that's just my opinion, not Masoud's. He caught the irregularity and discovered the broker who'd handled the transactions had not only retired, but cashed out and disappeared. And when he pursued it further, he was murdered."

"How do you know?"

"Know what?" she asked, feeling her temper beginning to rise again.

"How do you know he was murdered, and how do you know it had anything to do with Erskine Ross?"

She felt that flash of anger again, but swallowed it just as quickly. Lachlan's questions made sense. But remembering that night, Masoud's voice as he ran, the certainty that he wasn't going to make it. And that his final phone call had been to her. To tell her he loved her. Tears pressed against her eyes and she looked away, not wanting the vampire to see. She had a feeling he saw more than he admitted. And it was too much. She took another sip of wine, waiting until she could talk without giving anything away.

"He called me," she said, giving him no more than a quick glance before lowering her gaze to her hands. "The night he was killed. He was running for his life, trying to reach the Saudi embassy. There was no time, and he was so scared," she finished in a whisper. When she continued, her voice was flat, all emotion leeched out of it. It was the only way she could do this. "He told me about Erskine. Not the details, but that they'd just met and why. But mostly, he told me where I could find his files, proof of what Erskine had done."

"You think Erskine Ross killed your boyfriend—"

"He wasn't . . . That's a stupid word. Masoud was far more than a boyfriend."

"All right."

He was studying her, his gaze careful, as if waiting for her to begin screaming. She was stronger than that. She'd had to be. But Lachlan didn't know it yet.

"Erskine's a very powerful vampire. If he didn't want you to know he'd killed Masoud, you wouldn't."

"You're defending him?" she demanded in disbelief.

"Not at all. But I'm a vampire, too. And I know how easily people blame us for crimes we didn't commit, especially when they involve murder."

She closed her eyes then, her heart throbbing in pain as she remembered every one of the three gunshots, the sound of Masoud's final breath.

"Julia?" Lachlan said softly, one big hand reaching out to cover both of hers, where she'd twisted them into a knot. "Tell me what happened."

"I heard him die," she said dully.

"When you say you heard him die . . ."

Her heart broke all over again. How many more times would she have to relive the nightmare? "He was shot. Three times. I heard the shots," she whispered. She looked up. "I hear them every night in my dreams."

"I'm sorry, princess." He paused, then asked, "What'd the police say?"

She rubbed her face with both hands. "Three bullets to the heart, point blank range. Death was instantaneous." Her throat squeezed on the last sentence, but if Lachlan noticed, he didn't show it. "The official finding was that it was a robbery gone bad. His wallet and watch were taken, to make it look good, I suppose."

"Did you tell them about the files? About what he'd told you?"

She remained silent a long time, then, "No."

"Why not?"

She lifted her head and gave him a cold stare. "Because I knew Erskine was going to get away with it. Money can make a lot of evidence disappear in my country *and* yours, and I want him dead."

Lachlan looked away, staring at the London skyline, as if in thought. "Erskine wouldn't have done the hit himself. Vampires, especially the old ones, aren't big on guns. And besides, he'd want to keep his own hands clean. He'd have brought someone in to do it for him. You know that, right?"

"Of course, I know that," she snapped. "But I don't care who pulled the trigger. Erskine ordered it, and I'm going to kill him."

"Okay," he said cautiously. "But let's talk about this a bit. Does Erskine know you're on to him? Does he know Masoud was on the phone with you, specifically?"

She shook her head. "He shouldn't. Masoud was one of the few who knew about my job and had my private number. Anyone running a trace would go back to a cut-out that would return a pre-paid exchange. Like one of those phones you buy at the corner store."

"And how long were you on the phone with him?"

"I told you, they wouldn't be able to trace it."

"How long?"

She looked away and thought about it, avoiding the painful details and only focusing on the time. "Two minutes, maybe a few seconds more."

"And in those minutes, Masoud told you all this?"

She scowled. "Look, forget it. We'll go to Malibu, so you can meet Raphael. And when we come back, we'll go our separate ways. I never expected you to be a part of—"

"Hold up, princess. I'm not backing out of our agreement. I'm looking for facts. And one of those is that if Erskine killed Masoud to conceal his crimes, he'll do the same to you."

"If?" she snarled, done trying to convince him of the truth. She gathered herself to get up, but Lachlan wasn't finished yet.

"I had a conversation with your erstwhile kidnapper last night."

Julia paused, waiting to see what he'd discovered, or at least, how much he'd tell her.

"It was buried deep," he said, meeting her gaze somberly. "But they *were* hired by Erskine, and he wanted you alive. My guess is he knows Masoud called you, and he wants to find out what you know, and whether you've shared it with your government bosses."

"He can't know where I work. Maybe his contacts *here* are that deep, but not in the US."

"Aye, let's say you're right about that," Lachlan agreed, but in a tone that said clearly he didn't think so. "Why else would he want you?"

Julia thought about it, then looked up and met his skeptical gaze. "Because I'm the executor of Masoud's estate, his trustee," she said in sudden realization. "The trust itself wouldn't be public record, but there were many necessary transactions that would be. His home and most of his assets were held in the US, to keep his family away from them. The sale of the house, and the liquidation of certain investments, for example, would be in searchable databases. It would be a short step from that to discovering me as his trustee."

Lachlan nodded. "So Erskine's fishing, trying to find out what you know." His gaze sharpened. "What was in the file?"

"File?"

"Don't do that. Don't lie to me. You know which file. Did you look at it? Wait, first. Is it safe?"

Julia drew a deep breath. This conversation had already gone much deeper than she'd planned. She'd told Lachlan more about Masoud's final moments than she'd told her own father, much less Masoud's. Why the hell had she done that? She looked up and found him waiting patiently. For what? For her to decide if she was going to fully trust him. This was so hard. But damn it, she wanted Erskine dead, and Lachlan might be—no, *was*—her best chance of seeing that happen.

"Yes, I looked at it. But I'm no financial wizard. I trust his conclusions, but I couldn't tell you how he got there, even though I have all the data. And, yes, it's safe."

"I hope you're good at covering your tracks."

"I am. It's kind of my job, you know."

"Not really, but I believe you. Did you share it with anyone?"

"No. I didn't know whom to trust. You're the first person I've told, and I don't even know why I told *you*."

"Well, at least you know I won't tell Erskine."

"Is that supposed to reassure me?" she asked dryly.

"Hell, no. Just letting you know."

His straightforward response, and even more, the fact that he hadn't demanded she turn the docs over to *him*, made her want to trust him. Or at least, made her believe they wanted the same thing, which was close enough.

"So where do we go from here?" she asked softly.

"Malibu. Where else?" he said with a grin as he stood. "Are you staying in tonight?"

She stood to face him. "I guess. I hadn't thought about it."

"Well, think about it. And don't go out without letting me know." He turned and started for the door.

"Ex*cuse* me?" she said to his back, waiting until he spun to face her again. "*Don't go out without letting you know?* Who put you in charge?"

"Erskine Ross, princess. You don't stand a chance out there if he's after you. And I need *you* to get *me* to Malibu tomorrow night." He winked, then strode for the door and was gone.

Julia stood there staring at the closed door. "Arrogant asshole," she muttered, then shrugged. She'd planned to enjoy a long soak, then go straight to bed, anyway. She'd just been fucking with him, not wanting him to think he'd be calling all the shots.

Turning away from the door, she flicked off the lights and went to run a bath.

THE COUSINS WERE waiting for Lachlan at the hotel. They hadn't been happy about him going off alone, but if it was up to them, he'd be wrapped in plastic and kept on a shelf. How the hell he was supposed to run a clan like that, he didn't know. Much less destroy Erskine Ross and become Lord of Scotland.

"Welcome back, my lord," Lennon said, playing his role as the hotel's night porter.

"Lennon. Anything I need to know?"

"No news. The cousins are both upstairs."

"Are they alone?"

Lennon chuckled, apparently mistaking his meaning. It wouldn't have been unusual for Fergus or Munro to entertain a lady or three, but that wasn't what he'd been worrying about tonight. There was too much afoot right now, between the attempt on Julia's life, his own maneuvering to destroy Erskine, and now the upcoming visit with Raphael, which was an important first step to his move against Erskine. His question to Lennon had been aimed at any unwelcome or unknown visitors, whether they were friend or foe. No one other than Lachlan and his cousins needed to know clan business, much less his personal comings and goings.

The door to his suite was open when he stepped out of the elevator. Fergus appeared a moment later, gun in hand, but held down next to his thigh. Lachlan rolled his eyes. "A gun, Fergus? I just finished telling Julia how vampires don't like guns much."

"It's not my fault you lied to the lady," Fergus said, sliding the weapon into the shoulder rig he was so fond of.

"You watch too much television. Start acting like a vampire, for fuck's sake." He clapped Fergus's shoulder as he walked by. "Get Munro in here. We need to talk."

"Shite. What now?"

"Good news and bad. Get Munro."

Fergus crossed the hall and pounded on the door. "Munro, get over here. Lachlan has news."

The door was yanked open to reveal a disheveled Munro—his eyes sleepy and his hair looking like someone had been running hands through it. Lachlan studied him. "Lennon said there were no ladies visiting."

"I wish he was wrong. But no, I've been working my ass off on these fucking financials. And you well know it."

"Any luck?"

"Erskine's hiding his money, but I'll be damned if I can figure out where. I'm beginning to think he's converted it all to gold coin and buried it beneath Ross Castle." Munro tossed something onto the table behind him, and closing the door, crossed into Lachlan's suite where he went directly to the bar. "So what's the news?" he asked, seeming more interested in pouring himself a healthy four fingers of whisky.

Lachlan tossed his suit coat aside and sprawled on the sofa facing the bar, shaking his head when Munro offered the crystal decanter with a swirl of the amber liquid within. "For one thing," Lachlan said, "I think I've found someone who knows more about Erskine's financial holdings that you do."

Munro gave him an evil look.

"Unfortunately, he's dead."

"Fuck you."

Lachlan nodded in agreement. "I might be able to access his records, though. Would that help?"

"Aye. Give me a place to start, instead of trying to dig out of the hole I'm stuck in. Where'd you come by this bounty of data?"

"Julia Harper." He lifted his chin in agreement with the surprised look on Munro's face. "I wasn't expecting it either. I knew she was hiding something, but not that."

"And would that be the only thing she'd be hiding?" Fergus asked, his tone more skeptical than surprised. "There's got to be more to it. How'd she manage to get it done?"

"All good questions. Sit down, Fergus."

It wasn't an order, but Fergus sat anyway, too accustomed to following Lachlan's commands to do otherwise. He took the glass of whisky Munro offered him, looking at it in askance when he saw how full it was and setting it on the table untouched.

"First, we heard from Raphael tonight, or his mate, Cynthia Leighton, anyway. She passed on our message, and Raphael has agreed to meet."

His cousins exchanged grins, with Munro toasting the news with a long sip of whisky. The vampire symbiote metabolized alcohol too fast for it to have any meaningful effect on a vampire's senses, but some of them enjoyed the taste and the burn as it went down.

"Aye, I'll be leaving for California tomorrow night, courtesy of Ms. Harper's private jet."

Fergus scowled. "And when you said, 'I,' you meant 'we.' Isn't that right, cousin?"

Lachlan made a face. "And there's the rub. He's only letting one other accompany me—"

"Take Fergus, then," Munro said immediately. "He's handier at such things."

"You'd both be good to have with me, but the other person will be Julia Harper."

Fergus exploded to his feet. Munro was right, he was the better hand when it came to military matters, or simple security. He also had a fierce temper that he rarely tried to contain, just as he didn't now. "*Gads, hae ye lost yer mynd?* You're taking that woman? If it's the damn jet, we'll get our own. We don't need her fecking charity. I can't believe—"

"*Sit doon 'n' listen.*" Lachlan was on his feet, too, the laidback cousin persona burned away by the authority of both clan chief and vampire lord surrounding him in a corona of raw power. "*Ye think a'm that stupid?*" he hissed, as Fergus took his seat, eyes downcast, but his jaw still clenched.

Lachlan drew a calming breath, then reached down and gripped his cousin's shoulder. He didn't like to use his authority over these two. Fergus and Munro had been with him from the very beginning, when the decimated clan had looked to them for leadership. Three vampires barely-turned were suddenly making life and death decisions for everyone they loved. But alone of the three, it was Lachlan who ultimately had proved he had the power to rule. He was their lord and sometimes he had to act like it.

He sat again, forcing himself to relax. "It was Raphael who dictated the terms," he said quietly. "It's natural for him to be suspicious. I would be, too, under the circumstances. He may have heard my name, but he doesn't know me. And Julia, as you well know, works for the American government. He probably wonders about the whole setup, given the hostilities lately between the continents."

Fergus's eyes met his, anger and suspicion still simmering in their depths. "You think we should have gone through Quinn instead? Raphael underwrote his takeover of Ireland, so they must know each other."

But Lachlan shook his head. "I would have come off as weak if I did that. *Quinn's na more powerful than a'm.* Why appeal to him? No, it had to be Raphael directly. You don't see it, but Julia's involvement is good for us. And I'm not talking about the damn jet. She's the one who knows where Erskine's money is hidden—or at least has the data trail for Munro to follow—and she got us through to Leighton and Raphael." He shrugged. "The private jet doesn't hurt either, especially when it comes to dealing with sunlight—which I'll have to, either on the flight or the runway when we arrive."

Fergus shook his head. "I still don't like it, but I see your point. Sorry, *m'laird.*"

Lachlan hid his reaction at the title from his cousin's lips. He didn't mind hearing it from Lennon and the others. He was their Sire, which among vampires was a relationship so critical that it was built into their DNA. But it still made him wince coming from Fergus or Munro.

"I wasn't all that happy myself," he admitted. "I would at least have liked more time to prepare, but it is what it is."

"How long will you be—?"

"Can I get her records before you leave?" Munro asked, talking over Fergus, who scowled at him. "What?" Munro demanded. "Those records are important. We need to know where Erskine's hid the territorial funds. *Lachlan's like tae need thaim.*"

"Not if he's dead," Fergus growled.

"Raphael has no reason to kill me," Lachlan said confidently. "If he doesn't think I'm up to the task, he'll just sit back and let Erskine take me out of the game."

"Erskine doesn't have the power or the balls to defeat you."

"I hope you're right."

"*Feck*. You know I am."

Lachlan grinned. "Let's talk about what I say to Raphael, then."

The three of them talked for about an hour, hunched over the coffee table, trading insults and advice. But in the end, it was all up to Lachlan. He was the one who'd be walking into Raphael's lair and stating his case. Though that wasn't right either. He didn't need Raphael's permission to take over Scotland. He didn't need *anyone's* permission. That's not how it worked among vampires. If you were strong enough, if you could take the territory and *hold* it, you were a vampire lord. Simple as that.

So why was he traveling so far to meet Raphael? Because once he became the Lord of Scotland, he didn't want to end up fighting a slew of skirmishes with his neighbors. Not Ireland, not England, and sure as hell not anyone from the continent. As far as he was concerned, those fuckers over there needed to clean up their own mess. And if they tried to use *his* territory to solve *their* problem, then they'd die. Simple as that.

Chapter Five

LACHLAN WOKE THE next night to a message from Julia Harper, giving him a choice. She'd calculated the maximum darkness for their flight to Los Angeles. By leaving London at roughly 10:00 p.m., they'd arrive in LA by 2:00 a.m. Lachlan didn't know if they'd hit daylight during the flight or not. Munro could have told him, but it didn't matter. He'd be stuck on the plane, one way or the other.

The choice she gave him was their departure date. Did he want to wait until the next day, or would he prefer to fly that same night? If so, he'd have about three hours to pack and get himself to the airport. Julia didn't know if that was enough time, but she was going to have the pilots file a flight plan and prep the jet, just in case. And would he please call her as soon as he got the message to let her know his preference? It was all said very politely, in her cool, unruffled Julia voice. The one that made him want to ruffle her a bit. He thought of all those hours they'd have together on the plane, and all the ways he could muss her up.

He hit return on her message. She answered on the third ring, sounding out of breath.

"Did I catch you at a bad time?" he asked.

"No. Well, not exactly. I was getting ready, in case you decided to fly tonight. I showered earlier, but I was packing."

The slight tremor in her voice told him she was probably lying. He suspected she was standing in her bedroom, still wet from the shower, maybe wrapped in a towel. He smiled. He'd told her she couldn't lie to a vampire, but maybe she'd thought that only applied to in-person conversations. For most vampires, it would have, but then, he wasn't most vampires.

"Are you still there?"

Julia's voice jarred him out of his thoughts. "I am," he said. "Just thinking." Which wasn't a lie. He smiled. "We'll go tonight. I doubt we'll need to stay more than a night or two. At least, I won't. You may want a lengthier visit with Leighton. If so, I can—"

"No. The shorter, the better. This is business. Cyn and I can catch up another time. But she did say something about *daylighting* at the airport? And that if you wanted, you could go directly to the estate for the day. She said they have plenty of room in the vault," Julia said, sounding puzzled. "Does any of that make sense to you? Because it doesn't to me."

He smiled. It was refreshing to discover something she didn't know, and given her overweening need to have everything all neat and tidy, he couldn't let this pass without comment. "A flaw in your intelligence gathering, princess?"

"I beg your pardon?" Her tone was all snotty upper-class. She even added a faintly posh accent, despite her American origins.

"I quite like the begging, as long as you do it right pretty-like."

"Fuck you."

He laughed. Mission accomplished. "Sunlighting is when we sleep on the plane, usually in an airport hangar, because there's no time to get to a safer place. And the vault simply refers to secure sleeping quarters, which these days resemble bank vaults more than bedrooms."

"Oh. That makes sense, then." Her reply was so stiffly polite, he had to swallow a second laugh, figuring it might push her right over the edge. And while he wouldn't mind seeing his princess lose her cool, he wanted it up close and personal. He'd wager she looked beautiful in a full temper.

"Glad you approve. I'll meet you at the airport, shall I? Which one?"

"London City. I'll be in the first class lounge."

"Of course, you will. See you soon." He hung up without giving her a chance to respond, though there was really nothing else to say, and he had to check in with his cousins. He'd throw together a duffle bag of clothes and supplies, but he wouldn't need much, because he didn't plan on staying long.

He took a quick shower, then walked out to the sitting room to find Fergus waiting for him. He'd updated both his cousins on the situation insofar as Julia had told him the previous night. They were no more happy about him going to California without them, but they agreed that her story made a lot more sense than it had. Especially since Munro had verified the basic details about Masoud's death while they'd been discussing it.

"You hear from the woman?" Fergus asked. He might have reconciled himself to not going on the trip, but he wasn't any happier with Julia's involvement, no matter what she'd revealed.

"I did. We're leaving out of London City at 10:00. If you drive, we can talk on the way."

Fergus glanced at the clock on the side table. "When do you want to leave?"

"Twenty minutes? Departure is at 10:00, but we'll board before that."

"I'll bring the car around. You want Munro in on this?"

"Aye. I'll talk to Julia before we take off, see if I can persuade her to share the records this Masoud guy left her about Erskine's finances."

"You think she'll go for it?"

"Depends on her mood. She doesn't trust me yet."

Fergus scoffed lightly.

"Ah ken," Lachlan agreed, telling them he knew the problem. "Hard to believe, but 'tis true. I might have to do some work to get in there."

His cousin gave him a knowing look.

"It's not like that. This is business."

"Uh huh. You forget I've met the woman, and I know you."

"Business, cousin. Now let me finish packing."

JULIA GLANCED UP from reading the morning paper—something she only ever did when she was traveling and stuck in an airport lounge—to see Lachlan making his way toward her. He was dressed much as he had been that first night, in black jeans and a t-shirt, a black leather jacket and boots. Julia couldn't decide if she liked him better this way, or in the suit he'd worn the previous night. He had looked quite handsome, and she did like a well-built man in a nicely tailored suit. But his chest was huge beneath the smooth t-shirt, and he sure filled out his jeans well. She wasn't the only one who noticed, either. Every pair of female eyes, and more than a few male, were glued to his progress through the lounge. Damn vampire. He had to be aware he was the center of attention, but you wouldn't know it to look at him. His stride was easy and relaxed, and his gaze was firmly fixed on her. She fought the urge to squirm under the power of his attention. He was just so *there*. It was the same sense of presence that had drawn her notice in the bar that first night. It had to be a vampire thing, and that made her wonder if he could turn it off. Could he be invisible if he wanted? Not literally, of course, but could he disappear into a crowd? She made a note to ask him. Not because it mattered, but because she was curious. She scowled. Asking "curious" questions might stroke his ego, and one thing for sure, his ego did *not* need stroking.

"Why the scowl, princess?" he asked, pulling out a chair and sitting down, without waiting to be invited.

She gritted her teeth, determined not to react to him calling her "princess." She didn't know why he'd settled on that, but suspected it was because he knew it pissed her off. So her new strategy was not to pay attention. She glanced up as if just noticing he was there. "Oh, I was just working some things out in my head."

"Like what?"

"I was running details of where to go when we land. I haven't been through LAX much, and not at all lately, but I arranged a limo pickup, so at least we won't have to deal with traffic."

"Is the limousine service reliable? Have you used them before?" It should have been a casual question—chit-chat while waiting for a flight—but Lachlan said it with such intensity that it took on new meaning.

"Like I said, I don't get to LA often, but it's the same service my dad uses, so they must be okay."

"What else did you decide?"

"About what?"

"About where we're going once we arrive."

"Oh, right. I confirmed our arrival with Cyn, and she said it's up to you. The jet will be moved into a private hangar, since we won't be here long. The pilots are pretty happy about having a couple days in LA, actually. Anyway, Cyn said you might want to sleep on the plane, although I don't know how comfortable that'll be. The bed's big, but the mattress . . . I mean, I've slept well enough on it, but you're a *very* big guy."

"No room for both of us?"

He said it with a completely straight face. Not even a twinkle of humor in eyes that were more green than brown tonight. Oddly, that made it more difficult for Julia to know how to respond. Maybe he was serious, saying they could share the one bed since she'd be stuck on the plane, too. But wait—he'd be in his vampire sleep. Wouldn't he be horribly vulnerable? Why would he want a stranger next to him? Then again, he had saved her from being kidnapped, so that counted for something. Maybe if you saved someone's life, they weren't a stranger anymore.

"You're thinking way too hard, love. It was a simple question."

Julia's internal dialogue ground to a halt. She hated to admit it, but he was right on this one. She'd been chasing her own thoughts like a hound after a rabbit. Except she was the rabbit. And she was doing it again. She decided not to answer his question at all.

"We could go straight to Malibu instead," she countered. "It might be better for both of us."

He smiled then. "Sturdier bed?"

"I'm sure it would be," she said, refusing to be baited.

"Sounds lovely, but I'll stick with the plane."

"You're kidding." She was honestly stunned. Why the hell would he want to be stuck on a plane all day?

"I like to control my surroundings, especially when I sleep. I trust Raphael more than I would *most* vampires that I don't know, but he probably has a small army of vamps on his estate, every one of whom is completely loyal to him. Let's just say that I'm not comfortable sleeping surrounded by someone else's warriors." He fixed that dark gaze on her. "Unless you'd like to sleep with me and keep me safe?"

Again, she couldn't tell if he was being serious. But she knew she didn't want to find herself in a bed with Lachlan McRae. And she didn't want to consider *why* that was, either.

"The plane it is, I guess," she said somewhat wistfully. It was a very posh jet, but there was only one bed. She'd have to make do with a reclined seat. There was a short bench seat in the back, but it wasn't long enough for her height, nor wide enough to curl up on.

He smiled again. "I'll be dead to the world, princess. You'll be perfectly safe if you want to share the bed."

No. Nope. Nyet. Non. She was *not* going to share a bed with him, no matter how innocent he made it sound. Because she had a feeling "innocent" and Lachlan did not *ever* belong in the same bed.

Her phone pinged with a message from their pilot, saving her from the need to respond to his offer. "We can board, if you're ready. Our scheduled departure is in forty minutes."

He pushed back the chair and stood, then offered her a hand. Her heart did a weird little dance, and before she knew it, she was placing her fingers in his broad palm. The touch of his skin, rough with callouses and warmer than she expected, gave her that same electric jolt, just as it had in the bar. She would have pulled her hand back, but his fingers curled over hers and it was too late.

As soon as she could, she slipped her hand away to reach for her briefcase. She expected to be relieved, but what she felt was closer to remorse for the loss of that contact between them. She cleared her throat nervously. "Did you bring a bag?" she asked, feeling stupid. What a lame thing to say.

He gestured toward the entrance. "I left it with the charming ladies up front."

Of course, he had. She'd seen more than one person ask to leave a case, and the "charming ladies" had declined. But they did it for Lachlan. Damn vampire.

LACHLAN STUDIED the jet's luxurious interior. No wonder Julia had wanted to take her father's plane. He routinely booked private flights on the rare occasions he flew anymore, but although they were exceptionally comfortable, they were nothing like this. The plane wasn't one of the Lear-type private jets he was used to. This was a full-scale 707, with conference tables, and seats for conversation groups, in addition to individual seats large enough that even *he* was more than comfortable. The hush of money infused the very air. If not for the pervasive hum of the engines, he wouldn't know he was on a plane at all.

He still wasn't looking forward to the long flight, but it had more to do with timing than equipment. He would almost have preferred to leave at a time that would put him in daylight for the entire trip, so he could sleep for the entire 11 hours. That didn't work when going to California, unfortunately, so he was going to be stuck wide awake for most of the trip. And at the end of it, he'd have the so very special experience of daylighting on the plane. This is why he rarely left the UK anymore. Oh, he'd done his time in the US, back in the 70s. The *19*70s. His princess would probably be stunned to discover he had an MBA from Stanford University. He'd had to negotiate a special program that permitted him to matriculate at night, but enough money could buy anything. He could have gotten the same degree at any one of the UK universities, but he'd seen the way the world was going, with ties among countries spanning the globe. His clan wasn't as wealthy as some, especially not back then, but they'd all agreed it would be a good investment. In return, he'd made sure he *earned* that Stanford MBA and had made good on the trust they'd given him. It was a trust he continued to reward, using his newly acquired knowledge to enhance the clan's investments. He'd discovered a talent for anticipating the next big trend, and between that and Munro's ability to read the market, the clan was now wealthier than ever—a wealth that translated into stability and security for the clan and all its members. It had taken all the decades since that one fateful evening to reach this turning point. The McRae vampires were safe enough, *strong* enough, to follow Lachlan's path of revenge. He *would* kill Erskine and become Lord of Scotland. And then, finally, their dead ancestors would rest in the peace they deserved.

Lachlan watched as Julia made her way down the aisle to the back of the compartment, dropping her briefcase on a couch-length seat along the way. There was a galley of sorts on the left, and on the right, a door which she opened to reveal a second shorter aisle. When she disappeared into the next compartment, he followed, making enough noise that she would know he was there.

She glanced back and pointed at the first door on his left. "Bathroom's in there." She kept walking until she reached a second door. "Fully equipped office. Phone, fax, computer . . . I rarely use it, so I'm not sure what else is in there. And this. . . ." She opened a door at the end of the hall. "This is the bedroom."

Lachlan walked close enough to look over her shoulder, but didn't enter the room. "That sure looks big enough for two, princess," he murmured quietly, placing his mouth against her ear. And it really did. He'd anticipated some back-of-the-jet platform that would leave his feet hanging over the edge. But this was a full-size king, complete with expensive linens and bedside tables.

"In your dreams," she muttered, then dropped her overnight bag near the door and walked past him back to the seating area.

He laughed and followed, to find her pouring herself a glass of wine. "You know, if you weren't such a control freak, we'd have a steward to handle this," she said.

"That wine bottle too heavy for you?"

She gave him the finger and sat on the couch where she'd left her briefcase. Lachlan grinned and sat in the seat facing hers. There was a stationary table between them, making this one of the conversation groupings, especially given its proximity to the bar.

"You don't want a drink?" she asked, placing her own glass in a deep niche, clearly designed to hold such things while in flight.

He shook his head. "I didn't expect you to be a nervous flyer."

She glared at him, then shrugged. "I'm not. I just sleep better if I have a little something. Especially out here," she added, with a doubtful look at the sofa.

"I told you, once I'm out, I'm dead to the world. There's no reason—"

"Forget it. I don't care how dead you are. I'm not sharing a bed with you."

Lachlan bit his cheek to keep from grinning, or mentioning that when she finally did share a bed with him—and he'd decided she would—he'd be very much awake for the experience. Julia didn't seem to understand that the more she resisted the attraction between them, the more she resisted even the *possibility* of it, the more determined he was to make it happen. He was a vampire. A predator. When his prey ran, instinct told him to chase.

The pilot's voice came over the intercom as the jet began to move, advising that take-off was imminent, and asking them to fasten seatbelts.

Lachlan waited until after takeoff to broach the subject of Erskine's financials. It was obviously a touchy subject for her, rooted as it was in the death of her friend—boyfriend? Maybe. Though she insisted not. But although he was curious about the relationship, it wasn't significant to their current joint undertaking.

"There's something we need to discuss," he said, after watching Julia sip her wine and stare at the same page of her book for more than ten minutes without moving her eyes.

She looked up, eyebrows raised in question, her pouty lips curved into a slight frown.

It was a good look for her, though he doubted she wanted to hear that. "When you mentioned your friend who discovered Erskine's money laundering—"

Her eyes clouded with sadness, making him add a plus sign in the boyfriend column.

"—you said he'd found a trail of suspicious transactions. You also said he was a math genius, a detail guy, right?"

She nodded, her solemn gaze never leaving his face.

"He must have kept records of everything he did."

"Of course," she said, sounding puzzled.

"And since he'd found something shady—possibly even illegal, depending on the jurisdiction—he wouldn't have trusted the firm's records to remain untouched. Especially since he knew someone inside the bank was involved."

She nodded, her expression no longer confused, but wary. She knew what he was talking about, knew where he was going with it, so Lachlan cut to the chase, as the Americans would say.

"He made a backup copy, Julia. Whether it's paper or digital, he kept personal records of everything, so the bank couldn't erase it."

"And if he did?" she said defiantly.

"I need those records."

She made a scoffing noise. "Look, I know about your Stanford MBA. . ." She smiled sweetly at Lachlan's look of surprise. "You're not the only one who investigates the people you do business with."

He shrugged. It wasn't as if he was hiding the damn thing. "Your point?"

"You're right, Masoud did make a backup. It was why he called me. That and—" She cut herself off before confiding Masoud's declaration of love. She'd always known he loved her. She'd loved him, too. She still did. Just not the way he'd loved her. *That* wasn't something she wanted to share, however. "He told me where they were, and said I had to get to them before anyone else did."

"And did you?"

"Yes. There was a file, but most of the data was on a pair of thumb drives. I've studied them over and over, but I just don't see the same thing he did. I can't find it." She looked up. "I doubt you will either."

Lachlan couldn't decide if he should be insulted, even though she was probably right. But in the end, it didn't matter, because he wasn't going to be the one looking at the damn files. "Your Masoud wasn't the only mathematical genius in the world. Give me the drives, or copies. I have someone who can make sense of them. Do you have access to them from the plane?"

She nodded. "Who do *you* know who's that good?"

Well, *now* he might have to be insulted. Her question was loaded with such skepticism, as if it was utterly unthinkable for *him* to know such an accomplished person. But he wanted those records.

"My cousin."

"Another cousin? How many do you have?"

"More than you, I'd wager. But as it turns out, you've met Munro."

Her eyes widened in surprise. "Munro? He seemed . . ."

"Normal? Dull?"

"No," she said impatiently. "He was just so . . . martial."

Laughlin laughed. "Martial," he repeated. "That's a good one. Yes, he can fight. But he's also a fucking genius. He'll make sense of your friend's data."

She studied him for a moment. "I need to be sure you'll help me, not just take the records and disappear."

He wasn't a patient man. It usually wasn't necessary. But he forced himself to reason with her. "I thought we agreed," he said with deliberate slowness, "that we were on the same side when it came to getting rid of Erskine Ross. We both want him dead, right?"

"Why do you need the records then? You think I'm lying?"

"No." He dragged the word out, practically grinding his teeth in frustration. "I think those records can help us shake Erskine up a bit, make him easier to kill when the time comes."

She studied him some more, then blinked slowly. "After we return to London."

"Aye, but you're wasting time. Munro's a genius, but even he'll need time to figure out what's going on."

She scowled, studying him closely. "I have to think about this."

Lachlan exhaled noisily. "Whatever you say," he conceded, then lifted his head as he sensed the sun breaking the horizon. Damn long distance flights. They were convenient, but they sure fucked with a vampire's instincts. "The sun's near. I'll see you in a very few hours." He stood and made for the luxurious bedroom in the next compartment. Stopping at the open door, he called, "Join me, if you dare, princess. You'll be perfectly safe."

IF SHE DARED? DID he think she was afraid of him? Bastard was way too sure of himself. So what if he was in there, taking off his clothes, sliding into bed. She wasn't going to think about that, wasn't going to imagine his muscles flexing on that broad chest and those beautiful arms, wasn't going to replay the soft whisper of his skin against the sheets. Would he sleep naked? Probably not, she decided. Not today anyway. He wasn't a man who trusted easily, and he was in a strange place, with someone he barely knew, and no control over where the airplane would go. She lifted the shade on the closest window and saw the barest glimmer of light on the horizon. Odd how he'd known the sun was near, even with all the shades pulled down. Must be a vampire thing.

Stop. The word filled her thoughts, as she ordered herself to cease this foolish daydreaming and do something useful. She hadn't told Lachlan, but she had Masoud's files on her laptop. She wasn't stupid, so they were encrypted and under password, but she could certainly access them. And now she had a few hours ahead of her with nothing else to do. Maybe she should have one more go at them. She wasn't a financial wizard, but maybe this time they'd make sense. And if not . . . she'd have to trust Lachlan and his cousin. The idea didn't set easily on her mind, but she was stunned to realize that it wasn't as foreign as it would have been only three days ago. Some part of her, some instinct or hindbrain response, was ready to trust the vampire. What the hell?

Shaking her head, she opened her laptop and pulled up the files, then sat there staring at row after row of dates and numbers in at least five different currencies on the first page alone. She swallowed her groan and started reading, but an hour later, she jerked out of sleep to find her fingers still on the keyboard and a cluster of meaningless text on the screen. Hell, it wasn't even text, just a jumble of letters. Was there such a thing as sleep typing? What the hell had she been trying to say? And to whom? Notes to herself, to Munro?

Realizing it didn't matter because it made no sense, she shut the laptop and set it aside, then did the best she could to make a bed of her couch. Stretching out on the cushy seat, she covered herself with a blanket, punched a pillow into shape under her head, closed her eyes, and let sleep take her.

She woke to the sound of her own cry of surprise, and just in time to catch herself from falling beneath the table. She sat up, rubbing her arm which had slammed into the wooden edge. That was going to bruise, she thought, pissed off and feeling stupid. The damn couch wasn't wide enough for decent sleep. She should have made Lachlan sleep out here, while she took the bed. On the other hand, he was about three times her size, so if she couldn't make it work, he sure as hell wouldn't be able to. But he'd said vampires were dead to the world when they slept, right? Did that mean they didn't move? Didn't roll, or toss and turn?

Hmmm. Her brain flashed on an image of Lachlan again, sleeping half-naked in the big bed. "Stop," she whispered out loud this time. "I'll just move to one of the seats, instead. Take a sleeping pill and put it in full recline." She realized she was talking to herself and shook her head, obviously more tired than she thought. Pulling her briefcase closer, she rummaged in an inside pocket for the small bottle of pills she always brought along when she traveled, especially internationally. When she didn't find what she was looking for, she ran her fingers over the bottom and side seams, as if the bottle could hide there, then checked all the other pockets to be sure.

"Well, fuck." Had she left it behind? Impossible. She never took it out of . . . . "Oh, shit." She knew where it was. In the overnight bag she'd dumped in the bedroom, thinking she wouldn't need it until they were closer to L.A. She sighed. She *wanted* those pills. It was either that or arrive in California looking like a baggy eyed rag doll. Maybe not *that* bad, but exhausted wasn't a good look for her. She thought some more, lips pursed in irritation. Damn vampire. This was all his fault. If he hadn't taken the bed . . . . Okay, so she'd insisted, but he could have put up a fight at least. Of course, Cyn had told her about the vamps' sensitivity to sunlight, so he probably preferred to sleep in a securely dark room.

Wait a minute, what about that whole dead to the world thing? She could slip inside the bedroom just enough to grab her bag, then leave. He'd never know the difference, and there were no windows that opened on the hallway back there, so no risk, either.

She thought about it another minute or so, but couldn't see any downside to her plan. Standing, she tip-toed down the aisle, for some reason, then into the short hallway, careful to close the compartment door behind her. Covering the short distance to the bedroom in the near dark, with only the dim light from the bathroom to guide her, she stopped and put her ear against the bedroom door. Hearing nothing, she turned the knob and pushed it open.

It was perfectly dark inside, with not even the usual power lights from electronic devices to break the blackness. There should have been a digital clock on the bedside table, so he must have unplugged it, or shoved it into a drawer. Maybe he didn't like the red glow of the numbers. She was with him on that. They'd always seemed rather hellish to her, and she wondered why they didn't go with something soothing at least. Green maybe, or a soft white. But she didn't worry about that for long, because her eyes adjusted to the little bit of light leaking in from the hall, and she found Lachlan.

He looked impossibly bigger stretched out on the bed. He wasn't under the covers, and despite her rather vivid imaginings, he wasn't half-naked, either. He was fully dressed, on his back and . . . Jesus, was he breathing?

Julia rushed over to the bed and was reaching for him just as his chest rose in a deep breath. It was so sudden and unexpected that she jumped back, feeling foolish all over again. What was with her today? She was twitching like a mare in heat. And why the fuck had she used that analogy? Just because he was beautiful and utterly masculine, and she hadn't had so much as a kiss in months .

"Get yourself in order, Jules," she muttered, then stood straight as she studied the vampire's long form. He truly was dead to the world. Otherwise, she was certain he'd have woken by now. She started to turn, to grab her bag and leave, but then her gaze lifted to take in the huge bed. It had been custom-made for her dad, and was wider than a normal king-size. Lachlan had chosen to sleep on the one side, rather than in the middle, and his still form didn't come close to taking up even half of the available space. He wasn't even under the covers, but had stretched out on top, without even a blanket. He'd removed his jacket and boots, but that seemed to be it.

Julia eyed the other half of the bed. He'd said she could use it. And he certainly wouldn't be disturbed by her presence. He wouldn't even know she was there, as long as she woke before he did. And since she didn't sleep all that well on planes—the constant noise of the engines buzzed against her subconscious—she'd be long gone before he woke. She'd even skip the sleeping pill. Even without it, she could get at least a couple of hours before they landed, and she'd set her cell phone alarm to wake her just in case.

Moving around the bed, she toed off her shoes and unzipped her jeans, but left them on. She was tempted to loosen her bra, but decided that might be stretching her luck, and so left the damn thing fastened. Then she pulled back the covers, put her head on the pillow, and went out like a light.

LACHLAN OPENED his eyes to the darkness of an unfamiliar room and . . . a soft feminine breath. He drew in the scent of Julia's perfume and smiled. So his princess had taken him up on his dare. He lay perfectly still for a few minutes, wanting to be certain she remained asleep. He could have slipped into her mind and made sure of it, even given her sweet dreams to keep her company. Or something erotic, instead. But he wouldn't do either of those things. He considered himself an honorable man. One who'd done horrible things when necessary to protect his clan, but honorable, nonetheless.

Still, that didn't stop him from rolling over, his pupils dilating as they adjusted to the dark, glowing softly like those of the wolves that used to run the hills of Scotland. She slept curled on her side, her soft breath stirring a lock of hair over the hand she had under her cheek. He reached out and brushed the hair back along her ear, then stroked her cheek with a gentle touch. Her skin was as soft as he'd known it would be, warm velvet against his fingertip. She stirred slightly, a smile curving her full lips while she rolled almost to her back, as if welcoming a lover. Lachlan froze for a moment, not wanting her to wake to find him hovering, but then she moaned again, and the scent of feminine arousal filled the air.

He stopped breathing, every muscle going still, except for his cock. That fucker went hard as a rock in two seconds. Her tongue slipped out and licked her lips, leaving them wet and shining, just waiting to be kissed. He swallowed a groan. He might be a damn powerful vampire, but he was also a *man*. Even he had limits.

Leaning over, he brushed his lips with hers just once, barely firm enough to be felt. More of an exchange of breaths than a kiss. She lifted her mouth to his and kissed him back, her tongue sliding along the seam of his lips, urging him to open. He did, opening his mouth and tangling his tongue with hers, until the kiss was hot and heavy, their teeth clashing as they fought to get more. Lachlan twisted his hand in her hair and pulled her closer . . . and her eyes opened.

She gasped into his mouth, cheeks hot against his skin. Lachlan lifted his head at once, fighting not to smile as embarrassment fought the lust still clouding her eyes, still making her heart pound and her nipples harden.

She pushed herself up, then reached over to turn on the bedside lamp. Lachlan closed his eyes instinctively, but it was a low light, just enough to see Julia staring at him accusingly.

"You said I'd be safe."

He allowed a satisfied smile to touch his lips. "I woke up. It's night-time out there. And you were dreaming. You said my name." It wasn't true, but there'd been her smile when he'd touched her, and that kiss, which was far better than any dream-spoken name.

"Probably a nightmare," she muttered, but she didn't deny it.

He laughed. He knew when a woman wanted him. He'd tasted her kiss, felt the hard press of her breasts against his arm, caught the sweet scent of her desire. She'd been dreaming of him, all right, and he'd answered.

"Go back to sleep, princess. I'll leave you alone." He tucked the covers around her neck, then rolled to the other side of the bed and got up. "I'll be out there, if you need me," he said, dipping his head toward the other compartment with a wink, then turned, and in two strides was out the door and into the hallway, ignoring her muttered imprecations against him, even as he licked his lips, savoring the flavor of her and wanting more. His cock twitched, agreeing with him. He dropped a hand to the front of his jeans, pressing on the damn thing. He had better control than this normally, but something about Julia Harper had gotten under his skin and stayed there. He sprawled on the couch, legs spread wide to ease the discomfort. He contemplated freeing his erection and stroking it to completion, but the last thing he needed was for her to climb out of bed, only to find him jerking off on her dad's precious leather couch.

Looking for something to distract himself and his cock, he eyed

Julia's laptop. He bet she had her boyfriend's files on there—the ones that captured Erskine's financial transactions. Munro could do a lot with those files. Julia didn't understand the importance of that information. Maybe if he told her, if he explained that the money Erskine was hiding belonged to all the vampires of Scotland . . . . Then maybe she wouldn't be quite so reluctant to share.

Of course, she was asleep now, wasn't she? And her laptop was right here. She had it protected with a password, of course. But he'd been watching when she opened it earlier and was confident he knew the keystrokes. He could access the files and send them to Munro. No need to wait until after they met Raphael, or even longer, until Julia felt she could trust him, whatever *that* meant. How long would it take? *What* would it take, before she trusted him to fulfill his end of their bargain? He couldn't afford to wait until after Erskine was killed. Too much could happen in the meantime, especially to bank accounts and investments. And Lachlan needed that money to build a better Scotland for his clan and for all of the Scottish vampires who would look to him for protection once he became lord.

He flipped open the laptop lid and repeated the keystrokes from memory, noting as he did so that they spelled out a saying from a classic fantasy series. Strange that she knew that saying. She'd have been only a child when readers had taken it up.

He shook his head. That was immaterial. He needed to focus. But he'd no sooner pulled up her directory than a voice in his head, the one that yelled at him when he was doing something stupid, something *wrong*, told him to stop. His fingers lifted from the keys, freezing in place, as he considered why. And none of it had to do with that kiss.

The reality was that the two of them would be spending a lot of time together in the coming days. It would be dangerous and stressful, and there might be times when lives were at stake. His and hers, and others, as well. She'd spoken of trust, but did she understand what that meant when you were fighting for your life? Had she ever killed someone? Could she?

She was right about one thing. They did need a basic level of trust. And if he stole these files, if she found out about it, it would destroy any chance they had of building a partnership they could count on. He scowled. Sometimes he wished that damn voice of reason would shut the fuck up. But it was right this time. She'd promised to turn over the files once they returned to London, which wouldn't be more than a few days. This trip to Malibu wouldn't take long. He'd meet Raphael and leave. One day in, one day out. And then the files would be his, with no complications, no breach of trust.

Pulling out his phone, he texted Munro, telling him the files existed and he'd have them once he returned. Then, cursing the hours left until they reached LA, he pulled up a book on his phone and began reading.

It was a good book, but not good enough. By the time the pilot's voice came over the intercom advising of their imminent arrival, he was pacing the aisle, feeling as though he'd been trapped in this metal capsule for days, rather than hours.

"Thank fuck," he swore when he felt the plane's nose dip as the jet began its descent. Slamming into one of the big window seats, he lifted the shade and watched the lights of California's high desert slip by. He'd flown this route so many times, he knew what to look for, even if he didn't always know what he was looking at. The pattern of lights and swaths of darkness were familiar and welcome.

"Did I hear the pilot say we were landing?" Julia's sleepy voice had an immediate effect on his libido, although fortunately, it was no more than a sharp awareness of her presence. If he'd popped a full-on erection, he might have thrown caution to the wind and kissed her until she surrendered.

She didn't wait for his answer, disappearing into the bathroom instead. When she came out, she was still deliciously mussed and sleepy looking—cheeks pink, hair tousled—as she made her way down the aisle to sit across from him.

"We're landing?" she asked.

"Yes." He stood and leaned over her to raise the shade on her window. "If you look out there, that empty black space is the Pacific Ocean. They've circled around to come in from the ocean side. You should buckle up. We'll be on the ground soon."

She raised her head to look at him. "I'm sorry about before," she whispered, not meeting his gaze.

"Sorry?"

"When I. . ." She moistened her lips. "I was dreaming, but I didn't mean to . . . ." She stopped, unable to look at him.

"I didn't mind," he said softly, genuinely charmed by her need to apologize. "You have a very kissable mouth."

Her shy gaze became a glare of annoyance. "Couldn't you be a gentleman about it? Just once?"

He grinned. "Sure. But not when it comes to kissing a beautiful woman. Being a vampire doesn't make me less of man, you know."

"Great," she muttered, digging for her seatbelt.

"Here you go," he said, pulling it up from where it had fallen to the side. "Buckle up, princess."

"Stop . . . ." She cut herself off, closing her eyes and snapping her seatbelt into place with jerky movements.

Lachlan smiled. He loved getting under her skin, but it was almost too easy.

ONCE THEY WERE on the ground and parked in a private hangar, Julia went forward to speak to the pilots and explain that they'd be remaining on the plane for a while. She didn't mention vampires, but she got the feeling that at least one of the pilots understood what was going on. They worked for her dad when he needed them, but they had other clients as well. Maybe even vampire clients? Julia had never thought about it, but it made sense. Vampires had to travel, too.

With the pilots gone, she closed and locked the hatch, then returned to the passenger compartment to find Lachlan watching her. She couldn't tell what he was thinking. She'd told him the kiss was a mistake, the confusion of a waking mind, but that hadn't been true. She'd known who was kissing her and had wanted more. Some of it was curiosity, but mostly, it was desire. Maybe it was only the exotic quality of him, the idea of kissing a vampire. But he wasn't just any vampire, was he? He was . . . magnetic. She'd been no more able to stop that kiss than to land this damn plane. And she hadn't wanted to. But now, she didn't know what to do with him. Didn't know what to do with a hunger the likes of which she'd never experienced with another man. A hunger that came to life every time she got close to him.

She sat across the aisle, purposely avoiding the closer seat that faced him. "I think we should go to Malibu," she said, glancing up, then away. "We'll both be more comfortable there."

"You can go," he said with a dismissive shrug.

Julia *tsked* loudly in frustration. "I can't just leave you here."

"I promise not to steal the plane."

"Don't be stupid. It's not that. I just don't want to leave you un—" She couldn't say "protected." She was hardly strong enough to protect him, didn't even have a weapon. She switched tactics. "Why can't you go with me? They specifically invited both of us, and they must have special quarters that are safe for vampires, right?"

He turned to stare at her, and for the first time, she noticed that his eyes had a golden touch to them, as if there were sparks glinting in the light. Except there wasn't enough light for that. "I'm not going to daylight there," he said plainly. "I don't care how special their quarters are. Raphael is a stranger, and one who also happens to be a powerful fucking vampire."

"But he sleeps all day just like you do."

"*Not* just like I do. He's older and stronger, and that means he goes to sleep later and wakes earlier. He also has human fighters who are probably just as loyal to him as his vampires are. And then there's your fucking friend."

"Cynthia? What's she got to with anything?"

He gave her a scoffing look and shook his head. "How much do you know about her?"

Julia shrugged. "I don't know. *A lot.* What are you looking for?"

"Did you know she killed a vampire lord down in Texas? He wasn't as powerful as Raphael, but he was powerful enough, and a total psychopath, to boot."

Julia could only stare, as he continued.

"She's fought in every battle Raphael's had since they met. She's one of the best human fighters he has and certainly the most devoted. If you threaten him, she'll slice your throat and feed you to the sharks."

"Cyn?" she said weakly. "Are you sure?"

He laughed. "Yeah, I'm sure. Ask her. She'll probably tell you all about it."

Julia was still staring at him. "Jesus," she breathed.

"Yeah, well. I don't want to be the next notch on her bedpost, or wherever the hell she keeps tally. Until I know what Raphael thinks about all this, about going after Erskine, and upending Scotland, I'm not going place myself at his *or her* mercy."

She nodded. "Okay. Okay. I get it. I'll stay." She glanced around, then checked her cell for the time. "We have a couple hours 'til sunrise, if you want to get out and stretch your legs, or whatever. After that, well . . . I'll lock the hatch and stay inside. Maybe I'll watch a movie or catch some sleep, too. But you owe me."

He crooked a half smile and moved to the aisle, standing to his full height as he offered her his hand. "I'll figure out a way to make it up to you. In the meantime, come on, princess, I'll take you to breakfast."

She narrowed her eyes as she stood to join him. "Just remember, vampire. I'll be awake while you sleep."

His smile widened. "You going to take advantage of me while I'm helpless? Wake with me with a kiss?" he added with a knowing look.

"In your dreams."

"Or yours." He moved toward the hatch. "Come on, the darkness won't last forever, and you'll need your strength."

Julia was tempted to tell him what he could do with his sly looks and innuendos, but the truth was she was hungry, and nothing on the plane would be as good as a hot breakfast, American style. That was one thing she missed when she was out of the country. "Fine, but you're paying."

Chapter Six

Malibu, CA USA

LACHLAN SAT IN the backseat of the town car Julia had hired to take them from the airport to Malibu. Part of him would have preferred to drive himself. Vampires were all predators, but the truly powerful ones were as alpha as they came and hated surrendering control to anyone, much less a stranger. But Julia had cautioned against trying to find their way in LA's notorious combination of high speed and bumper-to-bumper traffic, and he'd conceded the point. He'd never driven when he'd been a student at Stanford, and it was far worse now than it had been back then.

At least there was plenty of room to stretch out in the big car. He'd changed into a suit for the meeting with Raphael—a charcoal gray wool blend, two buttons, and custom made down to the last stitch. He was too big to buy from the rack, even if he'd wanted to. He believed in dressing well when the occasion demanded, but more than that, he enjoyed it. He'd never want to dress like this every day, but once in a while, it felt good.

Julia seemed relaxed, but quiet. A little tired, maybe. He didn't push for conversation, instead using the time to examine their route and familiarize himself with his surroundings as much as possible. He'd studied a map on his cell phone and so knew the route they'd be taking. It ran along the coastline from Santa Monica to Malibu, though if he hadn't known the ocean was there, he wouldn't have guessed. Homes on the beach side of the Pacific Coast Highway were separated from each other by no more than a few feet. And with no moon in the sky, the few glimpses of ocean were nothing but black space between the houses.

They'd passed the downtown part of Malibu—such as it was—where they'd gotten their first look at the waves, courtesy of outdoor lights from homes and restaurants, and driven beyond, when the driver slowed for a sharp leftward turn. Lachlan's vampire sight showed him a slightly paler strip of road between dense trees, and he caught the sharp scent of eucalyptus.

"I hate that smell," Julia murmured.

He glanced over at her elegant profile. "Why?"

"It hurts my sinuses."

He was spared from coming up with a response when a very sturdy-looking gate abruptly broke the line of a tall wall they'd been paralleling for most of the driveway. There were no lights announcing the gate's presence. This was a vampire's estate, after all. But when the car lights hit the gatehouse, a dim light appeared and several heavily-armed vampires appeared from the shadows. *Lachlan* knew they were vampires, although there was nothing to distinguish them as such. At least, not until the headlights hit their faces and their eyes gleamed the tell-tale red of ordinary line vamps. Not that he thought these guards would be ordinary in any sense other than their level of power. A vampire lord of Raphael's strength and position would have only the very finest warriors in his security forces. And it was a sure bet that the ones manning the estate buildings inside would be magnitudes stronger.

That didn't worry Lachlan, however. He knew his own strength, too.

One of the guards approached the driver's side of the car, but ignored the driver's lowered window to tap on Lachlan's instead. Lachlan's mouth crooked in amusement at Julia's irritated, "What the fuck?" But there was no sign of humor when he gathered his power and lowered the window.

He studied the guard briefly, then said, "We're expected."

The vamp glanced from the screen of a cell phone strapped to his forearm, to Lachlan, and then back again. "Yes, sir." He stepped back and gestured at someone in the closed booth, who apparently hit the controls to open the gate. The other guards stepped back from their careful inspection of the car, eyeing the vehicle watchfully as it bumped over thick gate tracks and onto the estate proper.

Lachlan had been born and still lived in one of the most beautiful places on the planet. Scotland was a country of low mountains and green rolling hills, with stunning lochs and rushing rivers everywhere you looked. But even he was unprepared for the contrast between what he expected of this seaside estate and what greeted him beyond those gates. The road curved almost immediately to the left, forking after about fifty yards. Straight ahead, it disappeared into more trees, where he could see glimpses of another building. But to the right, the road dipped in a sweeping curve around a slope of perfectly manicured lawn, revealing what had to be Raphael's main estate house. Again, it surprised him. The house was a modern construct of clean lines, gleaming white in the light of what some might consider decorative lighting, though Lachlan eyed it from a security standpoint. A turquoise gem of a pool sat to one side, while the nearly invisible shadows of vampire guards surrounded the building. As they drove up to the main entrance, there was a large garage, with multiple bays to the left.

"From the road, it didn't look like there'd be this much land," Julia commented.

"Aye. And I'd wager we're not seeing everything, either. There's a basement under there. Maybe not the entire building, but a goodly part of it."

"A basement?"

"Vampires, love. That vault Leighton told you about? It'll be underground."

"An estate like this in Malibu? It's worth a fortune."

"No doubt. But Raphael's been alive and ruling this territory for a very long time."

"How long?"

"The territory? I can't say for sure, but I'd guess two hundred years or so. As for Raphael . . . I can't even guess. Vampires live a long time, especially the strong ones. He's centuries older than I am, anyway."

She turned to study him in the dim light of the backseat. "How old are *you*?"

He grinned, intentionally letting her see the flash of his fangs for the first time. "Let's just say, I hope you like your lovers to be older men."

A dismissive breath puffed over those sweet lips of hers. "Like that's going to happen."

He leaned in, put his lips next to her ear, and said, "Oh, it's happening, princess. It's only a question of time." When his lips touched the delicate skin beneath her ear in a soft kiss, she shivered in response, but didn't pull away. And Lachlan knew he was right. He was going to have her in his bed. But first, they had to survive Raphael.

The town car stopped at the foot of a set of stairs. "Stay inside," he told the driver, then opened his door and climbed out, holding out a hand for Julia to slide over and exit next to him.

She did so without complaint, which affirmed his confidence in her good sense. This wasn't a time for petty tantrums over protocol. This was very possibly the most dangerous gamble she'd ever taken, though she might not realize it. Lachlan could feel the immense power throbbing all around him. It was so strong that he was almost surprised to look up and *not* see the white walls pulsing in tune with the heartbeat of the vampire lord who ruled here.

And it wasn't only Raphael's power that pounded on him. He reached back and cupped a hand around Julia's slender hip, keeping her mostly behind him as he faced their greeting committee. Lachlan was a big man, but these two were even bigger. Having done his homework, he knew who they were—Juro and Ken'ichi. Twin brothers who formed the bedrock of Raphael's security apparatus. They were so identical that some might not have been able to tell them apart, but Lachlan could. Juro carried an air of authority and outward aggression, while Ken'ichi gave off a quiet confidence, one that said he'd listen before he acted. Regardless of their temperaments, however, the two were twins in power, as well as appearance.

But then, Lachlan had power of his own. Letting it rise just enough to make a point, without offering a threat, he held out his hand to Juro first. "Lachlan McRae," he said simply. "I believe Ms. Harper and I are expected."

Juro's dark eyes held his as they shook hands . . . and measured each other's strength. It wasn't a matter of physical muscle, although they tested that, too, doing their best to crush bones. But it was another test that truly mattered. Vampire power flared, and he caught a whisper of telepathic communication as Juro, no doubt, advised his lord of this new vampire's strength. But then, he gave Lachlan's hand a final squeeze that truly would have broken bones had he not protected himself with his vampire-enhanced muscle. Juro released his hand with a chuckle. "You should join us on the mats while you're here. It would be . . . interesting."

"An intriguing offer," Lachlan said, with the same touch of humor. "But perhaps another time. I doubt our visit will be long enough." He tightened his hold on Julia and stepped aside, letting her move up next to him.

"Julia Harper," she said, not waiting for an introduction as she offered her hand.

Juro's grip was visibly gentler. "Juro. Welcome to Malibu."

She smiled, then turned to Ken'ichi who'd just finished with Lachlan. There'd been no test of power in their handshake. It hadn't been necessary. And when he greeted Julia, his grip was even gentler than Juro's had been.

"Follow us," Juro said, starting up the stairs, while Ken'ichi gestured for one of the other vampire guards to deal with the driver.

The doors at the top of the short staircase were tall and elaborate, cut glass with a dark wooden frame and age-darkened brass hardware. They were opened from the inside by two guards who regarded Lachlan with open suspicion as they crossed into a marble-floored foyer. He was rather surprised that none of the guards viewed Julia as a threat. One would think living on an estate with Cynthia Leighton, they'd be more aware of the danger a human woman could represent. In this case, their judgment was warranted, since, to his knowledge, Julia wasn't even carrying a weapon. In her view, she was visiting an old friend, not entering the lair of a viciously powerful vampire lord.

She didn't fight him when Lachlan took her hand, however, so perhaps she wasn't as relaxed as she appeared.

They were across the foyer and halfway up the inside stairs to what, in America, was called the second floor when a stunning brunette rounded from the upper floor with a shouted, "Jules!"

Julia looked up with the biggest smile he'd seen from her so far. "Cyn!"

The two women ran toward each other, ignoring the undercurrent of vampire aggression as Leighton pushed past the two huge vampires to greet Julia with a joyful hug. "It's been forever," Leighton said, without loosening her hold.

For Lachlan's part, he simply stood there, admiring the sight they made. Two beautiful women, hugging and kissing each other's cheeks, their faces beaming with happiness. He glanced over and met Juro's gaze with a shrug. The big vampire made a huffing sound that might have been a laugh, then said, "Cynthia."

She turned to look at him, eyes rolling with impatience. "I know, I know. Come on, Jules." She pulled Julia up the stairs, past the twins, and turned left down the hall.

Lachlan doubted the friendly atmosphere would last long once they reached Raphael's inner sanctum, but didn't say anything, just kept to his well-guarded place between the two vampires and followed the women to what was obviously Raphael's office. The doors were open, but that didn't stop Lachlan from admiring their sheer magnificence. They were tall enough to grace any cathedral, the wood nearly black with age and grain. He wanted to stop and admire the intricate carving, but the impulse didn't last.

Because Raphael was waiting. There was no heartbeat of power like the one Lachlan had sensed outside. The vampire lord sitting behind his desk didn't need any blatant demonstration. His strength was like the heat of a distant star. Get too close and it would destroy you.

Lachlan didn't let any of these thoughts show on his face, however. Walking directly into the office, he stopped behind the two chairs placed in front of the desk and nodded his head in respect. It wasn't the greeting of equals, and not because of Raphael's simmering power, either. It was because Raphael was a vampire lord, and Lachlan wasn't . . . yet. "Lord Raphael." He didn't bother to introduce himself. That would have been redundant, since Raphael obviously knew who he was.

"Lachlan McRae," the vampire lord greeted him, proving the point.

"And this is my friend Julia," Leighton interjected, pulling her forward.

"Julia Harper," Julia clarified, taking her cue from Lachlan and not offering to shake hands.

Lachlan waited an awkward moment for Raphael to speak, while the vampire lord studied Julia with a moment's open curiosity, before it was concealed behind a blank expression. What was that about? Was it because she was human, and he didn't want her to be part of their discussions? This was vampire business, after all, and Raphael was unaware of Julia's desire to kill Erskine.

It was Leighton who finally broke the strange silence. "Come on, Jules. We don't need or want to stay here for this vampire bullshit. They take twenty words to say what you or I could manage in two." She rounded the desk and exchanged a kiss with Raphael. "See you later, my lord," she said, giving him an additional smacking kiss.

Lachlan could tell by the teasing way she used the honorific that it wasn't her usual title for him, and it made him like her. Made him think differently of Raphael, as well. Not that he thought the vampire lord was any less dangerous or deadly, but it *humanized* him. Which was a strange thing to say about a vampire as powerful as this one. But the fact that he indulged this public display, not so much the kiss, but the easy teasing between them, said something about who he was. And how confident he was in his power.

Lachlan turned and caught Julia's eye. She'd been watching the exchange with the same close attention and now met his gaze with more than a little puzzlement. He held out his hand, and she took it, letting him tug her closer. "Are you okay with this," he asked softly, more for her sake than anyone else's. Every vampire in the room would have heard the question, no matter how quietly he spoke.

Julia took a moment to respond, but then gave his fingers a squeeze as she nodded. "I'll spend some time with Cyn. You'll be okay?"

Her presence wouldn't stop Raphael from doing any damn thing he pleased, but her concern had been so sincere that he swallowed his automatic grin. The truth was that if it came down to it, Lachlan would fight, and he'd do some damage before he died. But die he would. Even so, it warmed his cold vampire heart to know she cared. "I will," he assured her.

"Don't worry, big guy," Leighton said, tugging Julia away from him. "I'll bring her back safe and sound." And with that, the two women left the office, Julia giving him a last scrutinizing look before letting herself be pulled away.

Lachlan's gaze didn't linger on the empty doorway once Julia was gone. He wasn't that foolish. The biggest threat in the room wasn't his lovely princess leaving him for a few hours. It was the powerful vampire sitting behind the desk. His eyes met Raphael's.

"Have a seat, Lachlan McRae. Tell me why you're here."

The doors closed behind Lachlan as he sat down. It was time to speak of murder and mayhem.

"SOOOOO," CYN SAID, as she settled onto an overstuffed couch in front of a huge fireplace. It was the kind of hearth Julia imagined was used, back in the day, to spit and cook whole goats or pigs. It was certainly big enough. Although, while this house was grand, it wasn't nearly old enough to have hosted a medieval feast. Besides, as far as she knew, vampires didn't eat regular food anyway.

"Sooooo," Julia echoed, sitting on the opposite end of the couch. "You've mated with a vampire," she said, using Lachlan's word.

"Looks like you've hooked up with one, too," Cyn said slyly.

"What? Absolutely not. We only met a few days ago, for God's sake. We're partners, nothing else."

Cyn laughed. "If you say so, but I know vamps, Jules. They're relentless when they want something, or some*one*. And that boy wants you."

"He's hardly a boy," she muttered. "He's old enough to be my great-grandfather, at least."

"Doesn't look like anyone's grandpa to me. That's one fine male specimen."

"Hey! You're a married woman. Or close to it anyway."

"Yep, thoroughly taken, and by the most beautiful man in the world. But that doesn't make me blind. Your Lachlan is a hunk, and you'd be a fool not to tap that, even if it's not long-term."

"Tap that? Jesus, Cyn."

She laughed again. "When did you become such a prude? Or I am hitting too close to home?" She stretched out a foot and nudged Julia with her toe. "Admit it, you're attracted to him."

Julia let out an exasperated breath. "Okay, fine. He's gorgeous, he's smart, and can be charming when he wants. But he's as moody as hell, and he keeps secrets."

"They all keep secrets. Raphael did, too, at the beginning. But . . . well, you know me. Trust doesn't come easily. We had a crisis of sorts, a serious one. And he doesn't do that anymore."

Julia reached down and squeezed Cyn's foot in a gesture of understanding. She did know the other woman, knew about her solitary childhood, her absent father, and the mother who'd abandoned her. Cyn had always been beautiful and smart, but Raphael was the first serious relationship she'd ever had, as far as Julia knew. So maybe the vampire really was good for her.

"Tell me about Lachlan," Cyn said, changing the subject. "Hey, you want something to eat or drink? Vamps tend to forget about us mere humans, but there's a full kitchen downstairs for the daytime guards. I can order up something, if you want."

"No, I'm fine. Lachlan took me out for breakfast after we got here, and I had a sandwich on the plane. We used my dad's jet."

Cyn nodded. "Yeah, there's no such thing as flying commercial with a vamp. And the food thing . . . it does make it easier to stay in shape. Plus, my trainer now is a vicious female vampire who loves to make me hurt." She waved away Julia's look of concern. "I'm kidding. Elke's my nighttime bodyguard and she's great. I'm in better shape than I've ever been."

"That makes two of us," Julia said dryly. "I've been planning this since Masoud was killed." She froze, realizing what she'd just said. She glanced over at Cyn to find her friend staring at her.

"Planning what, Jules? And what does Masoud's death have to do with it? I thought he was killed during a robbery gone bad?"

Julia sighed. There was no point in keeping her suspicions a secret from Cyn. The question of how she and Lachlan had met, and why Julia had helped arrange this meeting, was bound to come out eventually. Besides, Cyn was too smart not to see through some convenient story, and Lachlan would probably just tell Raphael outright. Especially given that whole 'you can't lie to a vampire' thing.

"I never bought the robbery story," she admitted. "He was murdered."

Cyn stared at her. "What? Who'd want him dead?"

"Someone who thought he was too close to uncovering their crimes."

"Explain please. Masoud was with his dad's investment group, right?"

Julia nodded. "And he was good at it. Too good. He discovered a money laundering scheme. Multiple currencies, but in the high nine figures if counted in US dollars. He was in London to meet with the client—to give him a chance to explain, I guess—but the night before the meeting, he was murdered. That's no coincidence, Cyn."

"Convenient timing, I admit." The other woman frowned. "But what does that have to do with Lachlan? Or vampires in general?"

Julia sighed, but there was no choice but to go all in. "The supposed investor, the one hiding the money, was a Scottish vampire. Erskine Ross."

"Erskine," Cyn repeated softly, thinking, then stared with wide eyes. "Raphael mentioned him when he talked about this visit. But he's not just any vamp, Jules. He's the Lord of Scotland. Really powerful. And dangerous, too. He'll have an army of vamps at his beck and call. If he killed Masoud . . . . You have to leave this alone, or he'll kill you, too."

Julia didn't raise her voice, just gave her friend a long look and asked, "Would *you* be able to leave it alone?"

"It's not the same. I have Raphael to back me up."

"And if you didn't? If Raphael had been the one killed, or even hurt? Would you just let it go, then?" she asked, still speaking quietly.

"Fuck, no, and you know it. Damn it. Does Lachlan know?"

"Of course, he does. Why do you think I called you? We have a deal. I help him get a meeting with Raphael, and he helps me get my revenge."

"What does that mean? What exactly is your revenge?"

"I want that bastard dead. And I want to be the one who does the killing."

Cyn was silent for a long moment, then said, "He won't let you do that, you know."

Julia frowned. "What do you mean? Who won't let me do what?"

"Lachlan won't let you kill Erskine. If he wants Erskine dead, it's because he's going after the territory himself. That's why he wants to talk to Raphael."

"Why does that make a difference?"

"Because it means he has to do the killing. It's a vampire thing. There's no way around it. He might let you get in a shot or two, but the death blow has to be his."

Julia thought about it. Lachlan had told her about how someone had to be ready to step up and take over the territory if Erskine died. And he'd never come right out and said she could kill Erskine herself. Only that they both wanted the vampire lord dead. She thought about it some more, then said, "As long as I get to hurt him before he dies . . . I can live with that."

"Well, okay, then," Cyn jumped to her feet. "Come on, I'll show you our armory. You can fire a gun, right?"

"Of course, it was part of my training at—" She stopped before she gave away her CIA connection, even though she was sure Cyn already knew. "Let's just say I was well-trained. And I don't need your armory. I have my own gun."

"A back-up's always necessary. And I have these special bullets. Well, they're not *mine*—I didn't invent them or anything. But I call them my vampire-killer rounds. One clean shot to the head and it destroys their brain. After that, you just walk up to them and blow out their heart, and you've got one very dead vampire. It doesn't matter how powerful they are, either. Come on, babe," Cyn cried excitedly. "Let's go kill some motherfucking vampires!"

"Cyn. Sit down, and stop using that word. Your language is even worse than it used to be."

Cyn laughed, but didn't sit down. "I'm serious, Jules. You need those bullets, and they might be harder to get in Europe. What size is your weapon?"

"It's a 9mm, and yeah, I'll take the bullets, thanks. But there's no need to visit the armory, even though I know it's probably your favorite place."

Cyn gave her a big grin and made a "pew pew" noise as she shaped her hand into a gun and shot it around the room.

Julia shook her head. "I don't need an extra gun. I'm sure Lachlan's cousins have more than a few hanging around."

Cyn flopped back onto the couch. "We could go to the shooting range. We can't do anything serious about this plan of yours until Raphael and Lachlan finish *talking*." The way she said the last word made her attitude clear, but a moment later, she was stretching out like a lazy cat, her feet practically in Julia's lap, her head on a big throw pillow.

"Since you won't let me kill anything, let's talk about Lachlan. I want details."

Julia would rather have discussed killing vampires. "There are no details."

"Don't give me that. You may not curse much anymore, but you're not a nun, either. I mean, come on. Look at the man!"

"Lachlan is . . . tempting," she admitted. "I'm not blind. I know he's gorgeous. And he's smart. You know how much I like brains in a man. But . . . it's a risk. And I don't know if I'm ready for that." She looked up. "I don't want any more pain, Cyn."

Cyn sighed. "You have to let that go, Jules. You have to move on."

She nodded. "You're right. And I will . . . as soon as Erskine Ross is dead."

LACHLAN BREATHED a private sigh of relief when Julia left the room. She thought she was ready to take part in Erskine's assassination, but it was one thing to desire a person's death, and quite another to strike the death blow, to watch your enemy's life blood spurt thick and red from the wound, to see his guts spilling over desperate hands in steaming heaps while he tried to hold them in. To watch life fade from his eyes. They never got that part right in movies. A man's eyes didn't close peacefully in death or stare blankly into space. The lids rolled up and a film covered their eyes until there was no question of life remaining. More than anything, it was the eyes that had haunted Lachlan when he'd killed his first man. It was so long ago that he'd still been human, but the details were as vivid as ever.

Of course, vampires simply dusted before their eyes could do anything.

"Why are you here?"

Lachlan didn't react when the sudden question interrupted his musings, just cursed himself for getting lost in useless memories. If he didn't want to join his unmourned dead, he needed to pay attention. Raphael had been the very picture of polite sophistication up until this point, but now that it was just vampires in the room, all bets were off. This was no time to fuck around, but to simply come out and speak the truth.

"I'm going after Erskine. He'll be dead within the month."

Raphael tipped his head sideways. "I don't know Erskine personally. What I do know of him isn't terribly impressive, so I don't really care what happens to him. But just out of curiosity, and since you came all this way, is he a bad lord, or simply too weak and incompetent?"

Lachlan concealed his surprise at the question. It must be a slow news day in Malibu, because vampires didn't give a shit about who died and who lived, unless it affected them personally. That's why he was here, after all, to make sure Raphael didn't have any designs on Scotland. He had no need to justify killing Erskine, otherwise. But since he *had* come all this way, he'd answer.

"Erskine's a bad ruler. He hoards the territory's riches for himself and his few cronies, while requiring tithes from even the smallest shopkeeper. But when that same shopkeeper comes to him for investment to expand, or for protection against a stronger vampire, he sends them away. I can't name the last time he invested in a new vampire enterprise that didn't benefit him personally. He claims there's not enough money, but I've done the math and there is. He's using it for himself and hiding what he can't use. I don't know his motives. Maybe he plans on a peaceful retirement. If so, he's going to be disappointed." Lachlan met Raphael's black gaze and smiled slightly. "But I'll be honest, Lord Raphael. I'd kill the fucker even if he was the best vampire lord in the universe. It's personal for me. He owes my clan a debt of vengeance, and I'm going to claim it."

Raphael nodded silently. "Then I'm confused. What does this have to do with me?"

Lachlan would have laughed if the stakes hadn't been so high. The vampire lord knew *exactly* why he'd come to Malibu, but he wasn't going to help Lachlan make this any easier. Bastard. "Let me be blunt, then," he continued, forcing himself to maintain his casual posture, the very picture of confidence and unconcern. "We all watched the recent events in Ireland with great interest. Scotland's not so far away, so what happens in Ireland is very relevant to our own piece of earth."

"Relevant how?"

"Relevant as in everyone knows you backed Quinn."

"Do they?" The two words sounded almost like a threat coming from Raphael, but Lachlan refused to be cowed.

"They do. *I* do. We also know you've had problems with some other European lords who thought to expand their territories at your expense."

"Not only mine."

"No. It was all of you here in North America. So we weren't surprised when you blew up the balance of power in France, or even when you put your boy in Ireland." He met Raphael's eyes across the wide expanse of his desk. "This is a courtesy call, Lord Raphael. I intend to take Scotland. I'd much rather be, if not friends, then at least not enemies, either. But I will kill anyone you send to oppose me, whether it's in support of Erskine or simply a candidate of your own. Scotland is mine."

"Is that a threat?" Raphael's eyes were the cold of a moonless winter night.

"Not at all. Simply the truth. I would, frankly, hope to ally with Quinn. Our countries have much in common, and we could help each other with issues that are unique to our people, to vampires. I would even expand that alliance to fight alongside you and Quinn against the old guard in Europe. Too many of them are stuck in the ancient ways that hold our people back, deny them the prosperity that could be theirs. But Scotland belongs to the Scottish. That much is set in stone."

"England would differ," Raphael said dryly.

"Humans and their governments are irrelevant."

"Until they make war on vampires," Juro said, speaking for the first time.

Lachlan glanced up at him. "Which has not happened in more than a thousand years. Even then, it was the sorcerers who led the charge. And where are *they* now? While vampires are so numerous they've taken to stealing each other's territories. Or trying to."

"Sorcerers are still out there," Raphael commented, then lifted one hand in a negligent gesture. "Although in significantly smaller numbers."

"My point."

"Yes," the vampire lord agreed. "What about Julia Harper?"

Lachlan's attention sharpened. "Julia?"

Raphael gave a small, indulgent smile. As if he already knew everything there was to know about Julia, and wanted to see if Lachlan had done his homework. That pissed him off. He was too smart to show it, but he wasn't some raw schoolboy come to plead his case before the big vampire. No one here—not Juro or his twin, and not Raphael—had yet tasted the full strength of his power. He wasn't Raphael's match. No other vampire currently alive had that kind of power. But Lachlan would be a fucking strong vampire lord. He could rule the entire United Kingdom, if he chose. That he didn't intend to was a matter of his choice, and it irritated the fuck out of him to be treated like some beggar come calling.

"Julia works for the CIA," he said coolly, "which has nothing to do with why she's here."

"No? Why *is* she here?" There was an edge to Raphael's tone that said this was the nub of why the vampire lord had insisted she fly to

Malibu. He wanted to know if the American government was prying into his affairs.

"Erskine killed someone important to her, someone she loved."

Raphael grew very still. "A family member?"

"A boyfriend," Lachlan corrected, surprised by how much it grated to admit that. "To my knowledge, her only living family is her father. Your mate probably knows more than I do."

"Yes." It was one word, but it made clear that any further discussion of his mate or what she might know was off the table. Raphael exchanged a glance with his two advisors, then said, "Are you going to permit Ms. Harper to do this?"

Lachlan almost laughed at the assumption he could control Julia. Not that he wouldn't try. "To be involved? She already is. She was ready to take off on her own when I met her. But to kill Erskine? No. Not least because I need to do it."

Raphael stood with a smile. It was the first genuine smile Lachlan had seen from him since Leighton had left the office. "Rest assured I have no sights set anywhere but on my own territory," he said. "As for Quinn, when last we spoke, he had his hands full undoing decades of damage his predecessor had inflicted on Ireland. You have that in common, and he might very well make a good ally for you in the future. I've learned to value such alliances lately." He turned to address Juro. "We'll move to the conference room. Ask Jared to join us." He turned back to Lachlan. "My lieutenant. He and Juro are very talented when it comes to strategic matters. And we might as well invite my Cyn and Julia Harper back in to the discussion. It's quite pointless to try to protect such strong women."

Lachlan had come to his feet when Raphael did. "That's very generous. Thank you, my lord."

Raphael waved a hand as he headed around the desk. "You were right about too many of our people being stuck in the past. The rest of us have to join forces if we're to drag vampires into a stronger future." He pulled a slender cell phone from the breast pocket of his elegant suit and pressed a single digit. "My Cyn," he greeted. "Would you and your friend like to join us in the conference room?"

THE MEETING DIDN'T end until an hour before dawn. Lachlan was convinced that Juro and Jared could have happily gone on much longer. To say they knew a lot about strategic planning was a vast understatement. They not only knew it, they loved it. They were obviously both fans of military history and had a story for every possible scenario that they, or anyone else, could dream up. Lachlan was grateful for their willingness to help, but he'd come all this way to get Raphael's word that he wouldn't interfere in Scotland, not for military advice. He knew his territory as well or better than anyone else, and he certainly knew his people better. More than that, they trusted him to lead them, to value their lives as much as he did his own.

And now that he'd done what he'd come to Malibu for, he wanted to get back home. Unfortunately, given the unreliability of traffic conditions between this estate and the airport, it was too late to reach the safety of the Harper jet before sunrise. Besides which, under those circumstances, it would have been scurrilously impolite to reject Raphael's offer of safe haven.

Julia leaned into his side as he walked her to the bedroom she'd been assigned for their stay. Truth was, he'd have rather had her in the vault with him, but since they weren't even lovers—yet—he didn't want her to be trapped in a locked vault with no escape. It had been different on the jet. She'd had the option of leaving at any time.

He smiled, enjoying the warm length of her body against his, but even more than that, he appreciated the casual way she leaned into him, with his arm around her shoulders. As if they were already lovers. "Tired, princess?"

She didn't even comment on the "princess," but only nodded her head with a wordless hum of agreement.

It made him grin, and then nearly miss a step when he realized he enjoyed simply being with her, even though they weren't lovers yet, and weren't going to start tonight either. He frowned and decided that was going to change. He had no intention of getting stuck in some weird friend zone with this woman. He didn't want sparkling conversation with her, or not *only* that, he wanted to hear her scream while he thrust between her silky thighs, going deeper and harder than any man had ever gone before. Including the permanently sainted Masoud.

She stopped outside a door that was just like every other door on the corridor, and looked up at him. He crowded her a little bit, not enough to threaten, but enough to make her aware of him as a man. Her look turned solemn, and when she spoke, it was in a whisper. "Will you be safe here?"

He gazed down at her, keeping his expression every bit as solemn as hers, and asked, "Are you worried about me?"

Her mouth tightened. She was obviously uncomfortable having

asked, and didn't realize he was teasing.

He stroked a finger down her velvety cheek. "I'll be fine."

"You're sure? I can stay with you, if you need me to," she said, sending a searching glance down the hall and looking embarrassed as hell while doing it. He was going to have to teach his princess how to hide what she was thinking before they went up against Erskine.

"I'll be fine," he repeated. "But thank you." He had a terrible urge to kiss her, but didn't honestly know if he'd be able to stop. And the coming dawn was an increasingly hot brand on the back of his brain. He reached behind her and twisted the door knob. "If you go out with Leighton tomorrow, take a bodyguard."

She rolled her eyes, but said, "Raphael insists Cyn do that, too, so we're covered."

"So you *are* going out."

"Probably. Cyn's a world-class shopper. I'll just tag along for the experience."

"Well, buy some warm clothes while you're there. It's going to be wet and cold when we get back to Scotland."

She frowned. "I have plenty of clothes for London at the apartment."

"But we're not going to be in London, princess. We're heading for the Highlands." He winked. "See you tonight."

And then he did what he'd told himself not to do. He leaned in and took her mouth. Her lips were as soft as he'd known they would be, opening in welcome as she gripped his shirt. He pressed closer, one arm going around her waist, the other up her back, his fingers tangling in her hair as her head tipped back farther, exposing the lovely line of her neck. His cock twitched and he knew he had to stop, but first . . . his tongue swept into the warmth of her mouth. She met him with tentative twists of her tongue in response, growing more frantic as the kiss went on, until finally Lachlan tightened his hold on her hair and gently pulled his mouth away from hers.

"Bad timing," he breathed against her lips.

"Right." She was out of breath, which pleased him no end. She licked her lips, and he had to bite back a groan.

"Tomorrow night," he murmured. "We have that big bed . . . and a long flight back to Scotland."

"Tomorrow," she repeated, her fingers still clenching his shirt, as if she couldn't let go.

He kissed her again, gently, but closed his teeth over her lower lip before letting go. "Be safe."

"You, too."

"I've gotta go, love. Or they'll lock me out."

"Right." She loosened her hold, stroking her hands over his shirt as if to smooth out the wrinkles she'd caused. "Where will I meet you?"

"I'll call as soon as I wake."

"Right. Cell phone." She smiled. "I'm going now." She pushed on the already opened door and backed into the room.

"Close the door. Lock it."

She shook her head in mock disgust, but blew him a kiss before closing the door. He waited until he heard the click of a lock, then strode quickly down the hall to a stairwell that Juro had pointed out to him, the one leading down to the vault. Once there, he strode down a second short hall to the vault entrance, where another vampire waited.

"Lachlan McRae?" the vamp confirmed. "This way," he said when Lachlan nodded.

Three minutes later, he was closing and locking the door on a very private, and very comfortable, sleeping chamber. He stripped off all but his boxer briefs, not wanting to show up tomorrow night in a wrinkled suit, then slipped under the covers just as the sun crested the horizon.

JULIA LAY IN THE big bed and watched the pale gray light of morning sneak over the ocean. She considered closing the drapes, but that would involve climbing out from beneath the warm covers. She'd much rather lie there, staring up at the ceiling and replaying *that kiss*. Had it meant something? Lachlan seemed like such a blank slate much of the time. He had to have emotions just like anyone else, but he kept them so well hidden. Oh, sure, he could be sarcastic, cynical, even clever. But that kiss . . . had it been nothing more than counting coup? Proving that she wanted him? It hadn't felt that way. His body had certainly been a willing participant. His erection had been impossible to miss. She pushed the covers down a fraction as heat raced over her face and chest, leaving her damp with perspiration. What the fuck was that? She was too young for hot flashes, wasn't she? But her nipples were hard and her chest wasn't the only thing damp. So. Not a hot flash, but a Lachlan flash. Just great.

She threw the covers all the way back, got up and pulled the drapes, then headed for the bathroom and a shower. She stripped off her sleep shorts and tank, and was reaching for the water controls, when she stopped. A hot shower wasn't going to make anything better. It might even make it worse. She stood there naked, then decided. She was going for a run. It had been ages since she'd run on the beach, and the sand made for an excellent workout. If she had to sweat, then she was going to get something out of it besides sexual frustration.

She was halfway down the steep stairs below the cliff when she heard Cyn call from above.

"Hey, Jules, wait for me!"

She watched her friend skip downward and felt the tiniest bit of jealousy. Julia was a pretty woman, some would say more than pretty. But there'd always been an effortless quality to Cyn's beauty. She didn't need makeup or an expensive haircut to draw attention. Cyn could be wearing grubby shorts and a t-shirt, hair yanked unstylishly into a ponytail, and heads would still turn. Maybe it was nature's compensation for having such a nightmare family life. Julia had lost her mother and brother, but at least she had memories of them, and she still had a dad who loved her without question.

"What are you staring at?" Cyn demanded, jumping the final two stairs to the sand.

"You, you beautiful bitch."

Cyn laughed. "Are we running or comparing make-up tips?"

Julia snorted. "You run here every morning?"

"Nah. I'm way too lazy. Most mornings I sleep a few hours with Raphael, then do some work, then go back to bed. He likes me there when he wakes up." She batted her eyelashes. "I bet Lachlan wouldn't mind waking up to you."

"It's not like that. We haven't . . . you know."

"Fucked? Come on, Jules, you can say it. I'm the friend who knows who popped your cherry."

She felt a blush coming on and laughed at herself. When had she become so proper? "I think I've been spending too much time at work," she said dryly.

"What, no one swears at the agency?"

Julia gave Cyn a sharp look, then shook her head. "Lachlan warned me about you. Well, not *you*, but Raphael and vampires in general. He claims they have spies everywhere."

"Not spies, really. Just people who work the night shift."

"Sure. Vampires gotta eat, too."

Cyn chuckled. "I just had a flash image of a vampire going from cube to cube, sipping on his late shift co-workers, like a tasty buffet."

"As if. At least that would make it interesting. All we have is a lady who should have retired five years ago and hushes us like a librarian. Especially when we curse."

Cyn patted her arm. "Don't worry, three days around me and you'll be swearing like a sailor. Now, are we here to have a fucking tea party or to run?"

"Bitch." Julia took off.

They ran then. No conversation. Just long even strides while the sun climbed over the hills enough to break up the morning fog. Cyn was a little taller than Julia, but not enough to matter, and contrary to their earlier jesting, they were both in great shape. By the time they finished, they were covered in sweat and breathing hard, but grinning like maniacs.

"Fuck, that felt good," Julia said, in between breaths.

Cyn laughed as she sank onto the steps. "Shit, that didn't even take a day. You're already cursing like a sailor."

"Might as well," she said, sitting next to her. "Lachlan and his cousins don't exactly censor themselves. Why should I?" She didn't look up, but she could feel Cyn's gaze upon her. She turned and met that green stare. "What?"

"Be careful, Jules. You're smart, and you just proved you're in good shape. But vampire wars are nothing to get involved in, especially for a human."

"No war is."

Cyn shook her head. "That's not what I'm trying to tell you. Vampires don't fight the way we do. It's close-up and brutal and always to the death. Make sure you know what you're getting into."

She nodded, even though she didn't agree. Killing was killing, wasn't it? She'd seen the crime scene photos before she'd even made it to London. Masoud's blood had stained the sidewalk for days after he'd been shot. Until someone—the city probably—had scrubbed it away. Julia was sure she could still see the outline of it whenever she walked past that spot. Which she did almost every day, even though it took her out of her way. "Don't worry," she assured her friend. "I'm not planning on leading the charge. I know my limits."

And that wasn't a lie. She *did* know her limits. But she had every intention of breaking them.

Chapter Seven

BY THE TIME LACHLAN walked out of the shower in his private underground room, the vault was echoing with voices and footsteps, enough to tell him that most, if not all, the vampires who slept down there were awake. He'd opened his eyes an hour earlier and had immediately texted Julia. He'd been subtle about it, suggesting a time and place to meet and arrange their departure that night, but he'd needed to know she was all right. Raphael hadn't exactly been friendly, but he'd been gracious and not at all hostile. And Leighton had seemed to be genuinely happy to see Julia. But it wasn't in Lachlan's nature—as a vampire or the future Lord of Scotland—to take safety for granted.

Toweling off his wet body, he walked out of the steamy bathroom and studied the room, wondering if he could transform his own basement quarters into something like this. He had sleeping quarters for any vampire who lived in or came to visit either his personal estate or the ancestral McRae fortress, but while the furnishings were nice enough, they weren't as secure or finished as these. He'd have to look into it once he was lord.

Right, because that was the important thing for him to consider tonight. Fancy sleeping quarters. He donned clean underwear, socks and a t-shirt, then decided to ditch his suit for more comfortable clothes. Pulling on jeans, he retrieved his leather jacket from the duffle, and shoved in the suit and shirt with little regard. After a last look around, he opened the door and joined the general trend of traffic upward. There was no guide waiting for him tonight. He didn't need one. Taking the courtyard exit, he walked across the wide driveway and over to the outdoor pool. It was large and well-lit with underwater lights, while the surrounding deck was darker, just a few landscape-type lights hidden in clay pots of trees along the house wall. There were three tables, all with closed umbrellas. He supposed the daylight guards made use of the pool in their time off, or maybe Leighton liked to swim. *He* only cared about the woman waiting for him at the farthest table. It was also the darkest table, since it was on the edge of the pool area closest the ocean cliff, though a wide expanse of green lawn stood between the pool and the cliff's edge.

Julia looked up when he stepped onto the pool deck, after crossing the narrow verge from the driveway. She had the remains of a meal pushed to one side of the table and a cup of coffee in her hand. When he reached her, he ran his fingers over her white blond hair, which was lying loose and silky down her back, then pulled out the chair next to her.

"Did you get any sleep?" he asked, helping himself to a cup of coffee from a tray on the table. There were two cups—hers and the one he was using—and a thermal decanter, along with the usual cream and sugar. She'd either anticipated his arrival, or she was expecting someone else. If it was the latter, they were going to be disappointed.

She studied him a moment, her pale blue eyes reflecting the turquoise water like bright jewels in the dark. Her smile was slow, but welcoming. "Cyn and I ran on the beach this morning."

"What were you running from?"

"Ha ha. You don't fool me. Cyn says vampires have to work out to stay in shape just like regular humans do."

"You think I'm in good shape, then?"

Those jewel-like eyes rolled in disgust. "Searching for compliments is beneath you."

He smiled. "Okay, you ran on the beach. What's that got to do with whether you slept?"

"It wore me out enough that my brain shut off. I slept better than I have in months."

"I'll have to remember to wear you out then. In the interest of good health," he added with a wink that he wasn't sure she could see.

"So you're going to jog through the Highlands with me?"

"Not what I had in mind, no."

She took a sip of coffee which concealed her reaction to his words, but she couldn't conceal the rush of her pulse or the press of hard nipples against her silk blouse—both perfectly clear to his vampire senses.

She put down her cup. "I assume from your message that we're going back to London tonight?"

"Tonight, yes, but not to London. Your jet—"

"My *dad's* jet."

He gave her an impatient look, but said, "Your *father's* jet should have no difficulty flying directly to Edinburgh. That'll save us some time, and there's no reason for us to be in London anymore. Unless you need to stop there?"

She shook her head. "No. I packed enough for three days on this trip, plus I keep a few supplies on the jet. Nothing warm enough, though, according to you. It's too bad Cyn and I didn't end up going shopping. I could probably have found some serious winter gear in the ski shops." She gave a dismissive shrug. "I'm sure they have lots of stores in Edinburgh."

"Good enough. If we leave late tonight—eleven or so—we'll hit Edinburgh just after dark. We can rest there for a night or two, then go home."

"Home?"

"*My* home. In Inverness."

She gave him a puzzled look. "I thought your clan castle was on that island near Dornie."

"Ach, that's just for the tourists, lassie," he said in his heaviest brogue. "The real yin's in Killilan, and a wee bit better defended." He laughed at her expression and added, "But that's not where we're going anyway."

"What's a yin? Never mind. We don't have to hike anywhere, do we? Because if so I'm going to need—"

He laughed. "A four-wheel drive is useful, but we've plenty of those, not to worry."

She leaned in close enough to whisper, "Do we need to say good-bye to Raphael first? You know, thank him for his hospitality and stuff?"

He breathed in the scent of her skin, before whispering back, "You can probably skip it, but I'll need to pay my respects. In fact, I expect to be called before his lordship any minute now."

She gave him a disbelieving look. "Should you say stuff like that?"

He couldn't resist giving her a quick hug. "I do believe you're worried for my safety, again, princess. But don't fret yourself. I know my manners."

Julia elbowed his side with a muttered, "Asshole," then said, "I'll give the pilots a heads-up. They'll need to file a flight plan for Edinburgh, as well as fuel up and do whatever else it is they do. Are you packed?"

"Yes, Madame," he said in a teasing voice.

"You're in an awfully good mood. Not your usual strong and silent self." She gave him a squinty-eyed look. "I heard there was a party last night. Cyn says they happen all the time, that they bring in lots of 'blood donors,'" she raised her hands in finger quotes, "for the guards who can't get away. Did you join the party before—?"

He straightened abruptly, shifting away from her with the same move and feeling oddly insulted. "I did not." He stood without notice and said, "You should make those flight arrangements. I see Juro coming this way. I want to speak with him before we go, and then I'll probably meet with Raphael." He stood. "I have your number. I'll call if you're expected to join us."

She stood to face him, seeming bewildered by his sudden shift in mood. "We'll need to leave for the airport by 8:00 if you want to fly at 11:00. Traffic's unreliable, and the airport itself can be a zoo."

"Shouldn't be a problem. See you later." He spun on his heel and walked away, heading for Juro who was now waiting just inside the foyer. He could have told Julia he was in a good mood because he was going home. He might even have hinted he was looking forward to spending time with her. But then she'd made that sly insinuation, implying at a minimum that he'd taken blood from some unknown woman's vein, or more likely, bedded her in the process. It shouldn't have pissed him off, but it did. He'd never been one to hop from bed to bed. Munro had once called him serially monogamous. He never got seriously involved, but he did tend to stick with one woman for a while. Until she started talking marriage, at least.

Vampires didn't get married, for the most part. Mating satisfied the urge to claim a woman or man as their own. But mating linked two people in an exchange of blood, which was far more serious than a marriage ceremony. In addition, marriage required a license from the human government, and vampires had spent too many centuries in the dark to trust human authorities. Give them a vampire's address, and they were as likely to burn the house down with everyone in it, as to perform their civic duty. He was certain that some in government still saw the burning as *part* of their civic duty. In recent years, however, he'd seen more vampires following the human tradition of marriage, maybe in addition to mating, maybe instead of. He didn't know. He assumed it was mostly to please their human mates. But whatever the reason, he wasn't going to be one of them.

Of course, his newly dark mood had nothing to do with marriage rites. It was Julia's assumption that he'd been in another woman's bed when the two of them had, fairly obviously to his mind, been heading in that direction themselves. He still had every intention of bedding her. But he was also going indulge his insulted ego for a while. He smiled, amused at his own thoughts.

"Good news from home?" Juro asked, holding out a hand in greeting.

"Yes," Lachlan said, shaking his hand. He could hardly tell the big vampire that he'd been brooding about a woman now, could he? "We'll be heading back there tonight. Julia tells me we need to leave by 8:00 to be certain of our 11:00 departure time."

"Unfortunately true. Come up. Raphael wants a final word." As they started for the stairs, Juro continued, "I'm sorry you've had such a short visit. We have a warrior here who's a genius with the blade. I'd have loved to see the two of you fight."

Lachlan had plenty of sparring partners back home. Every one of whom was more than two centuries old and a formidable opponent. But he appreciated the sentiment. "I'm always open for a challenge. Perhaps after things are more settled in Europe."

"Perhaps," Juro agreed, as they arrived at the open doors of Raphael's office. "My lord," he said, walking over to the desk and sitting in one of the guest chairs.

"Gentlemen," Raphael said, then gestured for Lachlan to take the remaining chair. He was dressed much more informally tonight, but then, so was Lachlan.

"Lord Raphael," Lachlan said, bowing his head in respect before sitting.

"Jared briefed me earlier on your discussions from last night. It sounds as if you and your warriors have things well in hand."

Lachlan gave a short nod. "We've had our share of battles over the centuries. This isn't so different. It comes down to weapons and tactics, and I'll pit my clansmen against his any time. He's grown foolishly confident in his Edinburgh castle. He's forgotten what it means to be a warrior."

Raphael shot a grin at Juro. "Ah, yes, castles. We don't have many of those over here. Modern houses are much easier to deal with."

"Aye, castles are bloody cold and damp," Lachlan agreed dryly.

Juro chuckled. "And bloody expensive to upgrade, I'm told. Lucas spent a fortune on that castle of his in Ireland."

"There's that," Lachlan agreed. He could have said more, but as pleasant as the company was, he was eager to be back on his way to Scotland. He doubted that Raphael, hundreds of years older and sitting in his wildly elegant ocean-front estate could understand the practical issues that Lachlan and his cousins dealt with every day. So instead, he said, "Julia and I want to thank you for your hospitality, Lord Raphael. And I want to thank you personally for your assistance, and for the opportunity to consult with your advisers." He smiled briefly. "Once

Scotland is mine, perhaps you'll visit our Highlands, see some of those castles you remember so fondly."

"Perhaps," Raphael said noncommittally.

Lachlan wasn't insulted. He'd known such a visit was unlikely, which was why he'd felt free to offer. He also knew that Raphael had supported Quinn in Ireland with an eye toward using that country as a staging area to move on the rest of Europe. That might be good for Quinn, whose loyalties were divided between America and Ireland, but Lachlan had no such divisions and no intention of permitting Scotland's vampires to get involved in another European war. Scotland had already bled a thousand lifetimes of blood. His invitation to "visit" made it clear, in vampire-speak, that he wouldn't welcome anything else.

Leighton and Julia walked in at that moment. Raphael glanced up and said, "My Cyn, you've come to join us." He didn't stand. He didn't need to. Leighton again ignored everyone else as she gave Raphael a lingering kiss, then leaned against his chair while the vampire lord wrapped his hand around her thigh.

"You guys were having so much fun that Jules and I just had to join in," she said, with a look of such skepticism that her true feelings were made perfectly clear. She glanced at Julia, who pressed her fingers over her lips to hide a smile. "Raphael," Leighton continued, "Jules says we should visit Scotland, that it's beautiful there."

"Yes," Raphael commented with a blank face, "lots of castles with bad plumbing."

His mate laughed. "Don't tell Lucas that. He spent a fortune—"

"—on his castle," Raphael finished. "We were just talking about that."

"Oh, God," she said. "You're talking about castle renovations. You need us even more than I thought. Can we at least drink a toast before Jules and Lach have to leave?"

Lach? he repeated to himself. No way in hell or on earth.

"If you insist," Raphael said, although it was imbued with so much affection that it reinforced Lachlan's view of the deadly vampire lord's relationship with his mate. Of course, Leighton was deadly, too.

For some reason, that thought made Lachlan look up at Julia, who'd moved closer to him, almost as if she was following her instincts in this room of predators. Because every vampire was a predator. If they hadn't been before they were turned, the symbiote remade them into one. But Leighton was a predator, too. Maybe the most dangerous kind, since she hid her more vicious instincts behind a façade of feminine beauty. Julia, now. . . . He studied her as she walked over to help Leighton pour a round of vodka shots. His princess claimed she'd be able to kill Erskine when the time came, or at least draw blood before Lachlan struck the fatal blow. But even though she'd been trained and seemed confident enough with a gun, she'd never done field work, and her job as an analyst certainly didn't expose her to a lot of bloodshed.

He shrugged inwardly, thinking they'd find out about her tolerance for bloodshed soon enough. Because once the two of them returned to Edinburgh, the battle would begin. Erskine had spies, just as Lachlan did. The Scottish lord had to know Lachlan was planning a coup. The visit to Raphael would have been the final stroke. If Erskine had an ounce of strategic skill left—which might be doubtful—he'd attack first, trying to cut the head off the snake. Lachlan would have to be ready from the moment they touched down in Edinburgh. If Julia truly meant to come along, she'd be getting her bloody baptism far sooner than she might expect.

A slender feminine hand slid a shot glass into his view. He looked up to find Julia giving him a hesitant smile. "A toast?" she asked softly. "To a successful partnership."

He held her gaze for a moment, then took the shot glass and clicked it against the one she held. "To us," he amended. He had a lot more in mind for her than one successful venture.

Her pupils widened, but she held off her blush until after she'd tossed the shot back, then blamed it on the alcohol. "Whew." She fanned herself with one hand. "I don't do those often."

Lachlan stood and reached for her glass. "You'll need another now, for Leighton's toast."

"Oh, I don't think—"

"Don't worry, princess. You'll be perfectly safe with me."

Was that disappointment he saw in her eyes? Or maybe it was simply the first signs of inebriation, and his ego was overinflated. Nah. Chuckling to himself, he crossed to the bar and picked up the bottle of vodka. Leighton ambled over as he was pouring.

"You know, I've been on Mr. Harper's plane. He has vodka there, too," she commented.

Lachlan gave her a lazy glance. "Since your toast was meant to wish luck on my endeavor, I thought it only polite to partake."

"Yours and *Julia's* endeavor."

He dipped his head in silent acknowledgement as he poured.

Leighton came even closer and leaned into whisper, "If you get her hurt, I'll hunt you down."

He looked up, unperturbed by her threat. "If you really care about your friend, you'll persuade her to stay in Edinburgh, and let *me* deal out the revenge."

She blinked, obviously not expecting his reaction, then narrowed her eyes. "But then you wouldn't have her daddy's fancy plane, would you? Or her money."

Lachlan's own gaze narrowed. He got it. Leighton thought she was protecting her friend. Or maybe she was testing him. But she was pushing it too far with her suggestion that he was somehow using Julia for her money. As if Julia would ever permit that to happen. Either Leighton didn't know her friend very well, or she had a low opinion of Julia's courage. And neither of those was acceptable to him.

Straightening to his full height, he regarded Raphael's mate and slammed down a shield over his anger, lest the vampire lord sense a threat. "Look," he said tightly, keeping his voice low enough not to be easily overheard by the vampires in the room. "You've got it all wrong. Julia came to *me*, not the other way around. She offered to facilitate contact with Raphael, in exchange for me letting her join in on my hunt for Erskine Ross. As for the other—" He set the vodka bottle down and screwed on the cap. "I'm nearly two hundred years old, with a knack for spotting market trends, woman. I don't need Julia's plane *or* her money. So like I said, if you really care about her, you'll persuade her to let *me* do the vengeance seeking."

Picking up the two brimming shot glasses, he gave her a final look. "My thanks for your assistance and hospitality. Now, I'm going to join the others for the toast that *you* suggested." So saying, he crossed back to stand next to Julia and handed her one of the drinks, which she accepted, holding one hand under the glass as she balanced the full shot.

"What'd Cyn say to you?" she asked, with a suspicious glance that told him she'd probably guessed what the exchange had involved.

"She's your friend. She's worried about you."

Julia *tsked* in exasperation. "I swear, she thinks I was born and raised like a hot house orchid. Don't believe her. I'm not that fragile."

"I never said you were."

"And I'm sorry I embarrassed you earlier, about the whole feeding thing. I didn't mean to make a big deal of it."

He studied her sincere expression, not knowing whether to be angry or amused at the idea that he'd been *embarrassed* when she'd asked about feeding from a live donor. Or had it been fucking the donor afterward?

"Let's get a few things straight, princess. One, I didn't feed from any of the provided women. I wasn't hungry. Two, I sure as hell didn't fuck any of them, and three, I don't fuck any woman when I have my sights set on another." He lowered his head and brushed his lips over hers as she stared up at him. "And now, I believe Raphael is about to speak."

He swung around to face Raphael and Leighton, who stood together behind the desk, as the vampire lord raised his glass. "To the next Lord of Scotland."

"*Slàinte,*" Lachlan said. He raised the glass to his lips, tossed the smooth liquid heat down his throat, and turned to Julia. "Time to go, love."

She drained the last of her own vodka, then walked over and set the glass on the bar, upside down. "I'm ready."

Chapter Eight

On a plane, somewhere over the Atlantic

JULIA SAT ACROSS from Lachlan, trying to study him without being obvious about it. He'd opened his laptop almost as soon as they'd boarded, saying something about making use of the jet's Wi-Fi now that they were away from Raphael's estate. She took that to mean he didn't trust the vampire lord, even though they were allies. Or were they?

"What happened in that secret vampires-only meeting you had with Raphael? Are you guys allies or not?"

"It wasn't secret," he said, without looking away from his keyboard. "You could have stayed, if you'd wanted."

"I probably got more information out of Cyn. She says you guys talk in circles. I don't know about that, but I can tell there's a lot more going on than what you say out loud."

Lachlan looked up then, with a smile that took her breath away. He didn't always smile like that, but when he did . . . . Damn.

"Vampires are mostly old. Raphael's somewhere around five hundred, Jared and the others at least as old as I am. People spoke differently when we were human. And then there's the cultural and language differences. We speak in circles to be sure everyone's hearing the same thing."

"Uh huh. Nice try. I think you're testing each other by saying the same thing ten different ways."

He laughed. Wow. This was a banner day for Lachlan viewing. That was also the first time she'd seen him really *laugh*. What little breath she had left fled her lungs. Thinking she had to get away before she embarrassed herself, she stood saying, "I'm going to get some tea. You want anything?" *Bad choice of words, Jules!* she chastised herself as Lachlan let his gaze travel slowly up and down her body, before meeting her eyes.

"What's on the menu, princess?" he purred.

She stood there, staring at him in unaccustomed confusion. Her chest was tight, her nipples tighter, and rush of desire had her thighs clenching against a sudden, sexual hunger. She'd had plenty of lovers, but couldn't remember a single time when she'd wanted a man like she wanted Lachlan McRae. And the look in his eyes said he knew it.

He stood without warning, his big body so close, so damn *masculine*, as he stared down at her, those changeable eyes seeming limned with gold in the dim light. "What do you want, Julia?" he murmured, not touching her, not even reaching for her, and yet she could feel the weight of his gaze like a firm stroke of his fingers along her bare skin.

She licked her lips, admitting to herself that she was nervous. Scared? Maybe some of that, too. Hell, maybe all he wanted to do was kiss her. He'd done that right in front of everyone in Raphael's office, so why not here? She moved a tiny bit closer, placed a hand on his broad chest, and tilted her head back to meet his golden stare. "A kiss?" she whispered.

He studied her silently for so long that Julia sensed the heat of a blush creeping up her neck. Feeling foolish, she was just about to back away when he placed a hand on her hip, holding her in place. His grip wasn't tight, but his fingers were so strong and gave off so much heat that she felt them like hot iron against her skin. Weren't vampires supposed to be cold? She banished the stupid thought. This wasn't some movie special. This was real life, and vampire or not, Lachlan was a *real live* male who was about to kiss her.

He lowered his head slowly, as if wary of startling her into shying away. But she wasn't going anywhere. She wanted this vampire, wanted to know what it would be like to make love to a man who'd had near two hundred years to hone his kissing skills.

In retrospect, she should have known better.

Lachlan put his lips against hers, softly at first, and Julia had a fleeting moment of disappointment. Maybe he didn't want her at all. Maybe—*Oh, God.* The kiss deepened, his mouth pressing harder, tongue sliding along her lips, demanding entry. She opened her mouth and his tongue swept in, skimming over her teeth, teasing her tongue, tempting her to dance. Julia heard herself moan as she went up on her toes and accepted the invitation, her tongue stabbing into his mouth hungrily. Her arms went around his neck as she fought to get closer, her fingers tangled in his hair, breasts brushing the hard muscles of his chest.

He kissed like a man who knew precisely how to please a woman, how to stroke his tongue over hers with a sensuality that made her yearn for more, how to pull his mouth away so that she was the one pushing for another caress of his lips. But he didn't yank her nearer, didn't crush her against his much bigger body. Didn't give any sign that he wanted something more from her.

Maybe she hadn't gone looking for anything more. She wasn't sure herself. But why didn't he want her? Her thoughts churned, too lost in the sensuality of his kiss to see the illogic of them. She finally bit his lip in confused frustration, not hard enough to break skin, just enough to get his attention.

Lachlan growled, low and dangerous, a rumble of sound that vibrated against her chest as his hold on her hip tightened even further. She suddenly found herself pressed against the long length of his body, her breasts crushed against his chest, aroused nipples pushed against him so hard that she knew he could feel them through his t-shirt. His hand moved from her hip to her back, pulling her impossibly closer, squeezing the breath from her lungs, until she was gasping into his mouth. But Lachlan didn't stop. His other hand dropped to her butt, fingers spread wide, slamming her against him until there wasn't so much as a wisp of air between them. Then the thick jut of his cock settled against her belly like an ultimatum, a statement . . .

You started this, princess. Now finish it or step away for good.

She should do the latter. She should step back and forget all about him. Walk away when they reached Edinburgh, and wait until news came that Lachlan had killed Erskine for his own reasons. But that wasn't what she did.

Rising up on her toes, she bit him again. Harder this time, until she felt her teeth sink into the flesh of his lip, felt the warm rush of his blood against her tongue. Desire stormed through her body like a flame, heating every muscle, lighting up every nerve ending, filling her with a carnal hunger that had wet heat pooling between her thighs. She ground herself against him, frantic in her need to vanquish her body's craving.

"What do you want from me, Julia?" he murmured against her lips.

She cried out wordlessly. Why wouldn't he give her what she needed? Why was he forcing her to beg for it?

"Say it, princess. And I'll give it to you. I'll give you everything."

"Bastard," she whispered.

His only response was an evil chuckle before he bent his head and sucked on her neck, while his fingers pinched the taut peak of a swollen nipple, the lace of her bra scraping the delicate skin and heightening the sensation unbearably. And still she pushed against his hand, wanting more.

"Damn it," she breathed. She didn't know what to do with all these feelings, all this raw lust. Then his fingers slid to her other breast, squeezing hard as he strummed her nipple to an engorged peak of need. She growled out a scream of surrender, then thumped her fist against his shoulder and cried, "Fuck me."

Before she could draw her next breath, he'd swung her up into his arms and was striding down the narrow aisle as if it was a marbled hall, pressing the latch and shoving through the doorway to the back section of the plane without losing a step, pushing the bedroom door open with a swiveled hip.

Julia was aware of the blackness settling around them as Lachlan carried her into the bedroom, her lips fused to his, their mouths caught up in a kiss that was as much a battle for dominance as any kind of affection. They might not be in love, maybe they didn't even like each other, but they sure as hell wanted each other. Lachlan placed one knee on the bed and lowered her to the mattress, following her down until his full weight rested on top of her. One muscled thigh slid between her legs, his knee shoved up until he was grinding against her pussy, heightening the soaring need screaming through her body, taking her right to the edge, and then backing off, refusing to give her release.

"Lachlan," she demanded angrily, although it came out as more of a breathless plea.

"You're wearing too many clothes," he murmured. "I want to see every inch of that creamy skin, those hard nipples. Are they pink like your lips?"

Julia would have ripped off every stitch of clothing if it would have gotten her the climax she needed.

He bent his head, his lips against her ear. "What about your pussy, princess? Is it pink, too? And tasty? I'm going to find out."

She nearly came when his knee rolled firmly over her clit while he whispered those dark, erotic words. Nearly screamed in fury when he stood, leaving her alone on the bed, desire a storm that threatened to bleed through her pores.

Lachlan chuckled, and she almost came to her knees intent on mayhem, but then he ripped his t-shirt over his head, baring a fabulous chest that she could barely glimpse in the darkened room. She reached for the light, wanting more, when she heard the slide of his belt, the rasp of his zipper.

"Take your clothes off, or I will," he said, his voice so harsh with desire that it was more animal than human.

Julia abandoned the light, rolling to the other side of the bed and coming to her feet, fingers already on the buttons of her blouse while she kicked off her shoes, leaving her blouse half undone as she reached for the zipper on her jeans, thumbs hooking into her panties as she shoved everything down and kicked it aside. She was fumbling with her blouse, when Lachlan knelt on the bed and reached for her, lifting her easily, sliding her beneath him as he tore her blouse open, scattering buttons and making her heart pound with excitement. A moment later, the front catch of her bra was gone and his mouth was on her breast, his arm under her thigh, pushing it high and wide as his hips settled between her legs. The heavy weight of his erection rubbed the slick flesh of her sex and she thrust her hips upward, wanting him inside her.

He closed his teeth over her nipple in warning. "Not yet. Not even close." She felt his lips stretch into a smile a moment before he slid downward, licking and kissing every inch of her skin until he met the swell of her mound, waxed to a silky perfection. "Oh, I like this, princess." His whisper brushed over her bared pussy, making her shiver.

And then she could only struggle to breathe, to swallow the screams of passion as she clutched the sheets, switching her grip to his hair when she thought she'd go mad if he licked her one more time, if his teeth grazed her clit or his clever lips sucked that sensitive pearl just to the edge of ecstasy one more time without letting her climax. Tears were rolling down her cheeks, her thighs slick and sticky, when he finally slid up her body, his cock sliding through the lust-swollen lips of her pussy as if to cover it in the hot, wet cream of her arousal.

He kissed her, long and slow, letting her taste herself on his lips, on his tongue, before lifting his head to stare at her with that golden gaze. "What do you want?"

"Fuck me," she whispered again, hoping this time he would, that he was done teasing her.

He smiled and pushed his cock into her body in a slow and steady glide, as if aware of his thickness straining against her tight sheath. But Julia didn't want slow and steady, and she didn't give a damn about how tight she was.

"Harder," she demanded.

He stared at her, his eyes flaring a brilliant gold, and then he pulled his cock back and slammed it into her greedy, drenched pussy, not stopping until he was balls deep and her inner muscles were stretched achingly tight. But Lachlan didn't hesitate. Didn't pause to let her body adjust. He simply dragged his cock back and pounded it in again, hooking her legs over his arms and holding her wide as he fucked her harder with every thrust.

Julia reached over her head, clinging to the headboard with eyes closed, unable to do anything else, even if she'd wanted to. She loved the weight of him crushing her to the mattress, the raw fury of his fucking, the driving strength of his powerful body. She was a slender woman, delicately boned, with pale blond hair and skin to match. Past lovers had always treated her like a fragile thing that would shatter if they pushed too hard or squeezed too tightly. But not Lachlan. For all that he called her "princess," he didn't fuck her like one. He *fucked* her. It was deep and hard, and rode the edge of violence. He made her feel like a desirable woman, a woman who could push a man to the kind of madness that left him thinking of nothing but sex.

"Open your eyes, princess," he growled.

She did and was not even surprised to find herself staring up at eyes that gleamed solid gold. She had the stray thought that it must have something to do with what he was, but vampire physiology was the farthest thing from her mind. "Why?" she whispered, in response to his command.

"I want you to know who's fucking you."

She gave him a slow, delicious smile. "Oh, I know that, Lachlan McRae."

He slid deep inside her again, her sheath pulsing around him . . . and stopped. Bracketing her head with his forearms, he leaned down and kissed her lightly, before murmuring against her lips, "That pretty pale skin and perfect blond hair is just a disguise for the real Julia, isn't it?"

She slung her arms around his neck and pulled him into a hard kiss, sucking his lip into a slow release as she finished. "You don't like my skin?"

"Oh, I like it well enough." He pulled out slightly and thrust into her once more. "Not as much as your tight pussy, but . . ." He winked.

"Are we going to talk?" she asked, narrowing her eyes. "Or are you going to finish what you started?"

"Oh, princess, I've barely gotten started with you."

Julia's entire body clenched, her inner muscles flexing to squeeze Lachlan's cock so tightly, she didn't know if he'd be able to move. He smiled, as if reading her thought, then slid out and back in again, stimulating the delicate tissues lining her channel and sending fresh shivers rolling over her skin. She moaned quietly, knowing he'd only delay her orgasm further if she asked for release.

"You want to come?"

Julia swallowed on a dry throat, not knowing what to say. She knew what she *wanted,* what she *needed*, but she didn't know how to get it. "Don't you want me to?"

"Oh, yes. Over and over again. I love the way your pussy feels around me, the way you squeeze me *so* tight." He winked. "But I bet it feels even better when you climax."

She licked her lips, staring up at him, nails digging into his shoulders as if he would do what she wanted if she only held on tightly enough. She thrust her hips against his experimentally, closing her eyes and breathing at the delicious friction of his cock. "You want to find out?"

He began fucking her without warning, his big cock shoving deep inside, pulling back, and slamming back in, over and over, as her muscles clenched and her pussy spasmed. Her entire body went rigid when the climax struck, back bowing, and muscles clenching so tightly that it hurt for a fraction of a second. And then it was nothing but pure, screaming pleasure as Lachlan continued to ride her, his cock pounding in and out, plunging through the tight squeeze of her inner tissues, setting off fresh waves of carnal pleasure until that was all Julia knew. Delicious sensation crashed over and back, one part of her body easing down as another jolted with ecstasy, only to switch off as a fresh swell of pleasure crashed through her.

"Jesus," she whispered, hanging on to him in desperation, barely able to think beyond the intense passion filling every inch of her being, and wondering if she'd survive the night. Lachlan was still fully aroused, his cock thick and hard, and unlike her own panting breaths, his were deep and even, as if he was just getting started. Just as he'd said.

"I'm sorry to cut this short, princess." He spoke softly, his iron-hard shaft buried inside her, as random shivers and quakes of sensation pulsed through her body. "The sun will be with us soon," he continued. "Next time, I'll take it slow."

Julia made a mental note to make sure her papers were in order, because if this was Lachlan's idea of fast, there was no way in hell she'd survive the slow version.

He started fucking her hard, a man intent on achieving climax, his hips pumping, cock driving, as she wrapped her legs around his waist. He grunted his approval, reaching back to shove her leg even higher over his back, and she did her best to meet him thrust for thrust. She caught a glimpse of his fangs a moment before he reached between them and pinched her clit, sending her into another raging orgasm. But this time, he came with her, the hot rush of his release filling her clenching womb as the pounding of his cock slowed to a luxurious glide through the mixed evidence of their climaxes, until he finally collapsed on top of her.

She wrapped her arms around him, holding him as tightly as she could, his heart thundering against her breasts—evidence that he, too, had been affected by their lovemaking. That she hadn't been simply a convenient hole to relieve the boredom of a long flight.

He didn't stay on top of her for long, however. He rolled over, taking her with him, until she lay on his chest, her nipples snug against his warm skin. She leaned down and kissed his neck. "Are you going to sleep?"

"Soon," he said, opening his eyes just enough that she could still see some of the gleaming gold.

"Do all vampires' eyes go gold when they're . . ." She reached for the right word, but he spoke first.

"Fucking?"

"Well, yeah."

He smiled. "No. Most vampires' eyes shine red when the lights hit them, or when they're using whatever power they have. Only powerful vampires have distinctly colored eyes, and we're the only ones whose entire eye gets involved. Not only when we fuck, but when we experience any strong emotion, or use our power."

She registered the pronoun change and asked, "Does that mean you're a powerful vampire?"

He gave her a puzzled look. "Of course. How else would I think to claim a territory?"

She shrugged. "I don't know how all that inside vampire stuff works."

"Well, that's how. Vampire lords are the most powerful, as in we have serious magical power."

"Magic?" she repeated doubtfully.

"And what would you call it, then? How many men do you know who can read minds? Or kill an enemy by ripping out his heart, then making it burst into flame with a thought?"

"Uh, that would be no one."

"You know one now, princess," he reminded her, putting a big hand on her butt and pushing his still prominent shaft against her.

Grateful for the dark, which hid her blush, she said, "Present company excluded. Besides, I never even met a vampire before you, much less a vampire *lord*."

"And now you're in the thick of it. You sure you won't change your mind and wait for me in Edinburgh? Or even better, in London?"

"No." It was one tiny word, but she said it forcefully enough that there was no doubt about her intentions.

He sighed. "I knew you'd say that." He closed his eyes briefly, then opened them and said, "No time for a shower. Not for me, anyway. Guess I'll be sleeping with the delicious smell of your pussy to sweeten my dreams."

"The things you *say*." She shook her head primly, privately pleased.

The truth must have shown on her face. Or damn, maybe he was reading her mind, because he gave her a crooked smile and said, "I think you like it." He slapped her butt smartly. "Ten minutes, Julia, and I'm out."

"You want me to leave or—?"

"Please yourself. It won't matter to me." His eyelids fluttered. "Whoa," he said, slurring slightly. "I forgot we're racing *into* the sun."

And then his eyes closed, his breathing slowed, and his heart forgot to beat for what seemed like a long time. But she remembered when they'd been flying the other direction, and how she'd nearly panicked, thinking he was truly dead. So she waited until his heart finally pounded out a single beat and after a long time, another. Then she kissed his still lips and climbed off the bed.

It wasn't until she was in the shower, with hot water sluicing over her body, that it hit her. He'd hadn't taken her blood. Cyn had told her about the incredible high of a vampire's bite, but Lachlan hadn't bitten her. She scowled as she washed her hair, wondering what that meant, and nearly pounding the wall in frustration because she'd have to wait to ask him until the sun went down . . . in Edinburgh.

THE THING ABOUT eastbound flights, Lachlan thought grumpily as the jet finally crossed enough time zones to take him back into darkness, was how it screwed with his sleep. People might think vampires didn't *need* sleep, since it was forced on them by the sun. But those hours of daylight gave the vampire symbiote a chance to repair whatever damage his body might have sustained during the previous night, in addition to simply resting his muscles and major systems. Vampires might be higher on the evolutionary chain than humans, but they weren't indestructible. They needed rest just like any other living creature. A need that was totally fucked up by an eastbound flight into darkness.

Fortunately, when his eyes opened on this particular flight, there was a soft sweet-smelling woman curled up next to him, all warm and familiar. He rolled toward Julia, tucking her lithe body beneath his as he bent to kiss her neck. His fangs pushed at his gums, drawn by the delicious scent of her blood rushing hotly beneath his lips. So close. He ran his tongue along the line of her vein, making it nicely plump and ready for his bite.

"Lachlan?" Her voice was slumberous and sexy as hell, as one knee rose to slide next to his hip, and her arms went around his neck.

"Who else, princess?" He meant it to be lighthearted, but even he heard the snarled demand underneath the words. Did she have another lover? Not any more, she didn't. He didn't share.

"Stop grumbling at me," she said, slapping his shoulder. "I was questioning your intent, not your identity."

"My intent should be clear."

She laughed gently, a sweet feminine sound, as her arms ran over the long muscles of his back. "I have a question."

"Now?" Realizing she'd changed into something silky while he'd slept, he reached down to find her naked beneath a short slip-like nightgown. His hand slid up her bare thigh and pushed it wide, making room between her thighs as he rubbed his already hard cock in the growing wetness of her pussy.

She made a soft, wordless sound as her hips flexed upward. "Damn, that feels good. Are you always this hard?"

"Not always. That'd make it a chore to get around, wouldn't it?"

"I don't know," she said absently, seeming focused on making him even harder the way she was grinding herself against him. "I've never tried."

"Well, thank the gods for that, love."

She snorted a less than graceful laugh, realizing what she'd said. "Sorry. Good thing you're not the delicate type."

"Are we finished talking now?" he muttered, closing his teeth over the delicate bones of her jaw, then licking away the bite and kissing his way back to her neck. He hadn't bitten her when they'd fucked before, because they hadn't discussed it. And he'd learned very early in his life as a vampire that it was always better to practice what would now be called "full disclosure" before sinking his fangs into a woman's neck.

"Yes," she breathed, her body all but vibrating beneath him.

"Good." Pulling back his hips, he slammed his full length into her sweet body in a single, long stroke, relishing the tight grip of her inner muscles as they strained around his intrusion. The delicate tissues almost vibrated in a combination of shock and excitement as her body adjusted, growing slick and welcoming when he pulled out and plunged in a second time. He remained buried inside her as he reached down and gripped her ass, tilting her hips just enough to permit him to go even deeper.

She groaned breathlessly, her fingers tangled in his hair, her breath hot against his cheek. "More," she whispered.

He grinned. He'd wondered if her demands on their first go-round had been just that . . . a wild demand of a first-time lover. But it would seem his princess liked it rough all the time. That was fine with him. Tightening his hold on her ass, he rolled over, putting her on top, straddling him, her beautiful breasts swollen with arousal, pale pink areolas and rosy, hard nipples just begging to be sucked until they ached.

"Lachlan!" she gasped, surprised at the sudden move. Her gaze found his and whatever she saw there had her sucking in a long breath and pushing her chest out, as if offering her breasts to him.

Her thighs flexed as she rose onto her knees, sliding her tight pussy up his cock, but when she would have slid back down, he dug his fingers into her hips and held her there. Leaning forward, he took a breast into his mouth. It was too full to fit all the way, but he sucked harder, rasping his tongue over and around her nipple until it was swollen with blood, until her fingers in his hair didn't seem to know whether to pull him closer or to tug him away. And then he switched breasts, giving her second nipple the same pleasure, sucking and swirling his tongue, until it, too, was pulsing against his lips. But instead of freeing her this time, he closed his teeth over the swollen nipple. Just enough to be felt, enough to cause an erotic pain, but not enough to draw blood.

Julia gasped, her grip on his hair going painfully tight as she crushed his face against her chest, and soft wordless moans fell from her pretty lips. Her heart was pounding so loudly that he could feel it drumming against his cheek, could hear the thrumming rush of arterial blood as it pumped from her heart, hard and fast. Without warning, her pussy clutched around him, and she cried out, crashing into an orgasm while she pleasured herself on his cock.

Lachlan watched her eyes close, her expression suffused with such savage desire that his cock stiffened to a furious hardness. Half of him wanted to slam into her until he climaxed and relieved the pressure. The other half wanted to fuck her into oblivion, until she was limp and exhausted and begging him to stop.

Tightening his hold on her hips, he thrust up into her hot body, her pussy so slick with arousal that it slid like silk over his throbbing cock. Using the power of his vampire nature, he jackhammered into her, while she screamed his name, hands twisted in her own hair, her face wild with helpless passion, breasts bearing the mark of his teeth as they swayed with every upward plunge of his straining erection.

He snarled when he felt the tightening of his balls, the ferocious pressure giving no more than a moment's warning before his release roared down his shaft and into her welcoming body. Julia cried out, trembling as the pounding heat of his climax threw her into a second orgasm.

Lachlan rolled again, tucking her beneath him, his cock gliding lazily through her throbbing wetness. Her blue eyes, darkened with lust, met his in disbelief when his penis hardened again, growing thick enough to push at the walls of her tight sheath. "Fuck me," she breathed. She meant it as a comment on his stamina, but he took it literally.

"That's the plan, princess."

"My God, how do you—?"

"Let's fuck now, talk later."

"If I live that long."

He leaned down and kissed her. It was slow and luxurious, the claiming kiss of a man who knew how to make a woman feel beautiful and sexy. She was breathing hard against his lips when he whispered, "You're going to live. I'll make sure of it." He began thrusting again. Long, deliberate strokes, while her pussy shivered around him, and her body grew taut, her fingers digging in his shoulders.

"Lachlan," she whispered almost desperately, her nails drawing blood as she held onto him, almost as if afraid she'd fly apart.

"I've got you," he murmured, fighting the push of his fangs. Damn, but he wanted to taste her. "Julia."

Her eyes opened when he said her name, going wide when he let her glimpse the bare tips of his fangs. "Do you want . . . ?"

"Oh, yes." There was an eagerness to her agreement that surprised him, but he forced himself to be sure.

"Do you understand—?"

"I know about the—" She moaned softly when he ground his groin against her clit. "—the effect of your bite."

"It will hurt," he warned, still unsure of her ready acceptance.

She smiled slowly. "Hurts so good, baby."

He'd forgotten again about his princess's penchant for erotic pain. Letting his fangs glide out to press against his lower lip, he bent his head to her neck and once again rasped his tongue along the line of her vein, over and over, until it was a firm swell of temptation against his mouth. He didn't give her any warning. His fangs slid with smooth ease into her satiny skin and punctured her vein with a tiny pop of resistance. Her blood surged, filling his mouth and rolling down his throat, a caress of warm, dark honey. It was sweet and thick and delicious, and he knew instantly that one taste of her would never be enough.

He didn't know how long he was going to keep Julia Harper. But he did know that he wasn't going to let her go until he'd had his fill—body and blood.

Chapter Nine

Edinburgh, Scotland, UK

LACHLAN WOULD have known they were in Scotland even if he'd been locked in the darkness, blindfolded, with headphones muffling his ears. His soul sang the minute the jet touched down, the land of his birth—both human and vampire—welcoming him home. For the first time since he left for London, he was utterly at ease. He knew this place, drew strength from every mountain and field, every drop of water tumbling down to fill the lochs. No one could defeat him when he was home. Not even Erskine Ross. The evil bastard might be Highlands-born, just like Lachlan, but something had twisted inside him. He'd replaced loyalty to the lands of his birth with a mendacious hunger for the trappings of wealth, so much that he'd sacrificed the well-being of his own people to enhance his coffers. But more important, in Lachlan's estimation, was the complete lack of honor, the kind Lachlan had been lectured on daily, even before he truly understood what it meant. An honor that had its roots deep in the Scottish Highlands and the clans that grew there. Erskine couldn't possibly hold that kind of allegiance to the lands that had birthed them both. If he'd had, he'd never could have forsaken honor so cravenly that he'd used humans to attack and kill the McRae vampires while they slept, helpless to defend themselves.

He drew in a deep breath and reached out, spreading his considerable telepathic awareness to ensure there were no enemies waiting to ambush their arrival, no unwanted spies lurking about to report. He didn't care so much for himself—he had more right to be in Edinburgh than most—but he didn't want Erskine's filthy eyes on Julia. The Scottish lord would know everything about her soon enough. That couldn't be helped. But there was no need to help him figure out why she was with Lachlan and where they'd been in the meantime.

"Do you have a hidey-hole here in Edinburgh, or should I call a hotel?" Julia asked as she sat next to him, her long legs making a silky sound as she crossed one over the other beneath the tight skirt she'd donned for their arrival. It seemed a questionable choice to him. Edinburgh was cold this time of year. But he couldn't fault the view. Or what the smooth slide of her skin did to his cock. Her fingers tightened on his, as if to demand he answer her question.

He turned with a jaundiced look, one eyebrow raised in cynical response. "Hidey-hole?" he repeated. "Does that mean you think I have some dank basement with a moldy mattress waiting for me?"

She *tsked* loudly, pale eyes rolling behind thick lashes that he knew she'd darkened with some kind of makeup. "Of course, not. Let me rephrase . . . Lord Lachlan, do you have an estate nearby, where we might rest from our journey, or should I, your faithful lover, secure accommodations suitable to your august self?"

"I lost you at 'Lord Lachlan.' I think you should always address me as such."

She snorted her opinion of that. "Fuck *me*."

Her pale skin reflected the golden glow of his eyes as he scanned her elegant form, from her sleek legs and firm thighs to the full breasts barely contained behind a virginal white blouse. "With pleasure, princess. Shall we start now, or wait until we reach the basement?"

Julia laughed, the sound once again full of an innocent joy that made him want to protect her from a world that would do its best to destroy her. Given her job, and the sorrows life had already visited on her, he didn't know how she'd managed to maintain that touch of innocence.

"I'm serious, Lachlan. Do we need a hotel?"

The jet pulled to a rocking stop, as the pilot spoke over the intercom. "We've arrived, Ms. Harper. If you want to avoid entanglements, I can go straight to the hangar, and you can deplane there."

Julia looked over at him.

"I don't think it's necessary, but why risk it?" he said, in answer to her silent question.

She nodded and pushed the intercom button. "The hangar, please, Captain. Thank you."

"It'll be a few extra minutes. Remain seated, please."

They sat in companionable silence, fingers intertwined as they took a tour of the Edinburgh airport via plane, ending up at a small private hangar whose door rolled back as they approached. Ten minutes later, the jet halted again, the engines winding down with a high-pitched noise that made him wish for ear plugs.

"Can I get up now?" he asked playfully, squeezing the hand she'd kept clasped with his, as if afraid he'd escape.

"I just wanted to be sure you didn't try to walk about the cabin while we were moving. I know your type."

"I don't have a type, princess. I simply am."

"Groan," she said, putting sound to the word.

He laughed as he stood and pulled her into a tight embrace. "If you don't get me off this plane soon, I'm going to drag you back to that uncomfortable bed and fuck you until you can't walk."

She gasped in mock outrage, but there was nothing artificial about the hot flush that stole over her fair skin. "Where are we going?" she asked, somewhat breathlessly. "You never said."

"Inverness," he said, drawing a frown from her.

"Inverness? But that's—"

"A three-hour drive for mere humans. Less for someone with a vampire's reflexes and night sight."

"What's in Inverness?" she asked, still scowling.

"My second-favorite hidey-hole."

"Drop the hidey-hole crap," she groused. "Where's your favorite, by the way?"

"I'll have to show you that one. You'll never have heard of it."

She sighed. "That's true of most of Scotland, but I'm game. Your car?"

He checked his cell phone. "It's already there."

"You know," Julia said conversationally, "I think I want to be a vampire when I grow up. I like the way everything just shows up when and where you need it."

Lachlan yanked her close, her breasts crushed against his chest as he lowered his head and put his lips to her ear. "There is no way in hell I'm letting you go vampire. I like you just the way you are, all hot and sexy and filled with delicious blood."

"It's not up to you. It's my—"

"I'll kill any vampire who touches you."

She went perfectly still for a moment, then went up on her toes and kissed him, brushing her lips over his once, twice, and then lingering to slip her tongue into his mouth, barely grazing the tips of his fangs. "We could spend the night in the city," she murmured, her voice husky with desire. "Make the drive tomorrow night instead."

Lachlan was tempted. He hadn't gotten anywhere near his fill of her sweet body, and was beginning to think he might *never*. But that was a thought he wasn't prepared to face. And there was also the fact that

Edinburgh was Erskine's city, his main base of operations, as close to a lair as he ever got. Although his activities more closely resembled those of a human mobster than a vampire lord. By choice, Lachlan thought. Even though it was his vampire blood that had brought Erskine power and wealth, Lachlan had always believed Erskine would have rather been a human king or prince, someone who ruled absolutely, with no care for the people, or the vampires, who looked to him.

With Julia warm against him, Lachlan calculated the time and distance to his home in Inverness, and the fact that sunrise came late this time of year in Scotland. And the truth that he'd been gone too long. He wanted to be home.

"Edinburgh's not a good city for me, lass."

She studied him for a moment. "Erskine?"

"Aye."

Julia gave a sharp nod. She might be sexy as hell and always ready for him, but she was also a woman on a mission to avenge her dead lover. And that thought gave him pause. She must have loved that Masoud fellow a great deal to pursue his killers like this. Maybe she still did. Before she'd met Lachlan, she'd been ready to seduce her way into Erskine's bed and kill him while he slept. She'd never come out and told Lachlan that was her plan, but he'd caught the fleeting thought in her mind that second night when they'd met at her apartment. He hadn't pried intentionally, but she'd been projecting strongly at the time, weighing her chances of going it alone, rather than working with him.

"Let's go," he said, more harshly than he'd intended, but the possibility that she could be in love with someone else, even a dead man, made him furious. It was an emotion he hadn't experienced often. Cold rage? Absolutely. But not this directionless fury that he didn't know what to do with. He grabbed her small suitcase, along with his own and started down the aisle.

Julia clearly sensed the shift in his mood—how could she not? But she didn't say anything, only gave him a surprised look, then wordlessly picked up her briefcase and followed him to the open hatch and down the deployed stairs.

He waited for her on the ground, swallowing the unwanted feelings, channeling them into something he could use. It was rare for him to have any kind of emotion surface so abruptly, to the point where it affected his behavior without restraint. He was all about discipline and control. He had been since almost two hundred years ago, when virtually everyone and everything he'd known had been wiped out in a single night's slaughter. He'd lived twenty-five years as a human, a single night as a vampire, and in the blink of an eye, he'd become the one his clan had looked to, to impose order in the chaos of disaster, and to lead them into a better future.

He held out a hand as Julia took the last few stairs. She didn't need the help, but then it was more than support he was offering. She placed her slender hand in his much larger palm, squeezing back when he closed his fingers over hers.

Having no bags but the ones they carried, they walked quickly through the terminal, bypassing the crowded passport control in favor of the more discreet, and much faster, portal available to passengers arriving on private aircraft. Julia kept up with his long strides, despite the high heels she'd chosen to wear for reasons known only to her. Lachlan didn't mind, since they were sexy as hell and made her already long legs seem even longer.

"Where's your car parked?" she asked, seeming puzzled when he headed for the pick-up zone right outside the terminal building.

He headed for a familiar black Range Rover. "Right here."

"Isn't someone supposed to be *in* the car when it's parked there?"

Lachlan shrugged as he opened the passenger door. "Not in my world." He watched her eye the high step of the running board and the even higher seat, probably wondering how the hell she was going to climb up there in that tight skirt. He sure as hell was. But since he didn't want her to flash every man in the vicinity by pulling her skirt up to free her legs, he put his hands on her waist and lifted her onto the seat. She made a surprised noise that he would never call a squeak—at least not to her face—then tucked her legs into the cab with a graceful slide. She reached for the door handle, but he beat her to it, closing the door with a firm push, then heading around the front of the car and sliding behind the wheel.

They were on the A9, heading north towards Inverness in the thin, late-night traffic, when Julia asked, "How *does* a person become a vampire?"

He shot her a hard glance.

"Don't get all pissy with me. I'm just curious."

"It's a process," he said grudgingly. "And most vampires can't do it. Your blood is drained to the point of death, then replaced by the vamp doing the turning. And it doesn't always work some people die. As any vampire will who dares to touch you," he added in a low growl.

She patted his leg. "Point made. No touching." She left her hand there, rubbing his thigh, as if soothing him. When they'd gone several more miles, she spoke up again. "How would Erskine have known you were in Edinburgh? The airport's not huge but it's too big for him to have spies on every gate. And private flights don't show up on the arrivals board."

Lachlan glanced over, amused by the idea of Erskine needing watchers to look out for him sneaking into the city. But she wouldn't see the humor, since she'd undertaken her pursuit of vengeance without having met any vampires. He frowned. Or had she? She'd said she'd spoken to Leighton, but had she also visited the Malibu estate? He eyed her silently. Had she ever indulged? Had some random vampire tasted her blood already? That same fury tried to strangle his throat again, but he choked it back down.

"Why are you looking at me like that? Is the Erskine thing a deep secret or something?"

"Was that your first visit to Raphael's Malibu estate?" he demanded.

"What? Where'd that come from?"

"Was it?"

She sighed impatiently. "The estate, yes. Malibu, no. Cyn used to live just down the beach from where they are now, in a condo right on the sand. I visited her there before she met Raphael. I'm guessing she's sold it by now, although I don't know for sure. Why?"

"You ever meet Raphael before?" he asked, instead of answering.

"Sure. But not there. Cyn and I met for dinner a couple of years ago, not long after she first hooked up with him. He stayed long enough for drinks, then left with Juro and some other guy. Why are you asking me these questions? What does Raphael have to do with Edinburgh?"

"Nothing. Erskine doesn't need spies to know when I'm in his territory. It's a vamp thing. I'm powerful enough that if I cross certain boundary lines, he knows I'm there."

Julia scowled at him for a moment, clearly unsatisfied with his decision to ignore her question about Raphael, but she didn't push it. Smart woman. Instead, she asked, "But isn't all of Scotland his territory? Does that mean he'd know even if you entered from somewhere else?"

"Aye. But he wouldn't care as long as I stayed where he thinks I belong." He paused. "Well, that's not true. He'd like me dead no matter where I am, but Edinburgh's his lair. It's where he runs all of his businesses from."

"Does that mean you can't sneak up on him?" she asked, her words threaded with disbelief. "How are you going to kill him then?"

Lachlan chuckled. "I've no need to *sneak*. It's not the way we do things, even if it were possible. When I kill him, it will be face-to-face, his power against mine."

She reached across the center console and laid her hand on his thigh. His cock twitched. "That's why you should let *me* kill him," she said softly. Her fingers squeezed his leg. "I know I didn't think this through originally, but I didn't know what I know now, either. We could still do it together, but you could simply distract him. Pay him a proper visit, and while he's swamped with your presence, I could sneak up and kill him from the shadows. He won't sense me at all, and no one will be able to blame you." She paused. "I don't want you dead, Lachlan."

He covered her hand with his, partly to keep her from moving any closer to his growing erection. "Ah'm no gonnae die," he said in his best Scottish burr.

She muttered something under her breath that he doubted was flattering, but didn't argue. They drove that way for the next hour, with Julia so quiet next to him that he thought she might have dozed off. She'd eased her seat back and appeared to be on the edge of sleep, her gaze on the passing darkness.

It was as he was moving his eyes back to the road that he glanced in the mirror and by pure happenstance caught the red gleam of a vampire's gaze in the small sedan coming up behind him. Cursing himself for being caught unaware, he cast a targeted whiff of his power at the car and swore silently at what he found. Four vamps. Undoubtedly Erskine's, though none of them presented a challenge, which made him frown. The vampire lord would have known these vamps had no chance against Lachlan. So what was his game? There was nothing to be gained by having them follow him to Inverness. His home wasn't a secret, and again, they couldn't take him anyway. He glanced at Julia. They'd tried to grab her once. Could she be their target? But how did they think to get her with him sitting right next to her?

"Princess," he said softly, sliding his hand over her knee and up her thigh just under her skirt.

She jerked out of her semi-doze, looking from his hand to his face. "Lachlan?"

"We've got visitors. Do you have any weapons on you?"

She started to shake her head, but then hesitated and said, "Just my shoes."

Lachlan took a second to think about it. Those spike heels of hers would be brutal in a fight, if she knew how to use them. A big "if." But it didn't matter, because he had no intention of letting her get that close to the vamps behind them. "Your gun?"

"In my case in the back, and Cyn gave me some special ammo for vampires." She twisted in her seat to look behind them. "Who is—?"

She never finished her sentence as a glint of light on metal had Lachlan's head swinging around, just in time to see a second vehicle, this one a much bigger black-on-black SUV, with no running lights of any kind. It sped into sight, seemingly out of nowhere, coming up on his right and swerving toward their vehicle. Lachlan swerved away from him, avoiding a collision, as he slammed his foot down on the accelerator in an attempt to outpace the black SUV. His Range Rover's V8 responded sweetly, pulling ahead of the SUV, far enough that they couldn't try the same maneuver again. For now.

Lachlan's Rover had more horsepower, but the same modifications that had made it more secure had also made it heavier. He glanced back. Both the enemy vehicles would catch up in a matter of minutes. The question was, were they kidnappers or killers? Either way, he didn't intend to let them succeed, but it would be nice to know.

Flooring the pedal for one more burst of speed, he spoke to Julia without turning. "I'm going to pull over and—"

"What? No. They'll kill y—"

"No, they won't. Trust me. Lock the doors, stay in the car, no matter what you see. This vehicle's armored to hell and back."

"I can climb over the seat. Get my gun and—"

"No. You have to trust me. Stay in the car. Please."

She stared at him for long enough that he was about to knock her out—which he really didn't want to do. But finally she snapped, "Fine. But if you die—"

"I won't. Hold on tight."

She made a growling sound, but gripped the armrest with one hand and the strap of her seatbelt with the other. Lachlan grinned, rather enjoying himself. Things had gotten almost dull over the last few months while Quinn had been stirring things up in Ireland. But now it was his turn. Every potential vampire lord—that is, vampires powerful enough to hold a territory and all that it meant—possessed a unique gift. There was no predicting what it would be, any more than one could predict which vampires would wake on their first night strong versus weak. Quinn was rumored to possess the ability to manipulate fire—to kill or to torture. That bastard Erskine possessed a talent for fire as well, though by all accounts his was no match for Quinn's. Nonetheless, he had enough to make him a vampire lord, enough to kill lesser vampires and humans. Lachlan glanced automatically at Julia, grateful that Erskine wasn't in either of the trailing enemy vehicles. He was confident of that.

With a final check on the small sedan behind him, and just as the black SUV slipped up to his side one more time, he braked hard, slid behind the SUV and over to the grassy edge of the road, which was nothing but empty space in the dark night. The SUV's brake lights flashed red as they zoomed ahead, then skidded into a 180 degree turn, and started back.

The first enemy car—the small sedan with its four vampires—wasn't able to respond that quickly. It slid right past the spot where Lachlan had pulled over, and unintentionally blocked the black SUV which was trying to get back to Lachlan.

While they were honking and cursing, trying to maneuver around each other, Lachlan yanked Julia over for a hard kiss, then jumped from the Range Rover, and ordered her in a hard voice, "Remember what I said. You lock the doors and stay inside, no matter what." He started to close his door, then added, "And keep the windows rolled up."

As he slammed the door, she shouted, "Don't you fucking die!" He grinned, then turned to face his attackers.

Lachlan took in the scene and calculated his strategy in a matter of seconds. The original four in the small sedan—the ones who'd revealed their presence by getting too close and giving him that chance reflection of their eyes—were out of their car and approaching on foot. It was possible that the glimpse of their eyes hadn't been a mistake, but rather a calculated risk, a way to distract him from the real threat in the second attacker's black SUV. But either way, it told Lachlan that their master considered them disposable. They were the weak point in the attack, a nuisance to be gotten rid of.

Focusing hard, he took all four down with a single, powerful blast of his power, blowing them to the ground and leaving their brains temporarily fried, neurons firing erratically as the vampire symbiote struggled to repair the damage. They would recover eventually, if Lachlan chose to let them live. But they were out of this fight for good, leaving him free to take on the real threat, which was the two vampires in the black SUV. They'd turned their vehicle around and were now storming back his way, seeming determined to run him over as a first strike.

Lachlan was certain they'd been shielding themselves earlier. There was no other way he could have missed them coming up behind him in the first place. If they had the power to do that—to successfully shield a big, moving SUV—then they might be strong enough to knock him out long enough to take him out of the fight for a few minutes. They couldn't kill him, but they wouldn't have to. Knocking him out for even a short time would leave Julia vulnerable. If he let these assholes take him down, they'd grab Julia and take her to Erskine. He couldn't imagine a worse fate. But then, that was never going to happen to his princess.

The SUV's engine roared as they sped closer, eating up the ground between them. But Lachlan wasn't going to stand there and wait. Reaching out, he struck the oncoming vehicle with a hammer-blow of power that crumpled the engine and sent the big SUV skidding off the roadway, where it came to a hard stop, as if they'd hit a physical wall. Howling furiously, one of them ripped the passenger door off with a shriek of tearing metal, then tumbled out of the car and jumped to his feet, a moment before the driver did the same, blood pouring down his face.

The two vamps took up position facing Lachlan, standing so close together that their shoulders touched. They stood waiting, glaring a fierce hatred at Lachlan, though he didn't recognize either one of them. He knew the moment their shields came up, and raised his own. These two might be weaker than he was, but stranger things had happened in his long life.

Like right now.

Because a moment after he sensed the flare of their power, he knew it was far stronger than it should have been. And then he understood the close stance, the touching shoulders. The two vampires were linking their energies, combining their power into something stronger than either of them could produce alone.

"Son of a bitch," he swore, even as every part of him settled into total focus. No emotion, no ego. A simple calculation. Do whatever it takes to kill the enemy. Something must have shown in his expression, or the lack of it, because where a moment earlier, there'd been nothing but smug confidence, there was now fear in the attackers' eyes.

Guns appeared without warning, pulled from under their jackets, fired in the same movement. Telepathic coordination, Lachlan thought. Clever. But not nearly enough against his ability to walk into their brains and make them see things that weren't quite where they should be.

He laughed at their shocked cries when their bullets sailed into empty space, because he simply wasn't there. No, he was much, *much* closer. He grabbed the first one from behind and ripped out his throat, catching his gun as it fell. The second vamp, the driver, heard his partner's gurgling scream and turned, gun up and firing. Lachlan's skin heated as bullets whizzed past, grunting when one hit its target and grazed a rib. Far too close. He'd underestimated his opponents and dropped his shield to avoid giving away his position. Stupid mistake. But not a fatal one yet.

He surprised the enemy vamp yet again, when instead of pushing him away, he yanked him closer. The vamp didn't have time to cry out before Lachlan slammed a fist against his chest, shocking his heart into a full stop for a critical moment, enough time for Lachlan to put a gun against the vamp's heart and blow it to shreds. As the driver vamp dusted to nothing, Lachlan leaned over the first vampire, who was still struggling to breathe through his ruined throat, put the gun to his head, and emptied the clip, destroying his brain, and leaving a second pile of dust.

He stood and tossed the gun away in disgust. He hated the fucking things, but they came in handy sometimes. His preferred method of execution was to break the enemy's ribs and crush the heart between his fingers. But if he'd done that this time, his hands would be as bloody as his jacket, and he thought Julia would be shocked enough by the raw violence he'd let loose on these two. She wouldn't appreciate—

The rapid sound of gunfire had him spinning around to see a lone vampire crumbling to dust no more than two feet behind him, what looked like an iron crowbar in his moldering fist. Lachlan looked up to see Julia, in her high heels and tight skirt, legs planted as far apart as the skirt allowed, a gun held steady in both hands as she eyed the pile of vampire dust. Lowering the weapon as he stared, she pantomimed blowing on the barrel of the gun, then calmly backed up to the open door of the Rover and reached inside to do . . . whatever. Re-load her weapon? Fix her make-up? Christ. He'd misjudged *her*, too, hadn't he? Good thing she was on *his* side, because she'd probably just saved his life.

Spinning on his heel, he headed back to where she waited in the Range Rover, glancing down at the three remaining vampires who'd been riding in the sedan. He considered killing them, too, and knew he probably should. But it would be too much like kicking a dog. They were drones in the vampire lord's army—fighters Erskine had been willing to let die, to be nothing but a distraction so that the two much stronger vamps in the black SUV could succeed.

Lachlan glanced up as he drew closer, and saw Julia watching him once more, her eyes taking in the blood on his clothes, the bodies on the ground. Yanking open the cargo hatch, he ripped off his jacket and shirt, tossed them inside, then dug into his duffle for a clean t-shirt. He was pissed about the jacket. It had been his favorite, but it could be replaced.

Slamming the hatch, he walked around to where she stood waiting. "I told you to stay in the car."

"Good thing I didn't, huh? You're welcome."

He studied her a moment. "Who taught you to shoot?"

"A very good instructor at the CIA."

"A boyfriend?"

Her smile was way too smug as she stepped close enough to put a hand on his chest. "A friend." She kissed his chin. "We should probably leave before someone sees this wreckage and calls the cops."

He nodded. "Fine. But we're going to talk later. You've been keeping secrets."

She scoffed. "Like you haven't. You want me to drive?"

"No," he growled, then yanked her close, held her tightly, and gave her a long, tongue-tangling kiss. "Thank you," he murmured against her wet lips.

JULIA DIDN'T KNOW what shocked her most—the casual violence of their encounter, or the fact that Lachlan had thanked her. For saving his life. Christ, had she actually done that? Killed a vampire? Her first. She should feel something, shouldn't she? Well, she'd certainly felt it when Lachlan had kissed her. Had he known she needed that hug? That his kiss would jump-start her into reacting to something other than horror at what she'd done? What she'd seen *him* do? She glanced over. He was a dark profile against the black night outside the window, nothing but the instrument lights on the dash to highlight the sharp line of his jaw, the surprisingly straight bridge of his nose. Shouldn't a two-hundred-year-old warrior have had his nose broken more than once? She smiled at the ridiculous thought, and saw his mouth curve slightly as if sharing the joke.

"You okay, princess?" he asked, without looking away from the road.

"Yes," she said without thinking. And that was another thing. Why didn't it bother her anymore that he persisted in calling her "princess?" She'd have verbally castrated any other man who dared to use that. It was sexist and condescending. And it *had* been the first few times he'd used it, but now . . . it seemed sincere. Endearing, even. Hell. A few good fucks and she'd practically canonized the guy. She needed to get away before she started wearing sensible pearls with a shirt dress, and wielding a feather duster instead of a gun.

"How much farther?" she asked, needing to get out of this car and put some distance between them. He was too big, too masculine, too . . . *Lachlan.* If she had to sit this close for much longer, watching the way his strong hands controlled the big SUV, the flex of muscles under his tight t-shirt every time they rounded another curve, the gleam of his eyes taking in everything, seeing every danger, every . . .

She gave herself a mental slap. And heard a soft masculine chuckle. That was twice he'd reacted to her thoughts. What the hell? Giving him a narrow-eyed stare, she hissed, "What's so funny?"

His eyes went wide with surprise when he looked at her. "Private joke. The cousins and I had quite the encounter with a red stag hereabouts. It was rutting season and Fergus got too close. The stag thought he was a competitor and came after him. Of course, Munro and I took great pleasure in telling him that the male was hunting up a new hind for his herd, instead." He smiled again.

"When was that?" she asked, somewhat embarrassed about her suspicions.

"A century ago, maybe more. Long before this road was what it is now."

There was a wistful quality to his voice that made her want to touch him, to provide a human link to the here and now. She should fight it. She'd just been warning herself against getting too close to this charismatic man who made her feel strong, feminine, and protected all at the same time. She shouldn't have been surprised. The more she learned, it was obvious that a disposition toward protectiveness was part and parcel with what Lachlan considered a good ruler. What surprised her was that she liked it. Liked the sense of being treasured, of being important enough to this dangerous man that his first thought had been her safety.

Yeah, he was dangerous, all right. That was a given. But the danger she worried most about wasn't the violence of his life. She was worried about her heart and what a man like Lachlan could do with it.

But she still reached out and rested her hand on his shoulder, wishing for one of those old-fashioned bench car seats, so she could scoot over, like in the movies, and rest her head on his shoulder.

"What's it like?" she asked him instead.

"What's that?"

"Living hundreds of years. Seeing the world change so drastically."

He seemed to think about it for a minute before saying slowly, "It was terrifying at first. I knew from the time I held my first sword that I'd eventually be made Vampire. The history books don't talk about it, but McRae always had vampires among its warriors. They were high up in the ranks, of course, being the best warriors simply by virtue of what they were. The vampire symbiote . . . You know about that, right?"

She nodded. "Cyn explained it back when she first started dating Raphael, and I did some digging on my own, although reliable information is almost impossible to find."

"That's because we want it that way."

"More of those friends in dark places?"

"Something like that."

They rode in silence for a while, with Julia waiting for him to continue his story. When he didn't, she prompted him, saying, "So what changed? You made it sound like things didn't happen as you'd expected."

He made a bitter sound. "You could say that. The night we were turned—the cousins and I—was the night Erskine attacked and wiped out virtually my entire clan. His human soldiers started the attack in daylight, killing everyone—women, children, old men—it didn't matter to them. And in the worst of the fighting, they went to the cellars where our vampire warriors rested, and killed them while they slept. Every vampire in his bed, and his mate, too, if she slept with him. By the time the sun set, and Erskine arrived with his vampires, it was a slaughter."

"Lachlan," she breathed. "I'm so sorry. How did you survive?"

"McRae had a separate chamber for a vampire's first night. We still do, though we're in a different place now. We discovered later that the first human attackers had tortured certain of our women to get their men to talk. The men held out longer than I could have, had a woman I loved been at a knife's edge, but in the end, they gave up the location of the main chamber where our vampire warriors slept. The few who survived confessed later, expecting to be executed as traitors, but I didn't have the heart for it. As it was, we'd lost too many, and I believe the McRae men hoped it would take so long for the enemy to break into the chamber, that our oldest vampires would already be awake and ready to fight." He shrugged. "But the Ross cowards didn't realize there was a first night chamber deeper in the fortress, and so the three of us lived long enough to drive away the attackers and save what we could." His jaw hardened. "It also revealed the enemy as Erskine Ross."

"Why you? Why'd he go after your clan?"

"There was an old slight. Irrelevant by then. But Erskine used it to justify his attack. The truth was that the McRae elders didn't fall in line and support the bastard's ambition to become Scotland's first vampire lord."

"When was this?"

"Early winter, 1846. Longer nights in winter."

"They're dark already this year."

"Aye, but it will get darker still before the days come back."

She squeezed his shoulder, feeling the tension in those hard muscles. "What did you do?"

He tipped his head, brushing his cheek over her hand where it lay on his shoulder. "We survived. I was the strongest surviving warrior, vampire or not. So everyone looked to me for leadership. You asked what it's like to live so long. It's not my own life that's difficult. It's all those other lives that I'm responsible for."

"Your clan?"

"The old clan is mostly scattered. Officially, Clan McRae barely exists in Scotland. I gathered what was left of my family, and a few others, and travelled deeper into the highlands until I found a place we could thrive. We're mostly vampires in this new place, with human relatives providing whatever daylight security is needed. It's taken us all this time to gather enough of us, to make the clan *secure* enough, that I dared take on Erskine, to finally make him pay for his crime, without endangering the people I love."

"He doesn't know where you live?"

"He knows. But we're not vulnerable the way we were then. We're far to the north, and while Erskine owns a house in Inverness for appearances, he's too settled in his fancy Edinburgh mansion to bother with a few Highland vampires. He hates me, and doesn't trust me any more than I trust him. But I haven't confronted him openly yet. He'd kill me if he could do it without anyone knowing, but I, and my cousins, make sure that will never happen. Privately, I think he still hopes to co-opt me into his little empire. He's been living the high life too long to remember what it's like to burn with the need for revenge, especially over something that happened nearly two centuries ago. Besides, the McRaes have been living quiet lives for so long, while we built up our strength, that I think he believes we're reconciled to his rule."

Julia frowned. "But then why'd he come after you back there?"

Lachlan turned to stare at her, long enough that she began to worry about his driving. "It wasn't me he was after, princess," he said, with a bare glance at the road. "It was you."

She shook her head in disbelief. "That makes no sense. According to you, that's twice he's tried. What the hell does he want with me? I'm no threat to him."

"Well, you do want to kill him, but I don't think it's you he's afraid of."

It only took her a moment to figure it out. "The CIA? What would the US intelligence community want with Erskine? Besides, I didn't tell anyone what I was doing or even where I was going, so he's not in danger from them. Not by my hand, anyway."

"So you say. But I've been thinking about this. He's awfully set on getting to you, and that doesn't compute if all he's worried about is what you know about his business with Masoud, and whom you might have told. He must have spies in the US who could get that information with a lot less drama. So it's something else."

"What?" she demanded.

"What if Masoud had something incriminating on Erskine? Something even worse than the money he embezzled. And what if he thinks your boyfriend shared it with you? Or maybe Masoud had a secret of his own, something Erskine's desperate to find out?"

"But I don't know anything."

"You don't *know* that you know anything. There's a difference. You need to let Munro see those files, Julia."

She sighed. He was fucking relentless. Not that it surprised her. Neither he nor his cousins would have survived if he wasn't. "Fine. As soon as we get someplace with Wi-Fi, you can send them to Munro."

He grinned. "That wasn't so difficult was it?"

"Not for *you*."

He sobered and said softly, "I've never told anyone that story."

Julia stilled. "What story?" she whispered.

"About that first night. About how it felt, how it still feels, to be responsible for so many lives, for their hopes."

She looked at him, caught his gold-rimmed glance at her. "Why tell me?" she asked, as he slowed for the A9 split, and they turned toward the northwest and Inverness. It was a moment before he answered.

"I don't know," he admitted. "I'll let you know when I do."

Well, *that* was frustrating, she thought. On the other hand, did she really want to know? Hadn't she just been warning herself against getting too close to this dangerous man? This vampire?

"Do you spend most of your time in Inverness?" she asked, intentionally changing the subject. "I know you said it wasn't your favorite place to live, but the city has to have advantages."

"True enough. I prefer the forest, but the Inverness house is comfortable and it's secure, which is more important."

"Do you live alone?"

"No such thing when you lead a clan. Especially not when that clan's mostly vampires. Vampire instinct is to live in groups for a lot of reasons, some of which are social. Those date back hundreds of years to when we hid what we were and tried to blend in with human society. That's not the case anymore, but the tendency survived. On the other hand, security is still a major consideration. All my vampires, whether fighters or other staff, live on the grounds. It's safer for them. A lot of the humans who guard the estate during the day live on site, too. Those who have families live in the city, but the ones who don't have their own building on-site."

Julia didn't know what else to say. She was intensely curious about the Inverness house—which sounded more like an estate—and she was even more interested in the house—or was it a fortress—in the forest. But she didn't want to sound like she was sizing him up as a potential suitor, so she didn't pursue the subject. That made the remaining drive to Inverness a quiet one, but the silence wasn't the awkward kind. It was oddly comfortable, even though they'd barely known each other a week. Okay, sure, a lot had happened in that week. They'd fought off a kidnapping—two, if you counted this last attack. They'd killed a few vampires together. Oh, yeah, and they'd had hot, *hot* sex. What was the line from her favorite movie? They'd "lived a lifetime's worth," in the few days they had together. She frowned inwardly. She sure as hell hoped they had a happier ending than the movie did.

She looked up when Lachlan turned off A9 and headed down what she could only call a dark country road. Huge trees hung over the narrow lane, which was barely big enough for two cars, and then only if they both edged off the pavement. It was midnight black under the trees, without so much as a stray moonbeam breaking through to lighten the shadows. It could have been creepy, but with a big bad vampire sitting next to her, it was fantastic. For a woman who'd grown up around the world, she sure hadn't done much traveling lately. Maybe she needed to start getting out of her cubicle more often.

"Is this still Inverness?" she asked very softly, not wanting to break the spell.

"Aye, we're only eight or nine miles out of the city center."

They emerged from the tree cover at that point, the road continuing down a long, gentle slope. In the near distance, a river sparkled under the moonlight of a now-visible, clear sky, and by the side of it was a large estate house lit up with warm, welcoming light.

"Beautiful," she murmured to herself, but, of course, Lachlan heard it.

"It didn't used to be. The land was always pretty, but the house had been left empty for decades."

"Did you do the work yourself?"

He laughed. "Not hardly. I've many talents, but construction isn't one of them. We lived in it as we found it for quite a while. But as our finances improved, we hired local craftsmen to begin updating it, and adding a few modifications of our own design. It's a job to renovate these old places, but it's quite comfortable now."

They pulled to a stop next to an arched walkway that stretched along the front of the house, reminding Julia more of Spanish architecture than anything she'd seen in Scotland so far. The walls were pale, the roof a darker tile, and as soon as their Rover pulled to a stop, several well-armed figures emerged from the shadows. One of them stepped into the light, and Julia recognized Lachlan's cousin Fergus as they exited the vehicle.

"Cousin." The two vampires grinned hugely as they hugged, pounding each other's backs so hard that Julia could hear the concussion as their fists hit. Not wanting to participate in the thumping version of a greeting, she stood by her open door until they'd disengaged, before stepping forward.

"Ms. Harper." Fergus's greeting was excessively polite, which made Julia suspect he didn't approve of her being there. Too bad for him.

"Fergus," she said just as politely.

"Where's Munro?" Lachlan asked, interrupting the awkward exchange. "We have those financials for him."

"Buried in his computer, where else?"

"Julia?" Lachlan made it clear that the next move was hers.

She locked gazes with him for a moment, noticing his eyes were an ordinary brown, with no sign of the gold that sometimes lit up like a small forge. A tiny voice in the back of her brain still wondered if she was being played. If she'd let herself be seduced into giving him what he wanted. It wasn't as if Munro was the only person she knew who could make sense of it for her. Even her dad could have made an educated guess at what was going on. But then he'd have insisted on turning the files over to the authorities, and done everything in his power to keep her out of it. Just as her CIA bosses would have done, if she'd turned them over to them. They would have been handed over to another division, and she'd never have seen them again, much less known how the situation turned out.

Lachlan and his cousin were her only chance of being a part of Erskine's destruction in a way that he'd *know* she'd done it, and why. Her need to do that, to personally avenge Masoud's death, was something no one else could fully understand. Possibly because she'd never told anyone the whole truth about the complex tangle of love and guilt that drove her. She'd hinted at it with Lachlan, but even he'd drawn the wrong conclusion, and she'd let him believe it. She was no longer sure why she'd done that. Maybe she'd simply been living the lie for so long that she didn't know how to unravel it anymore.

All those thoughts flashed in the few seconds it took her to fish the flash drive out of her laptop case and hand it over to Lachlan. He slid his hand over hers, caressing her fingers as he took the drive, and then immediately handed it off to Fergus.

"Get this to Munro, please. He'll know what it's for."

Fergus took it with a sharp nod, then strode into the house and disappeared. The other vampires had already faded back into the shadows, presumably taking up their guard positions after making sure of Lachlan's safety.

"Come on, princess," Lachlan said, grasping her hand. "It's been a long night."

She permitted herself to be pulled against his side, happy to have him there, feeling a little awkward at being the only human with so many vampires lurking about. Hadn't Lachlan said there were mates and human guards on the estate? Were they all sleeping already?

"You hungry?" he asked as they entered what might be called a great room in the US. The ceiling soared high, the floor was covered in beautiful rugs, and pieces of oversized furniture hugged the walls. In between, openings to other rooms arched nearly as high as the ceiling. It was an impressive room, except for one thing. There were few windows, and those were tall and narrow, reminding her of the kind of vertical aperture you'd see on an old castle. *Vampires,* she thought to herself. Lachlan had said none of his human staff lived in this main house, so the odd windows made sense. Not much to see at night, she supposed, and electronic surveillance would provide a much better view of hostile visitors than any window could.

As they crossed the great room, she caught a glimpse through one of the arched exits of a large room that had to be the place where Lachlan's vampires hung out. There was a huge, big screen TV on one wall, surrounded by furniture that was clearly suited for big men. In fairness, she admitted it would suit big women, too, but she hadn't seen any of those. In fact, female vamps seemed in short supply. The only one she'd seen among Raphael's people had been a pretty doll of a woman with spikey blond hair, who Cyn had insisted was a deadly killer.

"Do you have any women among your vampires?" she asked Lachlan as he guided her toward a second broad arch, beyond which she could see a beautiful, modern kitchen.

"No," he responded. "There aren't that many female vampires, especially among the fighters. That's not to say there aren't any at all, or that they have no power. There are still two or three very powerful female lords on the continent."

"Still?"

He gave her a puzzled look that quickly cleared into understanding. "Right. You wouldn't know this, but one of the oldest females, a French vampire lord, tried to assassinate Raphael not long ago. It didn't work out well for her. Obviously."

"Cyn didn't mention anything like that."

"She wouldn't. These things are always kept quiet, but rumor is the French bitch was vastly outclassed against Raphael and tried to substitute trickery for power. There's a reason vampires don't do things that way, which is why she's now dead and dusted, while he's very much alive and still ruling his territory."

"What about you?" she asked, pulling him to a stop and looking up with a worried expression.

"What about me?"

"You're talking about killing Erskine and taking his territory. It didn't hit me until now what that meant. Do you have enough power to 'outclass' Erskine?"

He gave her a crooked grin and pulled her against his body. "You worried about me again?"

She went to punch his gut, but ended up caressing rock-hard abs instead. He really did have a spectacular body. "Just want to be sure you can hold up your end of our bargain."

His hand slid down her back, fingers flirting with the swell of her butt. "I can hold up, love," he said, with an obvious double meaning. He patted her butt, there and gone so quickly she didn't have time to protest. "You hungry?" he asked, taking her hand again and pulling her into the kitchen.

Julia thought about it and realized she *was*. She couldn't remember the last full meal she'd eaten. Apparently, she wouldn't have to stress over her weight as long as she hung around with vampires. Not that she stressed overmuch anyway. "I am," she agreed.

"Graeme," he called as they entered the kitchen to find a stocky man in a white apron standing over a steaming stove.

The man turned with a welcoming smile. "My lord! Welcome home." Graeme had a full head of black hair, a round, pleasant face, and the well-fleshed body of a man who loved food.

Lachlan tugged her forward. "This is Julia Harper. Julia, Graeme Steward, the best chef in Scotland. Or so I'm told. Mostly by him."

"*Och, don't be telling lies tae th' bonnie lassie. I've ne'er said any sich thing. Bit if ithers say it, weel, wha am ah tae argue.*

"We have quite a few humans living on the estate," Lachlan reminded her. "Graeme keeps them all happy."

"Ah do that. How about you, Ms. Julia." He indicated Lachlan. "*Haes he fed ye today?*"

Julia's first instinct was to insist she didn't need Lachlan to feed her, she was quite capable of feeding herself. But she stifled that response and took the comment as it was meant. "Yes, but it's been a while since . . ." She couldn't remember the last meal she'd eaten. On the jet maybe? "I *am* hungry, Graeme. If you have the making for a sandwich, I can—"

"Uh oh. Now, you've done it," Lachlan muttered.

Graeme gave her a skeptical look. "*Ah'm sure you're a fine cook, bit there's one chef in this kitchen, 'n' it's me,*" he said firmly, then added, "*Now, I'd be happy tae make the sandwich up, 'n' send it tae Laird Lachlan's suite for ye.*"

"That would be most welcome," she said, smiling, because in truth, she *wasn't* a fine cook. Wasn't even a marginally good one. Mostly because she didn't find it worthwhile to cook for herself.

"I'll get on that," he said, then tipped his finger to his forehead in a salute to Lachlan and turned back to his stove, in clear dismissal.

Lachlan put an arm around her and hustled her in front of him and out of the kitchen.

"Is his food as good as his ego?" she muttered, letting him nudge her into a long hallway.

"You tell me. I'm not qualified to say."

"Right. Where are we going?"

"This way," he said, which didn't tell her much.

They passed a lone door on the right, which was more like something seen in a bank, or maybe a research facility where they handled dangerous things. It was sealed around the edges and there was no knob, just a very sophisticated-looking lock, which she recognized as biometric. Although it was much more complicated than the one on her London apartment.

"Basement vault," Lachlan said, as if that explained everything.

Remembering what he'd told her about vampires' daytime vaults, she assumed that was where Lachlan's various vampires slept. The basement location was self-explanatory, and no one was getting through that damn door. They kept walking until they reached the end of the hall. There was another door on the right, this one perfectly ordinary, but on the left was a second vault-like door with another biometric lock. Lachlan slid his full hand into the reader, and the lock clicked. Reaching back, he took her hand again, then pushed the heavy door open, pulled her into the room, and closed the door firmly.

Julia stood for a moment, taking it all in. Lachlan's suite, she assumed, was twice the size of her own bedroom in London—a room she'd always thought was too big. Of course, she didn't have an enormous four-poster bed, or yet another stone fireplace that had probably seen animals roasted whole back in the day. She turned and gave him a skeptical look.

"We do have guest quarters, if you'd prefer," he said, with a half-grin that told her he didn't think she would. She was tempted by that confident grin to take him up on his offer. She had a feeling Lachlan McRae was altogether too accustomed to getting what he wanted. But since she really didn't want to spend the night in a lonely guest bed, she'd be punishing herself along with him, and she'd never been one for self-flagellation.

"This is fine," she said pleasantly, then added. "But where are you sleeping?"

"Aye. Good one."

Julia wandered farther into the room, admiring beautifully carved furniture of a gorgeous mahogany with deep-red low lights. The four-poster didn't have a canopy, for which she was grateful. Every time she saw one of those, all she could think of was the dust it must accumulate and where that dust ended up. Yuck. The bedding, on the other hand, was a bold and beautiful blue, matched by heavy drapes on all the windows. Curious about the grounds, she walked over to one of the windows and pulled the drape back . . . only to find a wall. She turned a found him watching her.

"I'm a vampire," he said, by way of explanation. "There are shutters that close down all the other windows automatically, synced to a GPS that knows the solar calendar. But there are no windows past that first door to the basement vault."

"How do they like sleeping in the basement?"

"Don't worry. It's very comfortable, and they each have a private room."

"Then why are you up here, instead?"

He shrugged. "I like it, and I'm just as well protected."

Julia knew there was probably more to it than that, but figured that story could wait. "I like it, too," she agreed. "It makes a statement. What's with the giant fireplace?"

"It gets cold here," he protested.

Julia laughed. "I don't smell smoke. Is it wood-burning?"

He walked over and pressed a small switch on the wall. The electric igniter clicked briefly, and fire flared around a huge set of ceramic logs that were as close to real as she'd ever seen. Flames filled the big fireplace, giving off almost too much heat. As if he'd noticed her reaction, he did something at the switch and lowered the fire to a level that warmed the room without cooking the inhabitants.

"Better?" he asked, just as someone knocked on the door. Walking over, he opened the door to a very young woman who handed him a tray while craning her neck trying to see around him. She was obviously curious about his guest, since the food couldn't be for Lachlan. "Thank you, Bailey."

"*O' coorse, Lachlan. Is thare anythin' else ah kin git ye?*"

Even if she hadn't left off Lachlan's title—which, it was worth noting, her chef boss hadn't done—the adoring tone of girl's offer was enough to give away her obvious crush. One that Lachlan just as obviously didn't return. Probably because the girl couldn't be more than eighteen years old. Even if he hadn't been a 173-year-old vampire, he'd have been too old for her.

Okay, sure, he was a lot older than Julia was, too. But at least she was an adult, with life and, let's face it, *sexual* experience behind her.

"No, this is it. Thanks, Bailey. We'll keep the tray overnight."

"Oh." The girl's disappointment was plain. "*Weel, see ye th'morra, then, ah guess.*"

"*Aye. Th'morra.*" He closed the door without further conversation then turned, still holding the covered tray. He winced when he saw Julia watching. "She has a crush. She'll get over it."

Julia laughed as she took the tray from him. "Don't hold your breath. She's in love."

"Shite. I've known her since she was born, for Christ's sake."

She smiled as she uncovered the tray and found a ginormous sandwich. "I can't eat all this," she said, turning to give him a disbelieving look. "Do I *look* like I can eat all this?"

It was Lachlan's turn to laugh. "Definitely not," he said staunchly, then walked over to look over her shoulder. "Hell, *absolutely* not. Maybe he felt he had something to prove, what with you being a chef yourself and all."

"I'm not a chef," she insisted. "I'm not even a good fucking cook." She lifted the top piece of bread from half the sandwich, and removed most the meat—roast beef, nicely pink—then put the half-sandwich back together and took a bite. The bread was delicious and so was the rest of it, with a horseradish sauce that was divine. She took another bite and a sip from the glass of red wine on the tray before saying, "Your Graeme knows his food. This is great."

Lachlan was watching her like he wouldn't mind taking a bite.

"You want some?" she asked, holding out the modified half-sandwich.

He grinned and said, "I do," as he strolled over and put an arm around her waist, pulling her flush against him and burying his face against her neck. "But not of the sandwich."

Julia's entire body reacted to the crooning sound of his voice, the heat of his breath against her skin. It was as if every part of her remembered the thrill of his bite, the erotic feel of his weight on top of her, the sensuous push of his cock inside her. She shivered, and he pulled her closer, until his erection was a hard, thick rod against her belly.

"Lachlan," she whispered, dropping the sandwich to tangle her fingers in his hair, grateful for the irrelevant fact that she didn't have to reach as far to kiss him when she was wearing her spikey heels.

"Still hungry?" he growled, one hand dropping to her butt, pushing her even harder against his stiff cock.

"I can eat the sandwich later," she whispered urgently, then put her hands against his chest and shoved him back to the bed. He backed up obligingly, but she didn't have any illusions that it was her strength that moved him. The man was like a rock. A big, hot, muscled and beautiful fucking rock. And he was hers. At least for now.

LACHLAN LET HIMSELF fall back onto the bed, pulling Julia down on top of him. She kicked off those fantastic fuck-me heels, then pulled her tight skirt up over her thighs and straddled him. Her breath was coming fast and hard, her breasts pushed against her blouse in a way that accented the firm points of her nipples. He remembered the taste of those breasts and wanted more. Julia leaned over to kiss him, rubbing her silken-clad pussy against the ridge of his cock where it was crushed behind the zipper of his jeans. It appeared she was planning on being on top for this encounter, but he wasn't having it. Maybe later, but right now, he wanted to fuck her in the rawest sense of the word.

Hands on her hips, he rolled her under him, ignoring her protest. "Later, princess," he growled, and reached under her skirt to rip her panties away. Julia moaned and tried to help him free his cock, her fingers tangling with his on the belt buckle, until he took her hands in one of his and held them while he used his other hand to open his belt and shove down his zipper. His cock surged into his hand, more than ready to slide into her hot, creamy pussy. Freeing her hands, he shoved her skirt all the way to her waist and spread her legs even farther, making room between her thighs, as she thrust her hips upward, seeking the hard press of his cock.

"Here you go, love." Lining his cock up with her hot and welcoming sex, he inserted only the very tip, then with both his hands braced to either side of her head, he slammed his full length into her body, shoving through the tight slickness of her sheath as it surrounded him in a silky caress. He groaned when his cock slammed up against her cervix, hearing her sharp intake of breath as her arms closed around his neck. He started pounding her sweet pussy, fucking her with an urgency that had been hounding him since their fight on the highway with the enemy vamps. The violence and passion of their encounter, the sight of Julia standing there in her skin-tight skirt and sky-high heels, the steam still wafting off her gun barrel in the dampness of a Scottish night . . . he'd have taken her right then and there if they hadn't needed to get away before anyone saw them.

But now she was underneath him, half-naked, her pussy all slick and hungry, breasts heaving as he ripped her blouse open and yanked down the lacy cup of her bra, to suck a plump nipple into his mouth. Julia made a sound that could have been protest—for the bra or because she didn't want it between them. Either way, he ignored it. He enjoyed teasing her, not giving her what she wanted until it pleased him. He liked her desperate and hungry, nails digging into his flesh as she tried to draw him deeper, legs clasped over his ass.

He lowered his head and took her mouth in a savage kiss when her body rippled with the first waves of orgasm, drinking her scream as the climax grew and she bucked hard against him. She clung to his shoulders with desperate passion, as he never stopped thrusting, slamming through the hard grasp of her inner muscles, eased by the rush of satiny cream that flowed slick and hot over his shaft. He rode her climax until it surrendered, leaving her stunned by its power, her body shuddering in the aftermath. And then he flipped her to her belly, pulled her hips high, and spread her thighs wide, leaving her sweet pussy completely open to the furious demands of his cock.

Julia's cry was muffled by her arms as her body tightened in a fresh orgasm, her fingers digging into the sheets, twisting the fabric into knots as she held on, straining helplessly against the convulsing muscles of her abdomen, the clenching of her pussy, the tightening of her pretty nipples until they were as hard as the cock he thrust into her . . . until his body finally yielded. He groaned as the heavy pressure built in his balls, until with a final, agonizing grind, the hot rush of his orgasm roared down his cock and splashed into his woman. *His.*

Julia Harper was his and no one else's. His to fuck, his to protect. And in that moment, he knew he'd destroy anyone—man or vampire—who tried to harm her.

JULIA STOOD IN THE shower, face raised to the soft rush of steamy water, while heat of an entirely different sort seeped into her bones from Lachlan's powerful body standing behind her. She still couldn't understand her own easy surrender to his sexual demands, the hunger for him that left her helpless to resist. Of course, it was difficult to think beyond the pleasure he gave her, whether it was the unyielding thrust of his cock, or the brutal thrill of him flexing deep inside her as he came, the heat of his climax both a claiming and a triumph.

His arms came around her, turning her to face him as he reached up and did something to the shower head that turned the water's soft rush into a pounding heat against her back. She moaned with pleasure, resting her forehead on that fabulous chest while the water massaged muscles taut with strain from the long drive and the fight that had interrupted it. She kept replaying in her mind the moment she'd seen the enemy vampire rise up and go after Lachlan, the slow tightening of her finger on the trigger just as she'd been taught, the realization that killing a living, breathing person was vastly different than putting holes in a paper target.

She didn't regret killing the vampire, though. She couldn't, not with Lachlan's life on the line. It didn't trouble her that she'd killed, it troubled her that it *didn't* trouble her.

"You're thinking way too hard, princess."

She kissed his throat as the deep rumble of his voice sent shivers over her skin, despite the steamy shower enclosure. "The fight," she admitted. "I keep playing it in my head, trying to figure out if I should have done something differently."

"What else could you have done?"

"That's just it. Nothing."

He was quiet for a moment, strong hands sweeping up and down her back, adding to the massaging effect of the pulsing water. "Come on," he said, reaching around her to turn off the shower. "You need some food. It'll help you think."

Julia gratefully took the towel he offered from a heated rod just outside the oversized shower stall, wrapping it over her shoulders like a long cape, not even trying to dry the rest of her body. When Lachlan threw her another towel, this one smaller, she did a quick squeeze of her long hair and wound the towel around her head like a turban. Lachlan wasn't paying any attention by then, too busy drying himself with long seductive strokes that highlighted every muscle and sinew of that beautiful body. Was he doing it on purpose? Showing off? Teasing her with future intent? She swallowed a groan and turned her back to him, pulling the big towel from her shoulders and bending over to dry off her calves, her thighs, the soft, swollen flesh between them.

"You keep up with that, and you'll never make it back to your dinner," he commented matter-of-factly.

She raised her head and turned, eyes wide as she took in his relaxed slump against the marble countertop, and the hard jut of his cock along his thigh, while gold shards sparked like lightening through his eyes.

She stared. "You're insatiable! How do you do that?"

He smiled, seeming amused. "I'm not the one doing it, princess."

A surge of satisfaction warmed Julia's heart at the realization she wasn't the only one being swept away by their undeniable chemistry. It didn't make it go away, or lessen its pull, but at least she wasn't alone in it.

"Well, tell it to relax. I'm starving."

He laughed out loud at that, then straightened from his slouch and walked over to steal a wet and languid kiss that had her rethinking how hungry she was and whether dinner could wait. It was only a sandwich.

But he didn't give her the option, breaking off the kiss and saying, "I'll meet you out there," as he left the bathroom.

Julia sighed. Hopeless. That's what she was. Hopeless against the dark flame of his demands, the intense electrical spark of this damn sexual attraction between them. She told herself that's all it was. Hormones and mutual desire. A purely physical, chemical thing.

She finished drying off, then snagged the thick terry cloth robe hanging from a hook on the door. A slight twinge of something that might have been jealousy stabbed her before she realized the robe was much too big and was clearly meant for Lachlan's use.

Belting it around her, she padded out to the bedroom, the wood floor cool against her bare feet. Lachlan had pulled on a pair of sweat pants that barely covered him, hanging so low on his narrow hips that a soft breeze would have left him perfectly naked. Which wasn't an altogether bad outcome, but she needed fuel first, so those pants had to stay on for at least long enough for her to eat the sandwich. And maybe she'd add back some of the beef she'd taken off. She was going to need protein to keep up with her vampire lover's simmering sexuality.

Climbing up onto the big bed, she tucked the robe demurely around herself, then proceeded to devour every crumb of food from the tray. Not only the sandwich, but the freshly-made fries and creamy cheesecake with sweet strawberries. She put down her fork and pushed the empty tray to the foot of the bed, then leaned back on the pillows, still savoring the last delicious bite. If she'd been alone, she'd have crossed her arms over her swollen gut, feeling stuffed to the gills, as they said in the US.

"Feeling better?" Lachlan asked, looking up from the tablet he'd been working on while she ate. There was a definite note of amusement in his voice, but Julia didn't care. She'd enjoyed the food far too much, which was something she rarely did anymore.

"I do feel better, thanks." She sighed in satisfaction, then scooted over and pushed her head against his bicep. "What's that?" she asked, seeing what looked like a financial stock chart on his screen.

"Investment portfolio."

"For the clan?"

"And my own, as well. I keep the two separate."

"I thought Munro was your financial genius."

"Munro's good at making sure everything adds up and detecting nascent big picture trends in the market. But he's a numbers guy. I work more on instinct, which means I'm better at spotting future opportunities, new or revamped companies with an innovative product. Stocks we can get in on at the start and ride their wave upward."

Julia took all of this in, surprised even though she shouldn't have been. Lachlan was far more than a gorgeous body. He was obviously intelligent, since he'd pulled his clan out of disaster and led it back to prosperity. And she doubted his people would have followed him as loyally as they obviously did, even continuing their support as he planned for the overthrow of Erskine, if he hadn't had that indefinable quality that made leaders out of otherwise ordinary men. Of course, there was nothing ordinary about Lachlan. He was a vampire, for fuck's sake. But she couldn't help noting the differences between him and the enemy vamps they'd fought, or even him and his cousins. Maybe it was that magical power he'd talked about, but she thought it had more to do with who he was inside, the man he'd been even before he'd been made Vampire.

She turned her head and kissed the smooth skin of his arm. She'd intended to make it a quick kiss, but his skin was so thick and velvety, and he smelled so good, she found herself kissing her way up to his shoulder, then scooting higher, until she could nuzzle his neck.

"Hungry, princess?" he asked, his voice rough and rumbly, as he lifted his arm and pulled her against him.

"Not anymore," she murmured against his mouth, but then smiled when she realized what he'd been asking. "Dessert would be nice."

He chuckled, deeply masculine and smug, but Julia found she didn't care. She bit down hard on his lip, drawing a drop of blood which she licked up with a sensuous swipe of her tongue. Lachlan's grip on her tightened. "Careful what you start."

"I know exactly what I'm starting, Lord Lachlan. The question is . . . who's going to finish it?"

He reacted so fast, her head spun as she found herself on her back, with Lachlan pressing her against the bed, and the tray of dishes crashing off the edge.

"The dishes," she said without thinking.

"Fuck the dishes. It's time for dessert, and I know just what I'm after."

Julia moaned as his strong fingers made quick work of the tie on her robe, spreading the two sides to bare her naked body, as if presenting her for his pleasure. He ran a hand down the length of her, from neck to thigh and back again, lingering this time to squeeze her breasts, plumping them for his mouth as he bent his head and licked. She gasped, her fingers clutched in his hair, as his tongue rasped over a nipple that was still tender from their earlier lovemaking, swirling around the aching tip until she was arching her back for more. Lachlan hissed and took her breast, sucking hard until half the delicate flesh had been sucked into the wet heat of his mouth.

"Lachlan," she cried, not sure how much more of his erotic attention she could survive. Every inch of her body was on fire, consumed with such overwhelming pleasure that she didn't know what to do with it. Could a woman die of sexual ecstasy? She screamed as he bit into her breast, not from pain, but because it was a pain that felt so damn good. A week ago, she wouldn't have thought such a thing was possible. But a week ago, she hadn't met Lachlan. It stunned her to realize how much had happened in only a few days.

Lachlan's teeth closed on her flesh again, harder this time. Julia's eyes flashed open to meet his gold-sparked gaze. "You weren't paying attention," he growled.

Her body rippled when his warm tongue licked up the bit of blood from her breast, soothing and exciting her at the same time. But when he nudged his hips between her thighs, she surprised him by flexing her abdominals and shoving him to his back. "Not this time, my lord."

"Julia," he demanded, but she stopped whatever he'd planned to say by closing her mouth over his in a slow, wet kiss. It was the kind of kiss she'd wanted to give him since the first night they'd met, when he'd been grumpy but still delicious. He had succulent lips for a man, soft and full, but still firm, on a mouth that knew how to kiss. Her breasts scraped over his chest, her tender nipples feeling the soft touch like an electric shock. She moved until her entire length was stretched on top of him, his hands automatically going to her butt, though whether it was to hold her in place or assert his dominance, she didn't know. And she didn't care, either, because she had plans for this delectable hunk of a vampire.

His grip on her butt tightened when she began to move downward. But then, as if finally understanding her goal, his fingers loosened and slid up her back as she kissed her way over his chest, pausing long enough to lavish attention on flat masculine nipples that peaked to hardness under the stroke of her tongue. When she licked her way down even farther, to the hard ridges of his abdomen, he growled her name in warning. "Julia."

Her response was to glide her tongue in a wet spiral all the way to his groin, pausing only to take nipping bites of his flat belly, while her nails traced bright lines down his sides. His hand fisted in her hair, twisting until it was a sharp tug against her scalp. "Julia," he repeated, his tone demanding enough that she raised her eyes to meet his. "I don't have that much control," he warned in a rasping whisper.

She looked up. "That's all right. I do." She smiled, then lowered her head, and without warning, sucked his cock into her mouth, lavishing the iron-hard stretch of it with sweeps of her tongue as she struggled to take his full length into her throat. But he was simply too big. Surrendering to physical reality, she gripped the base of his erection, her fingers pumping tightly, as she slowly eased her mouth up to the tip. She closed her teeth teasingly there, until he growled a darker warning, his grip on her hair tightening to the very edge of pain. Smiling around his thickness, she raised up and kissed his tip in apology, before once more taking him deep into her throat, her head bobbing as she tried again to take all of him.

Lachlan's groan of approval told her she'd succeeded, and she reached for his balls, caressing them as she sucked, until his sac tightened and his hips jerked upward. Gasping for breath, she pressed her tongue against the heavy vein on the back of his shaft, licking and swirling around and around, loving the scent of him, the velvet thickness of his cock . .. Until suddenly, she was being lifted into the air and pressed flat on her back by the hard, masculine body on top of her.

"But I wanted—"

"I know what you wanted, witch. But it's my turn now." Not giving her a chance to protest, he positioned himself between her thighs and slid his entire length into her with a single, hard, flex of his hips.

Julia's body was so wet and ready that she took his thickness easily, her pussy drenched with slick heat as he began fucking her with steady, deep strokes. She wrapped her arms around his neck, holding on, the pleasure of their joining seeming unnatural in its intensity, making her feel as if her entire body was alive and about to float off the bed. She almost believed it would have, if not for the heavy weight of him, holding her to the earth.

She gasped back to reality when his teeth grazed her neck, shuddering with fresh awareness of the thrill yet to come, wondering if she'd survive, or if this would be the time her mind finally gave out under the electrifying high of his bite. "Lachlan," she breathed, trying to protest, to fight for her sanity, but his only response was a deep chuckle a moment before his fangs pierced her skin and went deeper, sinking into her vein until she felt the warm flow of her own blood.

She barely had time to process the sensation before the euphoric in his bite hit her bloodstream and drove away every thought, every feeling, on a wave of such intense, erotic ecstasy that she couldn't even scream, drowning as she was in such violent passion that her breath was driven from her lungs. It was Lachlan's kiss that forced her to breathe, his mouth hot and hard against hers, his breath slamming into her lungs, even as his cock shoved ruthlessly into her body.

His strokes slowed gradually, his eyes wicked and smiling, as he gazed down at her. "I love fucking your pussy after you've come. You're all juicy and trembling. Hotter than hell itself."

Julia was still too breathless to respond, her heart seeming to beat a thousand times faster than it should, while her lungs were only beginning to function normally. She ran her hands over his broad arms, gripping his biceps as if she had a chance in hell of controlling him. He kissed her with the same, slow, lush strokes as his shaft moving inside her.

"Delicious," he murmured, "but I want more."

Her nails dug into muscle as his hips flexed harder, driving his cock deep inside her once again, his balls slapping her ass with every forceful plunge. She cried out as fresh desire sparked to life, her arms sliding up to tighten around his neck, her legs crossing behind him as a renewed thrill had her lifting her hips, meeting every thrust, teeth closing over the hard line of his shoulder as she fought to hold on, to claim him as he was claiming her.

Lachlan grunted wordlessly, but he didn't try to pull away, only lowered his head to her neck once more and slid his fangs into her vein.

They climaxed together, his shout of orgasmic pleasure drowning her cry of joy as they tumbled over the edge and collapsed into each other's arms.

They lay silently while Julia wiggled her toes trying to figure out if feeling had fully returned to her appendages. She didn't know if Lachlan was doing the same, but she could feel his heart pounding against her chest as she lay sprawled half on top of him, too boneless to move. Eventually, he broke the silence.

"Dawn's not far off. You need to decide what you're doing today."

"Doing?" she repeated, wondering if she was expected to climb out of this soft bed and go be productive somewhere.

His hand slid down her back in a warm caress, ending up on her butt. "I'll be sleeping the day away. You know what that's like by now.

You need to decide if you're staying here with me, or moving across the hall. There's a guest room that's—"

"I'm staying," she said, interrupting his offer. "I'm not afraid of a little down time while you do your vampire thing. I'll probably sleep right along with you. I'm wiped." She expected some teasing reply about how he'd worn her out, but that's not what she got.

"You're sure? Once the sun comes up, there's no opening that door until I'm awake enough to do it."

"You might not have noticed, my lord, but I've been awake right alongside you these last few nights. I'm ready to sleep. And if I wake early, I'm not that easily bored. I can read or get some work done on my laptop. Just leave me the Wi-Fi password."

His chest moved in deep chuckle. "It's taped to the phone."

"Unbelievable. Great security. Well, then, I'll be perfectly entertained 'til sunset."

His phone rang before he could respond. He kissed the top of her head and stretched to pick up the cell from the bedside table, leaving Julia to listen to half a conversation.

"*Aye. Ye back?*" He paused. "*The fuck ye' say.*" He sighed, then, "*We'll talk th'morra.*" He nodded silently. "*See ye then.*"

She looked up at him with a grin. "I love the accent."

"*I'm nae th' yin wi' an accent, love.*"

She laughed. "I'm guessing that was Fergus. I thought he was already here."

"He was, but he drove over to Killilan to brief the others, and Munro came back with him."

"Killilan," she repeated, then remembered. "The clan fortress you like best."

"The same."

"You sounded pissed. What happened?"

"Erskine's suddenly decided to spend time in Inverness."

"He's here? But you said—"

"He's rarely here. Aye, and he snuck in, or I'd have felt him. Which means he's planning something. You sure you want to stay? You could go back to Edinburgh tomorrow. You'll be a lot safer."

She sat up with a glare. "I can't believe you're asking me that."

"Come here, princess," he said gently, pulling her down on top of him again. "I just want you safe."

"Fuck safe. What I want is to see him dead. Besides," she muttered grudgingly, "I'm safer with you." She waited for his gloating response, but it didn't come.

He simply hugged her close and said softly, "I'll protect you. No matter what."

"Hey," she said, lifting her head to meet his eyes. "No heroics, okay? I want you to be safe, too."

He gave her a crooked smile. "Still worrying about me? We'll keep each *other* safe, then." He tucked her head against his shoulder. "Sleep now. You're going to need it. Because I plan to spend tomorrow night inside you, before I have to consider the fate of every vampire in Scotland."

Chapter Ten

JULIA HAD BEEN right about how tired she was. She'd closed her eyes as soon as Lachlan dropped into his daylight coma—calling it sleep was simply ridiculous from her point of view. He wasn't asleep. He was unconscious. She'd had her e-reader ready to go, having figured she'd need at least an hour or so to fall asleep, since it was nowhere close to her usual sleep schedule. But she didn't manage a single page of her current book before falling asleep mid-read.

At some point, she'd rolled over and curled up next to Lachlan, which, in retrospect, she found odd. She wasn't accustomed to sleeping with anyone and hadn't had a serious relationship in years. She'd dated a couple of guys long enough to have sex with them, but when they'd spent the night together—which hadn't been often and spoke to the not very serious nature of the relationship—she'd never had the urge to curl up with any of *them*.

No, she'd waited until she was dating a *vampire* to do the whole cuddle routine. And dating? Was that what they were doing? Not much dating going on so far. It was more of a business agreement with benefits. Although it felt like more, damn it. She'd become a cliché. The rich daddy's girl who falls for the ultimate bad boy. It consoled her somewhat that her good friend Cyn had fallen down the same rabbit hole, but that didn't mean her story would have the same happy ending.

Thankful that she'd at least awakened before him, she rolled out of bed and headed for the bathroom, hoping she'd have enough time to shower and dress before sunrise. Lachlan would probably appreciate her absence when he woke up, too. Sure, they'd had lots of hot, sweaty sex, and God knew they had chemistry, but she doubted she was the woman he'd planned on to rule Scotland by his side. Some nice vampire chick would do better, she thought as she stepped into the shower. Someone who understood vampire society and customs. Even more importantly, someone who would live forever, just like he would. Her stomach clenched at the truth of that thought. Sure, Lachlan could be killed, but he was already nearly two centuries old, nearly indestructible and clearly powerful enough to defend himself against all comers. He'd go on living for a long, fucking time yet. Cyn had told her Raphael was even older. She'd wondered at the time how Cyn handled that, knowing she'd get old and gray while Raphael didn't. She hadn't asked, figuring it was too personal a question. But Cyn had volunteered the information, something about drinking Raphael's blood and remaining young as long as he lived. Of course, that she'd only known Lachlan a week, and they were lovers, nothing more. She'd be long gone and out of his life before gray hair became a problem.

The idea made her feel sad. No surprise there. The prospect of gray hair wasn't exactly a cheery thought. She leaned toward the mirror, rubbing away steam with her towel and checking her reflection. Probably a good thing she'd washed her hair tonight. In this mood, she might pluck herself bald searching for stray strands of age.

That was how Lachlan found her, naked, leaning over the counter, staring at herself in the mirror.

"Well, now, that's a pretty sight," he commented, sneaking up behind her and scaring her half to death.

She spun around. "How the hell do you do that?"

He grinned, eyeing her naked body. "Do what, princess?"

"Sneak up without me hearing anything. I mean, you're huge! How do you not make any noise?"

"I told you before. I don't sneak. As for the rest, it's a gift." He gestured at the mirror she'd been focused on earlier. "What were you doing there?"

She turned away to conceal her embarrassed blush. "Just wiping the mirror, so I could do my hair," she lied, reaching across with a towel to finish what she'd started.

He rested his hands on her hips and snugged his naked body up behind hers. She straightened in reaction, too aware of the temptation he presented, all charming and studly as he was. He could talk her into anything. He bent his head and kissed her neck in precisely the spot he'd bitten her the previous night. It was tender, but the mark wasn't as dark as she'd expected.

"You're bruised," he said, sounding truly concerned.

"It's not bad. I bruise easily. It's the curse of pale skin."

"I can fix that, if you'll—" His head turned at some sound she didn't hear. "Stay here. Get dressed."

"What is it?"

"It's my head of daylight security. He wouldn't interrupt me this early if it wasn't important."

Julia watched him go, worried, disappointed and relieved all at the same time. After her in-the-mirror pep talk, she'd been half-heartedly trying to avoid another round of sex. It was one thing to fall into bed with a vampire, it was another to stay there, knowing the relationship couldn't go anywhere. On the other hand, her body thrilled at the memory of him standing behind her, knowing what he could have done with his lovely cock and her in that position.

"Stop it, Jules," she hissed quietly. "You're supposed to be getting over him, not fantasizing about bathroom counter sex." She froze at the sound of the hallway door opening out in the bedroom and had a moment of panic, wondering if he'd overheard her muttering to herself. She shook her head. If he had, he'd never have let it pass. He'd have been back in there and between her thighs before she could say, "vampire."

Just in case, however, she didn't waste any more time searching for invisible gray hairs. Damn it, she wasn't even thirty yet. Cracking open the door, she peered out into the main room, and finding it empty, hurried out and grabbed her small suitcase, rolling it into the bathroom behind her. Dressing quickly in black jeans and a long-sleeved knit-top, she rolled her case back into the bedroom and sat down to pull on socks, along with the hiking boots she'd packed, but hadn't thought she'd need when she boarded the plane. She'd assumed they would be staying in Edinburgh until the next night, giving her plenty of time to change clothes. Fortunately, she wore heels often enough that they hadn't stopped her when the shit hit the fan on the way to Inverness. But that didn't mean she wanted to keep wearing them.

She finished tying her boots, then zipped her case shut and went looking for food. She didn't know where Lachlan had gone off to, but he'd already eaten well the previous night, thanks to *her*. She was the one who needed to replenish her reserves . . . for *both* of them. Besides, it would give her a chance to compliment Graeme on the sandwich, maybe win her way into his good graces, after apparently insulting him by suggesting she could prepare it herself. Although she didn't know why his good graces mattered, since she'd probably never see him again once Erskine was dead. She kept forgetting that she and Lachlan couldn't be a long-term thing, no matter how much it was beginning to feel like one.

"IT'S PROBABLY poachers, my lord," the head of his daylight security was saying, bringing up a series of photographs on his laptop in the main security office next door. "*We've had some few th' last six months or so. Caught a pair of 'em just two weeks past. Let 'em go a'course, but ah'm thinking this tonight might be connected. Maybe friends, maybe partners. Ah'll 'ave another go at 'em, find oot whit thay ken.*"

"They're still in our custody?" Lachlan asked.

"*Oh, aye. Davie wants to question'em himself,*" he said, tipping his head toward the vampire standing near, who was overall security chief for the Inverness property.

"I didn't like some of their answers, my lord," Davie said. "We decided to let them sit for a while, to contemplate their sins, as it were. But even if they're just poachers, we can't let this stand. People hereabouts need to know this property's off-limits."

Lachlan stared at the images of the so-called poachers, considering whether to take over the interrogation. Davie was a strong vampire and good at what he did. He was more than capable of wringing the truth out of human thieves, if that's what they were. On the other hand, there was Julia to consider. If these so-called poachers were Erskine's people in disguise, looking for a way to grab her while she was out on a walk, say, a much stronger response would be needed. Especially with his own plans against Erskine very much on a short timeline. His vampire fighters would have arrived from Killilan before dawn, and along with them Munro, who'd already be busy poring through Masoud's files that Julia had provided. Those financial records would be important for the future of Scotland under his rule. But they could *not* be the instrument that took Erskine down. Vampires didn't imprison their leaders for so-called "white collar" crimes. Vampires challenged and *killed* the current lord as proof of their power to rule. It had always been that way. The rule was, you keep what you can hold. If a vampire lord was incapable of holding his territory, he was no longer strong enough to be its lord.

Before the end of this night, Lachlan would be meeting with his cousins and senior advisers to finalize their strategy, though it really came down to two choices. Did Lachlan simply confront Erskine and challenge him to a one-on-one duel? Such a plan would save lives, assuming Erskine could be trusted to keep it one-on-one. Or, second option, did he launch a full-scale attack on Erskine, who'd now conveniently moved to his Inverness house? Some—Lachlan among them—saw the vampire lord's timely relocation as *too* convenient. It smacked of planning, more than coincidence, and it made him think Erskine had his own strategy afoot.

"Talk to them," he told Davie. "And if they say anything, or if you need me for any reason, call."

"Yes, my lord."

Lachlan strode back to the main house, taking his time, stopping to have a friendly word with several of his people along the way. He had a good group on the estate. They were accustomed to him being gone for long periods of time, but they still expected him to keep up with what was going on in Inverness. Once he became Lord of Scotland, he'd have to spend more time in Edinburgh, while the Killilan fortress would become even more the occasional getaway. He could see himself on some wintry future night, snowed in there, tucked up in his suite with Julia in his bed. The unexpected thought made him stop for a moment as he crossed the gravel drive. He didn't know if she'd still even *be* here by then, or if she'd *want* to be. Much less in his bed.

But that was the future. *Tonight*, she was here, and he wanted her.

He found her just coming out the kitchen. She had a smile on her face, although not for him. She was looking back, laughing at something Graeme had said. Dressed casually in jeans and hiking boots, with the braid of her pale hair even more striking against a dark sweater, she was just as enticing as she'd been in a tight skirt and heels.

"Princess," he said softly. Her head came around, and her smile faded.

"Lachlan," she said as coolly as if he was a guy trying to sell her a used car, instead of the man whose dick she'd been sucking just a few hours ago. What the fuck?

"Did you get something to eat?" he asked cautiously.

"I did, thank you. Graeme seems to have adapted to this weird schedule of yours."

"One person's weird is another's normal."

"Yes. Are you going out tonight?"

"No," he said slowly. "We're staying here. What's going on?" Lachlan had never been one to dance around a problem, preferring to confront it head on. And there was clearly a problem here.

"What do you mean?" she asked, as she headed back down the hall to his, *their*, bedroom.

Lachlan followed, closing the door behind him, watching as Julia quickly put the bed between them. As if that would stop him. Using the speed of his vampire nature, he moved and was next to her by the time she saw him take the first step.

Her eyes were wide and startled when she looked up at him. "How'd you do that?"

He slipped an arm around her slender waist. "All vampires can move fast. The stronger the vampire, the faster. And I," he tightened his hold on her, "am very powerful. Now, tell me what the fuck's going on with you."

Her entire body stiffened, eyelids lowering to shutter her gaze. "What do you mean?"

"I mean you went from sucking my cock to treating me like a stranger in the space of an hour. What happened?"

"Nothing," she said, still not looking at him. "I just . . . ."

He waited while her body softened against his, and she placed one hand against his chest.

"I'm not . . . *good* at casual relationships. I think maybe—"

"Who says this is casual?" he demanded, surprising himself.

She finally looked at him, her pale blue eyes clear and full of emotion. "Isn't it? We were supposed to be partners, both of us wanting Erskine dead, which meant spending time together. Then we flew to Malibu and back, and it was just the two of us, and you're so damn sexy. You have to know—Shit. I didn't mean to say that."

Lachlan tried not to grin, succeeded in keeping his lips tight, at least. Fortunately, Julia didn't see it, since she was avoiding his gaze again. But at least now he understood her reasons for treating him like he had the plague. "Come on," he said, sliding his hands down her arm and twining their fingers together. "Let's get you a jacket. It's cold out there."

"Out where?" she asked, but she didn't fight him as he pulled her over to the closet. "Where are we going?"

"I'm going to show you one of the most beautiful sights you'll ever see."

"Oh. Okay."

JULIA SAT ALL bundled up in her down jacket and wool scarf, gloves on her hands, but that wasn't what was keeping her warm. No, that would be Lachlan's strong arm around her, holding her to his side as they sat on a flat rock, overlooking a river that was gleaming silver in the light of a waxing quarter moon. Sure, her butt was freezing, but that was a small price to pay for what truly was a stunningly beautiful sight. Not to mention the gorgeous man sitting next to her. This was the most romantic moment of her life, although she kept that truth to herself.

Lachlan hadn't said much as he'd waited for her to put her jacket on. He'd just taken her hand and led her out past the wide-open space in front of the house, to a nearly hidden pathway that rambled through tall grasses that were as green and fresh as if it were spring, instead of fall. She'd realized why when they'd stepped off the path. The ground was soggy beneath her feet, which wasn't much of a surprise, since Scotland was a wet place, full of rivers and lakes, and waterfalls of all sizes tumbling over cliffs and down hillsides.

She and Lachlan had made their way through the grass to this pile of stones that seemed to appear out of nowhere, and now sat with their feet on the ground and butts perched on a stone. A cold, cold stone.

"Is this view the reason you bought the house?" she asked, leaning her head against his shoulder, ignoring her recent debate with herself, which had argued for putting distance between them.

"In some way," he replied. "Scotland is full of such places, but that this one came with a big, broken-down estate was a bonus."

"When did you buy it?"

"1963. Recent enough that we knew about indoor plumbing and electricity, at least. Though we've had to upgrade the phones more than once, and add all manner of digital connections, of course. But upgrades would have occurred no matter when we bought."

They sat without speaking for a few minutes, as her butt went from cold to completely numb, until Lachlan's arm around her shoulders squeezed tightly, and he said, "What you said earlier, about this being casual. It's not, you know."

Julia's breath caught, not only at what he'd said, but the *way* he'd said it. This wasn't some slick, say anything to get laid proclamation. There'd been a reluctance to his words, as if he'd been having the same doubts as she had, but had come to a different conclusion.

"I didn't plan on it either," he said, as if reading her thoughts. Again.

She reminded herself to ask him about that. Later. Right now, she wanted to hear what he had to say.

"I admit, at first, I just wanted you in my bed. I might be a vampire, but I'm still a man. When I meet a smart, beautiful woman, I want to fuck her."

Julia slapped his rock-hard thigh lightly.

"Aye," he admitted. "Neanderthal and all that. But that attitude didn't last long with you. We've been through some shit these last few days, all around the world. We secured the backing of the most powerful vampire in the world—"

"He is?"

"—fought off two separate attacks by people who want you for reasons completely different than my own. And now we're about to risk our lives to eliminate another very dangerous vampire lord." He paused, then continued, "I've got to tell you, princess, I never thought you'd stick with it."

"What? Why not?" she demanded.

"Look at you. You're all pretty and *pink*, with those needle-like heels and tight skirts that hug your ass. You don't exactly scream 'killer.'"

She didn't know whether to be pleased or insulted. She didn't want to scream 'killer,' but she didn't like the image of herself as pretty and pink, either. She *never* wore pink, for God's sake. "You seemed happy enough when I shot that vampire for you last night. Maybe I should buy a *pink* gun."

He shuddered. "Please don't. And that's not my point. I've discovered you're a hell of a lot more than my shallow, male mind first thought. I *like* you . . . more than I should. My life isn't . . . will *never be* anything close to normal. I'm a vampire. I'll soon be a vampire lord, with a world of responsibilities."

"Why do it then?" she whispered.

He sighed. "It's in the blood. Literally. The vampire symbiote makes every vampire more aggressive, more prone to violence. But for those few of us gifted with real power, the ones with the potential to become vampire lords—"

"Like you," she said, thinking she knew where this was going.

"Like me," he agreed. "For us, it's more than simple aggression. We're driven to rule, to conquer every vampire we meet. That's why vampire lords typically can't be in the same room with each other for very long. There are exceptions, and I'm told the North American lords have become true allies under Raphael's guidance. Although I suspect what's happened over there is that Raphael is so damn powerful, he's become like a super vampire lord, and the others follow his lead. But that's not what I want to talk about." He shifted on his seat, pulling her even closer. "What I'm saying is my life will always be dangerous, and I probably shouldn't drag anyone else into it, much less a pretty, pink princess."

She *elbowed* him in the gut this time, though she doubted he felt that much either.

He laughed. "Come on, admit it. You like me, too."

"What are we? Twelve?"

"Not for a very long time," he said solemnly. "Look, Julia, I don't know where this will take us, but right now, I don't want it to end. And it's not just because of your tight ass, either."

"You were doing so well before that." She sighed, trying to decide how to respond. He was right. She did like him. She thought it might be more than simple "like," but she wasn't prepared to face that just yet. She also wasn't ready to walk away, she admitted. Especially not now, when she knew his feelings mirrored her own. Her hand slid to his thigh and stayed there. "I don't want to end it, either. And since we're stuck with each other for the next few days anyway, we might as well see what happens."

"Well, that's insultingly practical."

She laughed. "We don't seem very good at this."

He lifted her onto his lap as if she weighed nothing—his wonderfully *warm* lap—then pulled her down for another one of his luscious kisses. Damn, he was a good kisser. By the time he'd finished, Julia's bones felt like they'd melted, and her arms around his neck were only managing to remain there because her fingers were linked.

"I'd throw you to the ground and fuck you right here," he murmured. "But it's wet, and I'd much rather—" He tensed abruptly, head tilted slightly as if listening to something. "Let's go." He placed her on her feet, then stood next to her, holding on as if wanting to be sure she was steady. "Are you armed?" he asked, his tone hard and no-nonsense.

"What's happened?" she asked, rather than answering his question.

"We have a visitor. Damn. I don't like—" He stared when she pulled out the small pistol she'd tucked into her jacket pocket after unpacking her suitcase. She'd forgotten it was there until they were leaving the house, but after the attack on the road the previous night, she'd decided to keep it. At only six inches long and weighing a single pound, the micro-compact Sig was barely noticeable, until she pulled it out. "Who is it?"

"You always carry a gun?" he asked, as he pulled up the jacket's black nylon hood to cover her blond hair and shadow her face. She started to explain, but he continued without waiting for an answer. "Never mind. Put it away, but keep both hands in your pockets, as if you're cold. I don't want him to know you're armed. Stay behind—"

"Who is it, Lachlan?" she demanded impatiently.

He stopped his fussing and lowered his head to meet her eyes. "His name is Tucker. He's Erskine's lieutenant, and he's nearly as powerful as I am."

She held his gaze for a moment, gripped by a fear so intense that she could almost *hear* the sudden, hard pounding of her pulse. Her throat moved in a dry swallow. "*Nearly*. That means you can take him, right?"

He slid a hand around the back of her neck and pulled her in. "He might not be here to cause trouble. He could simply be Erskine's message boy and nothing else. But I can't assume that." He kissed her forehead. "Remember what I said. Hands in your pockets, have the gun ready. I'd like to send you directly to the bedroom—"

"No way in hell am I—"

"—but I know you won't go without a fight. And there's no time. I should have sensed his arrival. That I didn't means he was shielding for all he's worth, hiding his presence. It could be just instinct when going into a hostile situation, but again, it could be more. Julia, please," he said, putting both hands on her shoulders, forcing her to pay attention. "Stay behind me, stay in the shadows if you can. I don't want him to see you."

She went on alert. "Why?"

"Someone's been trying to kill you. I think it's Erskine. If so, then Tucker probably knows about it."

Julia was about to argue. Surely this Tucker guy wouldn't try anything here, not while she was with Lachlan and all his security. But Lachlan was as taut as a horse in the chute, ready to get out there and run. So she nodded her head in agreement, then took his hand and let him lead her, at a much faster pace, back along the barely visible path through the wet grass to the house, where four vampires now stood outside the doors, waiting. Their heads turned in Lachlan's direction before she could even make out their faces, with one of them coming to meet them as soon as they hit the gravel of the drive.

"How many, Davie?" Lachlan snapped, without breaking stride as he continued toward the house.

"Tucker and two, Sire. I've got them in the great room."

"This have anything to do with the poachers?"

"No." Davie's response was firm. "I tore their brains apart. They really were poachers, nothing else."

"Shit. What the hell is this then? Maintain a guard out here. Tell them to keep a cautious eye. If they sense anything—and I mean *anything*—sound the alert."

"I'll see to it."

The vampire walked over to update his men, while Lachlan continued through the front door, his grip on her hand never easing. Focusing on her surroundings, she watched every movement, listened to every word. She didn't know much about vampire customs, but she'd read and listened to transcripts and videos of enough human meetings, especially the secret kind, that she knew what to look for. Every vampire had once been human. No question that they'd changed when becoming vampires, but from her limited experience, their body language and verbal giveaways remained mostly the same.

The great room was warm when they walked through the open double doors, with a fire burning on the huge stone hearth. Almost as soon as they walked in, sweat started pooling between her breasts and at the small of her back. But she didn't take her jacket off, didn't even push back the hood. Her attention was all for the newcomer—Tucker. She didn't have to ask which one he was, even though he stood with most of his back to her. The arrogant tilt of his head and the way he'd placed himself apart from the others, even his own men, told her all she needed to know.

Lachlan let go of her hand almost as soon as they entered, giving her hip a little nudge as they passed the first of four wide, faux pillars that propped up the compass points on the room's domed roof. The dome itself, she saw, was elaborately painted to mimic a view of the night sky. Whoever had done the painting was no Michelangelo, but *was* talented.

Julia remained next to the big pillar, her head lowered slightly, enough that the hood concealed her features, but without appearing to be hiding. Both hands were in her pockets, her right hand on the gun, finger on the trigger guard, thumb near the safety.

Lachlan kept going, giving no outward indication that he cared where she ended up. He didn't greet their visitor, either. He just strolled directly over to stand next to Davie who'd entered behind them, and now stood with two of his own vampire team, facing off with Tucker and his two. Lachlan's arrival unbalanced the numbers, but that wasn't all it did. She'd noticed an uncomfortable static charge when they'd walked into the room, almost like when the winds blew in the desert and the air became so dry that you could feel a tingle against your skin. Except that this was Scotland, and it was wet as hell.

Even worse, the moment Lachlan entered, *uncomfortable* had become threatening, as all the air seemed to be sucked out of the room at once. She was still breathing, but her senses were telling her she shouldn't be able to. The air itself was heavy with menace, pressing on her ears, her chest. A quick look around told her she seemed to be the only one feeling it. Or maybe she was just the only one who couldn't explain it.

Vampire magic, she told herself. And damn if it wasn't real.

LACHLAN TOUCHED his hand to Davie's shoulder as he walked forward to face off with Tucker. Davie was strong, but Lachlan could sense his relief that Lachlan had stepped up to take point. Tucker wasn't only a powerful vampire, he was also a prick. Lachlan wouldn't have put it past him to pull some asshole trick just to prove that he could. He wouldn't have gone so far as to challenge Davie, but he might well have tried to provoke him, simply to give himself an excuse to cause pain.

"Tucker, what an unexpected pleasure," Lachlan said, his tone making it clear there was no pleasure involved.

"Lachlan," Erskine's lapdog said smoothly. "I missed you in London."

"I didn't know you were looking. We could have had tea."

Tucker smiled insincerely.

"Why are you here?"

Tucker's eyebrows went up. "You're a powerful vampire who recently left Scotland to visit North America. Your return naturally caught Lord Erskine's notice. He asked me to inquire as to your intentions."

"My intentions? This is my home. I wouldn't think my return to it would be noteworthy."

"You encountered some trouble on the highway," Tucker noted, changing subjects. "Our lord is curious as to your new enemies."

"What makes you think they're new?"

The vampire gave an elegant shrug. "You've been gone before and returned home without incident. And yet now, you bring a guest, and people are shooting at you. That raises questions."

Lachlan shrugged. "It was nothing but a robbery gone bad. The fools didn't realize who it was they were trying to run off the road until it was far too late."

"Vampire highway robbers? How very tawdry of them," Tucker said absently, seeming to have grown bored with the conversation, to the extent that Lachlan was sensing a marked downgrade in the other vampire's power profile.

He was beginning to think Tucker really had been sent to do nothing more than snoop around and discover what he could about Lachlan's recent activities. It was no surprise that Erskine knew about the visit with Raphael, but he must be desperate to learn what they'd discussed. Might sacrifice *anyone* to find out. Even Tucker? Erskine's lieutenant had been with him a long time, but he'd become too strong for the vampire lord's peace of mind. Erskine would probably be just as happy if Lachlan took him out of the picture.

His thoughts were jarred back to the room as Tucker abruptly swung around and stared directly at the spot where Julia stood hidden.

"You're being rude, Lachlan. Introduce me to your guest."

He was aware of Julia sucking in a breath, of her heart beginning to race, her gaze so fixed on Tucker that she didn't so much as glance Lachlan's way. She was more stressed than she should have been. Why? He slid his mind into hers, his telepathy more than strong enough to pick up her thoughts. He generally tried to avoid eavesdropping without permission, but Julia seemed to have no shields at all, something he'd have to work on with her if they stayed together long enough. He'd also taken her blood, which always made the connection easier. But when he touched her thoughts this time, they were so skittish, it took him a moment to make sense of them.

Finally, it became clear. She knew Tucker. Or, no, she didn't *know* him, but she did recognize him. From where, damn it? He couldn't ferret that out, and she was so stunned by whatever the context was that she wasn't focusing on anything but her shock at seeing him here.

"Don't worry about her," Lachlan growled, letting the words carry enough power that they forced Tucker to turn around and face him.

"Who is she?" he demanded, raising his own power to match.

"She's mine. That's all you need to know."

"American, right? Where'd you find her?"

Lachlan's attention focused on that first question. How would Tucker know Julia was American? "I told you, she's mine."

"You go to Malibu and come back with this woman whom you seem determined to conceal. And you make no secret of your hatred for Erskine, who is, I'll remind you, your rightful lord. He wants to meet this American who is such good friends with Raphael, and I'm here as his emissary. Don't stand in my way, or you'll regret it."

Lachlan reached to the depths of his soul, where his magic burned hot and bright, just waiting to be called from the darkness. With a thought, he unleashed the full weight of it, letting power flow over him, glittering like diamonds as it formed an adamantine shield. He caught the heavy blade tossed to him by Davie, while every one of his people drew weapons and stood at his back.

Tucker had reacted in the instant Lachlan first reached for his power, drawing his own magic to the fore, sliding his shields into place, a swirling shimmer of gray that surrounded him, constantly moving.

A novice seeing the two shields for the first time might have thought Tucker had the advantage. An active shield was more flexible in a fight, able to react faster to a specific attack. But that novice would have been wrong. Lachlan's shields looked like solid glass, as light skimmed over them in a sparkling dance. But they were, in fact, multiple points of power, so many that their edges crossed and overlapped, shifting in concert with his attacks, anticipating the enemy's counter, and instantly responsive to Lachlan's need. He'd spent the last century honing his technique, blending his already unrivaled fighting skills with his vampire abilities, until he was a truly formidable fighter. He'd always known he would go up against Erskine someday, had lived every day since his first waking as a vampire, preparing to take down the coward who'd destroyed his clan and murdered almost everyone he loved.

Tucker wasn't Erskine, but he belonged to him. Once again, Erskine was trying to destroy someone who mattered to him. He might not know yet if he loved Julia, but he *did* know that she was *his*, and no one was going to hurt her as long as he lived.

He'd planned to urge Julia out of the room with a focused telepathic push, but when he turned, he saw that she'd shoved her hood back and was no longer bothering to conceal her identity. She stood with legs braced, her left hand in a fist at her side, her right in the pocket where he knew she held her gun. With face set and eyes blazing, blatant rage had replaced the fear that had stunned her earlier. He was proud of and terrified for her in equal measure, and he knew she wouldn't go anywhere until this fight was ended. Nodding his acknowledgment of her support, he turned to Tucker, and the first challenge that would set him on the vampire throne of Scotland.

JULIA KNEW THE moment Lachlan decided to fight Tucker. She read it in the tensing of his muscles, the cold light in his eyes. She wanted to scream when whatever it was that had been an uncomfortable pressure before, now became a force that threatened to rip the skin from her flesh and break her bones. How did Lachlan survive it, standing in the very center of this horrific battle . . . of magic? Christ, a week ago, she'd have said such a thing didn't exist. Sure, vampires lived longer and healed faster, but there were all sorts of medical explanations for that.

But this, this whirlwind of something that had sucked so much oxygen from the room that the huge fire was nothing but ash, while she, the lone human, found herself forced to drag every breath of air into her lungs . . . what else could it be but magic? She whirled, gun up and ready, when a hand grabbed her arm. But it was Davie, who dropped his hand as soon as he had her attention.

"Julia, you have to come with me."

"I'm not leaving—"

"Nor am I, but you'll get hurt if you stand this close."

Julia glanced at the two combatants. They seemed to be doing nothing but staring at each other, but she knew there had to be more going on. The air around them was distorted, the way it seemed when looking through heat waves in the desert.

"Julia, please. Lachlan can't concentrate if he's worried about you."

That got through to her as nothing else would have. She nodded and followed Davie to the far wall of the big room, where the ceiling hung lower and the hallway crossed just behind. It was darker there, but it didn't matter. The two vampires were lit up like meteors in the night sky, power swirling around them, the pressure shoving aside furniture, knocking over lamps. Letting go of her gun for now, she clenched both hands in her pockets and tried to follow the battle that Lachlan was fighting . . . to defend her.

LACHLAN WASN'T surprised when Tucker launched a risky first attack. He'd seen the vampire fight before, and the vamp was both impatient and confident. The confidence was well-founded against most vampires, but he'd never come up against an opponent who matched him in strength. Tucker had been gifted with the power to be a vampire lord. But so had Lachlan.

He saw the blow coming and did nothing to repel it, letting Tucker believe he'd succeeded. The strike hit Lachlan's shield with the sizzling crack of two powerful forces colliding, and though his shield held, he took a faltering step back, feigning an injury that wasn't there.

Tucker bared his teeth in a victorious snarl, dark eyes gleaming like black marbles as he raised his hand in a tight fist, muscles bunching as he built power and prepared to strike the same spot on Lachlan's shield, thinking it weakened and vulnerable. Lachlan waited until his opponent's hand was clenched so tightly that his bones were threatening to tear through his flesh, then with no outward sign, he reached for his power. With no gesture, no warning, he formed it into a mighty cudgel and slammed it into Tucker's head. The vampire's shield buckled and threatened to give way as he staggered, his eyes giving away the shock he was feeling, even as he forced a confident grin. His next strike was immediate, but weaker than it should have been, meant more for show than effect, as he recovered from the powerful head blow. As long as shields held, they protected a vampire from death, but a strong enough strike could still do a lot of damage.

Lachlan seized on this vulnerability, a rare advantage against an opponent of Tucker's might, and one not to be ignored. He hit him a second time, using the identical technique, striking the same spot. Then, while standing nearly motionless and giving away no sign of his intent, he leveled a third devastating blow to the opposite side of Tucker's head. The vampire lieutenant staggered visibly, but recovered quickly enough. Shaking his head as if to dispel the deleterious effects, Tucker snarled and straightened to his full height, hands rolling to form a globe of shimmering force at his chest—a globe that sparked with power to Lachlan's magic-enhanced senses.

Lips drawn back over bare fangs, Tucker pulled his arm back and shoved the sphere forward, aiming it across the short distance separating them, like a shot put targeted directly at Lachlan's heart.

Lachlan braced himself for the blow, manipulating his shield to add protective layers over his heart, the one spot most vulnerable on any vampire, even one as powerful as he was. But that didn't mean he couldn't fight back at the same time. While Tucker was aiming his deadly weapon against Lachlan's shield, thinking to shatter it and punch through to the exposed organs underneath, Lachlan was preparing his counterattack. Gesturing broadly for the first time since they'd begun fighting, he arched his arms out and upward, hands cupped as if gathering power from the air itself, and then he waited. The instant he sensed Tucker launching his assault, he stepped right up to the other vampire and slammed both hands against his head so hard, and with so much contained power, that the walls around them shuddered at the tremendous energy released when his hands crashed through Tucker's shield.

His shields shredded, their power scattering, Tucker roared in fury. Ignoring the blood gushing from his skull, he fought back, his face twisted with hatred as he fired a close-range punch of power. It was a desperate blow, aimed at Lachlan's heart, but he was too damaged and too close to target effectively. Lachlan grunted when it struck his sternum, but his shields held as he continued pouring power into his hands and reached once more for Tucker's head. Gripping as tightly as he could, he squeezed . . . and broke through. Bone shattered. Shards driven by every ounce of power Lachlan could muster, pierced Tucker's brain.

He screamed in agonized despair as blood streamed from his ears and eyes, as pink brain matter oozed through the growing cracks in his shattered skull. But vampire lords, even potential ones, have enough power to heal even the most devastating injuries, so Lachlan took no chances. Pulling back one hand, he slammed his fist low into Tucker's rib cage, then reached up into the vampire's body and grabbed his frantically beating heart. With it pulsing in his grip, he ripped it from Tucker's chest, trailing arteries of still pumping blood, and crushed it into a pulpy mess, before using a lightning strike of power to utterly destroy it.

Holding it in front of him for all to see, he opened his fingers and let the dust fall to the floor. Tucker's body instantly followed his heart, dusting in death, as the vampire symbiote in his blood acknowledged the inevitability of its host's demise.

Lachlan stared at the place where Tucker used to be, legs braced against an exhaustion that was both physical and magical. If an enemy had come at him in that moment, he'd have been hard-pressed to put up a good fight. But that's why vampires of his strength had loyal children and supporters of their own. Davie and most of the others deployed around him, while the two who'd accompanied Tucker were unceremoniously escorted off the property. He knew they'd hightail it back to Erskine with news of Tucker's death, although the vampire lord wouldn't need their confirmation. Tucker wasn't Erskine's child, but he was sworn to him by blood. Erskine would have sensed Tucker's death the moment it happened. And since he knew whom his lieutenant had been sent to deal with, he'd also know who'd killed him.

Lachlan wasn't prepared to consider that just yet. Not until he'd had at least a few minutes to recover. And maybe a few bags of blood.

Although fresh would be better. He couldn't stop the thought from filling his head as Julia shoved her way through the surrounding vampires to his side. He did have the presence of mind to stop her from putting a supporting arm around him, or getting too close. He was covered in the blood and gore of his opponent, which was disgusting. But he was also still buzzing with power, as if he'd been plugged into the un-stoppered electrical flow of a giant condenser, then shoved aside. It was residual power, not altogether useful, but still enough to deliver a nasty shock to anyone, but especially a human, who touched him.

Julia drew back, brows drawn in puzzled offense, before her gaze scanned his bloody form. She nodded in seeming understanding and raced away, only to return a moment later, her hands filled with wet kitchen towels. Lachlan nodded his thanks, while thinking completely irrelevantly than Graeme was going to be pissed as hell when he showed up in the morning and found his best towels covered in blood . . . and other things.

But then Julia was there, gently wiping his face clean, *tsking* over the cuts and bruises, taking his hands in hers and cleaning them, one finger at a time. He was vaguely aware of Davie ordering the others to various guard positions, just in case there were more of Erskine's people waiting nearby.

Lachlan thought it unlikely, but he knew this wasn't the end of it. Erskine would have to react somehow. The only question was how. Would he come after Lachlan with full force, using his killing of Tucker as an excuse to get rid of a dangerous threat to his own rule? Or would he simply growl his displeasure, but take no action? After all, powerful vampires killed each other all the time. It was the Vampire way of life. That argument would provide cover for Erskine, giving him a valid reason to avoid confronting Lachlan himself. Because the truth was, the vampire lord had never been eager to challenge anyone who might kill him. That's why it was Tucker who'd been sent to fetch Julia. Erskine had to have at least suspected that Lachlan wouldn't give her up without a fight, and he hadn't been willing to risk it.

Now that Tucker was dead, Erskine might send another of his people to finish the task, but Tucker had been his lieutenant, the most powerful vampire in his retinue. If Lachlan had killed *him*, then he was likely to kill any lesser vamp that Erskine might send, and with greater ease.

Julia slid her hand into his at that moment, breaking into his thoughts. Looking down at their twined fingers, he lifted them to his mouth and kissed the back of her hand. When she slid her arm around his waist, he draped his over her shoulders, surprised by the strength in her delicate frame.

"I'm taking you to bed," she informed him quietly.

He gave her a wicked grin. "You'll get no argument from me, princess."

She snorted. "You're in no condition."

"I'm a vampire," he reminded her, pride unreasonably pricked. "I will be soon enough."

He adopted a casual stroll until they were inside the bedroom, with the door locked. Julia took over at that point, ushering him into the bathroom, turning on the hot water and letting it run as she stripped off his clothes. His cock reacted to her nearness—he couldn't imagine ever being *that* tired—but she ignored it, simply shoving him under the hot water and closing the door to keep the heat in. Lachlan was miffed at first, but the pounding water felt so damn good on his various wounds and muscles that he groaned in pleasure.

The glass door opened at that moment to admit a very naked Julia.

"Did you start without me?" she asked, eyeing his straining cock as she closed the door. Stretching upward, she kissed him, but didn't linger. Instead, she soaked the wash cloth she'd brought in with her, then rubbed it with soap and proceeded to wash his body with firm but gentle strokes. He thought about telling her he could wash his own damn body, but decided it was much nicer to have her do it for him, wondering if this was only for post-battle occasions, or if he could persuade her to be his shower slave all the time. Probably better if he didn't phrase it quite like that, then he sucked in a breath when she knelt, took hold of his cock with soapy hands, and began washing *that* with careful strokes, too, one hand reaching even farther to take care of his balls. Closing his eyes, both arms outstretched and braced against the shower wall, head hanging between them, he fought the urge to drag Julia off her feet and fuck her senseless. Or even better, to fist his hand in her wet hair and show her what she could do for him while on her knees.

By the time she had finished with the soap and was using the hand-held nozzle to wash away the foam, he was hard as a fucking rock. Taking the handheld from her, he slipped it into the bracket, then looped an arm around her waist and lifted her up for a hungry kiss. He crushed her lips with his, his tongue sweeping in as he slammed her against the shower wall, and pressed his full body against her. She responded with fervor, her tongue fighting his, moaning as she pulled him even closer. Fuck, but he loved the way she moaned. It was soft and sweet, but laced with a raw sexuality that made his cock ache to be inside her. He kissed her harder, moving his hand down her side, circling her hip to slide between her body and the wall, caressing one rounded globe of her ass as his fingers stroked farther downward to push between the swollen lips of her sex.

Julia gave a small cry of surprise, the sound filling his mouth as he plunged two fingers into her body, feeling her pussy clench at the intrusion, the slick cream of her arousal hotter than the steamy water streaming over their bodies.

"Fuck," he cursed when she bit his lip, the sharp pain almost driving him into orgasming against her belly. No way in hell. Pulling his fingers out of her sweet warmth, he ignored her soft complaint to grip her thigh and position it higher on his hip. She brought her other leg up to match and crossed her legs behind him, thrusting her hips in invitation. One hand on her ass and the other squeezing a full breast, nipple pinched between thumb and forefinger, he slipped between her thighs and slammed his full length into her tight, tight body.

He slid out and back in a few times, until she was completely open to him, then plunged as deep as he could go, until his cock touched her cervix and his balls slapped her flesh with every thrust. Growling with the burning need to possess her, he shifted both hands to grip her butt cheeks, holding them tightly and arching her body upward to give him better access, letting him go deeper with every demanding shove. Julia's arms squeezed closer when he lowered his mouth to her neck and bit down, his muscles shuddering at the rush of her sweet blood while she held on, her mouth pressed against his skin and screaming into his shoulder.

Riding a surge of victorious fury, driven by the knowledge that he'd defended her, that she was *his*, he lifted his bloody mouth from her neck, and began to pound into her, ignoring the hard tile wall, hearing only her soft cries of pleasure as he fucked her, her slick inner muscles shivering with desire, caressing and stroking, coaxing him to come, to claim the ultimate victor's prize.

With a snarling roar, he climaxed deep inside her body, his release more than simple passion as his power reacted at the same time, collapsing back down to its hiding place deep within his body, while Julia orgasmed around him, her sheath squeezing his cock so hard he feared she'd never let go. Until, with another of those soft, sexy moans, she fell limp against him, her arms loose around his neck, her face still buried against his shoulder as her heart pounded.

Holding them both under the hot water, he washed away the fluids of their fucking, then stepped out, wrapped her in a big towel, carried her to the bed, and laid her on the cool sheets. Grabbing another towel for himself, he dried off quickly and climbed in next to her. She smiled, murmuring wordlessly, when he pulled her against him and tossed her towel to the floor. Yanking the covers up before she could get cold, he kissed her forehead, then settled back against the pillows with her in his arms, eyes closed as he drew a deep, relaxing breath.

He didn't intend to sleep, but he was tired, and she was sweet and soft in his arms. And while he slept, the sun rose and his sleep became something else as the vampire symbiote demanded its due. It did what it must to survive, healing, preparing for the next battle to come. The one destined from the moment he'd first awakened on that first agonizing night.

The one that would make him a vampire lord.

Chapter Eleven

JULIA ROLLED LAZILY when she woke, feeling warm and sated. There was a feeling a woman's body got when it had been thoroughly fucked. Or at least, *her* body got that way. The sensations always lingered for a little while, even after she woke and got started on her day. She wasn't in any hurry to do the getting started part tonight, though. Lachlan was in his deep sleep, and the estate was quiet around them. It made sense that a vampire's estate would run on vampire time.

Her stomach growled, and she considered going to the kitchen, but decided it was too much trouble. She pulled the covers up more tightly and grabbed her e-reader, then tucked her back into Lachlan's side and started reading. Or she tried. She soon discovered she was too drowsy to read more than a sentence or two, before her eyes wanted to drift shut. She put the reader down and simply enjoyed. It was rare for her to lie in bed doing nothing. Back home, she woke early, worked long hours, worked out at the gym or home, then went back to sleep and started all over again the next morning. Even weekends were busy, with more exercise, social obligations, and as often as not, more work.

The next thing she knew, events of the previous night began playing at high speed in her brain, like a cartoon on a candy high. She didn't know if she was dreaming or drifting, but when the cartoon got to those last few minutes, when Lachlan and Tucker had been beating the hell out of each other with invisible weapons, the fast forward suddenly ground to a halt, and all she could see was the face of a man she'd never met before, but that looked way too familiar. She'd seen Tucker's face somewhere. Her eyes popped open. Hell, she'd never sleep now. Not until she figured out where the hell . . .

She let out a small scream of discovery, shooting Lachlan a quick guilty glance, before remembering he wasn't truly asleep, then jumping off the bed and hurrying to her laptop case. Because suddenly, she remembered where she'd seen Tucker before.

An hour later, she was sitting at the desk, shuffling through papers from Masoud's blue file. She'd found Tucker's picture in there. Just one, and taken from a distance, but he'd clearly been meeting secretly with Masoud. She didn't know what it meant. Maybe he'd turned snitch on his boss for personal gain. Although she didn't see how jeopardizing Erskine's money would help him. It wasn't like Erskine would be going to jail. Masoud's father would never have permitted him to take it that far. The scandal would splash back on them and hurt their own profits. So why . . . ?

She threw down the picture and rubbed her eyes. Why the hell was she wasting time staring at a photo which told her nothing, when there was a gorgeous man in her bed? Well, mostly because the gorgeous man was a vampire and so not exactly . . . *available* at the present moment. She laughed and began gathering the various pages, trying to put them in some order for Lachlan later that night, after she told him about Tucker.

Her smile faded when her gaze fell one particular page. It was filled with Masoud's familiar script, the too-tidy writing of a mathematician who valued precision above all things. He'd been the youngest son of a controlling father, who'd already had grandchildren by the time Masoud was born. Raised to be more of a tiny adult than a child, he'd been hungry to be around children his own age when their families had first met. The three of them—Masoud, Julia, and her brother, Matthew—had been too young to be anything other than playmates, despite the two-year age difference between her and the boys. But as they'd grown older, and Masoud's father had pressured him to be increasingly studious, he'd been drawn to what, back then, had been Julia's free spirit, and too frequently cajoled into taking part in her schemes. Like the time they'd ditched their respective schools and spent the day on the indoor ski slopes of Abu Dhabi, or when they'd flown to Paris, not realizing how far it was and that they'd never be back before their parents missed them. They'd both gotten in serious trouble that time, but even Masoud had admitted it had been worth it. They'd had such a great time that no matter how many times she'd been to Paris since, the visits still paled next to the great Paris escape.

Of course, the crazy adventures ended once her mom and Matthew died. After that, her father had been so damn sad that Julia had done everything she could to be the perfect daughter, to make his life easier, especially once she'd understood that he was afraid of losing her, too. There were no more crazy adventures that would make him worry or have teachers calling to complain. No more risks. Not even the tiny ones, like crossing in the middle of the block to avoid the extra few yards of walking home.

Masoud hadn't said anything, though she'd always suspected he'd missed the crazy version of her. He'd even talked her into mild acts of rebellion, like drinking champagne along the Champs-Elysées on New Year's Eve, while reminiscing about the great Paris escape. Of course, everyone around them had been drinking, too, but since it was illegal, they could, strictly speaking, have been arrested. That was what passed for crazy by then, with Masoud all about his father-approved mathematical studies, and Julia, just as dutifully, following her father's footsteps to Washington.

She leaned her head on her hand with a sigh and felt the familiar twinge of guilt. Masoud had loved her so much. He'd planned their lives together. She'd loved him, too. Just not . . . . She raised her gaze to where Lachlan slept soundly and sighed again. Not the way she loved Lachlan.

JULIA WAS SLEEPING dreamlessly when Lachlan woke the next night. She knew this because one moment there was nothing, and the next, there were strong fingers gripping her hip and rolling her under a big warm body. "Lachlan," she murmured, still half asleep when his heavy weight settled between her legs and his lips went to her neck.

"What the hell are you wearing?" he muttered as a hand roamed over her breasts and down, insinuating between her thighs and pushing, to make room for him.

"Lachlan." It came out as a moan this time, when his penis, already thick and hard, pushed against flesh that was still tender from their earlier lovemaking, and yet soaking wet with arousal. When he reached down and positioned the tip of his erection against her opening, she didn't even have to think about a response. Her hips thrust upward automatically, eliciting a gasp when he met her move with a hard thrust of his own, sending his cock so deep into her that his balls slapped her butt. Lachlan hissed out a breath and ground his groin against her clit, the pressure so intense on the swollen bud that she thought she'd come right then. But he didn't let her. Seeming to understand what she was feeling, he lifted his hips at the last minute, making Julia want to scream at him for stopping.

"Patience, princess," he whispered against her ear, as he continued pushing himself in and out of her body, but being exquisitely careful not to brush against her aching clit.

"Patience, my ass," she muttered and wrapped her legs around his narrow hips. She wasn't a vampire, but she wasn't weak. Crossing her legs at the ankle, she held on to him tightly, forcing him to remain close.

Lachlan chuckled. "I love your ass. Want to do that next?"

A genuine snarl poured out of her throat as she flexed hard and rolled, succeeding in reversing their positions only because she'd surprised him. Putting both hands on her hips, he continued thrusting upward as she rubbed herself against him until she was breathless, hands squeezing her own breasts, pinching her nipples to painful hardness as she writhed above him.

"That's a fine sight," he growled, then flexed those fabulous abs and sat up, putting his arms around her, crushing her breasts against his hard chest and lowering his mouth to her neck once more.

Julia couldn't breathe, didn't want to. She wanted all her focus, every perception she possessed, on her vampire lover as his fangs sliced into her skin and pierced her vein, as she felt the first strong pull of her blood, heard his groan of pleasure at the exact moment every nerve in her body came to life, slamming her into the most intense orgasm of her life. She held onto him, her arms tight around his neck, her thighs tight where they straddled him . . . and shuddering with ecstasy when the liquid heat of his climax filled her, and they tumbled together into erotic bliss.

LACHLAN ROLLED to his side with Julia in his arms, trying to remember if he'd ever felt this kind of pleasure with a woman before. He'd been alive a long time, had enjoyed many lovers, so many it was possible he'd forgotten a few. But he didn't think he'd ever experienced such an *intense* sexual experience. Being inside Julia, feeling her body tremble around him, her pussy clutch at him with such vicious passion . . . . It was tempting to simply grab her and run. To forget about duty and responsibility and . . . . He closed his eyes, swallowing the sigh trying to force its way out of his lungs. It was pointless to think like that. He'd never do it. Too many people he cared about depended on him. His entire life, even before he'd been made Vampire, had been about responsibility to the clan. He couldn't change now. He didn't want to.

Deep within his embrace, Julia bit his shoulder.

"Careful there. If you break the skin, you'll be orgasming all over me again."

Her mouth opened, her breath hot against his skin when she said, "Really? You mean I don't have to put up with your torture when you bring me to the edge and let me hang there?"

He grinned. "You want me to stop?"

She punched his side, but was too close to put any power into it. "Let go of me."

He dipped his head down and licked her neck, sending a full-body shiver rolling over her skin. "You taste good."

"Lachlan," she said in a breathy groan. "We—" Her throat moved under his mouth as she swallowed. "We have to talk."

He scowled, not liking the sound of that. "About what?" His tone might have been a bit too unhappy, because her shiver this time wasn't one of pleasure. He lifted his head immediately and cupped her face in both hands, pushing sweat-damp hair away from her face. "Did something happen today? Tell me."

She shook her head and caught her breath, one hand reaching up to grip his wrist, as if to hold him close. "It's not bad. It's just . . ." She paused to take a deep breath, before continuing. "I recognized Tucker last night. I've seen him before."

Lachlan stilled to silent attention, but didn't let go of her.

"It wasn't me," she said quickly. "I mean, I didn't see him in person. He's in Masoud's files." Her eyes lifted to meet his. "I think he might have been giving Masoud information to help track Erskine's money laundering."

"Why would he do that?"

"I don't know," she said, with a shrug. "I thought maybe *you* would."

"Vampires are like humans when it comes to money. There's never enough. But if Tucker's goal was to knock Erskine off the throne, the last thing he should have wanted was for anyone to claw back Erskine's money. Maybe he and your Masoud had plans to split it when—"

"Absolutely not," she snapped, pushing away from him, until they were no longer touching. "Masoud would *never* be a part of something like that."

Lachlan studied her a moment, fighting a possessive rage that had nowhere to go. Was he jealous of a dead man? A ghost could be a powerful competitor, his flaws forgotten in the memory of those who'd loved him. "Did you love him?" he asked flatly, needing an answer.

Julia bit the inside of her lip, tears spilling over when she met his gaze. "Not the way he wanted me to," she admitted, as if it was a dirty secret, a terrible failing. "I found the ring in his safe after he died," she whispered, her cheeks wet as silent tears continued to flow. "He wanted to marry me. That's why he took the job, why he left the US."

"He wanted you to move with him?"

She shook her head. "He would have lived wherever I wanted. But when I said no, he took the job in London. And now he's dead, because of me. Because I couldn't love him enough."

"Fuck that," he snarled and pulled her close, ignoring her protests until finally she put her arms around him and held on tight. "You're not responsible for his choices. *He* chose to leave rather than fight for you. *He* chose to dig into Erskine's finances. You know how these things work. He could have turned it over to someone else, could have brought in a whole team to work on the problem. Why didn't he?"

She shook her head, her silky hair rubbing over his chest. "I don't know."

"I sure as hell don't, either, but I *do* know one thing. I'd follow you to the ends of the earth before I'd let you go."

She pulled back to look up at him, her eyes wet, nose bright pink, and just as beautiful as ever. "What if I don't want to go anywhere?"

He smiled. "Well, you know how I hate flying."

She nodded and gave him a watery smile in return. "You whined the whole time."

"I did not. Maybe I'll let you go after all," he grumbled.

"Please don't," she said softly and hugged him, settling her weight against his for a long silent moment. Then she sighed. "What do we do about Tucker?"

"Whatever Tucker was up to, he's no longer an issue. I'm more interested in how Erskine reacts to his death."

"Will he know by now?"

He nodded. "Tucker took a blood oath. Erskine didn't need anyone to tell him his lieutenant was dead. It's a vampire thing," he added when she gave him a questioning look. "We're connected to our vampire children—that's the vampires we personally turn—and to any vampire who's taken our blood in an oath of fealty. We feel their death deeply."

"You're head of your clan, right?"

"Aye, though there's a distaff branch that owns the castle for the tourists. It was in ruins long before I was born. They came along and restored it. And we had no quarrel. If anything, it was better for us. Foreigners looking to find their roots go to the castle, rather than looking for us."

"But the clan you were born into is yours, and you have a lot more vampires than when you were turned. So that means . . . how many vampire children do you *have*?"

He gave her a long, serious look. "Every McRae vampire alive is mine," he said quietly. "The only exceptions are Fergus and Munro, because they were turned on the same night I was. But they've sworn a blood oath to me as their lord, so we're bound by two ties of blood."

"All of them?" she asked, going back to her original question. "How many are there?"

"Fewer than 50 are sworn to me. But not all of my vampires are McRae. Others have taken a blood oath over the years, for reasons of their own." It was a slightly vague answer, but the instinct to maintain his secrets and protect the clan ran too deeply to be easily set aside. Even for the woman he was beginning to love.

She absorbed that information without looking at him, then lifted her head and asked solemnly, "Will it be a long war between you and Erskine?"

He shook his head. "This isn't an ordinary squabble. It's a challenge for the territory. No matter what he does, it'll very quickly come down to a duel between the two of us."

"But I get to be there," she said stubbornly. "Even if it barely hurts him, I get to shoot that fucker. You promised."

His jaw clenched. "You saw what it was like with Tucker. This will be worse. And Erskine will kill you, just because he can. And because he knows it will weaken me."

She scowled, then brightened. "I'll stay out of the way, just like I did last night. He won't even know I'm there."

Lachlan seriously considered locking her away in Killilan until the showdown with Erskine was over with. But she'd probably never forgive him, and he *had* promised. "All right, but you'll follow my orders to the letter, or I'll lock you up and leave you behind. You might hate me, but at least you'll be alive."

She gave him a sweet smile that he didn't trust for a minute. "I'm yours to command, my lord."

He leveled a narrow-eyed glare at her, which had no effect at all. "Come on, princess," he said, pulling her out of bed as he stood. "There's a few things I want to teach you while we still have time."

Or so he'd thought. His plans were sidetracked when Erskine sent a message, although it was phrased as more of a demand. The vampire lord's messenger was at his gate an hour after sunset, with an order for Lachlan to present himself to his lord. It grated on Lachlan's nerves to be summoned like a peasant, or even worse, reminded that Erskine was—whether he liked it or not—Vampire Lord over Scotland, with the power to order his appearance. But he had neither choice nor excuse. Especially with that fucking Erskine having decided to pay one of his rare visits to Inverness, a city that, given the vampire lord's infrequent visits, Lachlan considered to be his own.

"What is it?"

He cringed inwardly at Julia's question. She'd want to go with him to Erskine's, and there was no way in hell he could permit that. "It's a summons from Erskine. He probably wants to discuss Tucker's death."

She put a hand on his arm. "Will he punish you?"

Lachlan met her concerned gaze with a look that probably showed more love than was wise at this point, but he couldn't help it. "He doesn't have the power to punish me, princess. If he tried it, I'd fight back, and he might lose. He won't take that risk."

"Why call you in, then?"

"He'll make a show of it for his lackeys. Posture before the court and send me away."

"Okay. Let me finish getting dressed, and—"

He turned to face her directly and placed his hands on her arms. "You can't come with me tonight, Julia. It's not safe."

"*You're* going!"

"He didn't try to kidnap *me*. And we still don't know why he wants *you*. But that's not the reason. There won't be any humans allowed, not until after business is taken care of."

"So I'll wait in the car, then."

"Ah, no you won't. The after-business humans will be there for one purpose only. And you're not available."

She shrugged. "I'm not helpless. I wouldn't let anyone touch me."

He laughed. "*I* wouldn't let anyone touch you. But why dangle such a delectable morsel as yourself in front of an asshole like Erskine?"

She gave him a disgusted look. "Flattery, is it?"

"It's the God's own truth."

"Right. Who're you taking with you?"

"Fergus will be with me."

She made a face that conveyed reluctant approval. "Fine. But just so you know, this won't work the next time."

"And I'm a man of my word. When I kill Erskine, you'll be there."

Julia went up on her toes and kissed him. "Don't leave tonight without saying good-bye."

"*YE 'N' JULIA UR getting close.*" Fergus's statement was an observation, not a question.

Lachlan glanced away from the road long enough to judge his

cousin's expression. "Aye," he agreed, waiting for more.

"*Ye think that's wise?*"

"*Women ur ne'er wise, cousin. Ye ken that. What dae ye purely wantae say?*"

Fergus sighed. "*She's American 'n' works for their CIA. Not the best lassie fur a Scottish vampire laird.*"

Lachlan stopped at an intersection and stared at his cousin. "You think she'll spill our secrets to her government?" he asked, forgoing the Scottish slang of their usual friendly banter to make his point. "It's not as if they have no vampires of their own to gawk at. Raphael and the other American lords are like movie stars over there. Their pictures are on the society pages."

"Taking pictures in fancy gowns is very different than divulging private matters," Fergus responded in the same vein.

"Julia's not going to tell anyone what she knows. Besides, she doesn't know that much."

"She will if she hangs around long enough. She's smart."

"Fergus, I love you like a cousin—"

"I am your cousin, you arse."

"—but stay out of my love life. And don't be saying any of this shite to Julia, either."

He could feel Fergus's gaze on him and waited, knowing there was more his cousin wanted to say.

"You really do like her," he finally said with amazement.

"She's mine. Leave it at that." He was claiming Julia as his own a lot lately. It made him wonder what *she'd* think about it.

But it made Fergus throw up his hands in surrender. "Whatever you say. Now, what about tonight and our beloved lord?"

"He'll want to know how Tucker died," Lachlan said with a shrug. "We'll tell him and be done with it."

More plans forced awry, Lachlan thought an hour later when they'd finally passed through Erskine's paranoid number of checkpoints and were escorted into the great lord's presence. Erskine wasn't like some of the European lords he'd heard rumors about—those who put themselves on thrones and made everyone else stand in their presence. Or who surrounded themselves with guards as if they were too weak to defend themselves. In fact, someone who'd never met Erskine might have trouble figuring out which one he was in the crowded room filled with vampires. At first glance, it was more like a cocktail reception than a vampire lord's receiving room. But study it long enough and the truth emerged.

The attention of every vampire in the room was on Erskine. If one watched carefully enough, it became obvious who he was. And if you were a vampire, you didn't need to watch. An aura of power surrounded him if one had the eyes to see it. A combination of his personal power and the power of a territorial lord. Erskine could have contained it, if he'd wanted to conceal his identity. But he enjoyed his position and the attention it brought. If Erskine had a flaw, besides being a murdering thug who sent humans to slaughter opposing vampires while they slept, it was his overweening ego.

That would be his downfall, Lachlan thought, as he watched vampires circulate around the vampire lord. His belief in his own superiority. A belief he'd carry with him into death when Lachlan executed him for the murder of his clan.

"Lachlan." Erskine was all good cheer, as if they hadn't been enemies for generations. "Good of you to come so quickly. And Fergus, good to see you." Erskine was always very precise in his language, still fancying himself an English lord. No Highland brogue for him.

Fergus didn't feel the need Lachlan did to make a pretense of being polite. He simply stared at Erskine like he would a bug in his whisky.

"Always the loyal one, aren't you?" Erskine sneered. "The day will come, never fear." Dismissing Fergus with a glance, he turned back to Lachlan. "Come," he said, walking away. "We need to talk. Not you, Fergus. Just Lachlan. He'll be perfectly safe."

Lachlan shared a look with Fergus that said, yes, he'd be perfectly safe, but only because he'd make sure of it himself. The day he trusted his safety to Erskine was the day he'd surrender his own life and walk into the sun.

Erskine led him to what would have been the sunroom in a human dwelling, with windows filling the top half of three walls. A door led out to a beautifully maintained garden, visible in the bright wash of landscape lighting. Lachlan doubted Erskine spent much time out there, but it kept up the appearance of a normal home in this upscale Inverness neighborhood. Vampires preferred to keep a low profile, regardless of their growing acceptance among more progressive societies.

"Sit, please," Erskine said, indicating the chair next to his own.

Lachlan wasn't happy with that glass wall behind him, but he sat anyway. If Erskine wanted to kill him, he wouldn't do it in his own sunroom, with Lachlan an invited guest. He was much more a knife-in-the-back sort.

"So," the vampire lord began, "Tucker is no longer with us. A shame, really. He was a good lieutenant, strong and loyal, both."

"Not as loyal as you think," Lachlan commented, thinking about the dead vampire's meetings with Masoud. "Killing me would have cleared the field for when he came after you."

"But you killed him instead, thus saving my life in a way."

"Careful, Erskine, you're admitting he could have taken you."

His eyes burned with fury at the insult for a bare instant, before his gaze shuttered, and he shrugged. "I find myself in need of a new lieutenant." Continuing when Lachlan remained silent, he said, "The position requires someone like Tucker, maybe even stronger. The world is changing around us, the humans more aware than ever before."

"Humans worry you?"

Erskine eyed him intently, trying to determine if he'd been insulted yet again. Apparently deciding not, he answered. "They're a nuisance, but a clever one. They need to be kept out of our business."

"Agreed."

"I hoped you would. You're aware of this American woman, Julia Harper, who's been nosing into my affairs."

"I know her. She's not the one doing the nosing, however. It was her dead boyfriend."

"But she's got his files, and she works for the American spy agency. She needs to disappear."

Lachlan's gut clenched at the undisguised threat to Julia's life. But all he said was, "I don't see how she's a threat. Killing her might raise more issues than not."

"Maybe you have another reason for keeping her alive, heh? The two of you took a vacation recently, and she's a very beautiful woman."

He quirked an eyebrow. "There are many beautiful women in the world. Replacing one is hardly the issue. I'm more concerned with the blowback from killing this particular woman. Blowback that could fall on every vampire in Scotland. She's the only child of a very wealthy American, who also happens to be extremely well connected to their government."

"So you've investigated her."

"Of course, I have," he said, feigning insult. "You think I invite just anyone into my bed?"

Erskine chuckled appreciatively, which made Lachlan want to punch him. But he continued his deception, speaking with slow deliberation. "The point is, I'm not going to kill such a woman without good cause. Tell me what's worth that risk."

Erskine made a face as if he'd drunk bad blood. "I told you, she has Masoud bin Abu's files on my affairs, the *territory's* affairs, including details that could compromise not only Scottish vampires, but vampires around the world. Those files should never have fallen into his thieving hands, but they did and now *she's* got them. I want her dead, and I want those damn files."

He abruptly leaned forward to study Lachlan, his gaze eerily intense as he said, "Let's get serious, McRae. I want you to be my new lieutenant. You're stronger than Tucker. Smarter, too. You and I could rule all of the United Kingdom together."

"Quinn might have something to say about that," he replied mildly. "Not to mention Norwood down in London," he added, referring to the longtime Vampire Lord of England.

"So we'll let Quinn keep Northern Ireland," Erskine said indifferently, as if any of this were up to him. "But we'll take England. Norwood's never been a strong ruler."

Lachlan met the other vampire's fevered gaze. "Are you seriously planning this?"

Erskine waved a glib hand as he sat back in his chair. "Long-term planning, but then, we're vampires. We have the luxury of planning for centuries to come."

He was privately amused by the way the vampire lord seemed to swing between fearing humans on one hand, while dismissing powerful vampires on the other, but he only nodded without comment.

"What do you say?" Erskine asked.

For a moment, Lachlan thought he was asking about the proposed takeover of Scotland, Wales, and England, along with the various and assorted isles and islands. But he quickly realized that wasn't what Erskine was asking. He wanted Lachlan's response to the job offer.

"Our two clans don't have an amiable history," Lachlan said, giving the vampire lord what should have been an unnecessary reminder. "Why would you think to ally with us now?"

"Bah! That was almost two centuries ago. A new world demands new alliances. Think what we could do together."

Lachlan adopted a thoughtful expression, as if he was really considering this ridiculous scheme. The day McRae joined with Erskine Ross would be the end of their clan's honor, with a well-deserved slide into the dustbin of history after that. Maybe that was Erskine's plan, but he couldn't help thinking the timing of this offer was far too convenient. Either the bastard really did need him, or it was all a ruse to head off a future challenge for Scotland itself.

"I'm flattered, Erskine," he said finally. "But I'll need to think on it. It's not only me who'd be—"

"You're their chief, aren't you? It's the clan's duty to follow you."

What had been suspicion flared to flat-out warning. Erskine wasn't only set on getting McRae onboard. He wanted it in a hurry.

"They follow," Lachlan told the other vampire, "because they trust me. And they trust, because I value their advice."

"Well, I'm disappointed. But I understand your position. You became chieftain by default, after all. And you're still young for it."

Lachlan had to fight the urge to roll his eyes. How stupid did Erskine think he was to fall for such word games? He was nearly two hundred, not twenty. If he hadn't already been planning to kill this fucker, he might have done it now, just on principle. He stood abruptly. "If there's nothing else, I'll be leaving, then. My people are unsettled by the violence of Tucker's challenge. I'm still not quite clear why he did it, but that's neither here nor there. I'll get back to you—"

"What about the other?" Erskine's question was fired like a bullet, all pretense of friendship gone.

"The other, my lord?"

The vampire lord didn't stand, didn't even meet Lachlan's gaze head-on. "I want Julia Harper dead. If you don't have the *baws* for it," he snarled, using, in his anger, what, for him, was an unusual bit of Scottish slang for a man's balls, "I'll find someone who does."

Lachlan regarded him silently. Did the fool truly believe it would be that simple? Deciding on plain words since the roundabouts of diplomatic language weren't making his intent clear, he said, "I will not murder Julia Harper for you. If you find someone who will . . . *try*, they will not succeed." Having made his position as clear as he could, while still getting himself and Fergus out of the house without a fight, he spun on his heel and strode out into the main room. Fergus had been near at hand, waiting at the hallway's end, in the event he was needed. One look at Lachlan's face and he understood. Falling into step, they hurried, without looking as if they were doing so, through the gathering and out into the damp night.

Lachlan had parked the Range Rover near the gate at the exit end of the horseshoe driveway, anticipating the need for a quick getaway. Not because they couldn't make quick work of getting to the vehicle—they had vampire speed on their side, after all—but because he hadn't wanted the SUV to be boxed in. If it came down to it, he'd have smashed through any cars in his way without remorse. But that would have damaged the Rover, too, and he was rather fond of it.

Once on the road, he kept one eye on the rearview mirror for the first several minutes, but didn't see anyone following. "Call the house," he ordered Fergus, as an unwelcome thought intruded.

His cousin didn't ask any questions, just did as asked. "Munro," he said, without pleasantries. "Any problems?"

Lachlan's vampire hearing picked up Munro's reply of, "Quiet as a mouse," as easily as if the vampire had been sitting in the car with them. "Should I be worried?"

At Fergus's questioning look, Lachlan answered Munro's question. "It was an odd meeting. I'll brief you when we get there. Where's Julia?"

"Right here with me. You want to talk to—?"

"No. But keep her there, within sight."

"Of course, my lord. ETA?"

"Ten minutes. Maybe less."

"I'll let the guards know you're coming in hot."

Fergus hung up, then said grimly, "All of this tonight was just so Erskine could threaten Julia?"

Lachlan couldn't help noticing that his cousin now had his hackles up over the threat to Julia, when he'd spent much of the ride over questioning her presence in their lives. Apparently, all it took to relieve Fergus's concerns was having Erskine want her dead.

"Among other things. But I just can't figure out why he's so set on killing her. Why not simply steal the files and be done with it?"

"Files can be copied. And she's a smart woman—she'd still know everything that was in them. What the hell *is* in them, anyway?"

"He claims it's critical data that could end up hurting vampires worldwide. *Worldwide*. I'm insulted at his low opinion of my intellect. No question he's just covering his own ass. I just wish I knew why. Although there is one thing I know for sure—we have to be ready. Because Lord fucking Erskine isn't going to be happy with me after tonight."

JULIA HADN'T NEEDED to hear what Lachlan had said to Munro to know there was trouble, and that it involved her. Munro was a genius, just as Lachlan had said, but he'd make a terrible spy. He'd been on her like white on rice ever since that call, going so far as to linger by the door when she used the bathroom. She didn't bother asking him what was going on. Even if he knew, Lachlan probably would have ordered him not to tell, wanting to talk to her himself. More likely, though, Munro didn't know, either. Lachlan couldn't have grown up with his cousin and *not* known what a lousy liar he was.

She considered going back to the bedroom for some privacy, if nothing else, but didn't want to make Munro sit in the hallway to keep watch. Besides, the one piece of news Munro had imparted was that the guys would be home in minutes, so she could wait until Lachlan explained what the fuck was going on. And he would. She understood he wanted to protect her like the delicate "princess" he called her, but not this time. Not when it involved her personally. She could take care of herself in most situations, but not if she was kept ignorant of the threat.

So she sat in front of her open laptop and pretended to work, while listening for the sound of Lachlan's arrival. The moment she heard his voice, she stood with a wave of relief so strong, she had to fight the need to sit down again. What kept her standing was the determination *not* to look like a delicate fucking princess.

When he walked into the room, his gaze went right to her and stayed there, as he strode over, grabbed her hand, and pulled her away from the table and down the hall to their bedroom. Julia didn't bother protesting this caveman-like behavior. It wouldn't do any good, and if she *was* going to say something, she'd do it in private, not in front of a roomful of vampires with bat-like hearing.

Once in the bedroom with the door closed, he simply put his arms around her and held on tightly. She was happy to do the same, but it worried her. What the hell had happened with that bastard Erskine? "Lachlan?"

Pulling back enough just enough to tug her head back, he kissed her in that slow, delicious way of his, making love to her with his mouth as thoroughly as he did everything else. When he finally let her catch her breath, she gave him a worried look. "What happened?"

When she read defiance in his unusual eyes, she scowled and said, "Lachlan, tell me what the fuck happened."

He grinned. "I love it when you talk dirty."

"And I hate it when you treat me like an idiot. Talk."

He sighed long and deeply, the poor put-upon vampire. Then without letting go of her, said, "He offered me Tucker's job."

"He wants you to be his lieutenant?" she asked, making no attempt to mask her disbelief.

"Yeah. There's just one catch. He wants me to kill you first."

Her breath left her in a rush, and she gripped his arm.

"I told him I wouldn't do it," he hurried to add, as if she'd thought he would.

"I know that," she whispered. "But I still don't get it. Did he say why?"

"No. I pushed for an answer, but he wouldn't tell me anything we don't already know. He insists it's about Masoud's files and your government position, but he's lying. There's something else, something he doesn't want me to know."

She sighed. "It can't be anything to do with *me*, but the only other question is whatever Tucker was doing with Masoud, and he's already dead. Munro's still—"

Lachlan was shaking his head. "It's too late for that. Erskine's reasons don't matter anymore. He's not getting you. Come on."

Still holding her hand, they walked back to the dining room where Munro was frowning at his laptop, fingers flying over the keys. It was Fergus who looked up and said, "Are we staying put?"

"I was thinking Killilan," Lachlan replied.

"Best if we leave tonight, then, while Erskine's got a houseful of vamps just waiting to kiss his ass, and a healthy supply of blood donors on hand."

Lachlan snorted. "You're right. By now, half those vamps are so glutted with blood and sex that they'd be useless in a fight. Brief Davie. Tell him—"

"Lachlan," Munro called distractedly, his attention still fixed on his computer screen. "Take a look at this."

The three of them moved around the table to read over his shoulder. "I've been digging into Julia's family history, specifically—"

"Mine?" Julia demanded. "Why would you do that?"

Munro finally looked up. "Erskine wants you dead. Don't you want to know why?" he asked, appearing genuinely puzzled.

Her lips flattened with irritation. Sure she wanted to know why, but it would have been nice if he'd asked before snooping into her family. "What did you find?"

He shook his head a little, as if *she* was the one being unreasonable. "Your dad's the only *human* stockholder in Raphael Enterprises. Did you know that?"

"No, but I don't know specifics about any of his finances." She glanced from one vampire to the other, all with expressions that told her she was missing something. "Does that matter? What's Raphael—?" It struck her then. "Oh. Raphael Enterprises, as in Vampire Lord Raphael. What's that, his holding company or something?"

Lachlan nodded grimly. "Or something. Show me," he told Munro, who started pulling up images and financial reports, layering them one over the other.

Julia leaned over his shoulder. Although she couldn't follow Masoud's labyrinthine transaction trail, she *could* read a financial report. But Munro was bringing up so many images and reports, and they were coming so fast, that she gave up trying to read the numbers and focused on the photos. "Stop!"

Munro froze with his fingers suspended over the keys as he slowly turned his head to look up at her.

"Who's that?" she asked, pointing at an image two layers down.

"Um." He moved things around until the picture she wanted was fully displayed. "Oh. I just threw that in there, so I'd have it later. It's Erskine accepting some bullshit—"

"Erskine?" she whispered, one hand reaching back to grip Lachlan's thigh, as if to reassure herself that he was there, that this wasn't some awful nightmare. "He's supposed to be dead," she added, her voice sounding eerie even to her own ears.

Lachlan's arms came around her from behind, his voice in her ear. "What's going on? Who's supposed to be dead?"

"*That* man. He can't be Erskine Ross, because that man's dead."

LACHLAN TURNED her in his arms, waiting until she looked up at him to say, "I thought you'd never seen Erskine before."

"I haven't. But that's not Erskine. That's the man who killed my family." She stared at the three vampires, scanning their expressions one at a time, ending up with Munro. "What's going on? Why would you have a picture of him?" Her body was coiled tight in Lachlan's arms, her voice taking on a note of suspicion.

"Julia," he said, waiting until she met his gaze. "That *is* Erskine Ross. Tell me why you think he's the one who was in that accident with your family."

Her eyes narrowed in the first sign of anger. "Because he is. You think I could forget his face?"

"No, but you were young, maybe—"

"I didn't see a picture of him until years after the accident," she said absently, while patting her pockets looking for something. Not finding whatever it was, she searched the cluttered table until finally uncovering her cell phone. "I need to call my father," she said, all traces of anger buried beneath her cool surface.

"Wait." Lachlan covered her hand with his own, stopping her before she took a step, in the heat of the moment, that would make the situation so complicated that it couldn't be unraveled. To anyone else, Julia might have seemed remarkably calm, given the confusion of the moment. But he wasn't just anyone. He'd had her blood, and she'd had his, albeit a small amount. More importantly, he was a powerful telepath, and so he knew there was more going on behind the cool façade which seemed to be her go-to when she was stressed. The more stress, the cooler she got. Which was why he knew she was not only troubled by this new development, she was in pain. The death of her family had been a turning point, one that had altered the fabric of who she was and changed the entire trajectory of her life.

The truth was, Lachlan absolutely believed Erskine might have been the driver that fateful night in Florida. The vampire lord wouldn't have spared a thought for any deaths he'd caused, and he wouldn't have worried about the human authorities, either. Not then and not now. He'd obviously succeeded in disappearing without a trace after the accident. But that wasn't as extraordinary as some might think. Every vampire had a basic level of telepathy. It wouldn't have taken much more than that basic skill for Erskine to manipulate the investigators' memories just enough to forget his face.

"Munro?" He glanced at his cousin, wanting more details.

"I'm already looking," his cousin responded.

"Come on, princess," Lachlan said, kissing her forehead and hugging her against his chest. "You're cold." And she was. Her skin was as cool as her shatterproof expression. "Let Graeme fix you a cup of tea and something to eat."

"I'm not hungry."

"Just tea, then. With some sugar."

She got that stubborn look that said she wanted answers, but by now, she knew him well enough to understand she wouldn't get any until he decided the time was right. She rubbed her hands over her arms. "Okay. Hot tea would be nice. Thank you."

Lachlan nodded to Graeme who'd come to stand in the doorway. As the chef turned back into the kitchen, Lachlan guided Julia to the chair on Munro's right, where she'd been working while he'd been at Erskine's. It seemed like ages ago, but he'd been home less than an hour. He hadn't even sat down yet.

"I should call my father," she insisted again, fingers gripping his arm with urgent strength.

Lachlan sat next to her, laying a heavy arm over her shoulders. "Wait," he urged. "Let Munro dig out the details first, figure out how this happened. There are bound to be questions only your father can answer, but let's see if we dig out some answers of our own first."

"Maybe I shouldn't dig into any of—"

"I think you have to, but I will even if you don't," he said gently. "Your life is at risk, Julia. I can't accept that."

She met his gaze, her emotions written in her pretty eyes, but also clear to his telepathic sense of her. Those emotions warred between outrage that he thought he could tell her what to do, and warm pleasure at this proof that he cared about her. That last troubled him, because she shouldn't need proof of what he'd already told her.

Her attention shifted at that moment to Graeme, who placed a tea setting in front of her, along with a plate piled with freshly baked shortbread. She gave him a warm smile. "Thank you."

"If you need anything else, you let me know," Graeme said.

"This is plenty."

"Well. I'll be in the kitchen, just in case," he said and disappeared back into his realm.

Julia sipped the hot tea while giving Lachlan what she probably thought were surreptitious sideways glances. "All right," she finally informed him. "Tell me what's going on. I know you have a theory."

"Not a theory so much, as a partial explanation. But answer a question for me first. Why did you think Erskine—or the man who killed your family—was dead?"

"I can answer that," Munro said, fingers still flying. "The human police said he was, didn't they, Jules?"

"Yes," she said in surprise. "How'd you know?"

"Uh, maybe you don't know this about me, but I'm really good at digging into places where I don't belong."

"Explain," Lachlan snapped at Munro.

"The cops never arrested him, for one thing," his cousin said.

"It was a hit and run," Julia supplied.

"Right. But the car he was driving was a rental, and the rental company had a copy of the license he used. It was a fake, obviously, but the *picture* wasn't. That's probably what you saw. The rental car turned up a couple of towns over, with, according to police records, a very dead driver who was conveniently burned beyond recognition. The coroner's report claimed a fingerprint match, and that was that. One dead driver. Case solved. But it was all a lie. A little digging shows unexpected and very substantial deposits into the bank accounts of certain police officials, as well as the coroner. Deposits that are remarkably close to the crash timeline. And money talks, as we all know. Erskine bought off the right people to make himself dead. We vampires have a lot of experience with that sort of thing. But one detail stands out. How the hell did your father get a copy of the license photo?" he asked Julia. "I would have expected the cops to purge it from the records."

"They probably did, eventually," she agreed. "Just not soon enough. As you say, money talks, and my dad has money, too."

"Your father showed you the photo?" Lachlan was stunned. "You were a *child*."

"No, of course not," she said immediately, "not then anyway. But when I got older, and he still wouldn't answer my questions about the accident, I snuck into his office and found my own answers. I was fifteen."

"I got it," Munro said suddenly. They all turned to look at him. "Her maternal great-grandfather, Matthew Harris."

"What about him?" Confusion abruptly swinging to temper, she demanded, "How the *hell* do you know about my great-grandfather? *I* barely know anything about him. Look," she said, rounding on Lachlan. "I want answers. The three of you seem to understand a hell of a lot more than I do about this, and *he* . . ." she pointed an accusing finger at Munro, ". . . is telling me about my *own family*. So start talking. What the fuck is going on?"

"You're right," Lachlan said calmly. "Why don't we all—"

Her eyes narrowed. "Don't you try to *manage* me, Lachlan McRae."

He almost choked trying to swallow a grin. His princess was always beautiful, but fuck . . . with a temper on her, she took beautiful to new heights.

As if reading his thoughts, her eyes turned to slits of warning, blue fire.

It worked. Schooling his expression to perfect seriousness, he nodded and said, "Here's what we know. Erskine Ross wants you dead. *Badly*. He's tried twice, and when that didn't work, he tried to bribe first Tucker, then me, into doing it *for* him. But the one thing we couldn't figure out was *why*.

"And now," he said, running the back of his fingers down her cheek, as her gaze went from pissed off to thoughtful, "you're telling us that the man who killed your family in that accident and got away with it, is Erskine Ross. That can't be a coincidence."

"You'd be right about that," his cousin said, taking up the narrative. "You see, I had a thought earlier. Tucker kept going on about Lachlan visiting Raphael, which would have made sense if Erskine was worried about him getting Raphael's help in taking over the territory. But what really chafed his arse was that *Julia* was with you. Now, we all figured it was because of her job. Vampires are a secretive lot, especially when it comes to governments and their long memories. But then tonight, Erskine took it a step further when he came right out and told Lachlan that he wanted Julia dead. Why her? Why not Lachlan?"

"You think that's the real reason Tucker was here?" she asked.

Munro nodded. "Maybe you were his target all along. Kill Lachlan, deliver you—dead or alive—and he wins big points with Erskine."

Lachlan grimaced. "I don't know. Doesn't seem like much of a reward."

"Unless Erskine promised to help him win another territory. Like England. We all know Lord Norwood's too weak to hold against a strong challenge." He gave Julia an apologetic look. "Norwood's the current Vampire Lord of England," he explained. "He's held the territory for centuries."

"That could be," Lachlan agreed. "Erskine was nattering on when we met this evening, about seizing all of the UK for himself, and letting me have England. Maybe he made the same offer to Tucker."

"Great," Julia said. "But why kill *me*? I'm no threat to him."

"Aye," Munro said dramatically, "but what if you *are*?"

Julia gave his cousin such an impatient look that Lachlan was glad she wasn't armed.

"Sorry, lass," Munro hurried to say. "Right, so this is what I've discovered. Your maternal great-grandfather—Matthew Harris, as I said—purchased some land with Raphael way back in 1869. I don't know the circumstances that brought them together, but the property records are clear. It was a truly significant chunk of inland property that they caught at just the right time, and later sold to one of California's founding families for a sum that took them both from ordinary wealth to super rich."

"I never knew that," she whispered, turning to Lachlan. "I wonder if my father does?"

It was Munro who answered. "I think he must, because Raphael later returned the favor, giving your great-grandfather founding shares in what would become Raphael Enterprises. And *that* particular corporation, my lovely lassie, is worth billions by now."

"Wait, how do you know this? You said Raphael's holding company is privately owned. How do you know who owns what as part of it?"

Munro shrugged. "The corporation is privately owned, but the *shareholders* have to pay taxes and file returns." He grimaced. "I'm sorry to tell you this, but your taxing authority, what you call the IRS, is as porous as a sponge."

"My God," she murmured. "You could go to jail."

"*Pffft*. Only if they catch me."

Lachlan raised a skeptical eyebrow at his cousin's arrogance, but figured if the American government ever came calling, Munro could simply disappear. Legally, he didn't exist, since he'd been born nearly two centuries ago.

"The shares in Raphael's corporation are part of the Harris family trust which eventually passed into your mother, Marilyn's, estate, and from her . . ." Munro paused, as if aware he was treading on delicate ground. "To you," he finished softly.

"My father manages that trust," Julia said softly. "I never knew . . . . I see the annual reports, but the trust includes something like a hundred separate investments. I'm ashamed to say that I focus on the bottom line. I trust my dad and our financial adviser to handle the rest."

Fergus had been sitting quietly, taking in all this new information, but now he said, "What you're saying, Munro, is that there's a . . . *personal* relationship between Raphael and Julia's mother's family, and presumeably some loyalty attached to it. But if that's true, if Raphael was so close to the family, why didn't he hunt down Erskine a long time ago?"

"Because everyone involved—except the cops who took the bribes—thought the killer was dead," Munro explained, speaking carefully, as if he thought Fergus was a bit slow. "Raphael must never have seen the photo. And why would he? They had the driver's dead body."

Fergus gave his cousin a middle finger salute. "You're saying the accident was just that. An accident. Then why go after Julia now?"

"Too many coincidences," Lachlan spoke up. "First, she shows up as Masoud's executor, which is unusual enough. He cut out his family in favor of letting her handle his affairs, which put her in charge of all his files, including the ones about Erskine's finances. But then, she joins forces with me, smoothing the way to Raphael, to whom we immediately pay a visit."

"Exactly," Munro agreed. "Erskine would have known the identities of the people he killed back then, though he'd likely have forgotten it by now. But once he had his hackers start looking, they'd have turned up the connection to Julia . . . who just happens to be visiting Raphael with our dear cousin in tow. As Lachlan said, that's too many coincidences for a paranoid bastard like Erskine to handle. Too many reasons to want Julia out of the picture—beginning with what she might know about his shady financial dealings, and ending, in a very real sense, with the possibility that Raphael will discover who killed his old friend's granddaughter and her son, and wreak his own form of justice against Erskine."

"And we all know what Raphael's idea of justice is," Lachlan commented, thinking of the powerful vampire's visit to France, in the aftermath of assassination attempts by two separate French vampire lords, and the resulting decimation of that country's strongest vampires.

Julia sat silently for a moment, then looked at Lachlan in alarm. "My dad could be in danger, too."

"I don't think so, not after all this time. But you should call, just to be safe. Where is he?"

Her soft mouth curved into a rueful smile. "I don't know. I usually don't. But he always has his phone on, and he always answers when I call."

"This has been a lot for you to take in," he murmured, hugging her close enough to kiss the soft skin of her temple.

"Do you think Cyn knew about Raphael and my family?"

Lachlan took the non sequitur as an indication of her exhaustion, but he answered anyway. "No. I think she'd have said something if she knew. You two are close."

She gave him a narrow look. "Are you snooping in heads where you don't belong, Mr. Vampire?"

"No." Which was the truth, since he had little control over what she was broadcasting and could hardly help hearing it. "But I've been alive a long time and observed a lot of human interaction. You two have the kind of bond that survives."

She nodded. "I need to call my dad now. I won't be able to sleep until I do."

Lachlan nodded. "But you'll do it from our room."

OUR ROOM. JULIA liked the sound of that way too much. It made them sound like a real couple. She knew the moment Lachlan started down the hallway behind her. She didn't even have to look back. It was as if something connected them on a different level. Was there a vampire version of Bluetooth? Because that's what it felt like.

He didn't make any noise, despite the hardwood floors, but she knew he was there. His size and strength made her feel safer simply by being in the house. Not only because he'd protect *her*, but because he was a vampire. Odd that she'd never thought of this before. She'd always known her mother and brother's deaths had affected her. She'd told Lachlan as much. But she hadn't mentioned her reluctance to let anyone into her life, much less to love them. She'd never wanted the pain that losing them would cause. Because everyone died. Everyone went away.

But not Lachlan. He was tougher and stronger than anyone she'd ever met. He was also immortal, or so close to it, it didn't matter. She'd seen how quickly his vampires could heal, and that was on top of what Cyn had told her. Her friend had seen a lot of fighting during the four years she'd been with Raphael, a lot of horrible injuries healed.

Julia wasn't naïve enough to believe in absolutes. She knew Lachlan could die, too. But his chances were a hell of a lot better than most.

He caught up to her, a wall of muscle against her back as he placed his hands on her hips and turned her into the bedroom. "You should get comfortable before you call anyone," he said, closing the door behind him. She heard the heavy sound of the vault door locks sliding into place.

"Why?" She walked over to place her computer and files on the table before turning to face him. Her heart ached predictably at the sight of him. How the hell had he gotten so deep inside her heart so fast? She swallowed a sigh. It felt too much like surrender, and just because he couldn't die, that didn't mean he wouldn't break her heart.

He crossed the room and put his arms around her, pulling her against that magnificent chest. "Come here, princess." He held her silently for a moment. "It will be as painful for your father as it was for you to discover your family's killer is alive. And you're the one who's tasked with delivering that news. You'll have to bear his pain on top of your own. So yeah, I think you should take off your shoes and get comfortable on the bed, so I can be there beside you when you call."

She let the sigh come then. There was no fighting it. The heart wanted what the heart wanted, and apparently her heart wanted Lachlan McRae. Stupid bloody thing.

"All right. But I'm not taking off my clothes. I can't talk to my dad naked." She felt his mouth curve in a smile against the top of her head, heard it in his voice when he responded.

"Can *I* at least be naked?"

"Oh my God, no. Go away."

"No. I won't do that, but I'll be all proper-like."

She didn't believe him, but she kicked off her shoes and socks, and unbuttoned her jeans, then slid under the covers, holding up the quilt for him when he joined her. He pushed it away with muttered complaints of how "bloody hot" he'd be with "covers and clothes, too." But he still put his arm around her and tucked her close to his body, while she opened her contacts and called her father's number.

"Hey, baby," her dad answered on the first ring, as he always did when she called, no matter how early or late it was. Until she'd met Lachlan, her father's voice had been the sound of home, whether they were in the same city or thousands of miles apart. He still sounded like home. But so did Lachlan.

"Hi, Dad. Where are you?" It was an inside joke between them, the first question she always asked.

"I'm in London. I thought you'd be here, too."

"I left for Scotland a few days ago."

"Paid a visit to Malibu, too, I hear."

She almost asked how he knew, thinking immediately of his friendship with Raphael. But then she realized the pilots would have checked in with him to make sure he didn't need the plane when she'd wanted to use it.

"Yes. A quick trip to visit Cyn and Raphael. We weren't there long."

"We, is it?"

Shit. She'd known there wasn't much chance of him missing that. "Sort of," she admitted, her voice wavering, which earned her a pinch from Lachlan, who, naturally, could hear both sides of the conversation. She wondered if that was the real reason he'd wanted to be so close, then chastised herself with the next breath. Fuck, but she was a paranoid wretch. "Listen, Daddy—"

"Uh oh, when you break out the 'daddy,' I know I'm in trouble."

"Not this time."

He was silent for a moment, as if listening not only to what she'd said, but how she'd said it. He'd always known when she had bad news to deliver, although usually it had been nothing worse than trouble at school or a scratched car.

"Tell me what is, Julia."

She closed her eyes for a moment, trying to find the right words, as Lachlan's arm tightened around her shoulders and his lips brushed the side of her head. "You know why I was in London."

"To deal with Masoud's estate," he said, sounding puzzled.

"Right. But in the process, I uncovered something he was involved in, and I had to figure out what to do with it, and . . . ." She sighed. "There's no easy way to say this. The man who killed Mom and Mattie . . . . He isn't dead, Daddy. He's a vampire, and he's still alive."

Silence, then a soft question. "How do you know this?"

"I saw his picture, and, well, he's been trying to kill me."

"What?" That wasn't soft at all. It was an explosion of anger. "Did you call our London security firm? Do they have a team on you? Never mind, I'll call them. Where are you, and how soon can you get back to London? Jesus, Julia, you can't be running around Scotland with some crazed fucking vampire trying to kill you. I won't lose you, too. I can't."

It was the "fucking" that told her how upset he was. That and the pain in his voice at the end. But despite that, despite her own pain as she relived the first months after her mom and Mattie had been killed, what she noticed most was that he was more concerned about her safety than the news that Erskine Ross was alive. "I'm safe, Dad. Lachlan is with me, and he has his own security—"

"Lachlan who?"

"Lachlan McRae. His cousin Catriona introduced us when we met for a drink in London. She and I went to school together in France. He's . . . a vampire, which is why we were in Malibu. We went there to see Cyn, but also Raphael."

More silence. "Did you tell Raphael about the killer being alive and coming after you?"

"No. I didn't know then. We just worked it out tonight, when I saw his picture."

"What's his name?" he asked in a hard voice that she rarely heard from him.

"Daddy—"

"Don't 'daddy' me, Julia. Not on this. What's his name?"

"Are *you* going to call Raphael if I tell you?"

It was a loaded question, revealing that she knew about the family connection to Raphael, and there was a simmering undercurrent to her father's silence as he absorbed this new bit of information. "You and your vampire friend have been busy," he said finally. "What's he after?"

"Who?"

"This new vampire who's worked his way into your life and dragged you to Malibu."

"He didn't drag me anywhere, and before you ask, he has his own money. He's not after mine." Lachlan's chest heaved in an annoyed breath.

"What's he want then?" her father demanded.

"Me. I know it's hard to believe, but—"

"Stop. You know I don't think that, baby. And, yes, I *am* going to call Raphael."

"Please don't."

"Why? That murdering asshole killed your mother and Mattie and didn't even have the decency to stop and check on them. And now you tell me he faked his death. I want him dead. He deserves to be *dead*."

"I'm sorry," she whispered, feeling every bit of pain that Lachlan had predicted for her.

As if he knew what she was feeling, Lachlan pulled her so close that she was half on his lap and reached to take the phone. "Let me, princess," he whispered, but she shook her head violently and held on. This was her responsibility, not his.

"I want him dead, too," she told her father. "We *both* want him dead. Lachlan, too. But if you tell Raphael, he'll come over here and—"

"And make sure he's dead, that's what," her father interrupted. "Raphael's more powerful than you know."

"No, Daddy, I *do* know. Because Lachlan's powerful, too, and he's going to kill Erskine—" She stopped, but it was too late. It didn't matter that she hadn't told her dad Erskine's last name. Raphael would know.

"I'm calling Raphael, and then I'm coming up there, Julia. Where are you staying?"

"Please don't—"

"You're my daughter. The only family I have left. We're in this together, remember?"

"Dad. Please. Call Raphael first. Just ask him about Lachlan. He's a good guy, and he'll keep me safe. Raphael will tell you."

"I'm calling now. What the hell time is it?" She could hear him moving things around as he checked the time in Malibu, while she did the same, pulling up the conversion app she had already set on her phone.

"It's already past sunrise in Malibu," she provided. "You'll have to leave a message."

"Damn. I've always hated that about doing business with him. Why don't you want me to come up to Scotland with you?"

Julia was taken aback by the unexpected question and surprised into telling him the truth. Or at least part of it. "It's dangerous up here. Lachlan's taking care of me, but there's no need for both of us to be—"

"Let me get this straight. You're saying it's okay for you to risk your life, but not me?"

Lachlan was shaking his head, not at what her dad said, but what she'd said first. She glared at him. She was struggling here, doing the best she could.

"You know I didn't mean that. But why give Erskine—" No point in keeping his name a secret anymore, since she'd already blurted it out. "—another target? Lachlan thinks that's the reason he's after me, because he's afraid I'll tell Raphael. Of course, he doesn't know that I had *no idea* you did business with vampires. But it's too late for that, anyway. Lachlan's going to kill him before Raphael can get here."

"You're going to *kill* him?" He was either truly startled or doing a good job of faking it. Either way, she wasn't buying it.

"Come on, Dad. That's why you were going to Raphael. So he'd kill him. Well, there's no need. Lachlan's already here. And if you tell Raphael that, he'll understand what it means."

"Julia. This is a lot to take in. The news about that bastard being alive, the fact that he's after you . . . give me a day to digest it all. I'll call you as soon as I talk to Raphael. In the meantime, I'm sending some security up—"

"No, no." She didn't need to see Lachlan's shaking head to know that would never work. "I told you. Lachlan has his own guards, vampire *and* human. They have their routines. They know each other well. New guys coming up from London would only screw things up. "You go ahead and call Raphael, and I'll wait to hear from you."

"Promise."

"Of course."

"All right. Love you, baby."

"I love you, too. Go back to sleep."

When she disconnected, Lachlan was shaking his head and making a *tsking* sound of disapproval. "You lied to your daddy."

"I did *not!*"

"You told him you'd wait for his call."

"And I will. But I didn't say I'd sit here doing nothing in the meantime. And I didn't say *you* would, either."

"Hmm. You're much more devious than you look, princess. Should be interesting."

Julia pondered that. Should be interesting . . . fighting Erskine with her? Spending a few months together? Longer? Why did this have to be so complicated? And why was she worrying about relationship stuff, when they had a battle to plan?

"What's the plan for Erskine, then? Are you still going after him tomorrow night?"

"Definitely. He won't wait, and I'd rather take the war to him than sit here and wait for him to attack."

"I won't get in the way," she warned, "but I'm not going to wait in the car, either. I'm going in."

"I made a promise, and I'll keep it. But you'll go in on *my* terms, and not with the first wave."

She sat up and studied him closely. "Okay. But I'm trusting you. Don't let me down."

He cupped her face in his big hands, rubbing one thumb over her lips. "Never." He kissed her, as if to seal his promise, then said, "You hungry?"

"Why do you keep trying to feed me? Do you think I'm too skinny?"

He laughed. "I think you're perfect, but you've had a rough day, and I can't just come out and tell you what I'd really like to do."

She gave him a narrow look. "What's that?" she asked suspiciously.

He leaned in to whisper in her ear. "I want to pull you into a steaming hot shower, cover your sweet body with soapy suds, then rinse you off while I slide into your creamy pussy, and make you scream."

Julia's heart was pounding with excitement, her thighs clenching around flesh already swelling with desire. She swallowed the rock in her throat and whispered, "I could use a shower."

Lachlan's grin was pure masculine beauty. He didn't smile like that often, but when he did . . . good God, he was lethal. "Let's go." He was already stripping off his shirt as he stood and pulled her up to his side. A minute later, he was lifting her in his arms and carrying her to the bathroom.

"TAKE YOUR SHIRT off," Lachlan whispered. His breath sent tickling wisps of hair over her cheek, while he ran his tongue over the curves of her ear.

She got the buttons undone, but she couldn't get it off because he was still holding her. "I can't," she complained fretfully.

"Figure it out, love, or I'll tear it off."

"Don't you dare! I love this shirt." She wrestled with the shirt some more, then finally tugged it off over her head, leaving her in nothing but a pretty silk bra which was designed more for enticement than support. Her breasts spilled over so much that her nipples were barely covered. Lachlan took advantage, the fiend, lifting her high enough to run his lips and tongue over the bare flesh, then sliding his mouth down to suck one nipple through the lace. Julia moaned and tightened her arms around his neck. "Hurry," she pleaded, as she toed off her boots, letting them fall to the floor as he carried her.

He laughed under his breath as he set her down in front of the huge tiled shower, then knelt to unzip her jeans and strip them off, snagging her tiny panties along the way. She lifted her feet one at a time, tossing her bra aside as she did so, leaving her completely naked.

"Beautiful," he murmured, wrapping his big hands around her calves, letting his fingers run up the length of her legs, over the gentle swell of her hips, the curve of her waist, squeezing the full weight of her breasts. Glancing up with a wicked, little smile, he curled his fingers around to pinch her nipples, until they were rosy with engorged blood and aching for something she couldn't name.

Pushing her back against the tiled wall, he held her there with his body as he unzipped his jeans and let them fall. Hands on her hips, he lifted her slowly, letting her feel every inch of him, his erection a hot brand against her thighs, which were sticky with arousal. Her face flushed with embarrassment at how wet she was, hoping he wouldn't—She cried out, helpless against the desire flooding her body, as he dipped two fingers into her pussy.

"So wet for me, princess," he murmured. "Maybe I should bend you over the sink and fuck you there first."

Julia gasped in the last shreds of outrage she had left, but that didn't stop her body from clenching in hunger at the image of herself bent over and thoroughly fucked. She closed her eyes, savoring every touch, every kiss.

Lachlan's knowing chuckle was the only warning she got before his hands were on her hips, lifting her effortlessly, swinging her around and bending her over the sink, just as he'd said he would. His hand was gentle on her back, urging her downward, the cold marble countertop stiffening her nipples as he pushed his thick shaft between her slick and swollen flesh, going relentlessly deeper, until his hips hit her ass and his full length was buried inside her. His fingers dug into her hips as the room filled with steam, her forehead pressed into her crossed arms as she struggled just to hold on, to stop herself from coming too fast, even though her entire body was trembling in delicious anticipation. The climax struck like a bolt of lightning, muscles clenching to the point of pain as it blasted from breasts to belly to pussy in a jolt of pure sexual thrill. Behind her, Lachlan's grip tightened hard enough to bruise, but she didn't care, all thoughts swept away by the waves of pleasure coursing through her.

He groaned as her sheath clamped around him in a fierce embrace. "Your pussy is sweet perfection," he growled. "So hot and wet, like a silken glove." And all the while he kept fucking her, slamming in and out in an endless rhythm, until with a muttered curse, he reached around and fingered her clit, pinching it between his finger and thumb, until a second climax stormed through her in an unbridled ecstasy of nerves and muscle. The deluge of sensation was finally too much, as he roared to his own completion, his release filling her body as he collapsed over her back.

They hung there for a moment, too breathless to move, sweat coating their bodies, as Lachlan cupped her ass appreciatively and said, "God damn, princess. I could fuck you forever." Squeezing her butt cheek, he pulled his semi-rigid cock out and practically carried her the few feet to the shower.

Still shuddering with the vestiges of her orgasm, Julia stood under the hot water and tried not to moan every time her inner muscles flexed in remembered passion. She clung to the faucet handles when Lachlan did as he'd promised, washing her from head to toe with hands that soaped and scrubbed better than any loofah she'd ever owned. Leaving her pussy for last, he put his arms around her and soaped his hands with extra care as she watched, his thick chest pushing against her back, his tongue teasing the shell of her ear.

His sudsy fingers caressed her breasts, moving roughly over her nipples, sliding over her belly and downward until they slipped between the swollen folds of her sex. Julia moaned, one hand reaching up and around to the nape of his neck, fingernails digging in to anchor herself against the unstoppable wave of this sensual craving she had for him.

"Lachlan," she cried, not knowing if she was begging him to release her or never to stop. His response was to turn her in his arms and lift her against the tile wall, his hands behind her protectively as he entered her with a slow, steady slide of his cock. Her legs wrapped around his hips as her tender flesh, still trembling with her earlier climax, tightened around him, sending waves of fresh pleasure rolling through her body. He pounded into her, until with a growl of hunger, he lowered his mouth to her neck and fed.

Julia crashed into orgasm, giving him the screams he'd promised, fingers tangled in his long hair as she held on to her *self*, afraid she'd get lost in this man, this beautiful vampire. Without warning, he joined her in orgasm, his cock bucking inside her trembling sheath, while his fangs drew her blood and the heat of his climax filled her once again.

Lachlan stopped slowly, moving in and out of her in a slow, sensual glide, until finally he lifted his head and licked her neck, nibbling over her smooth skin to bite her jaw, before he kissed her thoroughly, lusciously. He kept on until they were both limp, holding on to each other to avoid crumpling to the shower floor.

Julia's legs were still wobbly when he guided her out of the enclosure and wrapped her in a big towel. She leaned against the wall, already half asleep, as she watched him dry off, his movements brisk and methodical, so very masculine. When he was finished, he tossed his towel aside and moved to her, using a fresh towel to dry her legs and feet, rubbing another over her hair, before carrying her to the bed, a towel draped over her shoulders.

Lowering her to the mattress, he tugged the towel from around her body and pulled the covers over to keep her warm. Julia snuggled under with a happy sigh and surrendered to a delightful sleep.

LACHLAN GAZED down at Julia, her hair a pale cloud around her face, eyes closed in the sleep of a well-satisfied woman. Well-loved, too, though he'd admit that only to himself. Once he'd survived Erskine, maybe he'd tell her. But he wouldn't wrap her up emotionally when he might die the next night.

Tossing aside the last of the towels, he slid under the covers next to her, pulling her sweetly naked body against his, as the sun lit a fire in his skull. A moment later, his eyes closed and he was gone.

Chapter Twelve

JULIA WOKE, FEELING groggy and sore. But it was the good kind of sore, in all the right places and all the right ways. She'd never had a man make love to her the way Lachlan did. It was fiercely passionate and *very* thorough. She wondered if it was because he'd had so many years to polish his techniques, to learn exactly what made a woman cry in pleasure. He did seem to like it when she screamed. She smiled at the thought and rolled over to check the time on her phone. It was just after noon, which meant she'd slept several hours, but now she was hungry. She'd been too stressed to eat much the previous day, but her growling stomach told her that was no longer a problem.

She got dressed and opened the bedroom door, which was more like a vault than any bedroom. Lachlan had given her the exit code, but no one, not even she, could get in once it was closed. She was locked out until after sunset. With that in mind, she paused in thought, then walked back into the room and snagged her laptop bag. She saw that her 9mm Sig micro was still in the side pocket, but then her eye caught on the second bag, this one a sturdy, canvas equipment bag with a heavy duty zipper. Cyn had given it to her, to carry the four boxes of Hydra-shok ammo she'd provided, the ones she'd called her vampire-killer rounds, and one more thing . . . an HK MP5 sub-machine gun. The hours she and Cyn had planned to use for shopping had been spent instead on Raphael's indoor shooting range. Julia was no sharpshooter, but according to Cyn, you didn't have to be, with an MP5 and enough ammo.

She considered the weapons. If she didn't need the Sig, she sure as hell wouldn't need a sub-machine gun. She was reaching for the Sig, intending to take it out, when her fingers froze midway. She couldn't have said why, but some instinct told her to take them along. The extra bag was heavy, but since it would only be sitting across the hall, the weight wouldn't matter. Dismissing the matter with a shake of her head, she secured her laptop in its bag, then picked up both and retraced her steps to the door. She had to put the second bag down to make sure the vault door was secure, but then she hefted it to her shoulder and crossed to the small guest room. Mindful of the guns, she placed the bags on the floor, on the far side of the bed, where they weren't immediately visible, and left.

Thinking she'd find something to eat, then come back and do some more digging on the internet, she made her way to the kitchen, surprised to see Graeme working busily. She'd expected the house to be empty, but maybe Graeme was an exception to the no humans rule. Whatever the reason, it made her happy because he was baking something that smelled absolutely heavenly.

"What is that?" she asked, feeling like a pastry bloodhound, with her nose up and sniffing the air. But it was such a delicious scent.

"Fresh shortbread, of course. This is Scotland, after all. The lads expect shortbread with their tea. Here," he said, putting a few on a small platter. "I've made a few new flavors. Give 'em a taste."

Julia slid onto a stool while she eyed the cookies greedily, her stomach grumbling its impatience as she stared at the treats piled high in napkin-lined baskets. These weren't the same as she'd had last night. "What are they?" she asked with breathless reverence.

He laughed and pointed to one at a time. "Dark chocolate with lavender, lemon with poppy seed, pistachio, and I've got the traditional butter ones in the oven."

"Can I eat them all?" she asked jokingly, but Graeme surprised her.

"Sure. I always bake plenty. I've got big lads to feed."

"Maybe one of each," she said. Then since chocolate was her go-to dessert, she bit into that one first and nearly swooned. "Oh, my God," she whispered, trying not to moan. "These are heavenly."

"The lads say my shortbread's better than their own mothers', though they've sworn me not to tell," he said laughingly.

"You should sell these. We don't have anything like it in the US."

"Nae, I'm happy enough cooking for th' lads."

"Well, I'm certainly happy you're doing it," she said, biting into the pistachio and thinking she should probably eat something more wholesome for breakfast than butter and sugar. But there were nuts, too. Nuts had protein, right? She was about to take another nutritious bite when the sound of gunfire had her spinning off the stool and racing out of the kitchen.

"Don't go out there!" Graeme shouted.

She didn't bother to correct him. He'd been hanging around the wrong kind of women if he thought she was stupid enough to run straight into a gun battle. Making a sharp turn out of the kitchen, she ran down the bedroom hallway, thankful she'd followed her instincts on the gun.

Sliding on the guest room's slippery wood floor, she skidded around the bed and grabbed the duffle, hitting the hallway again, just in time to hear the voice of Lachlan's daylight security chief. It took her a minute to remember his name—Kerr. She didn't know if it was a first or last, but it was the only name Lachlan had used.

And who gave a fuck about names?

"Who else is here?" he asked, slamming the front door behind him and stalking from window to window, checking that the heavy automatic shutters were down and the curtains pulled.

"No one but Julia and me in the house," Graeme said, as he emerged from the kitchen, wearing a ballistic vest instead of an apron, and carrying an MK5 much like her own.

"All right," Kerr snapped. "Julia, can you shoot?"

She nodded and held up the canvas bag. "I have an MK5 and a Sig micro 9mm, plus six boxes of ammo."

"Good. You get back in that hallway. I want a barricade set up as far ahead of the downstairs vault door as you can make it, and still be in the hall. Use whatever you need to. Chairs, tables, whatever. I don't expect it to be bulletproof, but make it as thick as you can."

"You're not going to hold the perimeter?" Graeme asked, surprise in every word.

Kerr shook his head grimly. "They outnumber us three to one, all heavily armed. Erskine must have rounded up every gunman in Scotland."

"Erskine?" Julia repeated. "But—"

"Human gunmen," he clarified. "He clearly meant to soften us up before sunset."

Julia was the one who voiced the nightmare, the truth that Erskine hadn't changed since Lachlan's clan had been slaughtered. That he hadn't grown a soul in all the years since. "Or take out the vampires as they sleep," she said flatly. "He's done it before."

"He has," Kerr agreed. "But he won't this time."

"No, he won't," she agreed, but the hard edge of her voice was nothing compared to the thoughts in her head. Erskine had taken too much from her already. No way in hell was he going to get away again with murdering someone she loved. She started piling furniture in front of the hall archway—tables and chairs from the great room, a dresser from the guest room—it all went into her barricade, each piece piled onto the next like a game of Tetris until there was nothing but a slender open slot, just big enough for her to slip through.

The sound of gunfire intensified outside, punctuated by screams and shouts of men who sounded much closer than they had been when Kerr had first come through the door. Bullets pinged off the metal shutters for the first time, making her cast a startled look over the barricade to where the daylight security chief was having a low, intense conversation with someone on the other side of his Bluetooth headset. He glanced up, as if feeling her staring at him, and said, "The shutters are ballistic. It'll take more than that to break through them."

"The door?" she asked.

He shook his head. "I can't secure it yet. This is the only safe retreat left for most of my men. The barracks are secure, but they pushed us back too quickly. Their target is clearly this house."

Julia nodded her understanding, then began closing up that last bit of open space between her and the main room. She'd just broken the legs off an elaborate side table, and shoved the top slab against the wall with a shriek of delicate wood, when Kerr strode over to give the construction a critical look.

"Good job."

He sounded so surprised that she was insulted. How much brain did it take to build a pile of furniture, for fuck's sake? "What about your men?"

"They'll be coming inside any minute. They've already started their withdrawal."

She nodded, as if she understood, which she did, sort of. She'd gotten the impression on her first day here, that the human guards never entered the house during daylight. But they couldn't be expected to die on their swords for no reason. Or maybe those rules went out the window during war. Because this definitely sounded like a fucking war.

Taking up her position, she laid out her ammo and weapons. She didn't worry about Lachlan sleeping right down the hall, because she didn't have to. They were never going to get past her.

When the first of Erskine's fighters finally broke into the house, the sun was still in the sky, streaming through the broken door to where Lachlan's human guards were waiting. The first rush was a suicide attack. Or maybe "sacrifice" was the better word, because those first invaders gave the men behind them a protective shield to hide behind as they slipped into the house and took up positions.

Julia didn't have time to do anything but kill after that. She ignored her little Sig micro-compact after seeing the sheer number of the enemy.

She was a good enough shot, but the Sig's 7 lousy rounds wasn't going to do much damage. Instead, she picked up the MP5 and started shooting, using short, controlled bursts, and avoiding the kind of spraying gunfire that was so popular in movies. According to Cyn, that technique wasted ammo and had a low kill ratio.

Kerr's men must have gotten the same training as Cyn, because they, too, were armed with sub-machine guns and were firing the same kind of targeted bursts. The front part of the house was being rapidly destroyed—furniture smashed, windows shattered in front of the still-closed shutters, and walls ripped apart—but Kerr's men seemed to be holding the line. Julia could feel the sharp pain of cuts on her arms and face, mostly from wood and glass shards, but she ignored them as she kept firing. More than once, Erskine's men attempted to rush her position. The first time they did it, she'd frozen. They were no longer faceless, armored figures firing from forty feet away. She could see their faces, their determination, and in some cases, the hatred as they forced their way closer. It was the hatred that pulled the trigger on her weapon. Unreasoning, thoughtless hatred. For Lachlan.

After that first time, firing became nothing more than a reflex. An automatic retargeting of her weapon from far to close-up and back again. It seemed to go on forever, until her arms ached and her fingers cramped. She knew the sun had to be moving down the sky, knew the battle would change dramatically once it did. But there was no time to think about that.

Not until she heard the bedroom vault door open behind her.

LACHLAN WOKE TO bloodshed and death. For a moment, a fraction of a second, he couldn't breathe, trapped in the nightmare of his first waking. But then reality kicked in. The soft bed beneath him, the scent of Julia . .. He slapped a hand out and found the bed empty.

"Damn it," he cursed and jumped up, grabbing the jeans he'd discarded the night before and pulling them on as he took stock. Gunfire replaced the clash of metal swords, but the screams were the same, the scent of blood and spilled guts on the air—faint now because of the vault door, but detectable all the same, carried through the vents.

Straightening to his full height, he gathered his power and blasted his still-sleeping vampires with a single command. "WAKE!" All around him they began to rouse early from their daylight sleep, their minds linking with his in a reflexive act as old as vampires themselves. He was their Sire and their lord. His power kept their hearts beating and their lungs breathing. Their first thought on waking was always to reach out to him. And as they did so, he arrowed knowledge of the attack to every one of them, calling them to fight by his side.

He didn't have to wonder who was behind this cowardly daylight attack, an act that violated the oldest rule of vampire society. Erskine Ross had failed in his desperate attempt to bribe Lachlan into killing Julia for him, and so had decided to come after her and everyone with her, regardless of the cost to his fighters—human and vampire. Erskine must have guessed that Julia hadn't yet told anyone of his involvement in the killing of her family. Maybe it was simply because Raphael hadn't shown up to kill him, or he could have a spy of his own in Malibu, watching the estate for unusual activity. But whatever it was, the Scottish vampire lord wanted to be sure Julia never spilled the truth. And so he ordered this cowardly assault. His fear of Raphael must be truly crushing.

Even so, an attack this reckless had to be driven by more than fear of Raphael's retribution. Because he hadn't attacked some low-level vampire, he'd attacked *Lachlan.* And in doing so, in bringing battle to him here, on *his* land, in *his* home, he'd set in motion a test of power between the two of them that had been nearly two hundred years in the making.

And just as he had then, Erskine had shown himself as a coward, eschewing honorable battle in favor of a craven daylight assault, and the murder of Lachlan and all his people while they slept.

But Lachlan was no longer a weak, day-old vampire. And the woman he loved was out there risking her life, waiting for him.

Opening the bedroom door, he found Julia crouched behind a makeshift barricade, blood-spattered and exhausted, surrounded by weapons and ammo. One of Lachlan's daylight guards lay next to her, alive, but unconscious, his shirt soaked with blood.

Julia twisted to look over her shoulder, giving him a faint smile above eyes that reflected weary relief, but it was no more than a glance, as several of Erskine's fighters try to rush her position. She spun back, but before she could fire, Lachlan slammed the attacking humans with a wave of power, dropping them to the floor before they'd gone three feet.

Furious and wanting more, Lachlan ripped apart the shield that concealed his true power, the one that kept other vampires from detecting just how strong he was. Vampire magic surged through his body in an exhilarating rush, firing his heart with renewed energy, flexing muscles that burned with new strength. And all the while, the symbiote in his blood raged, demanding he test himself against the enemy, that he destroy him and *rule*. It was fate. It was his purpose. He was Vampire.

His defensive shields rose around him in a flood of light, their multiple bright points surrounding him like diamonds as he strode openly down the hall to where Julia crouched. He wanted to scoop her up and lock her in the bedroom where she'd be safe. But even if he hadn't promised she could stand with him when he killed Erskine, she'd earned her place in this battle.

Extending his shield to protect her, he crouched and whispered, "Keep your head down, love." Then he stood and slammed a second wave of power out into the room, knocking everyone there—friend and foe—into unconsciousness.

Silence descended as he turned to see Fergus standing in the open door to the downstairs vault. "Sort them out, cousin," Lachlan said. "Lock up Erskine's, secure ours in the barracks. Graeme should have the infirmary set up by now. And Fergus . . ."

His cousin had already shoved a path through Julia's makeshift barricade, but now he stopped to give Lachlan a questioning look.

"No more of ours die tonight. Recruit as many vampires as you need to provide blood for the injured."

"And Erskine?" Fergus asked in obvious concern. "He'll be close."

Lachlan nodded. "I'll handle Erskine."

"He won't be alone."

"No. So move fast. I want you and Munro standing with me when he gets here."

"You'll need more backup than that."

"And I'll have it. Make sure the others are standing by, ready to lend me their strength if I call for it."

Fergus nodded in sudden understanding. Lachlan wasn't going to wage a battle with Erskine's forces. He was going to challenge for the territory, right now, right here. It would be a duel between the two of them, no one else. But they each would draw on their people for additional strength if the battle got too bloody or went on too long.

"Right. All right, lads," Fergus shouted, taking charge of Lachlan's vampires. "Let's sort these out and get them to the barracks."

Leaving that task to his cousins, Lachlan pulled Julia to her feet, cupping her cheek where several nicks of wood or glass had left a pattern of clean slices on her soft skin. "Come with me," he said.

"I need to help with—"

"No, you don't. Fergus and the others can handle that. You need to get ready for Erskine. He's nearly here."

She stared at him. "How do you know he's . . . . Oh, right. Vampire shit."

"Indelicately put, but yes."

"So what's to get ready for? He walks in the door, and I shoot him."

Lachlan smiled. He did like her style. "He'll have his shields up, just as I did. Human weapons won't work. Not at first, anyway."

He'd led her back to the bedroom as they spoke, and she glanced around, as if surprised to find herself in a room untouched by the attack. But then, her eyes closed with a deep sigh, and her whole body drooped.

"I didn't know if we'd make it," she whispered, before looking up at him. "When it started, I was counting the minutes, but then there was no time to do anything but shoot." She looked at her right hand, where her fingers were nicked and scratched. "I killed him." Her eyes met his. "In the first wave, there was a man, human. But you know that. He saw me and rushed the barricade, like he didn't believe I'd shoot him. But I did. I had to." Her eyes filled before she looked down again, holding both hands stretched out in front of her.

Lachlan pulled her into his arms, hating that she'd gotten involved in the violence of his life. "I'm sorry—"

"Don't say it," she growled against his chest, her arms around his waist. "I'm the one who insisted on being here. And it's not your fault, anyway. That fucker Erskine started it."

He choked back a laugh at her casual use of the obscenity as much as the childish insistence that the other guy had started it. It was true, but the way she said it reminded him of children on a playground. His princess had proven her courage many times over, but she wasn't yet a hardened warrior.

And if he had anything to say about it, she never would be.

"I can hear the gears turning in your head," she muttered. "Don't even think about keeping me away from Erskine."

"Sit down, I'll get you some water."

"What I need is a ham sandwich. Maybe some pickles and chips to go with it. Crisps. You call them crisps over here."

"I'd love to feed you, but there's no time, and you need to be ready. Erskine has no honor. He may have started all this because he was afraid you'd tell Raphael, but now he'll kill you just because you're important to me. I'm going to force him into a duel, but that won't stop him from lancing a bolt of power your way, or even ordering one of his men to attack you on the side."

"Well, fuck. I'm almost out of ammo."

Lachlan stared at her. *That* was her only concern? He'd never have thought, the night they'd met, that the cool blond in her tight skirt and spiked heels would be standing here next to him, bloodied, sweaty, and complaining about her ammo supply.

He sent Fergus a mental request, then turned to see Julia chugging a bottle of mineral water. Her head was thrown back, her elegant throat moving as she swallowed, water dripping down her chin to soak into her shirt. Christ, she was beautiful. He'd never wanted anyone as desperately as he wanted her. Damn.

"Fergus is bringing fresh ammo," he said, since he couldn't ravish her right then. He started to say more, but a sudden awareness had him going perfectly still. "Erskine is here. I'm going to meet him outside. You stay here in the bedroom, until Fergus comes for you." He gave her a hard, fast kiss and started for the door.

"What?" she demanded behind him. "No! I'm going to—"

He spun, power simmering in his veins. "You will do as I ask. This isn't a democracy. You, Fergus, and Munro will join me outside. But not until I give the word."

The mutinous gleam in her eyes faded almost at once. She moved in close enough that he could feel her heat against his chest, close enough that she could touch his face with one hand. "Be careful. I'm not done with you yet." She went up on her toes, and he lowered his head to meet her kiss.

"Don't worry, princess. I'm not done with you yet, either." He winked and was gone.

Lachlan stepped out onto the porch alone, his shields up and as strong as he could make them. As he'd told Julia, Erskine was not one to bother with rules or customs. If he saw a chance to kill Lachlan, he'd take it, whether it was warranted or not.

"Erskine," he said simply.

It didn't escape Lachlan's notice that the vampire lord wasn't leading his fighters. He had to thread his way through to the front ranks, finally stopping with several yards still between them. "Lachlan. I'd hoped you'd be dead this time."

"*Some* of us learn from our mistakes."

"Yes, unfortunately. What of the Harper woman?" Erskine asked with a studied lack of concern.

Lachlan chuckled. "Still alive."

Erskine gave him a dark look. "Give her to me, and this will all be over with."

"It's much too late for that. Besides, it wouldn't save you. She's already told what she knows."

A momentary flash of real fear lit the vampire lord's eyes before he blinked, and it was gone, replaced by hatred. "I should've killed you when I had the chance. My mistake in not recognizing how young you were back then. Who'd have guessed you'd turn out this strong?"

"My clan chief," Lachlan said, feeling the hatred burning his gut. "My uncles and cousins and all the others you slaughtered that day." And then he said the one thing that no Highlander could ignore. A title Erskine had earned, but never paid for. "You're a coward, Erskine. You were then, and you still are now."

Erskine's eyes lit with flames as his power raged forth so quickly that the vampires surrounding him stumbled back and crashed into the ranks behind them. It would have been comical had the stakes not been so high.

Lachlan did the same, with much greater discipline, telepathing his warriors waiting in the barracks to be ready, while ordering his cousins to combine their shields to cover Julia and prepare to step outside. He wanted the bastard to see her. To see her bloodied but standing strong, her courage like a blazing light for those with the power to see it, including Erskine.

"Fuck you," the Scottish lord spat. "And fuck Raphael, too." His vampires roared in response to Erskine's silent command, spreading out to enclose Lachlan in a half-circle of bristling teeth and weapons, while Erskine smiled smugly. "You McRaes are so predictable. I have all these." He gestured at his vamps. "While you've left most of your fighters in that crumbling Killilan stronghold you persist in maintaining. Shortsighted, Lachlan. Only five fighters to defend you. But I'll give you one last chance. Swear a blood oath to me, and I'll let your men live. The woman, of course, is mine."

Lachlan laughed, fangs bare and gleaming in the moonlight of a clear sky. "I'd offer you the same chance, but . . . ." He shook his head. "I'm going to do the entire world a favor and kill you, instead."

Erskine sneered, "This won't last long, then." He opened his mouth to give the attack order, but Lachlan's telepathic order was already given. His vampires stormed out of the barracks behind Erskine, screaming a challenge and hungry for blood. Most had friends or lovers among the humans injured, and they wanted revenge. If they couldn't have blood, they'd take dust, instead.

Erskine spun with a howl of outrage and readied a wave of power against the charging fighters, but Lachlan had anticipated the coward's response. Using a burst of vampire speed, he raced forward and slammed a fist of pure energy against Erskine's shield, aiming for his head. The vampire lord adapted his shields against the unexpected attack, but not quickly enough, as Lachlan's assault came perilously close to collapsing them. Erskine's cry was more a terrified scream than a roar of anger, as he ignored the battle in favor of defending himself. He spun with both fists primed to hammer Lachlan, only to find him standing, untouched, several feet away.

His flame-lit eyes widened in surprise when he caught sight of Julia and the two cousins stepping out to stand behind Lachlan. "You changed your mind?" he whispered, enhancing the words to be heard above the deafening sounds of battle.

Lachlan laughed. "Look at her. *Look* at her. *She* is the face of your death." And then he sent out a thundering challenge to Erskine, the words resounding in waves over the battlefield and whispering softly into every fighter's ear. As if time had stopped, every vampire—Lachlan's and Erskine's alike—froze to await the vampire lord's response.

The coward Erskine might not give a damn whether his followers lived or died, but *they* certainly did. And they also knew the protocol which had been set up a thousand years ago to save vampire lives. Challenges were the business of powerful vampires only, and they demanded a response—fight or surrender.

"Fine," Erskine snarled. "But know this, McRae. I'll have her before I kill her."

"You'll never touch her," Lachlan said calmly. No emotion, no bravado. Simple truth.

The two armies split and backed away from the two contenders, their rage a palpable thing. If this went badly, Lachlan knew Erskine would order his fighters to kill every one of his vampires, and they'd probably succeed, because he'd personally sired most of them. If Erskine managed to kill him, his vampire children would go crazy for a time, disoriented and lost, as they searched for the connection that was no longer there. Even those sworn to him by blood would be affected, though not as severely. Erskine would let his vampires slaughter at will. Every McRae would die.

"Kill the fucker."

It was the sound of Julia's vicious whisper that reminded Lachlan who he was. He'd survived Erskine long ago, and saved the McRae line of vampires from extinction, for just this purpose. To avenge the deaths of his clan—vampire and human. And now, for Julia's family, too. He turned and met her gaze with a confident wink. "Be ready, princess."

Lachlan had never faced Erskine in battle. He'd had the first-person stories of the people who'd survived the McRae slaughter—humans who were long dead, now—but vampire magic was a strange thing. What was obvious to most vampires was mostly invisible to humans. They might see the results of it in bloodied or dusted bodies, but even that could be so blurred by the vampire victors that human witnesses wouldn't remember.

But Lachlan had the evidence of his own eyes, the scorch marks on walls and doors, and on the human corpses. The vampire lord's power was fire, but Lachlan wasn't afraid of fire, and he sure as hell didn't fear Erskine. They'd met many times over the years, and he'd weighed his power against Erskine's many times. He knew he could take the Scottish vampire lord. But what Erskine might lack in raw strength, he made up for in trickery. That would be the weapon Lachlan had to guard against.

Erskine threw aside his human weapons in a show of confidence, discarding a basket-hilted sword, edges gleaming despite its obvious age, and an ordinary belt knife. When he stopped there, Lachlan scanned for signs of anything else, but there was nothing. No guns of any kind.

For his part, Lachlan had no weapons to remove. Waving his hands in a dramatic and unnecessary gesture, he grinned confidently, and while Erskine was still cursing, thrust a lethal spear of pure power at the vampire lord's heart. He hadn't expected it to succeed—it was a testing blow as much as anything else—but he was still surprised at Erskine's sluggish response. He wasn't fooled. The bastard hadn't survived this long by being slow. Reinforcing his shields by tightening their overlap, he sped forward and slammed both hands against the sides of Erskine's head, wanting to disorient as well as weaken his enemy. Erskine roared and shoved his fists into Lachlan's gut.

Lachlan had stepped back immediately after his own attack, but he was still close enough that Erskine's blow had his belly filling with the blood of ruptured organs. His personal magic went to work repairing the damage, but he couldn't stop the flecks of blood that coated his lips.

He heard Julia's cry from behind him, but ignored it. The damage wasn't fatal, and he didn't have time to reassure her, because Erskine had seen the blood, too. With a triumphant howl, the vampire lord moved in, one hand fisted and drawn back to his shoulder . . . and surrounded by flames.

Lachlan recalculated rapidly. He didn't know how much damage Erskine could do, or how close he had to get. And he wasn't going to wait to find out. Gathering his own magic, he pierced Erskine's mind with a needle-thin probe. Most shields didn't protect against an attack that small, especially not on the mental plane. It took too much energy and there were too few vampires who possessed the kind of telepathic power that Lachlan did.

Acting fast, before Erskine could sense the intrusion, Lachlan filled his enemy's thoughts with the image of a whirlwind of ice spinning around him in a blur of wet Scottish air. It was a simple trick, one that he'd learned in his earliest days as a vampire, but because it was simple, and because Erskine had no experience of it, he wasn't prepared to defend against it. He yowled like an angry wildcat, swinging those fiery fists around himself in a slicing motion, trying to break out of an ice storm that wasn't there.

Taking advantage of the other vampire's furious confusion, Lachlan slammed out a fresh attack of his own, taking one step forward and swinging a cudgel of raw power like an American baseball batter, aiming for Erskine's heart, midway on the left of his chest. The heart was his main target, but he'd settle for broken ribs, which could work their way into all sorts of bad places that Erskine's vampire symbiote might miss in its rush to prioritize its healing efforts.

Erskine grunted at the blow, then staggered briefly and looked around, his eyes displaying a moment's confusion before he straightened with one hand on his chest and fire-filled hatred now gleaming in his eyes. "You've learned a few tricks," he snarled. "But you'll have to do better than that, boy." He threw a series of fireballs, one after the other, that struck Lachlan's shields and clung, their flames dripping down the sides like water.

Lachlan felt his shields straining to protect him, and drew them in closer to his body, minimizing the power needed to keep them strong. He needed to figure out a way to end this. Normal fire wouldn't have been a danger, but who the fuck knew what Erskine was throwing? There were too many lives at stake—including Julia's to take a chance

Concentrating every ounce of power he could spare from his shields, he broadcast a telepathic image to every mind in the yard, a picture of him standing motionless behind the diamond hardness of his shield, as if he was waiting, preparing himself for Erskine's next attack. Once the mental projection was solid enough to trust, he worked behind the protection of his true shields, to shape a wickedly sharp blade of pure magic. Gripping it with both hands, he held it close to his body, where no one, not even Erskine, could see it. And then he waited.

The vampire lord attacked with another series of fireballs, smaller this time, but as they hit, they landed one on top of the other, eating away at Lachlan's shields as if they were feeding on his own power to do their damage.

When he felt the first touch of true warmth on his skin, and glimpsed Erskine's gloating grin at his weapons' success, Lachlan lifted his blade of magic, and in a lightning fast move, sliced through Erskine's neck until he saw the white of his spine.

Erskine dropped to his knees, his protective shield falling with him as he gripped his throat with both hands. It wasn't a killing blow. A vampire of Erskine's power could heal even that kind of a wound, given enough time and a fresh supply of blood. Lachlan could have cut the fucker's head clean off, and he would have . . . but he'd made a promise to Julia.

Keeping one eye on the choking vampire lord, he reached back and held out a hand. "Julia."

JULIA HAD WATCHED the vampire battle with what she hoped was well-concealed fear. This had been so much worse than the fight with Tucker. Forget her ears, the power being tossed around hurt her eyeballs, squeezing as if they were about to explode. She couldn't see the weapons they were using, but she *could* see the damage being done, and it was horrific. Blows were delivered that should have smashed their skulls or driven them to the ground. Blood dripped from their eyes, and faces in general, along with seeping through clothing that appeared untouched. She'd turned from Fergus to Munro more than once, prepared to demand they help Lachlan, but the intensity of their focus, and their pain when he'd been wounded, had made her realize they were as helpless as she was this time. She didn't know why. She only knew it was true.

When Lachlan swung his invisible weapon—although she'd have sworn she'd seen a shining arc just before it struck Erskine—she didn't know what to expect. But it wasn't the red gush of blood as the bastard fell to his knees, with his throat slit so far back that she didn't know how his head was still attached.

"Is he dead?" she whispered to no one.

Before she got her answer, Lachlan was holding out a blood-covered hand, keeping most of his attention on Erskine as he said, "Julia."

She blinked in surprise, but this was Lachlan. There was only one possible response. She stepped forward and gripped his fingers, letting him pull her to his side. She opened her mouth to fuss, to ask if he was okay and insist he let someone help, but before she could say a word, he met her gaze and said, "Take your shot, love."

She turned and stared at Erskine. How the hell was he still alive? Not only alive, but glaring at her with such hatred, as if this was all her doing. She had to force herself to hold that stare, but the longer she stared, the angrier she became. This creature had killed her best friend. He'd destroyed her family. He'd tried to kill her to cover his crime and would have killed others as well, if he'd had to. She thought about what it would have done to her father to lose her, and her head filled with ways to make Erskine suffer. But as she watched the blood flowing from his neck slow to a sluggish crawl, and saw the monster's lips draw back in a gruesome smirk, she knew she didn't have the power to cause him pain.

But she *could* kill him.

Squeezing Lachlan's fingers, she said, "What do I do?"

"You have a gun, use it. The heart's the most vulnerable target on a vampire."

"Will it kill him permanently?"

Lachlan tugged her hand to get her attention. When she met his eyes, now limned with the golden glow of his power, he said, "No, but I'll kill him in a way that will." Rage filled her in a wave before she remembered. Lachlan had to be the one to kill Erskine, or the territory would fall into a vicious war. Vampires and humans both would die needlessly.

She gave a short, sharp nod, then pulled her gun, and aimed at the injured vampire. "Fuck," she cursed. "He's so pathetic. I can't—"

Erskine sprang to his feet with a snarled oath, and everything changed.

Julia fired, striking him three times in the heart, but he kept coming.

Lachlan grabbed him by the throat, one hand buried in the gruesome wound as he used the other to punch a hole in Erskine's chest and tear out his heart. Julia stared as he dropped the gory piece of meat to the ground and pointed at it. There was a flare of light so bright that she closed her eyes against it, and when she opened them again, the heart was nothing but a small pile of ash. A soft whisper of sound made her swing back to look at Erskine. Or at least, where he'd been. Because there was now nothing but a much larger pile of *dust*, already beginning to disperse in the night air.

Swallowing a choking sound of disgust, she stepped behind Lachlan, not wanting any of the repulsive stuff to get on her.

"Are you using me as a shield, princess?"

"Yes," she snapped unapologetically.

He started to laugh, but then coughed abruptly and fell to his knees.

"Lachlan," she cried and dropped next to him, giving his cousins a frantic look. "He's injured, we should—"

Lachlan shook his head and muttered, "Silence."

Julia frowned. Well, that was rude.

LACHLAN KNEW about mantles, knew about the transfer of power from a dying vampire lord to his successor, who was usually his killer. There were cases of someone else inheriting, but they were a very few over the thousands of years vampires had been around. So he'd expected *something*. But this . . . . Fuck! It was as if someone was scouring his already damaged body from the inside, scraping it out to make room for the thousands of vampires living in Scotland. From bakers and shopkeepers to academics and professionals, from his own warriors to criminals preying on humans in the night. They were all his now. What the fuck had he been thinking?

"Silence," he muttered, mostly to himself, a wishful thought. But then he threw back his head and roared, "Silence!"

The voices stopped. The intruders withdrew. They were still there, on the edge of his awareness, but no longer demanding his attention. He resigned himself to the probability that they would always be there, but hoped that over time he wouldn't notice them as much. Lifting his head, he found Julia's pretty blue eyes regarding him with suspicion.

"Are you back?" she asked, eyeing him as if waiting for something to pop out of his chest, an American movie image that he was sure would be around for generations.

He grinned. "It's been a long night. How about a hot shower?"

"Yep. You're back. Come on." She propped her shoulder under his arm and helped him to his feet. He didn't need the help, but he liked the press of her body against his, and so let her "help" him all the way to their bedroom.

Chapter Thirteen

LACHLAN CARRIED a warm and naked Julia to bed, rolling her slightly to pull the covers over her sated body. He'd been surprised at the strength of his desire tonight. Not that he didn't always want her, but he'd been so exhausted after his battle with Erskine, bruised inside and out, that he'd anticipated some hot foreplay, possibly followed by mutual masturbation, and then a fast collapse into bed.

But once he'd gotten her naked, with the steam all around them, and the knowledge that he'd not only become Lord of Scotland, but had finally avenged the deaths of his clansmen . . . his sexual hunger, and his cock, had stirred. But it was the sight of her vein, thick and pulsing along the curve of her soft neck that had sealed her fate. The fight had cost him in blood and power, and there she'd been, his woman—because she *was* his—with her sweet body pressed against him.

He'd taken her then, lifting her without warning, her back against the tiles as her legs came around him and he slammed into her. No romance, no foreplay, just a hard, hungry fucking. She'd clung to his shoulders, her inner muscles straining around his thickness, her nipples hard points against his chest, and her breath hot against his skin despite the heat of the shower. He'd taken her vein, and they'd climaxed together, her nails digging into his neck, his fingers gripping her hips. They'd both done damage—blood ran down his back and bruises had already begun to show on her delicate skin—but they'd been too tired to think about counting wounds.

Finally joining her under the covers, he turned out the light, pulled her naked body against his, and slept.

JULIA WOKE THE next day . . . Was it daylight? She frowned and glanced at the clock. Shit. It was nearly sunset. She must have been wiped out. She lay there, remembering the previous night and the afternoon battle that had preceded it. No wonder she'd been tired. And then there'd been shower sex with Lachlan, which had wiped away any tension she might have been feeling. Not to insult him or anything—because he was a wonderful and tireless lover—but sex with him was the perfect sleeping pill. Or whatever. She probably shouldn't think "pill" and Lachlan in the same sentence. He would definitely take offense.

She was chuckling to herself when his arm stretched out and pulled her against his incredible chest. "What's funny?"

"Random thought," she lied, hoping he didn't have his vampire lie detector thing going. It was, after all, mostly a random thought.

"We need to talk."

Uh oh, she thought. That couldn't be good.

"You remember how we agreed we'd stay together as long as we were both still interested?"

"Are you breaking up with me?"

Lachlan stared at the ceiling and sighed deeply, as if . . . frustrated? "No, princess," he said slowly. "I'm asking you to stay with me. Permanently. I love you."

Julia's heart squeezed hard in her chest. Shouldn't joy feel less like a heart attack? She started to respond, to tell him she loved him, too, but then had to choke back a sob. It came out as a soggy hiccup, while tears streamed over her cheeks.

"Julia?" He rolled over so she was halfway under him, his arms bracketing her face. "Are you okay?"

She nodded, still not trusting her voice. "Happy tears," she managed to say, then pulled him down, hiding her face against his neck, until she finally squeezed out, "I love you," before emotion choked her into silence again.

"Come here." He rolled to his back, both arms around her as he tucked her against his side, her head on his shoulder. "I'm glad you're happy."

She nodded silently.

"We'll have to live in Scotland," he said in a warning tone. "You'll have to quit your job."

Her thoughts stilled. *Quit her job? What would she do instead? She'd be bored out of her mind.* She scowled. *On the other hand, her job bored her out of her mind already, so why not try something different? Life with Lachlan would never be boring. Plus, there was . . . Lachlan.* Her inner monologue continued, making her frown again. *Lachlan who never aged.* But then, according to Cyn, she wouldn't either if she drank his blood. *That* would be nice. The not getting older part, not the blood drinking. Although she'd bitten him once or twice during sex, and his blood had been an instant orgasm injection, kind of like his bite, although not as intense.

"What the hell are you thinking?" he demanded.

"All sorts of things," she admitted, then propped herself on his chest and smiled. "I love you. Did you get that part?"

He gave her a lopsided grin. "I did. I'm glad to hear it."

"And I don't care about the job, as long as you keep me busy doing other stuff."

He patted her ass. "I'll keep you busy."

She rolled her eyes.

"Fair warning, though," he said seriously. "It will take years, not months, to consolidate the territory. A lot of Scotland's vampires hated Erskine. I'll have to prove I'm different, if I want their support, which I do. There are major changes happening in the way vampires are aligned all over the world. Scotland will need to be a united front if we're to hold our own and remain independent."

She nodded, listening.

"That means more violence, more bloodshed. You sure you want to sign on for this?"

Julia smiled. "Give me a reason."

"I love you."

Her smile broadened. "Good answer. You'll have to meet my dad."

"I can handle that. Which reminds me, I need to call Raphael before he shows up on my doorstep."

"Oh, geez, yeah. You call Raphael. I'll call my dad. They're probably flying together."

THE PHONE RANG its usual one time before her father answered. "Julia, are you all right?"

"Hi Daddy. I'm fine."

"Daddy, again, huh? What's up?"

"Erskine's dead," she said bluntly, making it clear that she was serious.

Her father was silent for what seemed like a long time, but when he spoke, his voice was tight with emotion. "How do you know, baby girl?"

"I didn't kill him," she hurried to explain, abruptly understanding the reason for his reaction. "He attacked Lachlan, and they fought. Lachlan won."

"And you're sure he's dead this time."

"Definitely. I saw him die." She decided not to tell him about Lachlan punching through Erskine's ribs and ripping out his heart. "That thing about vampires turning to dust when they die? It's true."

"It is," her father agreed somberly. "When are you coming home?"

She paused. "I'm not. That's the other news. Lachlan and I are together." It sounded too corny to tell her *dad* they were in love. "I'm moving in with him, here in Scotland."

Her father sighed. "Damn vampires. Your great-grandmother had a schoolgirl crush on Raphael, except she was a grown woman. Did I tell you that?"

"What? No. You never told me any of this."

"Didn't change anything, did it? Where in Scotland?"

"Inverness for now, although we'll probably have to spend time in other places eventually."

"Inverness is good. I like the Highlands. When can I meet this guy?"

"Give us a—" She started to say, "couple weeks," then changed it to "—couple months. Lachlan has some business to take care of, and we need some time alone. Like a honeymoon."

"Emphasis on the moon. Okay, baby. I'll be leaving for DC tonight, then. I was going to meet Raphael first, but that won't be necessary now. I'm going to hold you to that two months, though. I'm your father. I need to meet this vampire of yours."

"I love you, Daddy."

"I love you, baby girl. Stay in touch."

IT WAS HOURS LATER before Lachlan picked up the phone in his office and punched in a number he had no business knowing. He only did because he'd entered Erskine's Edinburgh office a few years back, when the former vampire lord had been conspicuously on the phone. He'd made a big show of saying Raphael's name before he hung up. He'd then told Lachlan to wait while he passed on some intelligence that *Raphael* had shared with him, and left the office to stand out of view in the hall, murmuring to Tucker.

Lachlan had taken advantage of the moment to hit redial on the landline phone Erskine had been using. He'd memorized the displayed number, then hung up before the call went through. He didn't hang up this time, however. He waited as the phone rang. Raphael wouldn't recognize his number, but he wouldn't have to. Lachlan was calling on a rarely used phone, since it included an accurate caller ID.

"Lachlan, I presume," Raphael answered, his deep voice unmistakable.

"Raphael," Lachlan said, the absence of a title making it clear that they were now equals. Not in terms of power. No vampire alive matched Raphael's strength. But they were both vampire lords, and that made them equal in vampire society.

"Congratulations," Raphael said. "You've saved me a trip."

"So I hear. You are, of course, welcome to visit at some time in the future. Julia and I both appreciated your recent hospitality, as well as your assistance."

"In the future," Raphael agreed vaguely, though they both knew it was unlikely to happen. "My Cyn does ask me to pass on a request for Julia to call her."

Having heard Leighton's voice before Raphael had spoken, Lachlan knew the request had been phrased less delicately, but he said only, "I'll tell her. Thank you again."

"It was my pleasure, in more ways than one."

And then he was gone. A vampire of few words. But then, it wasn't as if the two of them had anything in common, other than a friendship between the women they loved. He looked up as his own love strolled into his office. "Leighton wants you to call her."

She smiled and walked around to prop her sweet ass on his desk. "Tell me, do I have to stand next to you now, like a proper bodyguard? Or do I sit on your lap?"

"The bodyguard is a definite no." He pulled her onto his lap. "But my lap is always open."

She rested her head on his shoulder. "Do you have to work tonight?"

"Not tonight." He stood, swinging her easily up into his arms. "Tonight, I'm going to teach you how vampires mate."

Epilogue

Somewhere in Europe

THE SCOTSMAN entered the bar with his usual caution, searching every dark corner before moving from the doorway. There was a modest crowd, but not unusual for a late Thursday night. Even dedicated drinkers needed to work the next morning, or at least most of them did. The rest sat at the few tables or lined the bar, some sharing the occasional laugh with a companion, the others focused solely on their drinks.

But none of these were what brought him to this place on this night. A glint of red from the vampire bartender's glance and a tip of his head toward a closed door on the far wall told the Scotsman where his purpose lay.

Opening the door, he paused to scan the room beyond and found exactly what he'd expected—a gathering of roughly twelve vampires, all of them strong, some more than others, although a few were almost certainly shielding their true strength. It was no matter to him. He was here as an observer only, sent by his own Lord Lachlan to judge the possible repercussions of this meeting for the vampires of Scotland. As he closed the door behind him, an unknown vampire addressed the group, speaking English, which was the best bet for a language they all understood.

"Look, if we do nothing, we'll end up with Raphael's hand-picked vampires ruling all of us." The vampire pushed his chair away from the table in disgust, then looked up to meet the Scotsman's gaze in silent accusation.

"Lachlan's got no allegiance to Raphael," the Scotsman said. His tone was flat, his stare uncompromising. He and his lord might have little riding on the decision these vampires made, but he wasn't about to let them insult the new Lord of Scotland.

"It's simple."

Several of the vampires twisted their heads from side to side, trying to figure out who'd spoken, before a dark-haired vampire sitting in the shadows below a shuttered window continued.

"You think you're the first to consider sending an assassin after Raphael? Have any of you ever even seen him up close?" When no one spoke up, he said, "Well, I have, and I've never felt such power. And that was at a formal affair with no threats about." The vamp stroked one finger along the grain of the table in what appeared to be a habitual gesture. "No," the vampire said, his face still obscured by the darkness. "What we should do is take a page from our North American brethren and organize ourselves the way they have. With an alliance. An agreement to stand together against outside threats."

"No one has suffered more from the foolish attempts by certain of our leaders to invade North America than my people," interjected a vampire with a strong French accent. "Attempts that not only failed, but cost hundreds of vampire lives. If anyone should want revenge on Raphael, it is the French." He sipped from the full glass of wine standing in front of him, one of several drinks along the table, many of which hadn't been touched. They were there mostly for show, in the event some human opened the wrong door. "But I'm telling you," the Frenchman warned. "The path of revenge will bring nothing but a quick death. Leave it alone. Raphael doesn't care what happens here, as long as it remains here."

"Agreed," the vampire in the shadows said, drawing everyone's attention back to him, despite his quiet voice.

That one has power, the Scotsman thought to himself, and turned his focus to studying the stranger. If anyone was going to unite these vampires in a common cause, that would be the one.

"We should create an alliance of our own," the vampire continued.

"There are too many of us," someone protested. "North America has only eight lords, we have—"

"Hundreds," the dark-haired vampire supplied. "Many of whom are too weak to be called 'vampire lord,' and everyone in this room knows it."

"You're proposing war."

"No, I'm proposing peace. Do what you want in your own countries, but I plan to rule mine. And no one else's. If you leave me and mine alone, I'll do the same. But if you attack . . ." He turned his head from side to side, making it clear that no one was excluded from his warning. "I will destroy you and everyone who followed you. I want peace, and I intend to get it if I have to leave mountains of dust across

Europe." He stood, fingertips pressed to the table in front of him. "I bid you fair traveling, gentlemen."

He left as quietly as he'd spoken, and would have closed the door, but spying the Scotsman leaving behind him, he paused to give a knowing smile. "My regards to Lachlan," he said, then walked away.

The Scotsman watched as the vampire left the bar, making mental notes of everything he'd heard from this one, knowing Lord Lachlan would want to know. He waited long enough to ensure the vamp wouldn't think himself followed, then exited to the street, eager to begin his journey back to the Highlands. Given the late hour, it would be the next night before he got there, but he could at least cover the distance to the port before dawn.

THE DARK-HAIRED vampire watched the Scotsman stride away, confident his message would be delivered—not only to Lachlan, but to Raphael, as well. He hadn't lied to the assembled vampires. He did want peace. But he intended it to be on his terms. Raphael's alliance wasn't the only model for what he wanted. Raphael himself was, too, though he didn't fool himself by thinking his power was equal. He didn't believe there was another vampire alive who could match the North American vampire lord. On the other hand, he'd weighed his own power against everyone in that meeting, just as he'd weighed it against every strong vampire he'd ever met. And he'd never found one he couldn't have killed, if it came down to it.

Yes, he wanted peace. He wanted an alliance. But he intended to be the one leading that alliance, the one making the critical difference, the tough decisions. Just as Raphael did.

Once the Scotsman was out of sight, the vampire moved out of the shadows, slid behind the wheel of his very fine European sedan and took off into the night to pursue a revolution.

To be continued . . .

Acknowledgements

As always I need to thank my editor, Brenda Chin, first and foremost. Especially on this book, she worked with me to make it so much better. I'd hate to do this without her. My thanks also to my publisher, the multi-talented Debra Dixon at BelleBooks, for her patience in working out my due dates, even when they slip, and for the always gorgeous covers she designs. And, of course, everyone at BelleBooks, all of whom work to keep things flowing in the right direction.

Love and gratitude to my friend and fellow writer, the brilliant Angela Addams (you really need to check out her Witch Hospital series) who's conveniently located in a different time zone, so she can "listen" to me moan and curse via messenger in the wee hours of the night. Thanks once more to John Gorski, who saved me from shoving the wrong kind of bullets into my characters' guns, to Annette Stone who cheerfully gets out newsletters and contest notices at the last minute (my fault,) and to Karen Roma who's the best beta reader an author could ask for, and whom I hope to be seeing in Brisbane 2020!

To Julie-Anne Wilson, a friend who goes back to our days on Kelley Armstrong's chat board, which is many more years ago than I like to think about, with apologies for my bastardized Scottish Gaelic.

To my lovely Leah Peterson who gave me so many tips about traveling in Scotland, including the best shortbread bakery you will ever find. It's worth a trip back to Edinburgh just for that.

To my large and extended family who are always there for me, in good times and bad, I love you all.

And finally, this book is dedicated to all the wonderful people I met in Scotland, who made my journey an enchanting and fascinating experi-
e, but especially to Jane Sanderson, Blue Badge Guide extraordinaire,
as an encyclopedic knowledge of Edinburgh. We walked all over
nd climbed to the very top of Edinburgh Castle, where she
wet and slippery Arthur's Seat and wisely advised me not

to try climbing it. And to Jean Blair, the incredibly knowledgeable Blue Badge Guide who traveled the Highlands and more with me, through rain and floods and the occasional sunshine. Through castles and luggage stores, from leaping salmon to whisky that almost killed me, and gorgeous vistas that filled my heart with joy. It was a wonderful and exciting adventure, and I can hardly wait to call you up and do it again.

About the Author

D. B. REYNOLDS arrived in sunny Southern California at an early age, having made the trek across the country from the Midwest in a station wagon with her parents, her many siblings and the family dog. And while she has many (okay, some) fond memories of Midwestern farm life, she quickly discovered that L.A. was her kind of town and grew up happily sunning on the beaches of the South Bay.

D. B. holds graduate degrees in international relations and history from UCLA (go Bruins!) and was headed for a career in academia, but in a moment of clarity she left behind the politics of the hallowed halls for the better paying politics of Hollywood, where she worked as a sound editor for several years, receiving two Emmy nominations, an MPSE Golden Reel and multiple MPSE nominations for her work in television sound.

Book One of her Vampires in America series, RAPHAEL, launched her career as a writer in 2009, while JABRIL, Vampires in America Book Two, was awarded the RT Reviewers Choice Award for Best Paranormal Romance (Small Press) in 2010. ADEN, Vampires in America Book Seven, was her first release under the new ImaJinn imprint at BelleBooks, Inc.

D. B. currently lives in a flammable canyon near the Malibu coast. When she's not writing her own books, she can usually be found reading someone else's. You can visit D. B. at her website www.dbreynolds.com for information on her latest books, contests and giveaways.

41246320R00156

Made in the USA
San Bernardino, CA
01 July 2019